HAPPY BIRTHDAY JESÚS

Also by Ronald L. Ruiz

The Big Bear
Giuseppe Rocco

HAPPY BIRTHDAY JESÚS

RONALD L. RUIZ

Houston, Texas
1994

This book is made possible through support from the National
Endowment for the Arts (a federal agency), the Lila Wallace-
Reader's Digest fund and the Andrew W. Mellow Foundation.

Arte Público Press
University of Houston
452 Cullen Performance Hall
Houston, Texas 77204-2004

Cover design by Eclipse Design Group

Ruiz, Ronald L.
    Happy Birthday Jesús / by Ronald L. Ruiz
       p.   cm.
    ISBN 1-55885-398-7
    1. Mexican American criminals—California—Fiction.
    2. Mexican American prisoners—California—Fiction.
    3. Mexican Americans—California—Fiction. I. Title.
    PS3568.U397H36 1994
    813'.54—dc20   93-45643
                                                        CIP

∞ The paper used in this publication meets the requirements of
the American National Standard for Permanence of Paper for
Printed Library Materials Z39.48-1984.

3 4 5 6 7 8 9 0 1 2   10 9 8 7 6 5 4 3 2 1

To Brother Sixtus Robert
who gave me orange juice
and read me T. S. Eliot
when I needed them most.

HAPPY BIRTHDAY JESÚS

Chapter One

They called me Jess, but my name was Jesús.

I could see the mountains on the other side of the valley. Three times they had taken me over this range and into that valley. They had taken me in their green buses with bars across the windows. Their buses didn't stop until they got to the next prison. Now I stopped.

Fog covered that great valley; soft, thick clouds of whiteness gleaming in the sun, giving no sign of the dreariness below. Somewhere down there had been my home. My people had lived there. They were buried there.

I drove down into the fog. The day darkened. I remembered its coldness and timelessness. It was there when I got up, a dark gray-white. It was there as I walked to school and at recesses, reddening my hands. It was there after school, still the same gray-white. Even the night had that gray-white. It was around the street lights and car lights and porch lights.

I came to a town I didn't know. I could see very little of it except for signs and roadside stores. The signs were new and I had money. I was going to stop; maybe walk around; maybe buy something. But I saw a police car and panicked and kept going.

I remembered officer Mooneyham as he opened the door

to the main line. He was grinning, but his voice was cruel.
"Well, Olivas, you lucked out. But you'll be back. It won't
take long. You ain't going to be able to make it out there.
You been in here too long." He opened the heavy steel door.
A young officer was waiting for me on the other side. "This
way, Olivas." I began walking down that long connecting
corridor. It seemed like years. Other prisoners were walking
about freely. I didn't recognize any of them. They began
staring at me. I was in brown dress-out khaki. They knew I
was going home. They started talking about me. They knew
I was going home from isolation. Then one of them said,
"Orale, Olivas," and raised his clenched fist in a power
salute. I smiled and kept walking down that quarter-mile
concrete corridor. They stopped as I walked, nodding and
smiling, "Orale." Even a black said, "Right on, brother."
    I was going home. But where was that? Not long ago I
had heard the first door to my cell open. It was too early for
lunch. I had just eaten breakfast and somebody had already
taken the tray. Then instead of talking to me through the
slot, the second door opened. Mooneyham stood there,
tossed in the khaki pants and shirt and the brown shoes,
and said, "Get dressed, Olivas. That idiot court says you're
going home." That was all.
    I wondered if this officer was really taking me out. I
looked down at the khaki pants, at the brown shoes: there
were no leg irons this time, no chains around my waist or
cuffs on my wrists, no white coveralls or heavy gray socks. I
was going home. Everybody knew it. They stopped as I
neared and passed them. Their faces told me. I was going
home. I wondered if my name had been on the radio. Someone called "Olivas," and I turned and didn't recognize the
face. I was sure my name had been on the radio.
    But where would I go? Besides what I had on, they
would give me a bus ticket, $44, and a jacket. Would I go
back to Fresno? It had been so long. My people were dead.
The people I knew would remember me, remember what I
had done. I didn't think I could face them. Where would I
work? Who would hire me? How long would the $44 last? It

was winter now. The cotton had been picked. There
wouldn't be any work in the fields.

They kept cheering me, "Orale, Olivas. Orale. Te aven-
taste." No one had ever cheered me before. I was nodding,
smiling, but I was afraid. And the closer I got to the green
door, the one that would take me to the visiting rooms, to
the offices and then to the gate, the more frightened I
became. I didn't want to go. There was no place to go. Their
eyes were bright for me. But now I didn't want to go. When
we got to the green door, I didn't think I'd be able to walk
through it. Then I saw my lawyer. She was alone, smiling.
"Jess," she said and she hugged me, and the fear was gone.

The sun was bright; I hadn't been in it for a long time. I
felt the wind. I turned and faced it and let it blow my hair
and flap my clothes. There were three women and a man
waiting for us outside the gates. They hugged me and
kissed me and shook my hands. I didn't know them. Two of
the women were crying. They asked me a lot of questions
and said a lot of things there in the parking lot. I was feeling the sun and the wind, turning and moving, free.

We got into a car. Cars had changed. It was my lawyer's
car. It was big and quiet and shiny and new. She asked the
man to drive so she could sit next to me and talk. She told
me the Supreme Court had decided my case that morning.
She explained a lot of legal things to me. I didn't understand them. When she finished the others asked her questions. Then they asked me questions. I tried answering, but
I got all tangled up. They waited for my answers, patiently,
understanding. But nothing came out right, and then I
didn't answer anymore. Everybody felt funny. They tried to
help me with the answers. Finally, I just put my head
down. Then she started answering for me. She told them
how long I'd been there, why I was sent there, how I had
come to be in isolation and what it was like there. She told
them about my family, about my life in Fresno, about my
education and religion. She even explained why I couldn't
answer, that anyone who had been through what I had been
through wouldn't have been able to answer either. Much of

what she told them she had gotten from my prison file.
Some of it had come from other prisoners and some from
myself. Much of what she told them was only partly true or
untrue, but it didn't matter much.

ooooo

 I had been in the valley for at least an hour. The fog had
lifted enough so that I could see maybe a hundred feet.
What I saw surprised me. All the fields were planted; they
weren't just white clay where the only living things were
jackrabbits. I wondered if I had taken the wrong road. I
began looking for road signs. The first sign I saw said
"Fresno 57," and below it "Firebaugh 36 Mendota 39 to the
right." I felt the hell-heat of Firebaugh, saw Mendota's few
weed-like trees wilting on its main street, and remembered
the bleak cold of the cotton fields around them.
 I went off to my right. I wanted to see Firebaugh and
Mendota again. Later I'd take the back road into Fresno.
After a few miles, I stopped on the side of the road and got
out to look at a field. I jumped over an irrigation ditch and
landed in some mud. I was sure I had ruined my shiny new
shoes, but I had a lot of money and it didn't bother me. One
side of that huge field looked like it had been planted in
alfalfa or oats, another in corn, and beyond it, cotton. Gone
was the dusty white. A car passed and slowed; the people in
it looked at me, and then it went on. I was afraid they'd
report me to the farmer. What would I tell him? That I was
Jess Olivas who had just gotten out of prison? That I was
standing in his field because I wondered? . . . He'd probably
look at me funny and ask where a little ol' Mexican with a
name like Jess Olivas had gotten the fancy clothes I was
wearing and that new car I was driving. It wouldn't be long
before the police would be there.
 I started for my car but the fog swallowed up the other
car. It was quiet again. I scooped up a handful of the wet
ground. It wasn't the mushy white clay we had walked on

so many mornings to get to the cotton. We started before dawn and I shivered all the way in the back of the truck, trying to sleep. But it was too cold to sleep, even with all the sweaters and pants I wore. Then, Don Miguel, the labor contractor, would holler that it was time and I would get down from the truck and drag that big sack over that white clay wishing I were still in bed. "Hurry up, boy. It's not even worth bringing you. You just take up a seat in my truck." And I'd move faster. I knew my grandmother would get mad if he told her.

I looked down the rows of dead corn stalks and thought of the brown cotton bushes. "Hurry up. Let's go. Everybody out. It's time. Let's go. Let's go." Slowly we would climb down and out. Don Miguel never moved. He would just stand at the back of the truck barking. "Hurry up. Let's go." Then he'd walk behind us barking. Somehow he always knew when it was time because just as we reached our rows and readied our bags, it would be light enough to see. Slowly the fog's grayness would lighten, pause in early afternoon, and then darken. The old men used to tell me not to stop, to keep moving, that it was colder if you stopped and thought about it. Soon I would fall behind and they would disappear into the fog. They weren't far; I could call them and they would answer. But as I moved from bush to bush and the sack got heavier and I fell further behind, I felt alone. At night I would stand next to the heater toasting myself. Those were the only times she let me just stand there. Without ever having talked about it, we understood that on those nights she would let me have the heater. So I would stand there, at times for an hour or more. Sometimes I would doze off and burn myself.

Another car slowed and passed me. I was sure this one would bring the farmer. In a few minutes I was in Firebaugh. I didn't recognize it. There were new buildings and homes, sidewalks and curbs and paved streets. I remembered the café, the blast of cold air from the giant, noisy cooler as you walked in from the heat. I remembered slouched men on stools staring out the bare windows into

the empty street. The heat stopped everything; it could only
be endured, waited out. There were three cafés now. I followed the main street out into the fields. I didn't recognize
them either. Everything had been planted, used. Even the
ranch houses were different.

I drove on to Mendota. In Mendota there had been an
old two-story wood-frame building at the center of town that
had faded to a light blue-green. Rooms were rented on the
top floor. On the ground floor there was a store in the middle, a café on one side, and a room that was used for the
Greyhound bus depot on the other side. It seemed like the
only trees in Mendota had been planted along the depot
side of the building. They looked like giant mesquite
bushes. They were flimsy in the summer and bare in the
winter and always seemed about to die. People stood under
them in the summer, but they gave little shade. Contractors
picked up and dropped off workers on the depot side. Everything happened at that building, and I had thought it must
have been there and would be there forever. But it too was
gone. The Greyhound bus depot was in a small new brick
building. I felt confused. I drove around the streets many
times. People were starting to notice me. It was getting
dark. I wasn't hungry, but after all those years it was time
to eat. I started looking at cafés, and then I chose one. But I
didn't go in. I didn't know if they'd serve me. I went to a
store instead and bought some bread, baloney, cup cakes,
and root beer. I ate in the car, my pockets jammed with
money.

It was dark when I finished eating, and the fog had
thickened. The car lights bounced back at me. I couldn't see.
I pulled over. I'd go to Fresno in the morning. I had slept in
the car last night, too. I had plenty of money, but I was
afraid they wouldn't rent me a room.

When I awoke the fog seemed even thicker. It was
always thicker. It looked like white gas, all around me, all
around everything. But now I was anxious to get to Fresno.
I drove on. I got more and more excited. I passed through
an intersection that must have been Kerman. The road I

was on was called Whites Bridge Road. As a boy, I had looked first for a white bridge and then for White's bridge. But I had never found it. After awhile I stopped, got out of the car, and walked a little ways into a field and along the road, trying to find what had been. But the fog was thick. I went on. Soon I could see the edges of small stores and businesses where grape fields must have been. The irrigation ditches were gone. Then there were front yards and houses where I must have laid the grape trays on the hot sand.

I passed the airport without seeing it because by then I was in the town I knew. I recognized what was left of the houses. Some had store fronts on them; others had been replaced by small buildings or vacant lots. Everything seemed dirty and tired. I remembered the old white people scrubbing their sidewalks early in the morning, sweeping the hard clean earth of their small front yards to make them cleaner. Now I saw mostly blacks and a few Mexicans. Papers, bottles and cans lay everywhere. Cars were parked on those tiny front yards.

I stopped at what had been Whites Bridge Market. The Coca-Cola sign said "Sam's Market." The people inside were black. The owner was black. He caught me staring at him. "What you want."

"Nothing," I said. But that wasn't true. It took me awhile to say, "Where's D Street?"

"Three blocks over."

I didn't look at him. The fir floors had always been soaked with oil; now they were dry and worn. The smell was different. "Thank you," I said and left.

I sat in the car alongside Sam's Market for a long time. "And where's home?" my lawyer yelled. I didn't answer. She knew I wouldn't answer. "And where's home?" At first she tried to educate me. During those first days at her apartment, it seemed as if everyone who came to meet me was a teacher or professor of some kind. They had special courses and programs. They had tutors ready. Money could be gotten. Everyone was sure I could do it and that I would "lead a fuller, more meaningful life." They even brought me a

Mexican professor. He introduced himself with a long complicated handshake, which I didn't let him finish, acting as
if he had hurt my hand. He let go and said, "Yo también soy
chicano." I answered in English, "What are you?" He didn't
say anything more, and she was angry with me. There had
been a lot of drinking that night, more than usual. I never
drank. Instead, I waited for the drink to work, for the pleasure of watching all those respectable people make fools of
themselves. John passed out, and finally just she and I were
there. She was tired, and the alcohol exaggerated the lines
in her face. Her words and thoughts stumbled badly. I had
watched her argue some of my case. She was a good lawyer.
The judges and prosecutors respected her; sometimes I
thought they were afraid of her. I had never paid her. She
had traveled all those miles and worked all those hours for
no money at all. Now she was trying to scold me. I watched
her closely. She was a drooping, drunken, middle-aged
woman. That gave me pleasure. She got louder. I just
grinned until I watched her stumble enough. Then I yelled
back, "You want me to be educated, huh!? What for!? So
that I can be like you and all your educated friends!? You're
educated! John's educated! Your friends are educated! Look
at you! You think I want to be like you or him or them!?"

The next morning before she went to work, she said
that I would have to get a job. The next day she took me to
a big store downtown. They sent me across an alley to a big
concrete building. There, a little old man told me to open
big boxes and stack the smaller boxes in them on shelves.
The work wasn't hard, and the old man was kind. But when
she picked me up that night, I told her I wanted to go back
to Fresno, back home. It wasn't the work, I said. It was the
building without windows, without doors, with artificial
lights and air. It was more of a prison than some of the prisons I had been in. At least they had windows. At least in
the fields I could feel the wind. She didn't make me go back
the next day, and I knew John was angry.

A few weeks later John went to Los Angeles on a case.
One of the nights he was gone, we ate early. She didn't

drink and we talked. Where was home? Who was there? They were all dead. What would I do there? It was winter. There wasn't work in the fields. We had been through this many times, but now for some reason, I said that home didn't have to be there; that it didn't have its beginnings there, that I had people in Mexico; that I could find my people, my family, in Mexico; that I could find out who I was and where I came from. She liked that, and before I knew it I was going to Fresno and then to Mexico "to discover my roots," as she later told her friends.

She had another party for me. This time to raise money for my trip. Lots of people came. The Mexican professor didn't. A woman named Jill came up to me and said, "Jess, I want you to have this. If you need more, there is more." It was a check for $25,000. She had offered herself to me that first night, and now she was offering her money. I couldn't believe it. "I want you to have it," she said. Something in me said "Take it, man, take it. Take it all. She wants to feel good. You're here and she's there. She wants to clean up her act. She's doing it for herself, not for you. It makes her feel good. So take it from the bitch. Take it all, and if there's more, get that too." I took the check, folded it, put it in my shirt pocket, and nodded.

I went back into Sam's Market. "Where'd you say D Street was?" This time I didn't stare. He pointed. I drove in that direction and saw the playground. I was eight or nine when I first went to that playground. I only went there a few times. One day a bunch of black kids came up to me and said that I had called one of them a nigger. It wasn't true. I hadn't used that word until I had gotten to the joint. They said one of them was going to fight me. He was the smallest, but they were all bigger than me. I didn't want to fight him, so they beat the shit out of me anyway.

I was on the B Street side of the playground. We lived on D Street. I went around the playground, past C Street. For twenty-two years many of my thoughts and much of my life had begun and ended on D Street. Then, out of the fog came a high cyclone fence. It was like a prison fence. On the other side of that fence, they had scooped away D Street. In its place, some twenty feet below, was a freeway, a concrete road on which trucks and cars were zooming back and forth.

Our house was five blocks from there. The fog wouldn't let me see. I got in the car. When I was half a block away, I knew it had to be gone. But I still hoped. Then I was there. It was gone.

I spent most of the day going up and down streets on each side of the freeway, trying to see my past. From across the freeway, I was able to place the house. The yard where I had rolled in, where I had watered corn, chili and squash summer after summer, hung in the air twenty feet above the freeway. The house was somewhere up there too. It was easier seeing it if I closed my eyes. In prison I didn't have to close my eyes. It was just there; it would pop into my mind no matter what I was doing. I wondered where they had taken that chunk of earth and all the things that had stood on it.

After awhile, I went to other places. I went to the railroad tracks and the loading docks. 'Amá didn't want me around on Sunday afternoons when the Guadalupana met at our house. "Go play," she'd say. I'd always go down to the docks. Each Sunday there were new and different things lying around. From the docks I'd climb onto the boxcars, and once on them I could go anyplace in the world. I'd check every door. One Sunday I got into a boxcar that was loaded with bananas, green bananas. I was really sick that night.

I stopped going to the docks when I was about thirteen. I started watching the passenger trains instead. I found a place almost across from the depot, next to stacks of poultry crates, where I could hide if I wanted. From there I'd watch the passenger trains come and go. Sometimes I'd wait hours for a train. Soon I knew when they'd come. The waiting wasn't long then, and I'd go on weekdays too. I wanted more than anything to be on one of those trains and never come back.

I found that place next to the tracks. The crates were gone, but the depot was there and it wasn't hard to tell where I used to hide. I even waited for a train, until someone came up and asked me what I wanted, what I was waiting for. When I told him, he just shook his head and said, "I don't know where you've been, but there ain't been many of those around here for a long time."

I saw the old two-story brick building standing alone on F Street. All the houses around had been torn down, but for some reason they hadn't leveled it. I stood in its doorway as I had on many Sundays on my way back from the tracks. All its windows were boarded up, broken glass was everywhere; there were gouges in the brick. It felt as if it had been left for dead. It had life and warmth and music, lots of it. When I'd pass it on my way to the tracks on Sundays, the black people would just be getting there. They seemed to come from everywhere, in fine cars and snappy clothes. The men wore suits and hats and shiny shoes; the women wore silk dresses that rustled when they walked, making sounds that drew my eyes to their big asses and big tits. They were happy. They were laughing and met each other with big handshakes and loud voices. On my way back, the music would be playing. Some were drunk by then, but they never bothered me. I think they liked me liking their music. I loved that music, loved the sound of those hard-driving drums nudging and pushing and forcing the others. I could hear it a block away, and when I'd get there, I'd stand by the door until somebody came out. Then I'd jam my foot under the door and feel the blast of those drums. It felt alive.

It was getting late. The fog hadn't lifted and in another hour it would be dark. I didn't know what to do or where to go. This was the Fresno I had wanted to be in, to come back to during all those years. There was nothing to come back to. There was the cemetery where 'Amá and my mother were buried. I didn't want to go to their graves. Not then. There was the church. I had often thought I'd do more to it now than on the night they had arrested me. And there was Chole. Maybe she still lived in that shack. If she was still alive, she'd be in her sixties, a babbling dried-up old woman. Was she what I had jacked-off to in the joint? I didn't want to see her. Let her rest in peace.

Chinatown was still there. It had always been easy to go there and it was easy now. I drove into that dirty, four-block square of stores and bars and restaurants and cheap rooms. There were very few Chinese in Chinatown; there were more Japanese. Chinatown was really Mexican-town and Nigger-town, only the owners were Asian or white. Everybody on those streets was Mexican or black. On Saturdays and Sundays it was jammed with brown and black people who had come to shop or drink or fuck or get lost. My grandmother had sent me there on special days from the time I was six or seven to buy whatever Mexican spice or treat she couldn't grow or make herself. It was three blocks from our house, and I liked going there. It wasn't like going downtown where I always felt dirty and dark; where the white salesladies would always ask if they could help me and I'd always say no because I didn't have any money, and they knew it, and I knew it, and I'd leave. That's what they wanted me to do, that's what they were telling me to do, when they asked me in their stiff voices if they could help me just as soon as I walked in the door. And I didn't have to interpret, and get embarrassed, for my grandmother when we went to Chinatown.

I ate menudo in Chinatown. It had been a long time since I had eaten tripe stew. I ate slowly, partly because I was wondering what to do and partly because I liked that restaurant. The Mexican woman who ran it was impressed with my new clothes and my big ring and my big bankroll, especially when I flipped her a five dollar bill and told her to play me some music. After that it was "Señor this" and "Señor that." I had three bowls of menudo and four beers and was feeling pretty good until her husband came in and asked her what the hell was going on, that two of the kids were sick and crying and that he had told her to close early. I wanted to take him on, rap his head on the counter. But what for? Once he walked in, she wouldn't even look in my direction.

I sat in the car for a long time. Where would I go now? It got cold. I turned on the engine and the heater. I'd rent a room tonight. But what about tomorrow? An old Chinese man kept coming to his window every few minutes to see if I was still sitting there with my motor running. "Fuck you, Chinaman," I said. "Fuckin' chinks are everywhere." It wasn't true, but there was no place to go. Finally he just stood at his window and stared. I flipped him a finger and left. It was too early to rent a room. The church was four blocks away. I knew where I was going.

When I passed it the first time, it looked just the way it always looked, high on its brick foundation, narrow and long. Aside from our house, I had probably spent more time in that building than any other in Fresno. I drove around the block. There was no one in sight. I drove around again, there weren't even cars in the streets. It looked the same. At most it had been painted, but it was hard to tell in the dark and the street lights were no help in the fog. I parked and walked up those high, narrow, brick steps. It wasn't locked. I went in. It was warm and dark, a darkness I knew. I went from the outer room into the church itself. I didn't bless myself; I didn't genuflect or kneel. Instead, I walked loudly down that aisle, and when the-dollar-and-ten-cent candles inside the altar railing gave enough light so that I could see the tabernacle, The House of God, at the center of the altar, I started mumbling, "You Motherfucker. You Motherfucker." I walked past the pews and the railing up to the altar, fingered and then jiggled that frail house of the Almighty, and laughed.

CHAPTER TWO

My grandmother, Soledad Olivas, was born and raised on a small rancho in Zacatecas, Mexico. She had come to the United States with her young daughter around 1910. They waded across the river at night. Her husband, Jesús, came before them. He had been a musician and a saddle-maker who was drafted into Villa's army when Pancho Villa marched through Zacatecas. He deserted that army and fled to the United States only to die, just after Soledad joined him, of pneumonia while working on a railroad gang. My grandmother always told me that he was a good man, a fine man, a hard worker and a good provider. My mother died when I was born. My grandmother seldom spoke of her and never spoke of my father. Still, I always knew that he had been a bad man, a good for nothing. It was Chole who told me I was a bastard.

The earliest memory I had of my grandmother was of a dark winter morning. I couldn't have been more than five years old because I had just started serving Mass and I had gone to church with her that morning. As always, she was dressed in black, layers of black that ended with a huge shawl she wrapped around her shoulders and over her head. She walked quickly and quietly and I followed, half running, half walking. She said nothing, but her lips were

moving in one of her first rosaries of the day. Under her
shawl she was fingering her beads. I followed her up the
brick steps into the lighted church. In the first row knelt six
black figures, nuns from Mexico who came to visit our
church each year. She blessed herself and passed through
the glass doors. Then, suddenly, she fell face down to the
floor and began moaning, *"¡Dios mío! ¡Dios mío! ¡Perdóname! ¡Perdóname!"* Slowly she rose to her knees and with
her forehead still on the floor and her arms and hands
stretched out before her, crawled toward the altar, moaning. Not once did the nuns turn. When she reached the communion rail, she fell flat again. The moans became gasps
and then only heavy breathing. I was scared, but the priest,
Padre Galván, took me by the hand and said, "Come, my
son. People who are close to God must suffer these things.
Your grandmother is a very holy woman."

Our day began with the six o'clock Mass. At five-thirty
she'd say, "Jesús, get up, it's time." She said it quietly but
she only said it once. Usually there were only the three of
us at the six o'clock Mass: Padre Galván, who said the
Mass; myself, who served as the altar boy; and my grandmother, who received Holy Communion. Under her first
black skirt she wore a large wooden rosary. At different
times during the day, as she cooked or mopped or swept,
she said the rosary, fingering the beads from time to time.
On our walls hung different pictures of Christ, the Virgin,
and some saints. Each room had its crucifix. In our front
room was an altar made of lug boxes which she had covered
with painted butcher paper. In the center of the altar was a
picture of Jesus dressed in red; He was pointing to His
flaming heart. To the right was a smaller picture of the Virgin of Guadalupe; to the left one of the Holy Family. Before
them were candles in glass vases and jars. There was
always a candle burning in honor of Jesus and His family.

On Saturday afternoons we went to the church to clean
and scrub it for Sunday services. At least once a day we
knelt at our altar and said the mysteries of the rosary.
When we finished, she spoke of the Goodness of God. On

Sunday mornings I served two Masses, and on Sunday afternoons the church ladies would come to our house. They called themselves the Guadalupana; they said they prayed and talked of church things, but they talked of other things too. On those afternoons, I wouldn't leave until just before five o'clock.

ᎦᎦᎦᎦᎦ

In the pantry behind the door were two red bricks. Under the bottom shelf was another brick, split in two. When the pantry door was closed, the tiny room was completely dark. It was one of the two punishments I feared most. There was never any telling which of the two she would pick. First would come the slap of her hand or a whack of the belt, and then she would grab me by the hair or the ear or the shirt and start to pull me towards the pantry. As soon as she moved towards the pantry, I would start to cry. In the pantry I would have to move the two bricks to the middle of that tiny room. Then I would have to take the broken brick, a piece in each hand, and kneel on the first two. Kneeling, I would raise them to my ears while she watched. Then she would motion how high she wanted them. Satisfied, she'd slam the door shut. Then she would wait, motionless, next to the door, sometimes for an hour, for the first sound of the bricks. When one dropped, or I let them fall, the door would fly open, and with her belt in hand, she would make me begin again. By the time I was twelve or thirteen, I taught myself not to cry. Years later in prison, when a guard would slam the door to an isolation cell shut, I would grope in the darkness for the hole where you were supposed to shit and piss because that was the center of the cell. Once I knew where it was, I could begin my stay. But there were times when instead of the hole, I felt those bricks again.

The other punishment I dreaded began when I was a boy and she would say I was acting like a baby. Later, when

I was in my teens, she used it when she said that I wasn't acting like a man. Anything could be proof of my guilt. After the slap or the belt, she would order me to put on my diaper. At first it was a diaper, later it was a towel. I would have to strip in front of her, fasten the cloth at my hips with huge safety pins. Then I would lie in my bed and she would bring a quart-sized milk bottle, capped with a nipple and filled with water, and jam it in my mouth. From my closet she would bring two sides of a big wooden crate. These she propped against the foot and side of the bed, making it into a big crib. Warm or cold, I'd lay in my crib for the rest of the day. I was not allowed to get out, and she brought me nothing to eat. When she did come, it was to taunt me or make fun of me or remind me that I hadn't been acting like a man. If I shit or pissed in my crib, she would make me change and clean myself while she watched. It was like in prison. There were times when I was thrown naked into an isolation cell, and when I first got there, the guards would laugh at the redness of my asshole and ask if they could punk me too.

For as long as I could remember she did these things to me. Often I thought I knew why, but I never could understand how she was able to do it and get away with it. She was not a big woman; she was under five foot and couldn't have weighed a hundred pounds. She was forty years older than me and by the time I was seventeen, I outweighed her by fifty pounds and was six or seven inches taller than her. It wasn't the slaps or the belt, because as I got older, I could have knocked her across the room and wrapped the belt around her throat. It was her eyes and something in her voice. But it was the eyes mostly. They were eyes that seemed to see into every part of me. They were brown eyes, common enough, quiet eyes even, until they looked for my eyes. Then they would strip me, and scare me, and convince me with their fierceness that, short of killing her, she was to be obeyed. There was something of that in her voice, too. She spoke softly, but with me at least, she only had to say things once. No matter who it was, they usually ended up doing what my grandmother said or wanted.

My grandmother worked as a cleaning woman for the San Joaquin Power Building six nights a week, from 6:00 p.m. to 1:00 a.m. From the time I was a baby, she took me to work with her, sneaking me in and out of the building when she went to and from work. It wasn't that the neighbors wouldn't have watched me; it was just that she didn't want to owe anyone anything. The boss was Mr. Mitchell, a small thin man who always wore gray khaki pants and a matching shirt. Once, even before I could remember, he had found me and had warned her not to bring me anymore. But she kept on bringing me anyway, hiding me more carefully.

Mr. Mitchell usually stayed in the building only until each of the three cleaning women had finished their first floors. Then he'd leave, and my grandmother or one of the other women would come into the women's restrooms on different floors and tell me that I could come out. Then I'd wander around the building until it was time for me to go to sleep in one of the cleaning closets. I liked going to the tenth floor; it made me feel like I was the tallest person in the world and could see forever. One night when I was in the first grade, Mr. Mitchell came back as I was looking out over the reddened west side. I ran, but he found me. He grabbed me by the arm and began yelling, "Soledad! Soledad!" She was scrubbing a hallway on another floor; she knew as soon as she saw us. She began nodding her head up and down. "Oh, yessa, Meesta Meetchel, yessa. Sorry, Meesta Meetchel, sorry." He was yelling that he had warned her, that he was sick and tired, that he should fire her on the spot. She understood, she agreed he was right: all of that as she shook her head from side to side with a sick grin. "No be mad, Meesta Meetchel, no be mad." She was on her knees; she shuffled the few feet between them and tugged at his pant leg, "No be mad, Meesta Meetchel, no be mad," with that grin. "No be mad."

CHAPTER THREE

The Fresno County jail was in the downtown park next to the courthouse. As a kid I remember the inmates always yelling at people passing below them in the park and at women as far away as Fresno Street. When I'd look up, I could never see them. All I could see were thick squares of glass and steel screens. But they could see me because as soon as I stopped, the yells would come down on me. "Get the hell out of here, sissy. Nobody's talking to you." They'd laugh. "Wanna fuck, boy?" More laughter. "Orale, *putito*, tráeme tus nalgas." I was sure they were the most evil men that ever lived, and as a boy, whenever I saw one of them outside the jail cleaning the park, I'd walk a block out of my way to get around him. Three days after my eighteenth birthday, I was one of them.

They said I was dangerous and put me in a maximum security cell. Across from my cell was C dorm. To look out of my cell was to look into C dorm. There were about fifteen inmates there: two blacks, an old white drunk, and the rest Mexicans. I recognized some of the Mexicans. I had seen them in Chinatown, around the church and on the street. C dorm knew of my crime. They didn't think I was dangerous; they just thought I was crazy.

A few days after I got there, a young white boy, not

much older than myself, was put in C dorm. That night I
heard a struggle and cries. Four or five inmates had thrown
a blanket over his head while he was still in his bunk. They
beat him and then stripped him of his underwear. "Don't hit
me. Don't hit me. Please, don't hit me anymore."

"Shut up, white boy. If that fuckin' bull come, we'll kill
you, hear? You're gonna suck a lot of cocks, white boy, big
Mexican cocks. You ain't ever gonna like no other kind after
you taste ours. And I'm gonna fuck you. That tight little ass
of yours is gonna feel good. It ain't gonna hurt too much."

They dragged him naked to the farthest corner of the
cell. He was crying; he was begging. Apache, a short skinny
Mexican, was their leader. When they got him to the corner,
Apache threw off the blanket and blindfolded him with a T-
shirt. With the ends of the blindfold in one hand, he knelt
over him. "You gonna suck cock, white boy?" Except for the
crying, the white boy didn't move; he didn't answer.

Then one of them kicked him in the stomach. "Answer,
fucker." The white boy doubled up and yelled out in pain.

Apache got mad. "You keep kicking him like that, asshole, and he ain't gonna be able to suck anybody's cock, and
you're gonna have the bull down on all of us, asshole." Then
he calmed himself and said gently, "Now you don't want
anymore of that, do you, white boy? You're gonna be a good
white boy and suck all our dicks and fuck a few of us, ain't
you?"

Yes, he nodded, yes. "Now get up on your knees. That's
a good white boy."

When they saw that, others got out of their bunks and
started for the corner. Apache said, "Hold it, you fuckers,
we're first. We did all the work. When we get ours, maybe
we'll let you have seconds."

The old white drunk stayed on his bunk, watching. One
of the blacks said, "What about me, Apache? Don't I get
any."

"Fuck you, nigger. You ain't getting shit. Get your own
white boy. You niggers better get back in your bunks before
you be blindfolded too. I always did like black ass." Every-

body thought that was funny. "Fuckin' niggers. Fuckin' pork chops. They always want a piece of our action."

Then they argued over who would be the first of the first. Apache got mad again. "Look, fuckers. Danny's first. He helped me the most. Without us, you guys would still be jacking off in your bunks. Bunch of chickenshits. After Danny it's Nacho, David, and Huero. I'll be last. I'll just watch and be last. See, I ain't greedy."

Someone said, "Yeah, but you like to watch." Apache didn't like that. He looked for the guy who said it. Everything got quiet; nobody copped to it and Apache let it pass.

Danny wiggled out of his shorts. His dick seemed gigantic. "Come on, man. I'm ready." Apache jerked the white boy's head up with a pull of the blindfold and grabbed his chin with his other hand. Danny said, "You'd better not bite me, cocksucker. Open it, open it." The mouth opened and Danny jammed his huge dick into his mouth. The white boy choked and his head shook. Danny got mad and punched him in the face.

The others didn't like it. "Cut it out, Danny. He ain't gonna be able to take us on if you keep beating on him like that. We want some too, you know."

They had lined up, like any chow line, except that some had taken off their pants and shorts and their dicks stuck out like giant handles. One of them I knew from the church. When he saw me watching, he said, "What you looking at, holy boy. Just wait 'till we get your ass over here."

I moved away from the cell bars. But not for long. Danny was saying, "Oh, that's good. Keep him like that. That's good. That's good." The white boy was still on his knees and Apache still held the blindfold, but now his other hand was on the white boy's forehead, tilting it back. And now another man was stooped behind the white boy grabbing him under the arms and moving him back and forth. The white boy seemed lifeless. Then Danny came, moaning, "Oh! Oh! Oh! Oh!" grabbing at the white boy's hair. The white boy started choking again, shaking all over, coughing and then vomiting. Danny fell to the ground, "Oh, that was good."

Nacho said, "Hey, man, make him stop puking. Get him
up again. Vomit was still drooling from his mouth. "Open it,
man. Open it." And then Nacho was pushing his dick in and
out of that lifeless mouth until he came and the white boy
vomited again.

The third man pushed Nacho aside. He was a much bigger man. Apache said, "Wait a minute, man, wait a minute.
Give us a chance to get him ready."

"Fuck that shit. I don't need you guys. I'm gonna fuck
him," the big man said. He moved over the white boy and
with one motion scooped him up so that the white boy's ass
was touching his swollen dick. Somehow the lifeless body
began struggling again. "Hold him. Hold Him." Apache and
his helper held him. The big man was anxious. He couldn't
find the hole. Then he couldn't get it in. He was mumbling
and gasping. His eyes seemed about to pop. He moved the
ass in every direction, but he couldn't get it in. His mum-
blings grew louder.

Apache said, "Cool it, man, you'll have the bull down on
us." The big man paid no attention; he got louder, cursing
the white boy and his white ass. Then, with one vicious
thrust he got in. The white boy let out a long scary moan.
Apache stuffed his mouth with a pair of shorts. The big man
could barely breathe, but he kept twisting and pulling and
wrenching at those white hips. Each thrust seemed to go
deeper. He was snorting. And then he came, falling helpless
on top of the whimpering white boy.

The next afternoon the guards found the white boy on
his bunk. "Jesus, look what they did to him." No one turned
in that direction. "Visiting day's tomorrow. Fucking Smitty
should never have put this kid in with these animals. Let
him go tell this kid's people that he's lost his visiting privileges because he's been a disciplinary problem. Let's get
him out of here. He's gonna have to see his people sometime." They didn't ask anyone what had happened.

A week or so later Pollo, the trustee, came running to C
dorm. "Apache, they just brought in some pervert. He
ripped up some four-year-old girl. Smitty's gonna put him in

here." Apache came to the cell bars. "Is he a *gavacho*?"

"Yeah."

"Find out where he's from. Check and see if any guys in here have done time with him."

"I already did, man. And I couldn't find out anything about him. Nobody knows him."

"How old is he."

"His jacket says thirty."

"Does he look like a fag."

"No, man, he's short. But he's a husky dude. Good build. Looks like he works out. Looks like he can be a mean motherfucker."

"Shit, that don't scare me." He thought about it. "So Smitty's putting him in here, huh? Wants us to punk him over. Don't worry, man. I always did like short husky *gavacho* dudes who think they're bad. Motherfucker's gonna have a big red sore asshole in the morning. We'll teach him to rip up little girls."

Within an hour Pollo was back. "He's getting his bedding now. They're gonna bring him pretty soon."

Apache said, "Okay. You guys get ready and let me do the talking," Apache said.

About six of them started playing cards at the cell's table; others gathered around Apache's bunk and some around Danny's. There was only one black in the cell now, and he and the old white drunk stayed in their bunks. Smitty brought him in.

He was a short man, at most five-foot-six, but he seemed as wide at the shoulders as he was tall. His thick muscles bulged under the faded green jail T-shirt. Shame weighed heavily on him and he carried it badly. His face was red and his blood-shot blue eyes seemed more red than blue. His head hung. And even though he kept nodding yes, he wasn't hearing Smitty. Finally Smitty grabbed him by the arm and pointed him to his bunk. "That's your bunk in the corner. Keep your sheets and blanket tucked in under your mattress. I think you'll like it in here. These are pretty nice guys." Smitty left.

No one spoke to him. When he reached his bunk he
looked around the cell. No one noticed him. He made his
bed slowly. Then he sat on his bunk facing the rest of the
cell. Still no one looked at him. He cleared his throat and
looked around the cell some more, back and forth. He
caught the old drunk's eye. He started toward him, but the
old man knew better and rolled over on his bunk as if to
take a nap. He sat on his bunk again and cleared his throat
some more. Then he went over to Danny's group. They were
talking in low tones of Spanish. When he got there they
stopped talking. Now he knew for sure. His head hung
again. He went back to his bunk and laid down facing the
wall. Apache let him lay there for awhile, then went over to
his bunk and shook him gently. "Hey, man."

The short man jumped up, startled. "Easy, man, easy."

"Oh, no sweat, no sweat. You just kinda caught me by
surprise." He was eager, smiling even. "I was just lying here
thinking." He spoke quickly. "Want a cigarette? My name's
Aubrey Perkins and . . ."

Apache wasted no time. "What you in here for, man?"

"Oh, just some chickenshit thing. Two-bit beef, you
know."

"Where you from?"

"Oklahoma."

"Done any time?"

"Yeah. Been to the reformatory and the joint in Oklahoma."

"What for?"

"Just some little ol' chickenshit car theft. Got a distant
cousin I was staying with while I was trying to find me a
job. But I pretty much decided to go back to Oklahoma."

Apache came back to it. "So what they get you for?"

"Oh, just some little ol' petty theft at some store, and I
roughed the people up a bit."

Apache flashed, his voice was loud. "Look, man. Don't
come in here bullshitting me. Don't think you're talking to
just another dumb Mexican. The only thing you ripped off
was a four-year-old cunt. And you didn't rip it off, you

ripped it up, you snivelling, filthy, fucking Okie cocksucker. Us Mexicans got ways of dealing with animals like you."

The other Mexicans surrounded them. One of them said, "We know all about it, asshole. Fucking white boys always coming in here lying to us. She was probably a Mexican, too."

"Yeah. You cocksuckers think you can do whatever you want to us."

Then Apache took over again. "Look, punk. We know you did it. Ain't anybody here that don't know that. Now you gonna cop out or not? I mean I want to hear you say you did it, pervert. And I want to hear it now."

He sat on the edge of his bunk, motionless, his head down. He didn't answer.

Apache kicked his leg. "Answer, cocksucker."

There was no answer. Apache waited.

"Want to do a little bleeding, pervert? Like you made her do? How *old* was she, punk? Four? How big was she, punk? About two, maybe three-feet? Was your dick big enough to handle it? Did you get off while you were ripping her little cunt and she was screaming? Can't do it with a woman, can you, punk? All them muscles. Look at all them muscles. Work out every day, huh, pervert? People think you're a man, then. But you know what you are, don't you, baby-cunt ripper? Now you gonna cop out, or you gonna make us make you cop out?"

There was a long pause. Apache kicked him again. "Tell us, punk."

He nodded, yes, yes, and then Apache began nodding too. "I knew it. I knew it . . . Alright, punk, we'll take care of you later. Get in your bunk now and stay there until we're ready for you. I don't want to see you walking around any part of this cell unless I say so, hear? I said, get over in your bunk. All the way over, right up against that fucking wall, fucker. And stay there and don't even be turning around. Don't even be looking at us, you filthy animal, hear? We don't want you contaminating any more of our cell than has to be, hear?"

He pressed against the wall, his huge back tight against the T-shirt.

Just before dinner Apache went to his bunk. He was still pressed against the wall. "Look, pervert, and I don't mean look at me, 'cause I don't want to see your animal white face. We're gonna go eat, but you ain't going. We don't want you going anywhere with us, hear?"

Smitty came and unlocked the cell for dinner. Everyone headed for the chow hall. Aubrey Perkins stayed in his bunk. Smitty said, "Hey, Perkins, chow time." He didn't move or speak. Apache stayed behind to watch. Smitty asked, "What's wrong with him."

"He's sick," Apache said.

They smiled.

Once they were gone, Perkins got out of his bunk and paced. He saw me watching him and came over to the cell door. I was at my door, and we were five feet apart. He started to speak to me, but he saw the sign beside my door that said I was crazy. He shook his head. What was the use of talking to a crazy man? Still, he didn't leave the door. He looked at me again, and then he looked away. His red eyes were full of fear. He looked at me again; he almost spoke, but instead he turned and went back to his bunk and faced the wall like Apache said.

Apache waited until the lights were dimmed, then he said, "Okay, Danny, get them moving." Three bunks were brought to the center of the cell. A table and a chair were placed on top of them. Apache had cloaked himself in a blue blanket and was waiting. When his platform was finished, he got onto it slowly. The bunk holding the chair swayed. He steadied himself and sat carefully on the chair. Three bunks had been lined up on his right; he motioned these closer. Two bunks were in front of him and below him, about a foot apart. Behind these were two benches and he motioned benches in the direction of Aubrey Perkins. Danny went over to his bunk and said, "All right, baby-cunt ripper. Get your ass out of that bunk. You're going to court. We're gonna show you a little Chicano justice."

Aubrey Perkins stumbled out of his bunk and Danny led him to one of the bunks facing Apache. It was the bunk to Apache's left, and seated on one of the benches was the old white drunk. Danny took him to the old man's side. "You stand here." Then Danny joined the other eleven Mexicans who were sitting on the three bunks to Apache's right. Behind the other bunk facing Apache sat the black man.

Apache said, "This court is now in session. This case is called The Chicanos versus A White Pervert. Are you ready, Danny? Mr. Foreman of the jury?"

"Are you ready, Mr. Prosecutor?"

"Yes, your Honor," said the black man.

"Is the defense ready, Mr. Defense Counsel?"

"Yeah," said the old white drunk. "You'd better show this court some respect, white man."

"Yes sir."

"All right, I have heard from a very reliable witness that you, white pervert, have fucked over a young beautiful Chicana child. That you got her alone and though she didn't even weigh forty pounds, you tied her and gagged her and then with your ugly hands forced her tiny legs apart. You laid your heavy, hairy body on that little Chicanita, and then, with that animal dick of yours, a dick that can't fuck no grown woman, a dick that you can't even jack off with like any normal person. Then with that diseased dick, you ripped her, tearing the skin between her cunt and her pee-hole and her asshole. She bled, oh, how she bled, but that didn't stop you. She screamed, but that didn't stop you. She passed out from the pain, but you kept on 'cause you can't ever do it to a real woman. You kept on 'till you made her three little holes one big one. You liked that, didn't you, pervert? You fucking white people think you can do whatever you want to us, don't you? And then you pumped your diseased jizz into that innocent child. And, if that wasn't enough, you wanted her to eat your filthy dick. Thanks to God that she passed out. And pig that you are, you raped her again and ripped her again. And when you were finished, you turned her over and you would have ripped her

ass some more except that she had shit all over herself and
it wasn't too pretty. But we got you now, don't we, pervert?"

Apache paused and glared down at the broad-shoul-
dered man. He was the only person standing. He stood with
his head down; his whole body drooped. He stood next to the
old drunk who also had his head down. Apache studied him.
"Fucking cocksucker." He studied him some more. "Stand
up straight, pervert. Straight, up, up. Show this court some
respect. Hold that head up. Take it like a man."

Aubrey straightened himself; he raised his head but not
his eyes. Apache stared at him for a long time. No one
moved; no one broke the silence.

Then Apache said, "What do you have to say, Mr. Prosecutor?"

The black man said, "I say what you say, Apache, your
Honor."

"And you, Mr. Foreman?"

Danny said, "Looks like a pretty cold case to me, Judge
Apache."

"And you, Mr. Defense Counsel?" The old drunk said
nothing.

Apache raised his voice, "I said, what do you say, Mr.
Defense Counsel?"

Still he said nothing.

Apache flashed, "I'm talking to you, asshole. You want
to see a little wine flow out of those veins of yours?"

The old drunk said, "Have a little decency, Apache. If
you guys want to rat fuck him, then do it. But why all of
this? He knows what he's done. Why don't you just make
him go down on all of you and get it over with."

Apache glared at the drunk. "You want to be sentenced,
too?"

The drunk shook his head no.

"Then I ask you, what do you have to say, Mr. Defense
Counsel?"

"I don't have anything to say."

"You will show this court respect. You will answer with
the same respect everyone else has."

"I have nothing to say, your Honor."

Apache turned to the jurors. "Gentlemen of the jury, you have a very serious responsibility here. It is your job to see that justice is done. You must be fair to all sides. You must be fair to me. You must be fair to yourselves and to all the Chicanos you represent. You must be fair to the black man and all the people he represents. And, yes, you must be fair, too, to that pervert. But most of all, you must be fair to that poor little Chicanita who suffered this horrible, outrageous act, and to all the millions of Chicanos who have suffered the same kinds of acts. Maybe we haven't had our cunts ripped, brothers, but it's the same. It's the same."

The jurors listened. He knew them; he understood them. And they respected him and even feared that wiry little Mexican who called himself Apache. He said his forefathers were Mayan princes. How he knew that, I never understood. He had the high cheekbones and thick black hair of any Indian, and while his nose was too small and fine, his eyes did have the slant, and his forehead had the mash of the Mayas. In those days in the Fresno County jail, no one doubted that he was a Maya. The name Apache came from other jailing days, before he knew of the Mayas. But he still liked the name, and he wore a red kerchief headband to preserve it. But some of them listened, hoping that the more attention they gave Apache, the sooner he would stop talking and the sooner they could get on with what they wanted. Some had already stripped to their shorts, and one had a hard-on.

But Apache was just beginning. "Long ago when the white man was still living in caves and covering himself with animal hides and eating raw meat, there was already a great and noble culture on this land."

Somebody groaned. This was going to take awhile. The Mayas were Apache's favorite subject. Each day he told C dorm something else about the Mayas, sometimes two and three times a day. I had never heard of the Mayas before I got to the Fresno County jail. The only Indians I knew about were the ones that cowboys chased in movies and

those that seemed to be all over Mexico and which most
people, or my grandmother at least, thought to be as low as
niggers. She had always reminded me that the darker the
Mexican, the more Indian blood he had in him. And the
more Indian blood he had in him, the dumber, uglier and
dirtier he would be. The drunks that slobbered around Chinatown were "Indios." "Mira ese indio." The whores were
"Indias." "Mira ese india." The tramps that came from the
railroad tracks and through the alleys to the back doors
begging for a tortilla and some beans were "Indios." "Aquí
viene otro indio." I was dark and hated my dark skin. I was
an "Indio," and it was easy to believe Apache.

He said the Mayan women were beautiful, more beautiful and fine and shapely than any white woman could be.
The world had never seen more beautiful women. And they
were devoted to their men. I had always thought that Lilly
Gómez was pretty, as pretty as a Mexican could be, as
pretty as a Mexican man could have, because he could never
have a white woman unless she was some old ugly whore
that no white man wanted anymore. But the Mayan women
were even prettier than Lilly according to Apache. I pictured myself walking down Fresno Street with a beautiful
Mayan woman. She clung to me. We walked through the
best parts of Fresno. I could see the white folks peeking
from behind curtains and bushes. She was more beautiful
than any woman they had ever seen.

Apache told of their cities and buildings: cities so well
thought out that no one had matched them yet, buildings
and pyramids that were being found in the jungle today,
that modern man with all his tools and machines and thousands of years of living could not copy or understand. The
Mayas lived in these cities and buildings at the same time
the white man was living in caves across the ocean. He
spoke of their science and mathematics. They knew the sea-
sons and they tracked the stars. They could predict the
weather and the sunrise and the sunset to the minute. They
planted and ate the best foods, foods that kept their bodies
strong and their minds razor sharp. They had a government

that really existed for the good of the people, all of the people. The ruling princes were chosen only after it was proven that they cared only for the good of their fellow man. Each Mayan knew that he carried a beautiful tradition, a duty to make the best use of his mind and body that could be made. And because of this, they loved and respected one another. It wasn't long before I was sure that I had some Mayan blood in me.

That night Apache wanted to tell Aubrey Perkins something about Mayan justice. "I know you don't know who the Mayas were. They were the greatest civilization known to man. The history books will prove that."

Whenever Apache spoke of the Mayas, much of his street talk disappeared. He became very serious, used big words, and slowed his speech. "They were our forefathers, and they lived on this land in palaces and cities while your forefathers lived in caves in other parts of the world. They didn't have crimes such as yours because a Maya would never do that to another Maya; there was too much love and respect. But if you were accused of a crime, you would get fairness no matter who you were. It made no difference if you were a prince or a farmworker or the son of a prince or an orphan. You were treated the same. There you didn't get one sentence because you were rich and another because you were poor. And it didn't matter who your friends were or how well they or you knew the judges. There you got what you deserved for what you did. There they didn't fool around with phony symbols like that blindfolded woman with her scales who can just happen to tell who the spics and niggers are. There you got plain and simple justice.

"And there you didn't need no lawyers. You didn't have some judge telling you not to talk to him, to talk through your lawyer, to 'address' the court through your lawyer, even though the lawyer they always give you never knows or cares about you or your case, or is too scared to tell the judge what he should hear. In the Mayan courts you talked for yourself, you defended yourself. There were no lawyers. You told the judge just how it was. Things never got so complicated that—even though it was your ass, your freedom, your life—there was nothing you could say that made any sense to the judge. You and the judge talked about what you did or didn't do, not about some silly rules in a book that you can't understand. And when you were finished, when it was all over, no matter what you got, you didn't feel cheated. You knew you had shot your best shot, and that he had listened and understood.

The Mayas never got so far away from each other that they didn't understand one another. If there had been junkies in those days, a judge would understand what it was like to be a junkie, what it was like to need a fix. He would have understood that junkies didn't just happen, that they came to be. That they weren't freaks or animals, but just people hanging around looking for something to do or something to be. At least he wouldn't look at them like they were some kind of scum that were smelling up or dirtying up his little courtroom. At least he would know that they were just people too, and that they needed and wanted the same things he did, but that somehow life had just gotten to be too much for them. Maybe a lot sooner than for most people. But it was the same."

Apache paused. He studied Aubrey Perkins. Whatever he expected to see, he didn't because Aubrey Perkins yawned. Apache flashed, "You rotten motherfucker! You no good Okified cocksucker! Try to spend a little time with you, try to teach you something!" Apache was loud now. "Try to give you a break, but you ain't interested. You know all about Messicuns, don't you, Okie. You been to Texas a few times, haven't you, asshole. You don't need to know any of this because you know all about Messicuns, don't you, fucker. Well, let me tell you. You don't know shit about this Messicun. I ain't like my brother or my mother and father and sisters. They all live in Texas. You know them all; they're all good lil' ol' Messicuns. Especially my brother. He went to school. You know, one of them schools they have for Messicuns. When they didn't want him in school no more, he chopped cotton. Then they let him wash dishes and support his wife and baby. And after three years of washing dishes they let him be a bus boy. I wouldn't do none of those things, so I was locked up a lot. Then the war came and they drafted his ass. They shipped his ass over to the Japs. The Japs blew his guts out. He's got to wear a bag to shit and piss. They blew his leg off. They left his face all scarred up. Well he came home, came back to Texas all dressed up in his pretty soldier suit with all his medals, purple heart and all that shit. Came back to Texas on a Greyhound bus. You're not gonna tell me you never been to Texas, are you, cocksucker? Sure you been to Texas. You know what it's like for lil' ol' Messicuns down in Texas. Sure you do. Well my brother was hungry, see, and he just couldn't eat any old thing 'cause of his stomach. They finally stopped the bus and he thought 'cause he had all those medals that they'd let him eat in the restaurant. He went in and the Okified bitch said, 'Can't you read the sign, greaser?' And he started screaming, and he showed everybody his bag and his plastic leg. And she said, 'Can't you read the sign, greaser?' And he took off his bag and threw it at her, all full of all that shit, and started tearing up the place. Then the sheriff came and then he was in jail just like me.

"But now you're in jail, Aubrey Perkins, and it's our turn. Mr. Foreman, I want you to be fair and just. Do you understand?"

"Yes, your Honor."

"Good. What is your verdict?"

"Guilty, your Honor."

Aubrey Perkins didn't move.

"Good. Now I'll sentence you. For the vicious crime that you and your people have committed against this innocent Chicanita, I sentence you to suck and fuck everybody in this cell every night for as long as you're here. And by everybody, I mean everybody, even that nigger sitting next to you."

Aubrey Perkins didn't show any emotion, and he didn't show any as he knelt down night after night to carry out his sentence. What was hard to understand was how that big back and that thick neck could bend over hour after hour without the slightest struggle. Later, I learned that this was how the Aubreys purge themselves. What scared me was that, as I watched Aubrey Perkins on the floor, I knew that someday, someplace, that would be me on my hands and knees.

CHAPTER FOUR

"**W**hy was I born?"

"I was born to know, love, and serve God in this world and to be happy with Him in the next."

"Who made me?"

"God made me."

"Why did God make me?"

"God made me to know, love, and serve Him in this world and to be happy with Him in the next."

"Who is God?"

"God is the All-Knowing, All-Powerful, All-Present, Eternal Good."

Once we knew that by heart, the nun told us about death. I remember the day it sunk in. I was on my way home from school. Everything had to die. The plants, the trees, the grass, the bugs, the cats, the dogs, me. Everything, everyone since the days of Adam and Eve had died. I didn't want to die. More than anything, I didn't want to die. I couldn't imagine what it would be like to be dead. It scared me. I wished I were a dog or a plant. It had to be easier to die if you were a dog or a plant. It was still hot in Fresno. The heat seemed to be killing everything. Everything I looked at was going to die. It seemed unfair. I would have rather stayed where I was before I was born, and

never have been born, if I was just born so that I could die.
I carried that terror around with me for days. I didn't tell
my grandmother. I couldn't tell anyone, and especially her.

Then the nun told us about heaven and hell. First she
told us about hell. If you sinned and died, you went to hell.
There you would burn in the hottest fire that had ever been
made, and you would burn forever and ever without end.
Death still seemed worse. It was the end of everything,
after that nothing mattered. But after awhile the idea of
burning forever and ever started to mean something. Now
there was something after death: a roaring fire that burned
you and burned you and burned you. Burning forever was
hard to believe or even imagine. Somewhere, sometime,
there had to be an end to it. Even my grandmother stopped
punishing me after awhile. I thought of making a deal with
the devil and becoming his helper. I thought that if I was
good while I was burning, that after awhile he'd let me off
the fire. Sometimes I'd think there wouldn't be a fire big
enough to burn all of us that went to hell, and that he'd let
me get off to the side while some of the others took their
turns burning. The whole thing was worse than death
because you lost twice. And I always knew I'd go to hell. A
lot of people would go to purgatory and just burn for awhile
and then go on up to heaven. The babies would go to limbo,
and others, like my grandmother and the priests and the
nuns, would go straight to heaven. But I always knew
where I was going.

Heaven was up in the sky. It was sunny, and people
walked around on clouds. Everything you ever wanted
would be there, except that once you saw God, you would be
happy forever and want nothing else. I used to see Him a
lot, in the sky, as big as the sky, with wild white hair and
cold blue eyes, but always angry, always shaking His head
at me, no. Sometimes I'd see Him at night in the dark of my
room. He was never happy with me and I'd hear that loud
voice, NO! NO! Sometimes I'd tell Him that I'd been good,
but He knew everything.

All of this led to Confession and Holy Communion,

which came at the end of the first grade. You could sin and be forgiven; you could sin and still get to heaven. There was hope. We learned the Ten Commandments, from these we knew what sins were. There were two kinds of sins: mortal and venial. Confession would wipe both of them away. But if you died with a mortal sin on your soul, you would go to hell. A venial sin would only put you in purgatory. One of the commandments said: Honor thy father and mother. That meant my grandmother; it meant that I had to obey, love, and respect her. If I didn't, it was a sin. I didn't ask any more questions about what that commandment meant because I didn't like my grandmother and I didn't want to give myself away. And just about the time I had convinced myself that I had sinned, I'd convince myself that I really did like her and hadn't sinned.

Just a few weeks before school ended, we went to Confession. The nun took us over to the church and lined us up against the back wall. The confessional was a booth split up into three parts, with curtains in each entry so you couldn't see in. The priest was in the middle, and we went into the smaller booths on each side of him. Then it was my turn, and I went in. There was a place to kneel right next to what looked like a small window, except that instead of glass, the window was covered by cloth. I couldn't see through it. I knelt down. By that time I had decided I had not liked my grandmother many times, that sometimes I had even hated her. I said what we had learned by heart. "Bless me, Father, for I have sinned. This is my first Confession. These are my sins . . ." Before I could go on, the priest said, "Yes, my child." It was Padre Galván. I knew his voice and I knew he knew mine. "Yes, my child, what are your sins?" I said nothing. I knelt there for a long time, saying nothing. I could never tell him my sins; I could never tell him I hated my grandmother. Then he'd know for sure that I was bad. Finally he said, "Jesús, there are a lot of children waiting. You must tell me your sins. I will forgive them." When he said my name, I said, "I don't like my grandmother."

"Why don't you like your grandmother, Jesús?"

"Because she's mean to me."

"Now Jesús, I know your grandmother very well. She
loves you very much. But she is a very holy woman, and her
ways are not our ways. She expects much of herself, and all
that she gets from herself she gives to God. Sometimes she
must seem hard, but these are the ways of the chosen ones.
I forgive you your sins. Say your Act of Contrition, tell God
that you are truly sorry and that you will sin no more, and
go in peace, my son."

Just a few weeks later, on a Sunday, after school had
ended, I served the seven o'clock Mass and went to Holy
Communion. I went back to serve the eleven o'clock Mass.
Before I left, my grandmother told me that she wanted me
home right after Mass because the Guadalupana was coming early. I heard her, but on my way home I passed by the
vacant lot on C Street. It was my favorite vacant lot. A
house had stood on it at one time and had either been
moved or burned down. What was left were cement steps
leading nowhere, the huge hole of the basement, and part
of the chimney. It was easy to get lost on that lot; you could
imagine many things. I stopped and played. When I got
home, she was mad. She slapped me as I came in the back
door and said that she knew what I was up to, that I wasn't
fooling her, that I didn't think she could punish me on Sundays because of the Guadalupana, that she had been noticing how I had been acting lately on Sundays, but she'd
show me. She grabbed me by the ear and took me into my
room and put on my diaper and set up my crib and forced
that big nipple into my mouth. Then she left, warning me
that she'd better not hear a sound out of me when the
Guadalupana came. In a little while they were there. I
heard her say that I was sick, and that they'd have to be a
little quiet. All afternoon I worried that one of them would
come in and see me in my diaper with my bottle. I hated my
grandmother, and I wished she were dead. I hated and
wished all afternoon. One of the women did start to come
into my room, but my grandmother stopped her. My back
was to the door and I didn't see her, but I was sure that she

had seen me. Everybody would know. I hated my grandmother.

Finally the Guadalupana left, and then she went to
work, but not before she came in and said she didn't want
me out of bed. Then the house was still, and I hated her
some more. I lay there for a long time, hating her. After
awhile I started sweating. The sinking sun was beating
against my side of the house. It was always hot on that side
of the house in the afternoons, but now with the door
closed, it seemed like all of the day's heat was trapped in
my room. The sun poured in. I got up and opened the door.
That didn't do any good. I went into the front room on the
other side of the house. It was hot there too. All the windows and the door were shut. Usually she would close them
late in the morning and open them just before she went to
work. Today she hadn't. I wanted to open the front door,
but someone might notice and she'd know I had gotten out
of bed. It seemed to get hotter; I could feel the heat in my
mouth. I wanted her to die and go to hell. I went into the
back porch, crawling so the neighbors wouldn't see. The sun
and the heat smothered the screen. It was hot there too,
but at least it was open. I laid on the floor, still in my diaper. From the speedway two miles from our house came the
drone of racing cars. There was racing every summer Sunday night, and for four hours the sharp droning of the little
cars speeding around the track would reach our house, ris-
ing on the straightaways and dying on the curves. It was an
awful sound, sad and long and sharp.

That night the droning brought a message of death. It
told me that I would die that night, that that was the last
sun I would see, that just as this was the end of a day, the
end of a week, so too it was the end of my life. It wasn't my
grandmother who was going to die, it was me. I laid on that
old worn floor not knowing how to escape it. The sun kept
sinking, and the time kept passing, and the drone kept
reminding me that this was my last day. I crawled back into
the kitchen and closed the porch door, but I could still hear
the droning, and with it too the commandment, "Honor Thy

Father and Mother." I was sweating again. I went back to
my room and knelt down and prayed. I prayed as hard as I
could; I squeezed each word for forgiveness. I tried to see
Him because if He saw me, He'd know how sorry I really
was. But even when I closed my eyes, I couldn't see Him. All
I could hear was the droning and the commandment, "Honor
Thy Father and Mother." I had sinned all afternoon. I had
hated her and wished she would die and go to hell. I told
myself that those were venial sins and, then as I faced
death, that I would just burn in purgatory for a little while.
But the more the sun sank and the longer the drone went
on, the more I knew that they were mortal sins. Praying
couldn't forgive mortal sins. I could feel hell's flames licking
my knees. I cried, but that didn't do any good either. I got
into bed and covered myself and buried my head under the
pillow so I wouldn't hear the droning or see the end of the
sun. The bed was soaked with sweat; I didn't dare get out. I
prayed under that pillow. I prayed and prayed, even though
I knew it wasn't enough.

The next morning I touched myself and then things in
my room. Then I thanked Him.

I stole a hammer when I was eight years old. It was a
special hammer, but once I stole it, I never used it. That
summer, missionary nuns held a summer school at the
church. Every morning after they taught us about God, we
did woodwork. There were two hammers, a big one and a
little one. I liked the little hammer and used it every
chance I could. I drove nails into everything. It seemed like
I could never use that hammer enough. I argued and fought
with other kids over that hammer until one of the nuns
would come and make me give it up. I wanted that hammer
more than anything. I felt that if I could just have that
hammer, I'd be happy. On the next-to-last day of summer
school, as we were putting the tools away, I stole it. I
pushed it under a platform, thinking I'd take it home after
Mass the next day.

I didn't take it home after Mass because Padre Galván
was around the whole time. Later that morning, the nuns

started looking for it. I knew what they were looking for
and I got scared. One of them looked under the platform,
but she didn't see it. Then they asked if any of us had seen
the little hammer; who had used the little hammer last.
One of the kids said, "Jesús always uses that hammer. He
hogs it. Nobody else gets to use it. He probably knows
where it's at. Ask him."

She asked me if I had seen the hammer. I shook my
head no.

After awhile she came to my seat and said, "Jesús, are
you sure you don't know where that hammer is?" I shook
my head no. It was hard to look at her. "Jesús, they say you
were using it last." No, no, I shook my head. She asked
again and I started to cry. That stopped her. Later, Padre
Galván came to thank the nuns. They talked for a long
time, and while they were talking, he looked over at me. I
knew he knew.

The next morning I went with Doña Petra's family to
the fields. I went every day for the rest of the summer. I
worked with her family and she gave whatever I made to
my grandmother. At first I thought of the hammer, thinking of ways I could get it home. By the end of the summer, I
had forgotten it. I worked up to the day school started.
Doña Petra said I had been good worker and gave my
grandmother something extra. That made my grandmother
happy. "You must be very tired," she said. "Doña Petra said
you worked hard. Sleep tomorrow. Don't serve the six
o'clock Mass. In fact, you should sleep late this whole week.
I'll tell Padre Galván that you won't start again until next
week."

When school started, I hadn't been to Confession and
Communion since summer school. On the first day, the nun
told us that Friday was First Friday, which meant everyone
in the school would go to Communion. On Wednesday she
started getting us ready for Confession by going over the
Ten Commandments one at a time. As soon as she started,
I remembered the hammer. I didn't know if it was still
where I left it or if someone had found it. I couldn't even

remember why I had taken it. But I did know that it was a
sin and that I'd have to confess it to Padre Galván the next
afternoon.

That same day, she told us about sacrilege. It was the
worst sin you could commit because it was a sin against
God Himself. It was most often committed by receiving
Communion when you were in the state of sin. To take
God's Body and Blood into your body while you were in the
state of sin was as horrible a sin as there was. If you went
to Confession and lied, or didn't tell all your sins, that was
a bad Confession and a sin itself, and you were still in a
state of sin. But if after that, you went to Communion, that
was a sacrilege. I had gone to Communion many times
since that Sunday in May in the first grade, and I really
believed that the Body and Blood of Jesus Christ was in
that host. It was a kind of bread that tasted like paper, but
whenever Padre Galván took one from the chalice and
blessed me with it and put it in my mouth, I could feel God
and Jesus and even the Holy Spirit coming into me. I would
walk away feeling lighter. Sometimes I'd hear singing.
Sometimes I'd feel like I wanted to burst. And sometimes
I'd even feel that He was smiling at me. Yes, I believed that
into that white, paper-thin, quarter-sized host, the whole
Body of that big Man that hung on the cross with all His
sweat and blood and crown of thorns, had been pressed. I
believed that the Man with the long flowing hair and full
beard who had sat at the center of the table at the Last
Supper, of whom they had asked: "Is it I, Lord?" was as
much in that tiny host as I was Jesús Olivas.

She told us that our bodies became tabernacles for the
Body and Blood of Jesus, and because of that, we had to be
pure, free from sin. God would never permit His Only
Begotten Son to be carried in the filth of our sins. He had
struck people dead who had tried it and had blinded others
on the spot. He had crippled some and deformed others. His
anger was great. I understood that well, and understood
also that the next afternoon, I would have to kneel and tell
Padre Galván about the hammer. I thought of that hammer

most of the day. I thought of sneaking into the church basement and giving it back. But to whom? The missionary
nuns were gone and it belonged to them. I could never
unsteal it; I had to confess it. Still, I wondered how long it
would take to make a sin go away without Confession. I did-
n't ask her because then she'd know. I'd have to confess it.

The next afternoon she marched us over to the church.
I got in line, near the end. I was going to confess it. One by
one I got closer to the booth. I kept thinking about that
morning on the last day of summer school when Padre
Galván came in and they told him and he looked over at
me. I wondered if he'd tell my grandmother and what she'd
do to me. Priests weren't supposed to tell anyone what you
said in Confession, but I knew he'd tell my grandmother.
The more I thought about it, the less afraid I was of what
she'd do to me, and the more worried I was of what they'd
think of me. Now he would know what I was and she would
be so ashamed. It wouldn't be long before everyone would
know what I had done. I left the line and went up to the
nun. "Sister, I don't feel too good, and besides, I don't need
to go to Confession because I don't have any sins to confess.
Can I be excused?"

She knew my grandmother; they all did. She knew I
served the six o'clock Mass every morning. "You're in the
state of grace?" she asked. Yes. I nodded. "All right, you can
go."

By the time I went to bed that night, I knew what I had
to do. I had to convince my grandmother in the morning
that I was really sick and couldn't go to school. If I went
into church, I'd commit a sacrilege. I didn't think He'd kill
me, but I was sure He'd deform me and I was already ugly
enough. I was awake when she said, "Get up, Jesús, it's
time," and I thought I was ready for her.

"Amá, I don't feel so good."

She didn't believe me; it was the way I said it. She
brushed it aside. "I don't want to hear that," she said. "Get
up. The trouble with you is that you haven't been to Mass
and Communion all summer. Today's First Friday. You'll

see how much better you'll feel after Mass. Besides, you've
been sleeping too much. Now get up." She left and I didn't
get up. I had to try again; this time I'd try to show some
pain. But before I knew it, she was back again. She was
getting mad. "Get up, I said." I got up. She watched me for
awhile, then said, "Did you confess yourself yesterday?" I
was bent over looking for my socks and shoes under the
bed.

"Yes," I said.

"Good." Then she said, "You know, I think I'll go to
Mass with you. It's such a fine thing to see all you children
receiving the Sacrament. There are few things I'd rather
see." I was sure she knew.

On First Fridays we met at the school, and then
marched over to the church in two lines. That morning she
walked with me. By then it embarrassed me to have my
grandmother walk me to school. But that morning, I was
scared; I wasn't worried about what the other kids thought.
She said nothing as we walked and I was sure she knew.
But if I went to Communion, then she'd never know for
sure. That was a sacrilege, and something in me sank. If I
didn't go, she'd know, everyone would know.

When we got to the school, I got into line and she
stopped and talked to the nun. She didn't speak much English and the nun didn't speak Spanish. But they talked for
a long time. The nun kept shaking her head no. I wasn't
close enough to hear, but I knew she was asking her if I
had gone to Confession. In church, the nun sat right behind
me; she was going to watch what I did. I looked back at my
grandmother. She looked mad. When we went into the
church, the morning sun was bright; it filled the church. As
the Mass started, as it went on, as we got closer to Communion, the church got darker. I tried not to think of Communion, but I could feel the thought. It was everywhere. When
the time came, when everybody rose to go to Communion, I
rose too. Slowly, pew by pew, the others went to the altar
rail. I watched each pew empty. No one, not one, stayed in
the pew. Everyone in the whole school was going to Com-

munion. When it was my pew's turn, I went too. God was everywhere, and someday, somehow, He would punish me. But my grandmother and the nun and Padre Galván were here now. The line moved slowly. I *had* to go to Communion. At the altar railing, as Padre Galván got closer, God and His punishments got closer. Would He punish me at the railing or in the pew, or at school or wait until I got home? Would He strike me dead, or just blind me or cripple me? Still, I couldn't leave the altar railing. They were all there and they would all know. When Padre Galván got to me, I was shaking. I expected some kind of thunder or blast just as the host reached my lips, but it didn't come and I swallowed hard and the host went down. And even as it was going down, He started struggling and fighting and kicking all that filth in my soul. My stomach hurt; the pain was sharp. He was twisting it and knotting it as He struggled. I felt hot. I wanted to puke, but I couldn't do it at the altar railing because they would know. I went back to the pew. He wanted to get out of that filth. I could feel Him and my whole stomach in my throat. I swallowed and kept swallowing because if I puked in church they would know. I held it until we got to the school hall, and then I puked at the breakfast line, all over the food.

I was sick for a long time. My grandmother tried every cure she knew. But for two weeks, I kept puking almost everything I ate. I felt weaker and weaker. I knew I was going to die. Finally she called a doctor. We couldn't afford doctors, but everyone told her it was serious. He examined me and said he didn't know what I had. I knew what I had. He gave me some medicines and said if I didn't get better by the end of the week, I'd have to go to the hospital. She didn't know how we were going to pay for the hospital, but if I puked all my breakfast Saturday, she said I'd have to go on Monday. I could hardly get out of bed. That afternoon before she went to clean the church and fix the altar, she told me that she was going to have a hard time confessing herself because Padre Galván was gone for two weeks and the priest who was replacing him did not speak Spanish. I asked her to take me to Confession. No one knew this priest. I could tell him everything and no one would l know. I begged her to take me. Weak as I was, I walked to the church and confessed everything. I ate when I came home and didn't puke. She said it was the work of God, and together we prayed our thanks.

Chapter Five

The first time I saw my lawyer was the second time I was in court. We had just been brought into the courtroom, and I was sitting in the first row of the jury box with the other prisoners when he came up to me, handed me his card, and whispered, "Jesus Olivas. My name's Ralph Fischer. The court's appointed me to represent you. I don't know much about your case, but today you're just up for plea. We'll just go ahead and plead not guilty for now and have it set for trial. I'll be up to see you in the jail in a day or two, and we'll talk about it." About all I noticed then was that he was young and wore big glasses and that when I tried to get up and shake his hand, my chains and leg irons bothered him. But I had a lawyer.

I fingered his card. RALPH FISCHER. And below it, ATTORNEY AT LAW. He had his office on Fulton St. in one of the big buildings. That made me proud and I looked over at him a lot. He was sitting with all the other lawyers as the judge called the cases. He looked like a lawyer; he looked like them. He wore a suit and white shirt and tie. Some of the salesmen in downtown wore suits in the winter time. The judge called my case. "The People of the State of California versus Jesus Olivas." It struck fear in me, but not like the first time. I knew enough to stand up this time.

I was going to have a hard time talking again. But this time
Mr. Fischer came over and stood in front of and to one side
of me. The judge read all the charges against me. It took a
long time. Then he said, "How do you plead, Mr. Olivas?
Guilty or not guilty?" Before I could say or do anything, Mr.
Fischer said, "As to each count, your Honor, the plea is not
guilty." Just like that. He sounded good. I was glad I had
him for a lawyer.

I started to sit down, but the judge kept asking, "Is that
your plea, Mr. Olivas?"

Mr. Fischer nudged me. "Say, 'Yes your Honor.' " "Yes,
your Honor." Then the judge said that I would have a jury
trial in sixty days. That was all there was to it. I was glad I
had him for a lawyer.

I was guilty. I had expected to plead guilty. I had beat
him until I thought he was dead. I could still feel the pipe
hitting his flesh. There was blood all over. He had begged
me not to, to stop. He had begged for mercy. I had spread
the shit all around, and I had started the fire. I had hit others, too. I was guilty. But when Mr. Fischer said, "Not
guilty," there had been a taste of hope. Maybe, somehow, I
wasn't guilty. It was the way he had said it, "As to each
count, your Honor, the plea is not guilty," strong and convinced.

I got up early and waited for him. It was the first time
I'd combed my hair in jail. I made my bed and picked up
and flushed all the bits of food and paper in the cell down
the toilet. Then I swept the floor with my hands and flushed
that too. I thought the guards would bring him to my cell,
and so each time I heard footsteps, I'd jump off my bunk,
straighten it, and then sit carefully back down on the edge
of it. After a time or two there was nothing to straighten,
but I kept straightening it anyway. Somebody in C dorm
noticed and said, "Hey, that guy really is crazy. He keeps on
getting up and making his bed and it don't need making." I
decided not to straighten it anymore, but as soon as I heard
footsteps I was up straightening it again. I waited that
night even after the lights went out, but he didn't come. He

had said in a day or two and I told myself that it was just the first day. I fell asleep waiting.

I woke thinking that he was coming. I washed my face and combed my hair and straightened my bunk again. I was sure he'd come that day. Everyone said I had a heavy case; that he'd want to start working on it. I could see him defending me in court. His voice boomed, and when it was over I would walk out into the street with him. But free meant that I was innocent, and I knew I was guilty. I didn't like thinking about being guilty and free. None of it made any sense.

By noon he still hadn't come, and I wondered for the first time why he had lied to me. There were fifty-eight days until my trial. The trustee brought my lunch tray and I ate everything. Then I swept the floor again. There had been days, especially at first, when I hadn't eaten; when I had taken the tray through the slit and put it on the floor. Once I had sixteen trays in my cell. The food changed color, it rotted, stank and drew bugs. The trustee would say, "Fuck you, crazy. If you don't want to put your tray up here where I can get it, I hope you rot with it, too. I don't really give a shit what you do." I didn't want Mr. Fischer to think I was crazy. The afternoon passed slowly. I found a way to sit on my bunk without messing it up. Then I didn't get up anymore when I heard footsteps. I waited for the rest of the day perched on the edge of my bunk, but he didn't come.

I hated him the next morning. I couldn't understand how, in a day of twenty-four hours, he didn't have five minutes for me. Still I washed and combed and ate and wiped my floor clean. He could come at any time. When he hadn't come by noon, I told the trustee, "Tell the guard to call my lawyer. Tell him I got to talk to him."

The trustee laughed. "The crazy's got a tongue. He can talk. Hey, you guys, look. The crazy can talk. But the first time he talks, he wants me to do him a favor. Well you know what, crazy? You've been nothing but a pain in the ass for me ever since you got here. I've had to clean up every one of your fucking messes. So you know what? Go

fuck yourself. I ain't telling no bull nothing." The tray was
still in the slit, and I grabbed it and started banging it
against the bar and yelling that I wanted my lawyer. Two
guards came running and wrestled me to the floor.
    "You fucking loony. You want to go to the hole!"
    I stopped struggling. I didn't want to go to the hole.
They talked about putting me in the hole, but finally
decided that I was just a crazy bastard. I didn't ask them to
call my lawyer.
    I laid on my bunk for a long time. He wasn't coming. I
would have cried, except I was afraid someone would hear
or see me. Sometime that afternoon, Apache called to me,
"Hey, crazy boy." He had never spoken to me before. He was
standing at the C dorm gate just a few feet from me, smiling. His slanty eyes were closed. I went to my cell door.
    "You ain't so crazy, are you, little brother?"
    I shook my head no.
    "I know that. I've been watching you. I seen what you
did today, and I seen what they did to you. I know this is
your first beef. I'm only talking to you 'cause you're one of
us, and it kind of gets to me when I see you doing what you
did because of your lawyer, and I wanna set you straight.
Your lawyer's not coming, not for a long time. And when he
does come, all he's gonna do is scare you and try to get you
to plead guilty. The judge appointed him to take your case,
right? Well, they don't make much money when they're
appointed like that. So you're not gonna see him much. And
mostly it's the young lawyers, the new lawyers that take
those kind of cases because they're not making much money
anyway. And they're not very good because they don't have
much experience.
    "And when it comes time to go to jury trial, they're
scared. Their asses start twitching, and they start scaring
the ones they're supposed to be defending. I guarantee you,
he's gonna make copping out look real pretty. He's gonna
make it so you don't think you got any choice. Don't do it,
little brother. You're looking at a lot of time. You might as
well fight it."

I waited for him, each day expecting him less. Then there were only 54 days until my trial. Then 36, 31, 28 . . . He didn't come. And Apache was steadily reminding me, "I told you so, little brother. He ain't coming. And when he does come, at the last minute, all he's gonna do is try to make you plead guilty."

I told myself that it really didn't make much difference if he came or not because I was guilty and there wasn't much he could do for me. Still, he had scraped on some hope, and I didn't want to be guilty. I wanted it all to go away. I wanted to wake up and have it be gone, to have it be a dream. Then 21, 19 . . . I threatened him. I'd refuse to talk to him. I'd tell the judge that he had never seen me, that he had done nothing for me. I'd punch him out, in front of the jury even, for trying to sell me out. But he didn't come.

ččččč

Tommy Lee Smith was a writ writer. They put him in the cell next to mine nine days before the trial.

It was late at night when they brought him. He caused a commotion with his chains and white coveralls and his arms cradling two stacks of yellow lined papers. I had been sitting on my bunk against the wall, shielding myself from the eyes of C dorm when I heard the chains. C dorm had it's nightly card game and clatter going. Their noise stopped, and the hush made me pay closer attention to the chains. Then he was standing just a few feet from me as the guards removed his chains. Our eyes met. They were blank dark eyes that said nothing, giving no hint of what they saw or if they saw. His dark hair was little more than stubble, joint-cut, and his skin was gray, joint-gray. Some of C dorm had come to the bars to look at him; but they came, from the beginning, with a kind of reverence: there was no jiving, no cuts, no smart-ass remarks; their eyes were wide, quiet and respectful.

Once the guards were gone, Apache squawked, "What
the fuck you guys staring at! Ain't you never seen a con
before! Get the fuck away from them bars!" He was setting
the stage, making it clear to the writ writer that he was in
charge. He waited 10, 15 minutes, and then he walked up to
the bars and spoke across the four-foot corridor into the
writ writer's cell.
"Where you from, man?"
"Folsom."
"Where in Folsom?"
"The adjustment center."
"You know Richard Rodríguez?"
"Yeah."
"Bobby Peña?"
"Yeah."
"Rudy Tafoya?"
"Yeah."
"How long you been up there?"
"Ten years."
Apache paused. I could see the respect. His face had
softened, and his slit eyes were as wide as I would ever see
them.
"How come they brought you back?" There was respect
in his voice as well.
"I got some action on a writ in the federal court. I filed a
writ of habeas corpus, and the federal court sent the case
here on an order to show cause why I shouldn't be released."
Apache was impressed. "Oh," was all he said.
The next morning, just after they took Tommy Lee
Smith to court, Apache didn't spare the praise, "That is one
heavy dude, one heavy dude. Let me tell you, I've been to
the joint many times and that's no phony. You bastards sit
in here and whine about your light-weight beefs, and that
bastard's been in the adjustment center, isolation, man, for
ten fucking years. And he's fighting his own case. And getting action too. You see those papers in his arms. You know
what those are? His library, and only part of it. The dude
must spend hours, and I mean hours, as many as he can

every goddamn day printing with those little stubs of pencils that they let you have in the joint. He prints from law books and legal newspapers and other writ writers' papers. He's printed thousands and thousands of pages with those tiny pencils. I've seen some of those guys print on toilet paper because that's all they could get their hands on. But they keep on printing, copying.

"And copying's just the beginning. Because then they bind those papers with string and use cardboard for covers and pretty soon they have books, lots of books, their own library, right there in their cells. That way they don't have to go any place to work on their case. And they work, every day, every night, all the time, reading that law, learning those books. They get so they know the law better than street lawyers. They're steady reading that shit. Their cells are filled with their home-made books. They get to having so many books that they have to make more books to tell them what's in the other books.

"They get to be like monks. They don't have any old ladies. They don't get loaded or drunk. They keep to themselves. Don't get into gangs. And they don't usually say too much; but when they *do* say something, it's usually worth listening to. Most of them are in the adjustment centers, or in some kind of isolation, and they're usually strong, tough motherfuckers. I don't mean physical. I mean you can't be that dedicated, that disciplined and not be tough.

"I mean you can see it in this dude. Just the way he stands, just the way he looks at you. There ain't no bullshit about him. He don't need those silly-ass card games, and he stopped whining a long time ago. And when a man gets action in them federal courts, then you *know* he means business; you know he ain't just talking shit."

I got only a glimpse of him when he came back. And again he looked at me as if I wasn't there, as if I was part of the cell, another set of bars.

Apache must have made it clear that nobody else was to talk to Tommy Lee Smith, because nobody else did. And talk to him he did, not constantly, but rather at intervals.

He would pick his times, probably when Tommy Lee Smith wasn't working or sleeping. Then he would casually move up to the bars and quietly begin a conversation. The first time it was, "Hey, Tommy, I had this here dump-truck public defender. I played hell getting rid of him. The judge said if I got rid of him I was on my own. Can a judge do that?"

Each time they talked, Apache wanted some kind of legal advice. At first it was only about his case, but then, after he had asked every question that could be asked about his case, he asked about the case of some of the others. He even told him about my case. "You know, that little brother next to you is facing some pretty heavy charges, Tommy. He just barely turned eighteen and he's never been jailing before and now he's looking at a life beef. And that dump-truck lawyer the judge appointed him ain't even been up to see him and he goes to jury trial next week.

"They keep saying he's crazy. That's why they got him in that cell next to you. But if the dude's crazy, then I'm stupid. He ain't crazy. He's just scared. Shocked, man. And I keep steady preaching at him to fight it, not to cop out, to take it all the way to a jury trial 'cause he's got nothing to lose. He's gonna get life either way, and if he fights it, he can at least appeal it. Ain't that right, Tommy? I keep telling him that when that fool lawyer of his finally shows up, all he's gonna do is try to get him to plead guilty. I don't know if I'm hitting home with him 'cause he never talks. Doesn't say a goddamn thing. But maybe he'll listen to you, Tommy, 'cause he sure as shit has to know by now that you know what you're talking about."

But Tommy Lee Smith didn't say anything. Not then. He waited until the night before he left, until five days before my jury trial to say anything. Even then he waited until the last of the card games was over in C dorm and we could hear the snoring and heavy breathing before he said, "I know you got to be awake, kid, because nobody sleeps that badly. Nobody can toss and turn like you've been doing and still be asleep."

"I'm awake" I said.

Tommy went on. "I killed a priest when I was about your age. I didn't just maim him, I killed him. I was probably a little older than you, but not much, maybe a year or so. I don't talk about it much, but then I never did. And I've wondered if I should say anything to you about it, if there was anything at all to gain by talking about it. Because I don't *need* to talk about it, and people learn so little from what others tell them. They've got to make their own mistakes. But there are so many parallels here . . . I mean, there are so many things about your case and mine that are alike, that it's probably worthwhile telling you what happened to me . . . Yeah, I think you ought to fight it. Of course, I only know what Apache's said about your case, and I don't get the feeling you're gonna add anything one way or the other."

"No."

"I killed the son of a bitch the week before I was supposed to go off to college. He was the parish priest, and I had known him most of my life. My mother was a Catholic, a good Irish Catholic. But when my father died—he was no Catholic—she really turned to religion. I was thirteen then, the oldest of four kids. I became the man of the family. That's how my mother wanted it, and I guess that's how I wanted it too. I got a paper route in the mornings and a job at the neighborhood grocery store after school and on weekends. My mother worked in a dry cleaners, and between the two of us—my Dad's insurance had paid off the house—we were able to give my brother and two sisters a pretty good life. I was a driven kid. I made time for study and studied hard. Before long, I was at the head of my class. Then I took on football and baseball, too. They let me switch my hours at the store so I could practice and play in all the games. I didn't get much sleep, but I was the star. In football, I was a halfback. I wasn't real fast, but I had good balance and was shifty and could run over most bastards when I had to. I knew I could dominate my classmates at anything. They were just kids. They didn't know anything about anything.

"And the girls loved me. They were always after me.

But there was no time for girls. More than that, I thought
they would weaken me. That if I gave into any pleasure
that didn't come out of struggle, it would only weaken me. I
know I thought that, understood that, even then, because I
feared it. My mother loved to see the girls chase me because
she knew I'd reject them. She was the only girl in my life.

"Some time after I was a football star, Father Joe
started coming to the house. Father Joe. That's what he
wanted me to call him, and that's what I called him, Father
Joe. His attention didn't surprise me because everybody
wanted to get next to me then. I was a success story. There
were write-ups about me in the paper: high school star,
holding two jobs, straight-A student, helping widowed
mother support a younger brother and two younger sisters.
It made my mother proud to see the interest that Father
Joe took in me. He'd come over to the house every night and
tutor me, show me short cuts and help me digest the mater-
ial. He was like a brother to me, an older brother. Not a
father, because by then I was the man of the house, no
doubt about it. The meals revolved around my hours: we
went to church when I was free; visitors came when I was
home; and my mother decided nothing, I mean nothing,
without first consulting me.

"Church and God weren't big deals for me. I believed in
God probably because everybody around me did. I didn't give
Him much thought. I knew He had to be on my side because
I did everything right. Everything I touched was right. I
went to church on Sundays. I liked going to church. You
could feel the stir when we walked in, everybody gawking
and admiring us as a family. But the admiration really was
for me. I knew that. I'd usher my brother and sisters into the
church and then walk beside my mother down the center
aisle. When we got to our pew, I'd stand beside it as first my
brother and then my sisters and then my mother entered it.
All eyes were on us, on me really. There wasn't a woman in
the place who didn't want her son to grow up to be like me.
The men respected me. I was big then, bigger than I am
now. I had more bulk and muscle then which made me more

of a man. It added the final touch. They all knew I was going to college on a football scholarship. What they wouldn't have given to be me!

"And Father Joe always added to the fanfare. When I would go up to the altar railing to receive Communion, he would raise his voice as he got to me. He would dramatize each word of that Latin prayer so that everybody in the church would know that Tommy Lee Smith was receiving the so-called Body and Blood of Jesus Christ. I know I felt that, everybody watching and admiring me. And in that last year, he would mention our family in his sermons, but really me, using me as an example of what anyone could do or be if he worked within God's will, if he used his God-given talents as God wanted us to do. If anyone said those things about me now, I'd be embarrassed. But I wasn't then. I expected it. That was normal. I was young.

"That last summer I worked full time around the church and rectory. Father Joe had worked it into his budget so that I could make enough money in those summer months to be able to leave my mother for the school year without any money worries. There was no place else in town that I could make that kind of money. I worked hard, and Father Joe worked alongside me much of the time. I remember thinking all summer long what a great guy he was. There wasn't any job I did that he didn't do. I never once thought or suspected that he could have been doing something else.

"Then that last week, the week before I was to leave for college, he took me on retreat. To prepare myself spiritually and mentally for the new challenge, he said. To let God into my life in a new and profound way. He went with me to help guide me to these new levels of God, he said. But the first night, I woke to him sucking my dick. My God, I was a virgin. The only thing I had ever known was my hand, and then to wake up to that, just before I was about to explode. Jesus, what a shock. But what a sensation, too. Anyway, he left without saying a word, and the next day neither of us said a word about it either. We went through all the ses-

sions of that retreat, through all the prayers, all the fire
and brimstone sermons, through all three meals sitting
right next to each other with our thighs sometimes touching. But not a word. And the last sermon of the day was
about the sins of the flesh, about the millions of souls that
were burning in hell for giving into lust. But not a word.

"He came again that night, again in the darkness, without a word. I was awake, probably waiting for him, my dick
was as hard as steel. I lay silent and motionless as he went
through this elaborate ritual that ended with my screams of
pleasure. Still, there wasn't a word spoken.

"The retreat ended at noon of the third day. I was in my
room gathering my things when he came again. At first I
told myself that I had killed him because he was a priest.
Because the whole idea was so evil and repulsive: he, a man
of God, doing to me what he said was the basest of sins. And
he was calling me his young god as he knelt there before
me. I've told myself that made it worse, that maybe it
wouldn't have happened if he hadn't kept calling me his
young god. I've told myself that it was because he had taken
advantage of and betrayed my family, my mother, me. That
he preyed on us, on me, for years. That he was evil, true
evil, because he cloaked himself in good. I've told myself it
was the light, that it wouldn't have happened but for the
light. It hadn't happened before when it was dark, and it
wouldn't have happened in the dark. Because then I would-
n't have seen his greedy eyes and his wet, weak mouth and
his sagging belly and this thick hairy hands. But now, in
the light, I could see the ugliness of it all. It was probably
some of all of those things. But the bottom line was that he
was stripping me of my manhood, and I was letting him, I
was enjoying it. He was stripping me of everything I was.
He was making me a faggot, a queer, and I was letting him,
I was enjoying it. And so I stabbed him. Oh, did I stab him.
There was a fish knife on the dresser. I sank it into the back
of his neck. He looked up at me, startled, and I stabbed him
in his eye. I tore up his face. I stabbed him again and again.
Because instead of dying, he was writhing, and I stabbed

him and kicked him to stop the writhing. I stabbed him when there was only twitching, when his face was no more than splattered bloody meat . . .

"The priests that ran the place knew what had happened when they found me naked and bloody and in shock, and him a gory mess. I remember them washing the blood off my body and then dressing me before the police came. Dressing me in clothes that had been in my bag, clothes that couldn't have been bloody, but sure as hell were when the cops got there. And they did one other thing before the cops got there. They put my things in his room and brought his clothes into my room to make it look as if *I* had gone into his room.

"You can imagine what the paper did with the story. I was so ashamed, so guilt ridden. Like you, I couldn't or wouldn't talk. It broke my mother's heart. It was weeks before she came to visit me, and then all she did was cry and beg me to admit my guilt and get it behind me for everybody's sake. And I did that, without a word, except for Guilty. Guilty and sentenced to life, without a word.

"It was years before I realized the mistake I had made. Not in killing the faggot priest, because then I probably couldn't have done anything else. No, the mistake I made was in pleading guilty without a word, in taking a life sentence without so much as a grunt. But I've been fighting ever since, fighting really for just the chance to go back and tell them what happened. Because going back probably wouldn't change anything. Yeah, I've slaved over these writs of mine, learned the courts' silly jargon, so that I could go back and, if nothing else, shove the ugly facts of my case down their clean, white, throats. And maybe some day, if nothing else, they'll understand that men aren't born monsters . . ."

Tommy Lee Smith was gone the next day. Just as soon as the court denied his writ, they sent him back to Folsom. They didn't even bring him back to the cell, and they didn't wait for the weekly prison bus. Instead they sent him by patrol car, chained and with two deputies. They wanted him out of there.

ŎŎŎŎŎ

My lawyer came the next afternoon. By then, I didn't
think I'd see him until my jury trial on Monday. It didn't
matter. I had already decided to fight my case through to a
jury trial.

"I'm sorry I haven't come sooner, Jesus, but I've been so
damn busy . . ."

I heard the words, but my mind was on the stink. I
stank. It had been weeks since I had showered and almost a
week since I had changed my clothes. I smelled like stale
piss. And I knew that my smell had filled every crack of
that tiny interview room. I could see his clean white
starched collar, and I knew that he knew that my smell was
rubbing up against it. Because of my smell, my eyes would
go no higher than his collar. But even without the stink, my
eyes probably wouldn't have gone any higher. Our eyes
would never meet. The only white men I had been alone
with before were the vice-principal and two teachers at Jefferson High School. I hadn't been able to look any of them in
the eye, and they were only teachers. This white man was a
lawyer.

". . . although in reality it wouldn't have mattered if I
had come to see you every day, two times a day, since you've
been here. They've got a cold case against you, Jesus. I suppose the only question is how badly you want to fall. You
know your grandmother testified against you before the
grand jury. They said she made an excellent witness even
though she doesn't speak English. She was there that night,
Jesus. She saw some of the things you did that night, Jesus.
She heard your ramblings and your threats. And she told
the grand jury everything, just as she'll tell your jury everything. No one will doubt her. She has no reason to lie.
Everyone that knew the two of you knew that you were very
close, that she loved you very much. She told the truth. She
took an oath to tell the truth, and that's what she did.

"You almost killed that priest, you know. But he's recovering and he'll be able to testify. They'll probably bring him in a wheel chair because he's paralyzed on his right side. He's lost his right eye and most of his right ear. Can you imagine the impression he'll make on a jury . . . in a wheel chair? And he *did* see everything. And there was no reason or excuse for any of it.

"There are also two women who live near the church. They both know you and your grandmother. They heard your rantings at the end. They heard your threats and your mocking of that lifeless priest. They saw the bloody pipe in your hand. They, too, were called as witnesses before the grand jury. No. Jesus. I could have come up here twice a day for the rest of my life to visit you, and it wouldn't have made any difference."

She hadn't come to see me. No letters. No money. I expected that. But I didn't expect her to testify. How could she? . . . Easy enough. I had humiliated her. And for that, I would pay. She would bury me . . . But the others, who were they? Maybe Agripina . . . And Padre Galván. The son of a bitch deserved everything I gave him. I was sure I had killed him. How many times do you have to hit someone with an iron pipe to kill him?

"You know, you made a pretty big splash in the paper, Jesus. You were on the front page for at least a week after it happened. Then it faded for awhile. But just this week, it started up again. Sunday's paper had a big write-up on you. It was trying to figure out what made you do it. Everybody who knew you was shocked. Except your grandmother. She said it was the work of the devil, that he had possessed you as completely as the saints are possessed by God, whatever that means. She said she had seen it coming for months, that it was the devil trying to get back at her through you. This is a high-profile case, Jesus. So much so that the district attorney himself is thinking of trying it. He has an election coming up next year, and sending you away for life would be a feather in his cap.

"And that's made it difficult to talk about plea bargaining, about dealing this case out. But I've made it my busi-

ness to talk to the district attorney about your case. In fact
I've talked to him several times, trying to convince him that
it's in everybody's best interest for him to drop the majority
of the counts if you plead guilty to just two or three counts.
This is a case that should be negotiated. This is a case that
should never be tried to a jury. This is a case . . ."

Somewhere Tommy Lee Smith was nodding, staring at
us with that blank stare. And behind him, in the C dorm,
Apache was grinning his slyest of grins.

He talked about the hopelessness of the case, about how
everybody knew I had done it and how badly they wanted to
hang me. There was nothing to gain by going to trial and
everything to lose. We had no witnesses, no defense, and I
could never testify—the D.A. would tear me to shreds. My
own grandmother would drive the stakes into my coffin. He
said the same thing over and over again: I should plead
guilty.

He got louder and louder. He stood up and sat down,
talking down to me when he was standing and putting his
face close to mine when he was sitting. He banged on the
table and clapped his hands. And then, in mid-sentence,
while he was standing, it occurred to him that I hadn't spoken, not once.

"What is it with you? You won't even look at me. Say
something! You're as strange as your name. People in this
country don't go around naming their kids Jesus. That's
almost like asking for it, like putting a curse on someone.
Look what it's done to you. You don't go around naming
your kid after the Son of God. Look, you can sit there as
long as you want with your head down and act like you
can't talk for as long as you want. But that's not going to
change anything. The fact of the matter is that you have to
make one hell of a decision real soon, like this afternoon. So
what's it going to be, Jesus? Speak to me, Jesus. I want to
hear your thoughts, Jesus."

He'd never hear my thoughts. I had no thoughts, other
than don't plead guilty, fight it to a jury trial. And he'd
never hear those because I couldn't talk. I was so dirty and

ashamed that I couldn't talk. I knew that I'd gag on my own words, on my own sounds, if I tried to talk. I lowered my head more. The smell from my crotch was rank, strong and rank. My hair was matted and crusted with old sweat and saliva and foodstuffs and drinks. I couldn't remember combing my hair in jail. How could I talk to that white man?

For a long while there was silence. Then, maybe I grinned. Out of awkwardness if I did, because he flew into a rage.

"Look, you silly bastard. There's not a goddamn thing funny about this case! Nothing! Only a twisted mind could find anything funny about this case. This was a brutal, savage act! Ruthless! Totally unprovoked and unexcused! You had absolutely no right to inflict your savagery on that defenseless old man. People like you deserve to be locked up. Society has to be protected from people like you. You're scum! Worse than scum! Because there's no remorse, no accountability, no . . ."

He stopped. Now he, too, couldn't speak, although he tried. Three or four times I heard him gather his breath to speak, but he didn't. For a long time I could feel him staring down on me. His eyes were burning holes in my head through my filthy matted hair. I pictured him with his nose wrinkled up, fending off the smell from my crotch. Then he sighed, and in one motion he stooped for his briefcase and stepped to the door. "I'll see you later, Jesus."

Apache was waiting for me at C dorm's door as my leg irons clanged on the corridor's concrete. "What'd I tell you, right? Didn't I tell you, right? Fucking dump truck, right?" Yes, Apache, I nodded. You told me. You were right, Apache, I nodded and nodded until he gave out from behind the C dorm door.

I laid on my bunk. It was late afternoon. I wasn't sleepy and I wasn't hungry. I knew I was in for another one of those times that just slipped by. They were blanks; voids, because the next day, or the day after, they would be gone, with no memory of any thought, sleep, or dream. Nothing. I would only know twelve, twenty-four hours later that a chunk of time had passed, and that I had no recollection, nothing, of it's passing.

During the next three days there were several of those chunks of time, and when I slept, I had a dream again and again. I had dreamed of my grandmother testifying against me. It was always the same. The judge would say, "Soledad Olivas," and somewhere from the back of the courtroom, from behind a bunch of white people, she would come out moaning, all in black, but tiny, half her size, and start crawling down the center aisle like she did in church, moaning, "¡Dios mío! ¡Dios mío!" I'd watch from my seat next to Mr. Fischer, mumbling under my breath, "Get up! Get up!" And the more I'd watch, the more ashamed I'd become. I'd see the white people looking at her. And then some of them would start to giggle and I'd scream, "Get up! Get up! Don't you have any shame!" The guards would gag me, and they'd gag her too because by then she had reached the railing that separated the lawyers from the people and had collapsed there, moaning, "¡Dios mío! ¡Dios mío!"

Then the guards would carry her up to the witness stand. It was like being in church again: she and the judge at his altar, three or four steps above us all and looking down at me. He would ask her questions, and, from the witness stand, she would give her sermon, which was about what I had done. She told them everything about that night, and she told them more. She told them about things—all bad—I had done as far back as I could remember. Things I didn't think anyone knew about, not even her. I put my T-shirt over my head. I felt the endlessness of prison, day after day, always locked up, night and day one and the same. I'd scream at her, "Don't you know what you're doing to me! Can't you see what you're doing to me!" But she wouldn't stop. She went on and on except that she got smaller. And as she did, I could see Padre Galván behind her on a stretcher, pointing at me. Half of his head was bashed in and one of his eyes and ears were gone. He couldn't move except for the finger he was pointing at me. His lips were mumbling, "¡Tú! ¡Tú! ¡Tú!" I had to shut them up. I reached for them, from behind the counsel table to the witness stand twenty feet at least. My arms stretched. They snaked their way to the witness stand, like two brown canvas fire hoses. My arms reached them and wrapped themselves around them, but I couldn't tighten my grip on them. My thirty-foot arms lay flat on them. As hard as I tried, as much as I tightened my muscles, it was no use. My arms just lay there. And she kept talking, and he kept pointing, and the jury saw what I was trying to do. "Guilty!" they said and the prison bus drove into the courtroom, up to the counsel table, and they put me on, chains and all.

CHAPTER SIX

I saw them just as the guards were putting me into the holding cell. They were coming into the courtroom. One of the guards said, "Here comes your jury, asshole." I didn't get much of a look at them. But I knew they were white.

I looked at myself. There were splotches of food on my T-shirt. I had worn it and slept in it for days, stretching the collar of the cheap cotton almost over my shoulder. My pants had slipped up into creases at my crotch. Smells of piss and jizz rose from the creases. I put my hands over my crotch, maybe to cut off the smell, maybe to hide the creases and the stains. Instead I felt the crust of more jizz. It was on the bottom of my T-shirt too.

I hadn't been in the sun for three months. Still, I seemed darker than ever. All my life I had been too dark. I scratched at my wrists, leaving streaks of white. That wouldn't fool anyone. When I hunched, the neck of my T-shirt hung down to my stomach. My hair was greasy. Now it hung almost to my eyes, greasing up my forehead. Grease was oozing out of my pores. Greasers were greasy. I tried to see the grease on my cheeks. I saw it on either side of my nose. I wiped my nose with my T-shirt sleeve. I ran my hands through my hair, trying to take the grease out of it. I wiped my hands on my pants. That just made my pants greasy, and I could still feel the grease oozing out of my pores. My wrists were slimy with grease, but not slimy enough to slip out of the chains.

The guard opened the door. "All right, Olivas." The courtroom light blinded me. I could hear every clink of the chains as I got up and started to shuffle into the courtroom. This time some of them gasped; some of them let out little cries. I shuffled toward them, my head down, not really knowing where I was going. Then I fell down the stairs that put the judge above everyone else. There were louder cries. I couldn't get up. I tried to get up. I didn't want to get up. The chains were twisted all around me. The guards picked me up. "Come on, Olivas." They sat me next to Mr. Fischer. Some of the jurors were still gasping. The bailiff rapped his little hammer, and they stopped. But I could feel them all around me. And I knew what they were thinking. Dirty Mexican. I was dirty. They could smell me. The lawyer could smell me. Dirty Mexican. My lower back felt bare. The T-shirt must have slipped up and my pants down when I fell. I was sure they could see the crack of my ass, a Mexicans ass, all brown and caked with shit. They were whispering about me. It was hot in there.

The judge came out, the bailiff rapped his little hammer. Everyone stood. I didn't stand. The lawyer nudged me and said something, but I didn't stand. Two guards came over and stood me up. "The Superior Court of the State of California is now in session. Judge Reginald Harrison presiding. Please be seated." The judge nodded and smiled. It was a smile for children or old people. He motioned for everyone to sit down. They sat down. I didn't sit down. The guards shoved me into my seat. I could hear the jurors behind me liking that.

"Good morning, ladies and gentlemen. The court would like to begin by apologizing for any delays or inconveniences you might have experienced in waiting for this case to commence.

"Often times, however, these matters are completely out of the court's control. So be patient with us. The court would

also like to thank you for taking time from your busy lives
and schedules to help us administer our American system of
jurisprudence. Jury duty, which may appear to some to be
solely an inconvenience, is in reality your most important
civic duty. For, without your participation, our system of
jurisprudence could not function. And the American jury
system, with all its shortcomings, is—I can assure you—the
best system of justice known to man. In this case, for example, the defendant—Jesus Olivas—is entitled to a trial by
his peers. Twelve of you—all members of the defendant's
community—will be selected to determine his guilt or innocence. It will be you—his peers—who will sit as judges in
his case because it will be you who will weigh the evidence
and apply the law to determine his guilt or innocence. Now,
the defendant sits there accused of certain charges. The fact
that those charges have been lodged are not proof of his
guilt or innocence. Rather, the district attorney must prove
those charges to you beyond a reasonable doubt and to a
moral certainty before you can return a guilty verdict. That
is not the case in other countries where, frequently, the
accused must prove his innocence. Furthermore, all twelve
jurors must unanimously agree before a guilty verdict can
be reached. If but one of you is not convinced of his guilt,
then a conviction cannot be had. Those kinds of rights, freedom, and protections cannot be found, I dare say, in many
other systems."

I didn't like him and I didn't like his big words. They
must have thought I couldn't understand, but I did. I understood all that crap about jury trials. Lies. They were just
waiting to hang my ass. They had come to get me. They
were going to make it look good. Hide behind those big
words and smiles and manners and clean faces and clean
clothes, and then stick it to the little greaser. They all knew
what I did. What was all this shit about him having to
prove anything? Everybody knew. The lawyer said it was all
over the paper. Everybody in C dorm knew what I did the
first night I got there, and they didn't get the paper. I
should have just copped out and gone to the joint. Gotten it

over with already. But I couldn't.

"In a few moments, the clerk will deposit slips of paper bearing each of your names into that cylinder on his desk. Then he will select twelve names at random from it, and the twelve of you will take your seats in the jury box here to my left. Then the attorneys for each side will ask you questions bearing on your qualifications to sit as jurors in this case. Essentially, they will be trying to ascertain whether or not you can be fair and impartial jurors. Each side has what are known as peremptory challenges. Ten for each. What that means is that each side can excuse up to ten of you for whatever reason he chooses. In fact, they don't have to have a reason to excuse you. Once they have selected twelve of you, you will be sworn. And once the attorneys make their opening statements, the case will be presented to you. But before the clerk selects twelve names, I have a few general questions and comments that I would like to put to you."

I knew what was waiting for me in the joint. Some of those guys wanted me. They were just off the streets, they had just left their women. But those guys up there had been there for long, long times. They liked young tender asses. And the smaller you were the easier it was for them to turn you out. There weren't too many guys smaller or skinnier than me. Once they turned you out, you were never the same. You'd always be a *puto* and everybody would know it. They could tell just by looking at you. And when you got out, when you came home, everybody at home would know it too. They had always said I was a sissy.

"Are there any of you who because of family considerations or job considerations or your own physical condition do not feel that you can devote as much as two weeks to the trial of this case?

"If you feel that any of these considerations may apply to you, would you please so indicate by raising your hand. Yes, Ma'am, and would you kindly state your name for the record?"

"My name is Ruth Ann Spalding, and I just want to say that I couldn't sit here for two weeks and listen to all the things that boy did that night without getting sick. Now, I'm a Catholic, and even though I don't go to that particular church, I know that this case has to be about that poor priest that was mutilated and almost beaten to death. I want you to know that I don't appreciate what this boy did. I've been reading all about it in the paper. It's downright disgusting and sickening what this boy did, and I just don't think I could sit through it. That's all."

She made it hotter. The heat pricked. It had been hot enough in there, but when she started talking it, got hotter. I wanted to scratch, but I couldn't. They were all watching. I could feel them breathing on me. They were just waiting for their chance. If I copped out, they wouldn't get their chance. I knew what she looked like without even looking at her. I hated her. I could tell by her loud voice. She was big and fat and ugly. Her nostrils got huge when she talked, and her eyes bulged. Her hair was pushed straight back, and the folds of fat under her chin matched the folds of fat around her belt.

"Mrs. Spalding, the court appreciates your concern. This could well turn out to be a case involving many sordid details. However, many of our criminal cases involve sordid details, and if the court were to excuse prospective jurors because of their aversion to criminal acts, then very soon we would find ourselves without a sufficient number of citizens to make our criminal justice system operate. Now, that is not to say that the court condones the sordidness that often accompanies criminal acts. Nor is that to say that the court is unsympathetic to the unpleasantness that the ordinary citizen must at times experience in listening to many of these cases. However, the court urges you to consider the importance of your task and to recognize the contribution that jurors make to our society in general and to our criminal justice system in particular. Now, Mrs. Spalding, given those considerations, and being mindful that at this stage of the proceedings none of us has any way of knowing what the evidence will be, can you truly tell me that it will be impossible to set aside any natural feelings of revulsion that you might justifiably have in listening to the facts of this case? That you couldn't set aside those feelings and render a fair and impartial verdict? Now remember, the entire process depends on concerned citizens like yourself."

I hated her more than him and his big words. They both wanted to get me. But she wanted me more.

"Well, if you put it that way, I guess I could not let it upset me too much. But I want you to know that it won't be easy, because I'm a good Catholic and a God-fearing woman, and I don't appreciate what that boy did to that church either. Now mind you, that's not our church because we don't live on that side of town and so we never go to that church. But still, there has to be some respect."

The more she talked, the hotter it got. They were all pressing in on me. Even the lawyer was too close. What was he there for? He was just sitting there. He didn't want to be there. "Good," she said. Where the fuck was He? He never showed up except to punish you or make your life more miserable. I was expecting Him any minute now. Catholics. They said one thing and did another. They had rules and sins and punishments for everything. Nobody stood a chance to get to heaven. I didn't stand a chance to get to heaven. Especially now. But I didn't care. Yes I did. She kept calling me "that boy." Every time she said that, they looked at me. Hot eyes. White man's eyes. Clear and smooth and blue. If I could just cool off someplace.

"Believe me, Mrs. Spalding, I can understand your concern. However, it does raise other points that I think are best gone into at this time. You mentioned that you have read about this case in the newspaper. You understand, do you not, that any verdict that is reached by any of you must be based solely on the evidence that will be presented to you in this courtroom. What that means is that you'll have to disregard any prior knowledge you may have about this case from whatever source, be it the newspaper or radio or friend or acquaintance. In other words, we start with a clean slate here. Do you think you can do that?"

Horseshit. How could they forget everything they knew?

How could they look at me in those chains and forget? I hated them all. They were supposed to look at me, smell me even, and forget. Bullshit. She'd never forget.

"I suppose."

"Of course you can. Now let me make it clear that the court welcomes these concerns. You may be seated, Mrs. Spalding. Now is the time to raise these concerns; not once you've found yourself sworn and listening to the evidence. Are there others of you who might feel that it would be a hardship to sit on this jury for perhaps as long as two weeks?"

"Yes, sir."

Two weeks. Why two weeks? It didn't matter. They could vote now or two years from now and it was going to be the same thing.

"Yes, your Honor. My wife and I run a little hardware store over on the eastside . . ."

He was an old man. I hated white old men. Most of them were drunks. And even when they weren't drunks, they might as well have been. They couldn't control their hands or their legs, and their eyes got milky and weak. But that still didn't stop them from looking at me like I was a piece of shit. What made them think they could still look at me like that when they were falling apart themselves?

"Would you kindly state your name for the record, sir."

"Excuse me, judge. My name's Russell Roder, and like I said, me and my wife run a little hardware store on the eastside, and if I'm going to be gone for two whole weeks, it's going to make it pretty rough on my wife."

What did they know about things being rough? Sit on their asses in a cool store while old Mexicans burned in the fields. What did they know about picking grapes, about knees buried in that burning sand? Sticky juice running down your arms. Streaks of dirt and mopped sweat on faces. Wasps on your sticky hands, chasing you and getting into your hair until you twisted your head in the sand. There was never enough water. The jug was always empty and the ranch house was over a mile away. Then the contractor was on your ass for always drinking water. While they sat in the cool of their store.

"Is there anyone else, Mr. Roder, who can help out in the store for a few days during the time you served on this jury?"

"Not really, your Honor. In fact, it's tougher now than it usually is because my wife's mother is out here visiting us from Iowa and she's getting up in years and her health's not too good. And as a matter of fact, she needs quite a bit of attention herself."

Who gave a shit about the old Mexicans in the fields. The old ones that they carried around with them from field to field, season after season. Those who could still move would find a tree or some shade and sit under it all day, sliding around as the sun shifted, waiting for the "dead ones" to come back each day about sunset. Those who couldn't move would lie in houses made of grape trays, boxes, and paper. It was hot in there, and the old Mexicans were always waiting. Flies crawled on their sweaty bellies. The little ones who just got in the way had to watch them and the babies. They gave them water.

"The court is not unmindful, Mr. Roder, of the sacrifices it sometimes has to ask the citizens of its community to make. There probably isn't anyone in this room who in one sense or another wouldn't be inconvenienced if he or she were selected to serve on this jury. And if the court were to excuse prospective jurors on the basis of inconvenience alone, then I'm sure you can appreciate the effects that would have, couldn't you, Mr. Roder? Now, that's not to say that you may not have a real problem, Mr. Roder. But what the court over the years has found is that oftentimes individuals in your situation, with just a little delving, just a little bit of resourcefulness, can think of a person or two who could provide them with a little assistance. Now just think for a moment or two, Mr. Roder. Isn't there anyone you know who could perhaps give you and your wife a hand during the next week or two?"

I hoped he'd leave. And after him, I hoped they'd all leave.

"Well, sir . . . not really."

"You're sure, now?"

"Uh, yes."

"There seems to be something bothering you, Mr. Roder. Is it in any way related to the proceeding here?"

"Well, nothing, your Honor, except that this is the third time I've been called for jury duty and . . . and . . ."

"Yes, Mr. Roder."

"No offense intended, your Honor, but I just feel that these criminals just get too much consideration as it is. They're the ones who break the law, and then we have to feed them and clothe them. And on top of that, you have to miss work or even shut down your business to come down here and listen to some runaround that they get up and give."

The old bastard didn't like me. I wasn't just a Mexican, I was a criminal, too. I didn't ask him to come. I didn't want the no-good fucker there to begin with.

"Well now, Mr. Roder. I don't know what kind of runaround, as you put it, you've gotten in other courts. But I can assure you that no one will give you the proverbial runaround in my courtroom. What we seek in this courtroom is the ascertainment of truth and justice. Let me remind you of an old adage that says it is better that ten guilty men go free than that one innocent man be hanged. What may seem to you, and perhaps understandably so, to be a coddling of criminals, is really an attempt by the courts of this land to protect the safeguards of the free and the innocent. This young man seated at counsel table is presumed innocent even though he is accused of a great number of crimes. That presumption remains with him until the district attorney, Mr. Cline, proves his guilt to you beyond a reasonable doubt and to a moral certainty. Now, our forefathers felt it was fundamentally important, in order to protect the freedoms of our society, that a man should not be convicted on mere suspicion or accusations alone, but rather after a full and fair trial by his peers. So you see, Mr. Roder, even though the court may seem to involve itself in unduly long and complicated trials in these matters, it does so really to protect you and other law abiding citizens of our society because someday you or one of your loved ones could conceivably stand accused of a crime, and then–I'm certain–that you would want all the safeguards that the system provides applied to your case."

I didn't know what that was all about.

"Well, sir, I've raised five boys and not one of them's ever been in trouble, and I've never been in trouble. We're just hard-working people who try to stay out of trouble. And it's real hard for me to believe that all those people sitting up in jail waiting to come to court are innocent. They wouldn't be there if they were."

They liked that. I could hear them liking that behind me. The bailiff rapped his hammer and they shut up. I thought of one person after another in C dorm. Was he innocent? Was he? How about him? No. No. I ran out of people. None of them were innocent.

"Well, Mr. Roder, without either indicating agreement or disagreement with your remarks, let me just say that I can understand your concerns. Now, as to whether or not I should excuse you, that is another matter. Normally the court is very reluctant to excuse prospective jurors for work-related reasons. I think you can all appreciate the court's reasoning in that regard. However, your case may be just a little different, Mr. Roder, and in light of the fact that you have already served on three prior juries, and in light of the fact that besides your duties at your store, you have an ailing mother-in-law with you, I'm going to excuse you from jury duty this time. But I'm sure our paths will cross again, Mr. Roder, and I hope that your mother-in-law will have recovered by then because the court has a long memory, Mr. Roder."

They laughed. They all thought it was funny.

I didn't think there was a fucking thing funny. Except maybe for that old fool.

"Thank you, your Honor."

"Now, is there anyone else who because of some . . . yes,

Mrs. Campbell."

"Judge Harrison. As you well know, Doctor Campbell and I have been planning a rather extensive tour of South America for some time now. We're scheduled to leave on the fifteenth, which is only two and a half weeks away. Now, Lord knows, I certainly know the importance of jury duty. You and I have discussed it many a time. But you also know how hard the Doctor works, what with all those long hours at the hospital. I truly would hate to disappoint him. And if this case were to go beyond two and one-half weeks, what with all this rationing still, we might have to just cancel our trip altogether."

Rich bitch. I wouldn't have been sitting there if I were rich. I would have had everything I had ever wanted. I'd be happy. I'd live in Plum Gardens with all the rich people. No, Mexicans didn't live there. Not even the rich ones. I'd live in Mexico then. Rich people in Mexico were richer than rich people here. That's what everybody said. There we would all be Mexicans. Lots of them were darker than me. The braceros in Chinatown on Sundays were all darker than me, a lot darker than me. The lawyer cleared his throat and scratched his leg.

"Yes, I'm aware of your plans, Mrs. Campbell. Mr. Cline, is there any possibility that this case could go beyond the projected two weeks?" He talked real nice to her. He smiled real nice at her. Rich bitch.

"Well, your Honor, there's always that possibility. As your Honor well knows, one can never be certain about these things. I frankly would hate to guarantee that we would be finished in two weeks."

"Yes, of course. The court has in fact been aware of Doctor and Mrs. Campbell's itinerary for some time now. Many of you, I'm sure, are aware of how dedicated and hard-working an individual the Doctor is. No, the court is not inclined to interfere with the Doctor's travel plans. The court is of the opinion that the Doctor has more than earned this well-deserved rest. You will be excused, Mrs. Campbell."

"Thank you, Judge Harrison. You can rest assured that

the Doctor and I will be seeing you and Mrs. Harrison
before we leave."

Rich bitch.

"All right. Is there anyone else who feels that, given the
projected length of this trial, they will be so inconvenienced
as to cause a bona-fide hardship on themselves? Seeing no
other hands, I would like to get into one or two other areas.
As many of you have probably guessed by now, the charges
in this case arise out of that horrible incident that was
alleged to have occurred not too long ago at Our Lady of the
Angels Church. The defendant in this case, Jesus Olivas, is
accused of—and I'll just summarize them for you now
because they'll be read in detail for you later—of having
assaulted, with intent to kill, the pastor of that church; with
having assaulted, also with intent to kill, several others
who were alleged to have been at that church; with having
set the church on fire—arson—with burglary in the first
degree; with a number of assaults with a deadly weapon,
and with numerous misdemeanors. Now, there's been a lot
of publicity locally—and I daresay, even up and down the
state—about this case. The Free Press has given it extensive coverage; it's been on local radio frequently; and I'm
sure it's been discussed a great deal in the community.
Now, I would like to see, by a showing of hands, how many
of you have heard about this case before coming here
today."

When he told them what I did, sweat poured out of my
head. I couldn't stop it. I couldn't wipe it. Because if I did,
they'd see and they'd know. I tried to hold it back, but that
made it worse. It dripped onto my pants and rolled down
my face. I could feel it on my back, feel the T-shirt sticking
to my back. They could see that. They'd know. If I copped
out now, I'd be in the joint tomorrow. The sweat seemed to
make me feel the chains more. They dug into my wrists and
into my ankles. As soon as school was out she'd buy me new
boots. If my feet were protected, I could work better and
make more money. The new tops cut into my legs. They left
red marks above my ankles until I wore the leather down—

I'd never wear the chains down. I thought of the new boots until he stopped talking about me. I heard what he said, and I knew when he stopped, but I was still thinking about new boots. They heard too. And now they knew.

"Well, I see by the show of hands that most of you have heard about this case. Now, you all understand that because of the presumption of innocence in a criminal case and the corresponding burden of proof that the district attorney carries, it will be necessary that each of you selected will have to put out of his or her mind anything and everything that he or she may have heard about this case outside of this courtroom. In other words, you'll have to decide this case solely on the evidence that is presented to you in this courtroom. Is that clear to everyone?"

I didn't know what he meant. How do you put everything out of your mind?

"Now, if you will all keep that simple rule foremost in your minds and work at it, we shouldn't have any problems at all. With that in mind, is there anyone here who does not feel that they can decide this case solely on the evidence presented in this courtroom?"

He was looking at them and nodding, and I knew they were nodding back. They were going to hang me. But they were going to do it the right way, the clean way, their way. And he would lead them.

"Good. Good. All right, let's move on to another area before the clerk selects twelve names and I turn the questioning over to the district attorney and defense counsel. In a moment, I'm going to ask both attorneys to provide the court with a list of their witnesses. I want you to listen closely to those names because, at the conclusion of that recitation, I'm going to ask all of you if you know any of the individuals mentioned. We will begin with Mr. Cline. Mr. Cline."

Defense Counsel. That sounded good. But what did he do and when did he do it? He had been writing or drawing something on his yellow pad from the time the judge started talking. Now I saw that they were pictures of men with big noses. Crooked noses, hooked noses, noses with warts on them and hair sticking out of them. He had begged me to cop out. What was he going to defend? Then there were the names.

"Father Pedro Galván."

I heard the Father and the Pedro too, but it was the Galván that hit me. I saw him as I had thousands of times, at the altar with his back to the tabernacle, opening his hands and his arms to the people. But I saw him too on the ground, grunting when I swung. I shook my head. I didn't want to see that. And I didn't because of the next name.

"Soledad Olivas."

No one else had that name. Soledad. Alone. Lonely. I didn't have to hear the Olivas. I knew. She was everywhere. The black of her skirt covered my mind. I could feel its black folds rustling against my brain. Soledad. Only I knew how alone she was. She made me alone. We were alone in that house. I knew I could never bring anyone there. She never said it, but I knew. Only the Guadalupana came. On Sunday afternoons. And then she'd go to work, and I'd be alone. Soledad. No matter what I did or where I went, she was there. She even came to the church that night. I saw her as they dragged me into the police car. Watching. No tears, no screams, no words, nothing. Watching, the way she always did. She hadn't been to visit me yet. She wouldn't come. She'd have less reason to come and see me in the joint. It was so far away, she'd say, and God knows, at her age it was so hard to get around. Except she was everywhere. I could never get rid of her. Soledad. He was mentioning other names. None of them mattered. The lawyer had said she would testify. That hadn't mattered then either. Now it did. She and me in this big room with all those white people. She would pull her shawl down so that all you could see were her eyes and her mouth and maybe her fingers on her rosary beads. Did she have legs? I would never have known except for the wounds. Did she have tits? I shook my head. I couldn't think of her like that, not even now. Did she? I shook my head. She was so small and skinny, I didn't see how she could. Even on the hottest days, the most she would take off was the black blouse. But under that she wore a white blouse that looked like the top of a nightgown. Then I could see her hands, not just her fingers. The green veins bulging under stretched and dried skin, and the wounds. Soledad. She was coming. She wouldn't miss it for anything. They would laugh at her, but she wouldn't notice or care. Or maybe she was used to it. They didn't have people that looked like her on their side of town. Every now and then gypsies used to come through town. After a while, I stopped laughing at them. She looked like them. Soledad. I was always afraid of her. I was ashamed of her too.

"Refugio Jiménez. Chavela López. Juan López. Carmela Inocente. Petra Díaz. And I'm not sure about this next pronunciation. Eufemia Negrete."

"U what? Why don't you just give us the spelling, Mr. Cline.

"Certainly, your Honor. E-u-f-e-m-i-a- N-e-g-r-e-t-e. Then of course we have the following investigating officers and peace officers: Captain John Humphries; Lieutenant Stanley Sexton; Sergeant David Jones; Sergeant Louis Craig. And peace officers Calvin Meyers and Jerry Whitney. Also, depending upon whether I think we'll need him, we may also call our fingerprint expert, Sergeant Ralph McIntyre."

"That's quite a number of witnesses. I hope the members of the panel can keep them in mind. Now, are there any of you who know any of these potential witnesses? If so, would you kindly so indicate by raising your hand. Yes, Mrs. Petersen."

"You probably know, Judge, that Captain Humphries is and has been our neighbor for fifteen years."

"Yes, now that you mention it, I do know that. But do you see them—do you see the Humphries—that often? By that I am not referring to seeing them over the backyard fence or on your way shopping or at church. Because sometimes one can be neighbors, even for several years, and not

really be close in a social sense. In other words, do you see
the Humphries on a social basis? Are you members of the
same clubs or church groups? Do you have them over to
your house for dinner?"

"As a matter of fact, Judge, we are very close friends.
And we get together frequently, not only in our homes, but
often we attend the same social gatherings together."

"Well, Mrs. Petersen, the purpose of this line of questioning is really twofold. First, it's designed to elicit any
bias you might have for or against a particular witness or
witnesses based on your friendship or acquaintance with
that person. In other words, the court is concerned that a
juror might unduly favor or give special weight to the testimony of one witness over that of others because of his or her
relationship with that witness. Secondly, it's designed to
determine whether or not a prospective juror has had any
communications with a potential witness about a particular
case. In a community our size it is frequently the case that
jurors will know witnesses and even will have had some discussions with them about the litigation. That is often
unavoidable, and if the court were to automatically disqualify individuals solely for those reasons, our system would
certainly suffer. The determining factor in the court's mind
is, therefore, whether the prospective juror can assure the
court that, regardless of whatever the relationship might be
between juror and witness, he or she will be able to judge
and weigh the witness's testimony by the same standard he
would any other witness. And also, that whatever the
nature of the communications might have been, he can set
it aside in reaching a verdict in this case solely on the evidence presented in this courtroom."

Her boss called her Sol. Good old Sol. "Ah, yessa,
Meester Mitchell. Good old Sol." She'd been there for thirty
years. She must have known every square of marble by
heart. "Ah, yessa, Meester Mitchell." From her knees, she
was all grins and nods with her bucket and her mop. Once
she went through those doors, it was all nods and grins and,
"Yessa, Meester Mitchell." He must have thought she was a

little crazy, weird at least. All those black clothes and not a word of English in more than thirty years. But she scrubbed faster and better than any of the others. She must have prayed when she scrubbed. She was always praying. She prayed for everyone and everything. That's what she said. She wasn't praying for me, not now. She was probably praying, but not for me. She was home now. She'd been to Mass. She'd eaten what little she ate. She'd knelt at her altar. She'd said her morning rosary. She'd cleaned and aired the house. Sometimes she read, either the New Testament or the Lives of the Saints. Her hands and feet had bled like Jesus. People said that she was so holy.

"Now, Mrs. Petersen, despite your friendship with Captain Humphries and his wife, do you think you could judge his testimony by the same standards you would judge all other testimony?"

"I think I could."

"You wouldn't favor Captain Humphries' testimony over others?"

"No. If I understand you correctly, we're not supposed to, and I don't think I'd do that."

"Have you ever discussed this case with Captain Humphries?"

"Well, when it first happened I'm sure we talked about it a little. The whole town was talking about it. But Captain Humphries is the kind of man who prefers not to talk about his work. Meriam, that's his wife, says that he just doesn't bring his work home with him. She's grateful for that, as you well might imagine when you consider what he has to deal with day in and day out."

"So any discussions you might have had with Captain Humphries about this case have not been extensive. Would that be fair?"

"Oh, no. And they were some time ago."

"And I take it that you haven't formed any opinion about this case based on whatever discussions you might have had with Captain Humphries or your friendship with him?"

"Oh, no."

"Thank you, Mrs. Petersen. Now let's get on to some of these other people who had their hands raised. Would you raise them again, please? Fine. Yes, ma'am. Would you state your name for the record, please?"

"Yes, my name is Linda Haley, and I know who Father Galván is because we used to go to Our Lady of the Angels on Sundays for the 11:30 Mass when my husband was working Saturday nights and we had to be out to his family's for lunch at one o'clock. It was the only Mass in town at that time. Father Galván used to say it. I remember it was him because he would always give those long sermons in Mexican, and we didn't understand a word he said."

The last time she put the diaper on me was when I was going to Jefferson. As I got older, it wasn't that often. I'd lie in my crib all naked and she'd put it on. As I got older I started getting hard-ons, not every time, but sometimes. But she never said anything. It was like she didn't see it. But she had to have seen it. Sometimes it was bigger than ever. It felt like it was going to pop. But she never said anything. Instead, it got real quiet. All you could hear was her and me breathing. And, then it seemed to take forever to put the diaper on. Lots of them said she was already a saint. There were people like that. People who didn't have to die before you knew they were saints. They had seen proof of it in church. The first time I saw it, I believed. It was in the summer, at night. It was hot. The open windows seemed to be keeping the heat in. It was benediction. The cassock was making me sweat. The sweet smoke of incense was making me sick. Then there was an awful scream. Padre Galván ran from the altar. She had fallen back in the pew. Every part of her was shaking. Her eyes were huge. She must have been looking at Him. Her mouth was open and jerking. Some of the old people said that they had seen living saints before, in Mexico, and that's how it was. But how could saints be evil?

"Now, Mrs. Haley, I want you to understand that the fact that you may know a certain individual is not reason of and by itself to disqualify you from serving on a jury before whom that individual may testify. What the court has in mind is any relationship you may have, or communication you may have had, with and individual that of and by itself would influence your decision in this case. Simply having gone to services at Father Galván's church does not appear to be, without more, what the court has in mind. Are those services the extent of your contact with Father Galván?"

"Yes, sir. And like I said, we couldn't even understand the man because he talked in Mexican."

"Who am I, 'Amá?" I must have asked her. I know I did. She never told me. "What was my mother like?" "Who was my father?" She never said. Some of the Guadalupana told me, but not much. "You look just like your mother and your mother looked just like your grandmother." She didn't like them telling me even that much. They knew it. She just had to look at them and they'd stop. Chole told me about my mother and my father. Everything.

"You needn't be concerned, Mrs. Haley. You may be seated. We have quite a few hands today. Yes, sir. And again, would you state your name for the record, please?"

"Yes, your Honor. My name is William Clark. I know Captain Humphries, Lieutenant Sexton, and Sergeant Craig. They're all in the Lion's Club with me, and we all have breakfast together every Friday morning at 7:30 at the Blue Eagle Café."

"How well do you know these officers, Mr. Clark?"

"Pretty well. I think we've all been in the Lions for over ten years. We've been on a lot of committees together; worked on a lot of drives together. Lou Craig and I have been on the club's softball team together every summer as far back as I can remember."

Chole stank. She smelled worse than me, even now. It was the smell of her come, I thought—jars and jars of it that must have dripped off her bed. She had no water in the shack. Just a bed and a heater. The walls were of cardboard, streaked and swollen by rains. She had pasted hundreds of movie-magazine pictures on those walls—women stars with hair-dos and makeup like hers. There were no windows, only a door and a single electric bulb. 'Amá hated her. I don't think she hated anybody worse. She lived across from the church. We used to see her in the dark of those winter mornings on our way to church, drunk, coming home from Chinatown. If she wasn't too drunk, she'd slow down and hunch up and slink off into a yard or into the street like some scared dog until we passed. In the daytime, when she wasn't drunk, she'd see us coming a long ways off and she'd cross over to the other side of the street right away. Then I'd watch to see if she'd cross back over. She usually did. 'Amá never spoke to her. She said she was the lowest of all women. Even when I was really small, I knew she was bad. All 'Amá ever did was look at her. That was enough to make her slink. Except when she was real drunk. Then she got pretty bad. Once she came up to 'Amá and grabbed her by the shawl, "I know who you are. You might be fooling everybody in this whole fucking town, but you're not fooling me. You're no better than me, Soledad Olivas. You're just a fucking whore, too. And your daughter was a whore, like you. And his father was a pimp who turned her out just like he turned me out. I know people who know you from Mexico. You're not fooling me with all this God shit." My father was so bad that I knew we would never talk about him. But she was worse. 'Amá loved to make her slink. It got so that 'Amá would wait until we were close enough to see how drunk she was. If she wasn't that drunk, she'd stare her into a yard and then slow down, pass by real slow. If she were real drunk, then we'd cross the street right away and walk so fast that she couldn't catch us.

"Have you discussed this case with them, Mr. Clark?"

"To be honest with you, your Honor, like the lady said before me, when this thing happened seems like everybody in town was talking about it. Nothing like this has ever happened here before, and I hope nothing like it will ever happen here again. But I do know that I talked to Lou about it, and I think I talked to Stan Sexton about it, and, if my memory serves me correct, I think I may have even

92 RONALD L. RUIZ

talked to the captain about it."

"Well, Mr. Clark, would any relationship you might have with any of these individuals affect the manner in which you would view their testimony as opposed to that of, say, a total stranger?"

"Oh, I don't think so."

"Would you be able to use the same standard in evaluating the testimony of all witnesses, and not use some special standard for these three individuals?"

"I don't think I'd have any trouble doing that."

"Would the conversations you've had with these individuals about this case influence you in any way?"

"Not really. To tell you the truth, I've pretty much forgotten what we talked about. And I learned a lot more about this case from the newspaper than I ever did from them."

"Could you set aside anything you might have read in the newspaper about this case and reach a verdict based solely on the evidence introduced in this courtroom?"

"Oh, yes."

"Thank you, sir. Yes, ma'am."

"Your Honor, my name is Christine Walker, and I just want to say that I know Sergeant Jones because we went to school together."

"Nothing more than that, Miss or Mrs. . . ."

"Mrs."

"Mrs. Walker. Other than being schoolmates did you have any other contacts with Sergeant Jones?"

"He used to come over to the house."

"How often?"

Chole liked me. I knew that after the first time she saw me alone on the streets. I was eight or nine. It was a Saturday afternoon. 'Amá had sent me to Chinatown. There were three men around her. When she saw me she left them. She was wearing one of those dresses. Her legs looked huge and naked. "Come here." No. I was afraid then. "Come here." She spoke in Spanish. No. She was bad. Then she took a dollar out of her dress. "This is for you, *m'ijo*. Come and get it. Chole likes you." It was the most money I ever had.

"Well, pretty often because he and my brother were real good friends."

"How often, ma'am?"

"Well, like every day because first he and my brother were real good friends and then I started dating him."

"I think I best excuse you, Mrs. Walker. Just a moment, though. Just a moment, please. Mr. District Attorney, without getting into the specifics of Sergeant Jones' testimony, can you give the court some idea of the relevance and importance of Sergeant Jones' testimony?"

No matter how drunk she got, she never let on to 'Amá about me. It was a long time before 'Amá even suspected that I talked to her. She never knew for sure. Not that I talked to her that much, at least not at first. She always gave me money. And she always touched me.

"Well, your Honor, as I understand it he was one of the first officers at the scene of the crime. He subdued and arrested the defendant and later took several statements from him. He's a very important witness."

"In light of the district attorney's representations, Mrs. Walker . . ."

Later I tried to stay away from her. It was the dresses. Her tits swelled out of the top and her thighs were so naked and big. It was the confessional. "And who have you coveted, my son?" I couldn't tell him it was her. "Who have you had these impure thoughts about, my son?" Anybody but her. "You must avoid the occasion of sin. Who is this girl, my son?" I wouldn't answer. "Is it one and the same girl, my son?"

"Yes, Father."

"Do you see her often?"

"No, Father."

"Well, you must see her even less. You must see her not at all."

"Yes, Father."

It was after the come. It never started with her. But when the rhythm and pleasure became one, it was her.

Then I would have given anything to cup those giant tits in my hands, to feel their weight and suck on them. Then it would have been enough just to put my hand between those juicy thighs. But after the come, as I lay there with my dick in my hand, there was no escaping it. It had been her, and the shame would set in. She'd fuck anything for three dollars. She spent hours at that street corner, leaning up against that building, one leg folded back under her, raising her cunt for all to see. Any drunk could have her. Any nigger or chink. All they needed was three bucks.

"Excuse me, your Honor, but I just want to say that it's been over eight years since I've gone out with Sergeant Jones. I haven't even talked to him in years. I only see him every once in a while when he drives by on the street in his police car. In fact, he always acts like he didn't see me. Or if he's staring right at me, like he doesn't recognize me. He never talks to me or even waves. I guess he thinks he's too good for me now."

"Mrs. Walker, what Sergeant Jones thinks about you is not before the court at this time. What is before the court is whether or not any past associations you might have had with Sergeant Jones would influence your decision in this case."

"No, sir, it wouldn't."

"My first inclination was to excuse you, Mrs. Walker. But I'm now having second thoughts about that. I think perhaps we had better pass on to some of these other hands. We have so many of them today. And perhaps we'll come back to you a little later, Mrs. Walker. Thank you.

"Ladies and gentlemen, let me make it clear that the court recognizes that in a case of this size and notoriety, with the large number of witnesses listed here, that many of you will know some of the potential witnesses. If the court were to summarily excuse all of you who have indicated by a showing of hands that you know one or some of the witnesses, then it's clear that we would have to summon a new panel. That would take at least a full day, and of course, there is no guarantee that the new panel wouldn't have the same problem. So let's proceed in this manner. You have all heard my questions to those who have indicated that they know some of the witnesses. The crux of the matter is whether or not the expressed familiarity would influence your decision in this case, and whether, as jurors, you could set that familiarity aside and decide this case solely on the evidence presented in this court. Now those of you who had your hands up before, think about the following questions carefully. Is there any one of you who does not think that he or she can set aside any familiarity or conversations you might have had with any of the previously-mentioned potential witnesses and decide this case solely on the evidence presented to you here in court? May I have a show of hands?"

He was wrapping the *chorizo* when she tapped me on the shoulder. Everybody in the store knew me. Everybody knew her, and everybody knew 'Amá. She was grinning. "I want to talk to you, *m'ijo.*" She stank of wine. "I have to talk to you, m'ijo." Don Fausto stopped wrapping the *chorizo.* The Señora Valdez was watching. She had on one of those dresses. That made it worse. "Leave that boy alone. Leave him." Agripina was in the store, too. This brought her out. "Get away from him," she said. They surrounded her. All that wine couldn't blot out the hiss of their words and the hate in their stares. She started to stammer. I took the sausage and left.

"Well, it appears that we've saved ourselves a substantial amount of time. Yes, ma'am."

"Your Honor, I know all those police officers, every one of them, because my son's a police officer and I . . ."

"Could we please have your name for the record, ma'am?"

"He was my Daddy, too," Chole said speaking of my father. He was the only Daddy I ever had. They say he's in San Francisco now, and that he's got lots of girls working for him. Some day I'm going to leave this town and go find him. I can still make good money for him. I don't look that bad, do I? When I'm clean and sober and all fixed up, even white men look at me. He couldn't have forgotten me. He used to call me 'Chunky.' He said I was one good chunky fuck. I used to be able to fuck ten or fifteen or as many as he wanted me to in one night. Sometimes he used to take me out to the labor camps. And when the night was over, all he had to do was touch me and I'd come. I used to dress him so fine. He looked so good. No Mexican in this town ever looked that good. He was my king. You can't know how much you remind me of him, ever since you were a little boy."

"I'm sorry, I forgot. My name is Carol Johnson and my son's name is Johnny Johnson. And like I said, he's a police officer, and I've know Captain Humphries for at least ten years and all the others, with the exception of the patrol-men for almost as long. Judge, you asked if we had talked to any of these people about this case. Well, I haven't talked to these officers, except maybe at first when I'd see them downtown or someplace, I probably said something like, 'My, isn't that an awful thing that happened at that church,' or something like that. But I did talk to my son about it. I'd be lying if I said I hadn't because I talked to him quite a bit about it."

"You don't have to talk to me. You don't have to be seen with me, m'ijo. It's all right. I understand. It doesn't matter. It doesn't offend me. You can come to my house at night when nobody will see. I'll give you anything, m'ijo. Money, anything I have. Anything you want. It's yours, m'ijo. Just come and take it."

"I guess what you're asking is if I would tend to believe these police officers more than some of these other people. Of course I would. Now, I know good and well that at least some of these officers were down at that church when it happened. What they saw wasn't too pretty. That boy was like some kind of wild animal. The district attorney says Sergeant Jones had to subdue him. Believe me, they had to do a whole lot more than that to subdue him. He was trying his best to kill people . . ."

They were talking about me. I heard her. Who was I

trying to kill? Maybe I was trying to kill Him. How do you kill Him? Where do you find Him to kill?

I waited for three days and three nights. I hid in the choir loft when they used the church. I drank the wine and ate the hosts. For three days and nights I ate His Body and drank His Blood. But He never came. I cursed Him. I called Him the lowest cock-sucking, cunt-smelling, pig-fucking dog that ever lived. There wasn't a peep from Him. The cunt-licker was afraid to come out. I broke open the doors to the tabernacle. There's your fucking house. He didn't come out. He wasn't home. I climbed up on the altar. I pissed in there. He didn't come out. I stuck my ass in there. I grunted and farted and finally shit in there. But, He didn't come out.

"Mrs. Johnson, please. The court would very much appreciate it if you would refrain from discussing what you think may or may not have happened in that church that night. Obviously, you weren't there, and I suspect that your son wasn't either. None of this is the product of your own first-hand knowledge. It's speculation at best and highly improper at this stage of the proceedings. Now . . ."

"I'm sorry, judge, but I thought you wanted us to tell you if we would believe police officers more."

"That's precisely one of the areas the court has been attempting to explore. But you've gone a bit far afield of that."

"Then I better answer you this way, judge. Those police officers are just going to tell the truth about what happened. They got no reason to lie. They don't know that boy from Adam. They are all God-fearing men, and that's more than I can say for that . . . for him. They're going to take an oath to tell the truth, and that's just what they'll do. Now for me to sit here and tell you that I'm not going to believe them more than him is just plain nonsense. Of course I'm going to believe them more. And as far as any conversations go, I haven't talked to any of them but my son has. They wouldn't lie to him, and I know what he's told me, and so, I know what that boy did, and it would be awfully hard for me to put that out of my mind."

I must have been waiting for Him. Who else could I have been waiting for? I waited for three days and three nights because after three days and three nights, He rose again from the dead. I took an old can from the basement and started saving my shit. I didn't sleep much, but I was careful to go up to the choir loft each night so they wouldn't find me in the morning in case I fell asleep. I was awake each morning when they came. It was just the two of them. If I was waiting for them, I could've gotten them on the first day. I wasn't waiting for them. I was waiting for Him. On the third day, He rose again from the dead. He didn't show up on the third day. It was funny. It was all I could do to keep them from hearing me laugh. The first morning he said that he was offering that Mass up to Him so that He could help me in whatever I had chosen to do. I doubled up over the can. The next morning she noticed it.

"What's that smell, Padre?"

When he came out for Mass, he said, "Something strange happened last night, Soledad. A lot of the hosts and much of the wine is missing, and I can't find any trace of anyone having broken in."

"And that smell?"

"I know."

I had forgotten the can downstairs. It was under the altar. He didn't find it.

After Mass she said, "I haven't heard from that boy. Nothing."

"God is watching over him."

"I know. But still I worry."

"God will show him the way." "I know. It's just that he was acting crazy. I'd never seen him acting like that before. He scared me."

"Do you have any idea where he could be?"

"No, he just said not too long ago that his father was in San Francisco."

"Is he?"

"Oh, Padre, how many times have I told you that his father died in Mexico before he was born."

"I forgot."

"Thank you for your candor, Mrs. Johnson. The court appreciates your honesty. However, I think it's my duty to excuse you. Please report to the clerk's office on your way out. They will give you a slip excusing you."

"Don't get me wrong, sir. It's not that I don't want to be on this jury, because I really do. I know what he's done and I think he should suffer the consequences. It's just that when you ask those questions, I feel like I have to speak out or I'd be lying."

"Thank you, Mrs. Johnson. You're excused . . . I thought I saw another hand . . . Apparently not. Now is there anyone else who does not think that he or she can set aside any familiarity or conversations they might have had with any of the potential witnesses in arriving at a verdict in the case . . . Good. It occurs to me, Mr. Fischer, that I neglected to ask for the names of your witnesses. Would you kindly provide the court and the panel with the names of your witnesses."

"May I have just a moment, your Honor?"

"Certainly."

He leaned over me and whispered. "Do you have any witnesses?" I heard him, but I didn't answer. He nudged me. I could hear them mumbling behind me. There was nothing to say.

"If the court please. It's not clear at this time, your Honor, who our witnesses will be."

They were giggling. I didn't have any witnesses. They knew it and they liked it. Dirty bastards.

"Surely the defendant will be testifying on his own behalf."

He leaned over me again. His breath smelled. "Are you going to testify or aren't you?" They liked him leaning over me. I could hear them. They liked me not answering. There was nothing to say.

"I assume so, your Honor."

"Very well. Gentlemen, it occurs to me that I haven't introduced you to the panel. Ladies and gentlemen, as most

of you probably know, the gentleman seated at counsel
table to my right is the District Attorney of Fresno County,
Matthew Cline. Would you stand please, Mr. District Attorney?"

"Good morning, ladies and gentlemen. My name is
Matthew Cline and I'm the District Attorney of Fresno
County."

Everything about him was right. The way he stood. The
way he looked. The way he talked. They would have done
anything he told them to do. And he was going to tell them
to hang me.

"Thank you. The gentleman in the dark suit seated at
the counsel table to my left is the defense counsel, Mr.
Ralph Fischer. Mr. Fischer, would you stand please and tell
the panel where your offices are located and with whom you
are associated?"

"Yes, your Honor. Good morning, ladies and gentlemen.
My offices are located in the Bidwell Building and I'm associated with James Marlowe and Frank Durrell."

He half-stood and half-turned, like he was in a hurry to
sit down again. Not like the district attorney. His voice was
quiet and he stammered. I didn't like it.

"Mr. Fischer, would you introduce your client and have
him stand and face the panel."

It hit me at the same time the lawyer was whispering,
"Stand up. He wants you to turn and face them." I'd hidden
from them all my life. I wasn't going to face them now. "For
Christ's sake, stand up, Jesus." No. He grabbed my arm and
I pulled from him. "Stand up." He grabbed again and I
jerked away from him.

"Mr. Fischer, I've asked you to ask your client to stand
and face the prospective members of the jury. Now that's a
simple request and it has a legitimate purpose. The court
has tried to be accommodating, but there's a limit to its
patience and it will not tolerate impudence. It is your client
who has demanded this jury trial, and it will be your client
who will co-operate with the processes of a jury trial. Do I
make myself clear?"

"Yes, your Honor."

"I would have you ask him one more time."

I wasn't going to stand up and look at those people for nobody. He was whispering hard and he had my arm again. He was shaking. He pulled up on me, and I pulled down. I could hear them all around the room. They were liking it. dirty bastards. Then two guards were there. "Come on, Olivas, stand up." They took my arms. I jerked. They tightened their grips. "Get up, boy." They pulled and I struggled. They lifted me and I went limp. But they held me up.

"Have your client turn and face the panel, Mr. Fischer. It's important that I be able to intelligently question the jury as to whether or not any of them might know him or have had any dealing with him."

He whispered at me again. I wasn't going to look at those people. One of the guards said, "Come on, Olivas, turn around." He wasn't whispering. They liked that. I heard them. Then they turned me around hard. I hung my head.

"It is important, Mr. Fischer, that the panel be able to get enough of a look at your client to be able to identify him. Would you please have your client raise his head. It's terribly unpleasant to have the deputies make him perform these common courtesies."

He whispered, and I buried my chin in my chest and tightened my neck. One of the deputies said, "Look at them." Then they yanked my head up, and I screamed and tore myself from them and fell on the floor screaming, "I don't want to look at them! I don't want to look at them!" until they dragged me to the holding cell, screaming, and slammed the door and kicked me and beat me where it wouldn't show.

After awhile, the lawyer came in. "Look, Jesus, he's threatening to do one of two things if anything like this happens again. He's either going to keep you locked up in here for the whole trial, and you can watch them convict you through that little window, or he's going to take you back in there and chain you to the chair and gag you."

"I don't want to look at them."

"What good is either of those things going to do? For that matter, what good is the whole trial going to do?"

"I don't want to look at them."

"Okay. We're going to break for lunch. When we come back, I'm going to tell him that you're going to behave yourself."

They kept me in the holding cell during the lunch break. I thought of Tommy Lee Smith. He was the only thing that was keeping me from pleading guilty. Much of what he had said I hadn't understood. But his message was clear: Don't plead guilty; you have nothing to gain and everything to lose.

I trusted him. His blank eyes and his gray-white face convinced me. He had no reason to lie, nothing to gain. Where are you, Tommy Lee Smith?

"Let the record show that the defendant, Jesus Olivas, is once again in the courtroom. Let the record also show that his absence was caused by his own disorderly and disruptive conduct which became so volatile that sheriff's deputies had to physically escort him from the courtroom."

He was scolding me, and they liked that. I could hear them. I could feel how glad they were. It was like I felt when she scolded me and they were around.

She always scolded me. It didn't matter who was around. I hated it, especially when white people were around when we went downtown. I'd try to walk a little behind her or maybe a little in front of her, so they couldn't be sure I was with her. But she knew. "*Espérame.* Wait for me." Her long black skirt and shawl and funny glasses. They'd stare. I'd see them shake their heads as we passed. Some would laugh. "*Espérame,*" she'd say, and I'd slow down. I'd wait, ashamed of her and ashamed that she knew. And then, as if to punish me, she'd scold me. Anywhere, on the street, in a store. In Spanish, but they understood. They could hear it in her voice, or see her hands waving at me. Then they'd laugh at us some more.

"Let the record further show that in the defendant's absence during a recess, I have discussed his conduct with his attorney and the district attorney. I have made clear to his attorney, Mr. Fischer, and have asked him to convey the same to the defendant, that the court will not tolerate any further outbursts. I have clearly set forth my proposed courses of action should there be a repetition of his conduct. Mr. Fischer has informed the court that the defendant has been made fully aware of the court's intentions and has decided to conduct himself as a gentleman during the balance of these proceedings. Is that correct, Mr. Fischer?"

"That's correct, your Honor."

In Chinatown they knew her. They were afraid of her. Anywhere we went on the west side, they'd bow to her. But the white people just stared and laughed. And there was no way that I could make them understand that I wasn't like her; that I was different; that I was just walking with her because I had to.

"Let the record also show that during the defendant's absence, the court inquired of the panel if any of them knew the defendant. We had only one positive response and that individual was good enough to assure the court that her acquaintance with the defendant was minimal at best. However, the court felt that further inquiry into the matter was probably warranted, but should most properly take place in the defendant's presence. So the court recessed, and ultimately had the defendant brought back into the courtroom with the understanding that he was going to behave himself. Now, Mrs. Ella Colari. You've indicated, ma'am, that you know the defendant. Would you tell the court something of that acquaintance?"

"Yes, your Honor. It's only that my husband and I own and operate Colari Brothers Farms, and ever since I started reading about all this in the paper, I kept telling my husband that he . . ."

I knew her.

"By *he* you mean the defendant?"

"Yes, your Honor. Anyway, I kept telling my husband that I was sure he used to work for us every summer. But since he was one of those that was brought in by a labor contractor, I had no way of knowing for sure because the labor contractor keeps his own payroll records. So yesterday, when I read in the paper that this case was supposed to start today, and since I had been called for jury duty, I thought maybe I might be on his jury. So I called the labor contractor, and he said sure enough, it was the same boy."

Don Miguel took me there every year. It was the lady of the peaches. She had the big shed with no sides and the big red and white roof. I hated it. They put me with the women. They said I was too small and skinny to do the boxes. The women talked to me like I was a girl, and the girls giggled at me. I ate alone. But they didn't leave me alone.

"You say he worked for you every summer?"

"Yes, sir."

"For how long?"

"For about five or six years."

"*Puto! Putito!* Where are you?" The boys on the boxes brought the girls with them. There weren't that many places to hide. "You better come out from wherever you're at, *putito*. If you make us look for you, we won't like it." It never took long for them to find me. "*Putito*, we thought that since you're going to be a *puto* all your life, that you should be able to dance like all the other *putos*. So we came to give you some dancing lessons. Get up on you feet, fucker! Now dance!" They threw rocks and rotten peaches. They had great fun when one of the peaches finally splattered on my shoes or my pants.

"For how long?"

"Oh, you mean how long every summer. Well, not too long. It was mainly in the peaches as I remember. Maybe two or three weeks every summer."

"How much contact did you have with him, Mrs. Colari?"

"Well, quite a bit actually, because I always work in the shed with the women, and we always kept him in the shed. He was so small, and then we never thought he could handle the boxes. We usually start the younger boys in the shed, culling and sorting with the women. As they get older and bigger, we move them outside or to dumping the boxes full of fruit. He never did seem to grow much, and though he was slow, he was careful, and he didn't damage much fruit."

Liar. I could have done the boxes except they never gave me a chance. I did boxes at the Logan ranch. Maybe not all day, but I did them. And they were heavier. Because they were plums and there are a lot more plums in a box than peaches—less space between the fruit. Some of the old men were smaller than me and they dumped boxes all day. One of them taught me to swing them. Don't pick them up, swing them. You don't get tired that way.

"How well did you get to know him? Did you, for example, have many conversations with him?"

"Not really. He was very quiet. I don't think he talked much to anybody. The most he ever said to me was probably just a nod. I had to scold him a little every once in a while because he was slow. But even then he wouldn't say anything. He'd just nod."

It was easier to be quiet. And when she was around me, when she was checking my fruit, she'd lean over me and her huge tits would press into my arm, my bare arm, and my dick would spring out like a snake, and I could hardly breathe. Her tits were bigger than Chole's, and Chole's were gigantic. She was older than Chole . . . but she was still good. Chole, she was probably in some alley in Chinatown, or on some ratty cot in one of those filthy rooms. I saw her one morning on my way to church in an alley with some drunken old Mexican. She was drunk too. They were both on the ground. They were so drunk they could hardly talk. He had her dress up and was trying to pull down her pants. She was struggling, rolling in the dirt. "Gimme the money."

"I gave it to you."

"Liar."

"I gave it to you."

He had his pants down around his ankles and he couldn't roll around like she could. She rolled, covering herself with dirt, except between her thighs. He could hardly breathe.

Somebody left five dollars for me at the jail. The guard said she wouldn't give her name.

"Would you say then, Mrs. Colari, that there was anything about this association you had with the defendant that you feel might influence your decision in this case one way or the other?"

"Oh, no."

"Thank you, Mrs. Colari. That just about completes my questioning. However, before I turn the questioning over to the attorneys, let me ask this final question. Is there any member of this panel who feels, for whatever reason, that he or she cannot sit as a fair and impartial juror in the trial of this case? . . . Good. All right, Mr. Clerk, select twelve names. And, ladies and gentlemen, as your name is called, would you please take your seat in the jury box beginning on the top row at your far left."

The short fat man called out names. One by one they came up. Some of them spoke to the district attorney on the way to their seats. Now they were on one side of me as well as behind me. There was little room to hide.

"You may proceed, Mr. Cline."

He walked slowly over to them.

"Mrs. Hutchison. Is that correct, ma'am? It's not *Hutchinson*, is it?"

"No, Hutchison, that's correct."

"Are you employed, ma'am?"

"No sir, I'm just a housewife."

"Have you ever worked outside the home?"

"No."

"And what does Mr. Hutchison do?"

"He's the assistant manager at Bryson's Department Store."

"I see. Do you have any children?"

"Yes, we have three children. But they're all gone now. Two are married and one is away at college."

"Have you ever served on a jury before?"

"No, sir."

"Mrs. Hutchison, this case is entitled the People of the

State of California versus Jesus Olivas. As the District Attorney of Fresno County, I represent the People of the State of California. That's my job and I try to do it to the best of my ability . . ."

She liked him. She nodded yes as he spoke. She smiled at him. He leaned on the railing and spoke softly. She was nodding to everything he said. My lawyer was drawing circles on a yellow pad and filling them with lines.

"And as the representative of the People of the State of California, I find it incumbent upon me to emphasize to you that there are two parties involved in this case. The defendant, who is sitting over there and about whom you'll hear a lot during the course of this case, is obviously one of the parties. But the People of the State of California are also a party to this case, and as such, they are also entitled to a fair and impartial trial. The People ask for nothing more or nothing less, simply a fair and impartial trial. Can you assure me, Mrs. Hutchison, that if you are selected to serve on this jury you will give the People of the State of California a fair and impartial trial?"

When he pointed at me, she looked at me. The smile disappeared and the face was hard. There was no nodding, just a straight, hard look. I looked away, but as I did I noticed the woman next to her and the man behind them. Their looks were the same.

"Yes, sir."

"Now, his honor has alluded to several legal concepts that are fundamental in our criminal justice system, concepts . . .

Why was I there? If I plead guilty, she'd stop nodding and go away. They'd all go away. I wanted them to go away. He'd stop talking, stop hanging me with every word and go away too. The lawyer was drawing his circles. If I told him I wanted to cop out, he'd be happy. What did it matter if I went to the joint tomorrow or two weeks from tomorrow. They were still going to jump me. Still, the slow, even words of Tommy Lee Smith circled in my mind.

"Mrs. Hutchison, you understand, do you not, that as

district attorney of this county I have very little control over
the types of cases I must prosecute? In other words, once a
crime has been committed, and the police have reasonable
cause to believe that a certain individual has committed
that crime, then it's my responsibility to prosecute that
case. Oftentimes the facts of a given case are not pleasant.
Whether they're pleasant or not, it's still my duty to present
those facts to the court and the jury. I anticipate that the
evidence that I will present in this case may not be pleasant. Some of it in fact may be downright brutal and shock-
ing and even obscene. It most certainly will include matters
that men do not normally like to discuss in the presence of
ladies. I'm sure much of it would tax any woman's sensibili-
ties. Now, without getting into the facts of this case, do you
think that, given the nature of the charges here, the possible obscenities and vulgarities that the evidence might
depict would so upset or offend you that you would not be
able to give this case your most careful and detached consideration?"

"Well, I would try my best."

She nodded when he wanted her to, shook her head
when he wanted that, got scared and shocked when he
warned her. She understood that he didn't have control of
the cases—the nod was slow then. She understood that he
was just doing his job—the nod quickened. She knew men
like him didn't talk about those things in front of ladies.
She took a deep breath when he mentioned those awful
things that she might have to hear. I looked from her to my
lawyer. He was still filling in circles on his yellow pad.

"Good, Mrs. Hutchison, that's fine. That's all anyone
can ask: that one try his best. But you won't hold it against
me, will you, ma'am, if it appears that I'm the one who
appears to bring out those vulgarities?"

"Oh, goodness no."

"Thank you, ma'am. Now, one other thing that I'd like
to point out, Mrs. Hutchison, is that at the conclusion of the
trial, the judge will instruct you, among other things, that
you are not to decide this case based on bias, prejudice, or

sympathy for or against either side. Now, I want you to look over at the defendant."

I felt myself burning. I kept my eyes down and held my head still. I hated them and I hated him. I held my breath and then tried not to blink. One of my legs quivered. I moved it to the other and stopped it. Dirty bastards.

"He looks awfully young, doesn't he? Maybe as young as fifteen. Certainly he could pass for sixteen. The information lists, and I'm sure we will establish, that in fact he's eighteen and must be tried as an adult. He's not very big either. In fact he looks frail. It wouldn't seem that he could hurt a fly. And those chains may seem to some of you oppressive. Just let me assure you that this court wouldn't permit those chains if it wasn't absolutely necessary. You've had a hint of that already this morning. And there's a sad look about him. One could, I suppose, even feel sorry for him."

My eyes watered. I wanted to cry for myself. The fields, 'Amá, our house, the ridicule, the sins and confessions, Chole, my mother and father, the church, the cell, the chains and finally the joint: they were all in those first tears. Except that I could never let those people see me cry.

"And that's precisely my point, Mrs. Hutchison. It might be very easy for some folks to feel sorry for this defendant. He might, if you please, even bring out that protective mothering instinct in some women. All that the People ask is that you be aware of, and guard against, that potential emotion, because to base the outcome of this trial on that or any other emotion is contrary to the dictates of the law. You understand that, don't you, Mrs. Hutchison? Of course you do. So that what the People ask is that you decide this case on the evidence and not on any feeling of sympathy, understandable as it might be, that you might have for the defendant. Is that too much to ask, Mrs. Hutchison?"

"Oh, no, sir."

They didn't need to feel sorry for me. I felt sorry for me. I felt sorry for every moment of pain in my life, and that seemed like forever. I looked over at them. I must have expected some of them to be feeling sorry for me. They weren't; they were watching him. He was leaning on the railing, talking softly, seriously. One of them saw me looking, and I looked away. There was nothing in his face that felt sorry for me. That made me feel sorrier for myself. Still I could hear the district attorney. The voice was smooth and right. She was still nodding. My lawyer was filling his circles with X's now instead of lines.

"Can you assure me that you'll be able to do that if you're selected to serve on this jury."

"Oh, yes, sir."

"Oh, yes, sir. Oh, no, sir. Oh, shit, sir. Let's fuck, sir."

"I'll pass this juror for cause, your Honor."

"Very well. Mr. Fischer?"

My stomach hurt. It was his turn. He stopped filling circles. Sweat ran down on either side of his ear. He straightened himself in his chair and scratched his head. I thought I could smell him. Did he stink or was it my stink? He looked scared.

"Excuse me, your Honor," the district attorney said.

It was my lawyer's turn to talk, that saved him.

"Yes, Mr. Cline?"

"Your Honor, it's occurred to me that I should have directed one general question to the panel as a whole. May I do so now?

"Ladies and gentlemen, can I by a show of hands have an indication of those of you who have served on a jury before? . . . Thank you. . . . Good. Will you please keep your hands up? . . . Thank you."

"Yes, please keep your hands raised until Mr. Cline has had an opportunity to note your prior jury service."

The judge liked him too. You could hear it in his voice. He motioned them to keep their hands up. He didn't talk to my lawyer like that.

"All right, Mr. Fischer, you may proceed."

He stood up, but slowly, and then he didn't move. He didn't walk over to them. He stood at the table and flipped through the pages of his yellow pad.

"Mrs. Hutchison, do you have any problems with the

concept that my client is presumed innocent?"

He spoke too low. I could barely hear him. And he stopped after every few words, like he couldn't remember what he had started out to say. He was afraid, and I was ashamed.

"I beg your pardon, sir?"

"Would you speak up, Mr. Fisher?" the judge said.

He cleared his throat. "Mrs. Hutchison, you understand that . . . that my client is presumed innocent?"

It still wasn't loud enough. He kept stopping and looking down at the yellow tablet like he was looking for his next word.

"Yes, sir."

I was surprised the juror heard.

"And if you had to vote on his guilt or innocence right now . . . you would have to vote him innocent."

"What was that, sir?"

I knew it.

"Please keep your voice up, Mr. Fischer."

He didn't talk to him the way he talked to the district attorney.

"If you had to vote on his guilt or innocence . . . right now . . . you would have to vote him innocent."

"I don't understand, sir."

I didn't either. Who was he trying to kid. Nobody thought I was innocent. He made me ashamed. Every time he stopped, I didn't think he'd start up again.

"What don't you understand?"

"That the law says he's innocent."

He cleared his throat again. "What I mean is that . . . if you had to vote right now . . . if you had to vote right now, you have to vote . . . not guilty because the law says that right now he is presumed innocent."

He stopped a long time after *vote*, I could feel them waiting. I thought he was going to say *guilty*. I wanted to say the hell with it and cop out right then and there. But I couldn't.

"But why would I vote right now? I thought we did that

at the end of the trial."

"Yes, I know, ma'am . . . but what I'm trying to . . .
point out to you is that the law presumes Mr. Olivas innocent at . . ."

"Mr. Fischer, you're confusing the lady. Please don't
question the prospective jurors on matters that the court
has already covered. The court has adequately covered the
concepts of the presumption of innocence and the corresponding burden of proof and reasonable doubt. Please
move your questioning into another area and try to refrain
from going into matters that the court has already covered."

The judge was mad. He was scolding him, but the way
white people did, real quiet and polite. I wished he would
have grabbed him, jumped on him, screamed at him,
punched him. Anything but those polite words so that he
would have done something for me besides mumbling.
While the judge scolded him, he kept his head down. We
both kept our heads down. Why was I always ashamed of
something? Long after the judge had stopped, he said, "Yes,
your Honor." Then he started turning the pages of his tablet
again. There was writing on these pages. He stopped and
ran over the words with the tip of his pen. His hand was
shaking and the pen drew lines through some of the words.
I started shaking. The pause was too long. I could hear
them moving around and whispering among themselves. I
wanted him to hurry up and say something, anything.

"Proceed, Mr. Fischer."

"Yes, your Honor . . . Did you say you read about this
case in the newspaper?"

"No, I didn't say that."

"Do you take the *Free Press*?"

"Yes."

"And you're saying you never read about this case in the
paper?"

She was mad. He was getting everybody mad.

"Mr. Fischer, please don't argue with the prospective
juror. The court has requested that you restrict your questioning to areas that it has not already covered. Now, I

spent a great deal of time on this subject, as you well know. The purpose of the court's questioning was not so much to elicit individual responses as to whether or not the prospective jurors had heard or read about this case. The court assumes most have. Rather, the court's questioning was an attempt to determine whether such prior information would affect their deliberations now. We can assume that Mrs. Hutchison has read about this case in the newspaper. That's not the point. Now, unless you can convince the court that you have some different and legitimate reason for wanting to go into this area again, the court would request that you move into other areas."

He was scolding him *again*. I didn't like it. That didn't matter. I kept my head down. The lawyer kept his head down. He started going through his yellow tablet again. This time he was turning and stopping at pages on which there was no writing. His hand shook more and the lines were jagged on the blank paper. He didn't speak and I didn't think he was going to speak. I thought I'd be in San Quentin by morning. They were moving behind me. I had wanted him to talk to them like the district attorney had. Now I just wanted him to talk.

"Do you have any further questions, Mr. Fischer?"

He didn't answer. He just stood there looking down at the blank tablet.

"Mr. Fischer, the court asks you if you have any further questions?"

I could hear them giggling. Answer, say something, you fucker. It's my ass, not yours.

Then he answered. "May I have a moment, your Honor?" I could barely hear him. He turned the blank pages some more until the judge asked him again.

"Mr. Fischer, does that complete your questioning?"

He shook his head and then he said, "No, your Honor."

"Then proceed."

He cleared his throat and the room became quiet. "Mrs. Hutchison, . . . are you the kind of person who . . . would change her mind because she's outvoted?"

"No, I don't think so."

"Well, what I mean is that . . . suppose that during your deliberations you . . . you feel that you are outnumbered . . . eleven to one . . . you wouldn't change your mind just because you're outnumbered . . . you wouldn't do that, would you?"

"No, I've never considered myself to be a wishy-washy person. And no one's ever even accused me of that, at least not until now."

They laughed. They all laughed. It was a long laugh. The bailiff rapped his hammer. The lawyer sat down. The son of a bitch was playing with my life.

"Anything further, Mr. Fischer?"

"No."

"Since you did not challenge Mrs. Hutchison for cause I assume that you have passed her for cause."

He didn't answer. Say something, you son of a bitch. It was *his* head I should have bashed in. The district attorney was up and at the railing again.

"Good morning, Mrs. Colari."

Shit. It was the one that knew me. I didn't recognize her all dressed up like that.

"Good morning, Mr. Cline."

I wanted him to know that this was the one who knew me. But he hunched over his tablet. He was filling in the lines now, no more circles, every other line with black ink. He was sweating.

"Mrs. Colari, I'm going to try not to be as burdensome on you or the other jurors as I was with Mrs. Hutchison. I take it that you heard and understood the questions I posed to Mrs. Hutchison?"

"Yes, sir."

"You heard my questions on reasonable doubt, and on the unpleasantries you may be subjected to as a juror in this case, and my questions on sympathy as a factor in deciding this case, did you not?"

Apache was right. He was scared. He couldn't talk to the judge. He couldn't talk to the jury. He couldn't even talk. Maybe he was ashamed, too. The way he was hunched over his tablet. Maybe it was all the same thing. Whatever it was, they could all see it, and it made me ashamed. I never felt good enough. Now my lawyer wasn't good enough. Now my lawyer didn't feel good enough.

"Yes, sir."

"Did those questions in turn, or any of the other questions I asked, raise any questions or doubts or problems in your mind that would lead you to answer them any differently than Mrs. Hutchison did?"

"No, sir."

I remembered the way the white people used to look at me on the streets. It was something in their eyes. I don't know what it was in their eyes, or what their eyes did. I don't know if their eyes got bigger or smaller, or just got fixed in a squint or a stare, or changed color or what. It took just a glimpse to see it and to know it. But I could have never described it or explained it to anyone who wasn't a Mexican. They knew. We never talked about it, we just accepted it. I saw the others do what I did when the white people looked at them. They looked away, too. They shuffled, got nervous, and did something with their hands. All of it was saying there was something wrong with us. We weren't good enough. None of us ever talked about it. None of us ever said it, but we knew. Our bodies said it for us. Our feet and our hands did those funny things. Our necks and our shoulders drooped. There was something wrong with us. We never questioned it. We were forever ready to admit it. All they had to do was look at us and we confessed right on the spot, in an instant, without speaking a word. There is something that is bad about me and there doesn't seem to be anything I can do about it. We all know that. It has to do with us being darker and smaller and our language and food and not being clean. 'Amá was always clean. She was always cleaning. She cleaned at work and she cleaned at home. She made me clean all the time. She made me take baths all the time. But around them, I never felt clean.

"Now, Mrs. Colari, I always try to be as open and above board as possible. With that in mind I'd like to ask you, or perhaps just make known, whether or not you know that your husband and I are members of the same duck-hunting club?"

"Oh, yes, sir. I know that."

"And it's true, is it not, that we've both belonged to that club for many, many years?"

"Yes, sir."

"But during that time, I personally have had very little contact with you, is that correct, ma'am?"

"Yes, sir. The only times we've been together is when the wives go up to the cabin and clean it up a few times a year and then we cook and have like a get-together, you might say. But aside from 'hello' and 'how are you,' I don't think we've talked very much."

It was their mouths, too. Not like the eyes. But it was there. The way they raised the edges, even the old ones.

"That's precisely what I'm driving at, Mrs. Colari. Do you feel that any contact we might have had because of your husband's membership in the duck club would influence your deliberations in this case one way or the other?"

"No, sir. About the only thing I know about you is that you're a real good shot. You're so good that at times it gets my husband upset. But I think he's just jealous."

They were laughing and I didn't know why. He was still coloring in lines even though he was looking at the district attorney. Her face was all lit up. She liked him too. She'd do whatever he wanted. My lawyer was coloring in the same line. His beard had grown since morning. His face looked dirty. Some of his sweat had fallen on the edge of his white collar. That looked dirty too.

"Good. Thank you, Mrs. Colari. Your Honor, it occurs to me that I neglected to ask Mrs. Hutchison a question, and with the court's permission, I'd like to ask it now, perhaps in the form of a general question."

"Very well, Mr. Cline."

"Is there anyone presently seated in the jury box who

has had a negative experience of any kind with a police officer? . . . Yes, Mrs. . . ."

"Phillips."

"Mrs. Phillips. All right. Would you tell us about that,
ma'am?"

"Well, once I was stopped for a speeding ticket and I got
pretty mad."

"Why did you become angry?"

"I don't know why I got mad. I just got mad."

This one liked him too. Was there any one of them that
didn't like him? My lawyer was so hunched over his tablet
that I couldn't tell if he was on the same line.

"I'm sure you're aware, Mrs. Phillips, that we will be
calling quite a few police officers as witnesses in this case.
Do you think that there is anything about the incident you
have mentioned that would carry over and affect your deliberations here in this case?"

"Do you mean will I still be carrying a grudge?"

"Well, if you want to put it that way."

They laughed again. Very funny. I wanted to kick that
fucking tablet away from him. He didn't even look up. If
they laughed again, I would. He was sweating more. I was
sure I could smell him.

"Oh, no. The man was just doing his job. And when I
stopped and thought about it, he acted like a real gentleman. In fact, he and his wife and two kids come in the store
every so often, and I like him real well. But I sure didn't
like that ticket."

They laughed again. I looked at him and at the tablet.
The whole thing was a big joke.

"But you wouldn't hold that ticket against any police
officer, would you ma'am?"

"No, sir."

"Thank you, ma'am, and thank you once again, Mrs.
Colari. I have no further questions of Mrs. Colari, your
Honor, and I'll also pass her for cause."

The judge was looking at my lawyer. It was his turn to
talk. He was waiting for him to talk. He stayed hunched

over the tablet.

"Proceed, Mr. Fischer."

He didn't hear him. He wasn't listening. Say something, man. It's my ass, not yours. It's not fair.

"Mr. Fischer, the court has asked you to proceed."

I could hear them behind me. I could hear them all over. They were glad he was my lawyer. They were glad it was happening to me. Then he got up, but slowly, and the room got quiet. He didn't look at them until after he started talking.

"Mrs. Colari, are you trying to tell me? . . ."

"Keep your voice up, Mr. Fischer. I can't hear you from here, and I daresay the jurors are having greater difficulty than I in hearing you."

"Are you telling me, Mrs. Colari, that even though your husband and the district attorney have been hunting partners for years, and you have been to several social gatherings with . . ."

"Objection, your Honor, that's clearly argumentative."

"Yes, yes. Mr. Fischer, don't argue with the juror. This is a court of law. There are proper and improper methods of phasing questions. You know that. Proceed."

"Mrs. Colari, how long have your husband and the district attorney belonged to the same duck hunting club?" He spoke softly, but he wasn't stopping.

"Oh, for quite a few years now."

"How many? Ten, fifteen?" He was pushing her.

"Probably at least fifteen."

"And you like the district attorney, don't you?"

"Yes."

"You don't know me?"

"No."

"And you don't particularly like me, do you?"

"I'll object, your Honor. Whether Mrs. Colari likes me or likes Mr. Fischer is really not relevant to this proceeding. Besides being improper, this whole line of questioning borders on being childish."

"Yes, yes, Mr. Fischer. Some of this may be remotely

relevant, but when you begin probing into whether or not a particular juror likes you, I not only find that improper, but I also question the service you're providing your client. Why don't you simply ask Mrs. Colari whether she'll be able to set aside any ties she might have with the district attorney in reaching a decision in this case? That's really the issue."

He started turning the pages of his tablet again. Past the lines onto blank pages, reading whatever there was to read on those pages. She didn't wait for the question.

"Oh, I could do that, your Honor. I really don't know Mr. Cline that well. I don't favor one side more than the other."

"You may proceed. Mr. Fischer."

He didn't answer.

"Do you have any further questions of this juror, Mr. Fischer?"

He sat down instead. And they were loud now, so loud that the bailiff rapped his hammer once.

"All right, proceed, Mr. Cline."

"Thank you, your Honor. Mr. Simmons, can you tell us a little bit about yourself?"

"I'm married. We have three children who are all grown and gone. I'm the superintendent of custodians for the Fresno Unified School District, and I've been with the District going on thirty years. That's about it."

He had gone back to the page he had been coloring. He was skipping every other line. He had a yellow and black flag. Sweat was pouring down his face. His collar's edge was brown.

"Were you able to hear the questions I posed to the first juror, Mr. Simmons?"

"Yes, sir."

"If I were to ask you those same questions, would your answers be any different, sir?"

"No, I don't believe so, sir. But there's one thing I think I'd better tell you."

"And what is that, sir?"

"My wife's cousin is a deputy for the Sheriff's Department."

"Do you have much contact with him?"

"Not really."

"Have you discussed this case with him?"

"No. He works for the Sheriff and I think the city police handled this. So he wouldn't know too much about it anyway."

"Mr. Simmons, is there anything about the fact that your wife's cousin is a deputy sheriff that would affect your ability to serve as a fair and impartial juror in this case? In other words, could you put the fact that a rather distant relative is a deputy sheriff out of your mind in deciding this case?"

"I don't see why not."

"Thank you, Mr. Simmons. I'll pass this juror for cause, your Honor."

"Mr. Fischer."

He turned the page and started another flag. The hum got loud. The bailiff rapped his hammer.

"Would counsel approach the bench?"

He still didn't move. The judge was staring at him. He was getting red. Then the district attorney came over. "Come on, Ralph," he said quietly and took him by the arm and led him up to the judge. The bailiff rapped again. They were glad.

They were standing in front of the judge when the door opened. The judge was scolding my lawyer; I heard the door over the humming of their voices. I heard it this time even though I hadn't heard it open all day. This time I knew it had opened. And then their humming changed. It became a hush. And I knew she was in the room. I knew it before she spoke. I could feel it. Then I heard her voice, not clearly, but just enough to recognize the Spanish, just enough to know that it was her. I looked back. She was in black, standing between two deputies, bewildered, not knowing where to go or what to do, looking all around.

"Stop it," I said. "I'm guilty."

Chole came on the day the judge sentenced me.

Except for the lawyers and the deputies, there was no one else in the courtroom. She sat way in the back, in the last row. She kept her head down.

"I have received and considered the probation officer's report. Do you waive the forty-eight hour rule, Mr. Fischer?"

"Yes, your Honor."

"Do you have anything to say on behalf of your client?"

"No, your Honor."

"Does your client have anything to say to the court?"

"No, your Honor."

How did he know? He hadn't talked to me.

Then the judge started preaching at me. I didn't listen. I stuffed my mind with pieces of anything I could find. But I did hear him say, "The Court therefore sentences you to the California Department of Corrections for the term prescribed by law."

Chole started crying at the back of the courtroom, screaming, "Oh, *m'ijo*! *M'ijo*! No! *M'ijo*! Don't do it to *m'ijo*! Please! He's a good boy! *M'ijo*!"

She ran toward us, but the guards stopped her. When they took me back to the holding cell, one of them asked, "Is that your mother?" The other one answered, "Oh, hell no. That's Chole Carabello. She's an old whore. We used to pick her up all the time years ago when some of the businessmen's wives complained that she was hustling their husbands. Now she knows better. Now she just works out of Chinatown."

"That's not his mother then?"

"I told you, she's just an old whore."

Then I said, "I never had no mother."

"Let's get this crazy asshole out of here."

CHAPTER SEVEN

I rubbed against it accidentally the first time. I must have been five or six then, maybe younger. I was in the closet changing. I had caught my foot in my pant leg and had fallen against the closet wall. It was hard and the rubbing felt good. There was nothing wrong with that then. Except that I closed the closet door and rubbed in the dark so she couldn't see.

After that I rubbed against a lot of things, a lot of times. But I couldn't remember touching myself until they started talking about it at school.

"Aw, go beat your meat."

"I can't, guy. I'm too tired. Why don't you do it for me?"

"You must have jacked-off ten times today already."

"No, guy, only nine."

They were in the eighth grade and I was in the sixth. When I tried it for the first time, all I got was sore and swollen. It was at night and she was at work, but I still locked the bathroom door even though I didn't think of it as a sin then either.

When we came back from summer vacation to the seventh grade, everybody was doing it. This time I tried it for two nights in a row. I beat it and beat it, but nothing came out. When I woke up after the second night, it was puffed

up like a small red half-blown balloon. It hurt. My shorts
felt like sandpaper. I could barely walk.
"What's wrong?" she asked.
"I hurt myself."
"Where?"
"At school."
"No, no. Where does it hurt?"
"Up here, at the top of my leg."
"Let me see."
"No, It's okay now. It really hurt yesterday, but it's okay
now. We better go. Padre Galván wants me there on time."
It still wasn't a sin, but it took two weeks for it to go
down. I thought it was going to be like that forever. I
wanted to tell or show somebody, see a doctor even. But I
didn't dare.

Later that year, near summer, I dreamed about Rosie.
She was the girl with the great big tits. She stayed in with
me one recess and stood in a corner where no one could see.
She wanted me to touch those great big tits. She motioned
to me. I got closer and closer. Just as I was about to touch
them, my insides started coming out. I grabbed myself and
rolled over, but they kept coming out. When they stopped, I
woke up. I was sweating and my body was wet. I turned on
the light to see what had come out. My hands and stomach
and thighs were all full of a sticky, smelly white cream. I
was relieved and decided that it felt good. The next night I
used my hand. That was a sin.

I confessed it easily enough the first time. But Padre
Galván changed that.

"You must guard against that, my son. It is a mortal
sin. It is called the sin of self-abuse. For those few empty
moments of pleasure, you would suffer the loss of your soul
for eternity if you were to die immediately after engaging in
that act. Also, the effects of repeated masturbation on your
mind and body in this life can be devastating. I would ven-
ture to say that ninety-nine per cent of all the boys who
died at your age and are burning in the flames of Hell right
now are there because of the sin of self-abuse. That's not to

mention those that are in the asylums. You must fight against it."

It wasn't easy. After a day of not doing it, it was always big and as hard as a rock. If I moved, it rubbed against my leg or sank into my stomach. Either one was bad. It felt raw and needed touching. And the slightest touching made me want to touch it more and more until it all spilled out and I was panting and tired. Even the sheet at night could make me want to touch it. And all I had to do was just see a hint of tits and it felt as if it was going to bust through my pants. Some days I'd do it when I got home from Mass. Then again when I came home from school. Having sinned already that day, what difference did it make if I did it again? So I'd do it again as soon as she left for work, and if it wasn't too sore again, when I went to bed. It soon caused problems.

She got suspicious. "Why didn't you go to Communion this morning?"

"I broke my fast."

"Again?"

"Yes."

"How did you break it?"

"I drank some water."

"Again?"

"Yes."

"When did you drink it?"

"Last night."

"I know that. When last night?"

"It was after midnight."

"I know that. When after midnight?"

"Just after midnight."

"That's odd. I was home before one and you were sound asleep. Are you sure it was after midnight?"

"Yes, because I saw the clock. I was real hot and sweating and I needed some water and I had just woken up so I didn't remember that I shouldn't drink until it was too late."

"That's the third time this week you've missed Communion because you've broken your fast."

She didn't believe me.

It became harder to confess it. Though Padre Galván couldn't see me in the confessional, I knew that he knew it was me. And once, just after I had confessed that I had done it again, he said, "Again?" I worried that he would tell her. Even though priests weren't supposed to tell, 'Amá and he talked about everything. One morning she said, "I don't know what to do about this boy, Padre. It's disgusting. Three times this week he's missed Communion because he's broken his fast." Padre Galván just looked at me.

It was about that time that a priest from St. Patrick's talked to the seventh- and eighth-grade boys.

"I have come to talk to you boys because I'm concerned about the number of times I hear the sin of self-abuse being confessed. I don't think many of you appreciate the seriousness of the sin. Each time you give in to the temptation, each time you give in to yourself, you are risking eternal damnation. For those few moments of pleasure, you could burn for eternity in Hell. But what most of you don't seem to know is that it's not good for your minds and your bodies either. I know of a boy who drove himself mad by repeated masturbation. And there are many, many more cases like him. This boy got into the habit of abusing himself at least once or twice a day. Often it was more. Now this sin is not called the sin of self-abuse for nothing. What you do each time you commit it, is that you abuse your whole nervous system and drain your body of its precious energy. And the body and mind are like anything else. They can just take so much. This boy got into the habit about your age. Each day, without realizing what he was doing to himself, he would strain his nervous system to its edge. Not once, but often several times. He drained his energy so much that he wasn't good for much; he hardly had the energy to move. And whatever he did do, he did clumsily and poorly. And like most vices, the more he did it, the more he wanted to do it. Picture stretching your nervous system each day as far as it can be stretched, and then just letting it snap. Well, that's what he did. More and more and more. His parents

didn't know what to do with him. On the one hand, he could
barely move. He ate less and less. In desperation, his parents took him to a doctor. But of course, a doctor cannot see
what he is not told about. And the boy didn't tell the doctor
about his self-abuse. He couldn't. He was too ashamed.
Finally the boy went mad. I was called into the case
because his family was so concerned about him that they
wanted me to give him his Last Rites. From what they told
me, it occurred to me immediately that this was a classic
case of self-abuse. But, of course, it was too late by then. I
only mention what my thoughts were at the time because
they did in fact turn out to be true. You see, once the boy
was in the asylum, it didn't take them long to find out what
the problem was. They put him under constant observation,
and within a day or two, it was clear what was wrong. But
getting him to stop was another thing. He was so bad by
then that they finally had to put a strait jacket on him to
keep his hands away from himself. But by then the damage
had been done. That was almost ten years ago, and they tell
me that this boy has to be kept in a strait jacket much of
the time even to this day. That's the only way they can trust
him to be by himself. Not that they let him wander around
by himself, because they can't. He walks into things, into
anything that's near him. Though his eyes are wide open,
he always seems to be staring far beyond. And he doesn't
talk anymore; he just sort of grunts from time to time. Now
I ask you, is there anyone here who really believes that the
momentary pleasure he gets from the sin of self-abuse is
worth that?

"Then there's the story of Blessed Father Damien, the
priest who went to the island of Molokai to devote his life to
working with lepers. Leprosy is a disease that eats away
first at the skin and then at the flesh and finally at the
bones of human beings. It usually starts in the hands or
feet and slowly rots away those parts of the body until it
leaves nothing but a stub of a man. Then his face starts to
scale away so that after awhile, there is just a trunk of a
man with a skeleton head that still manages to move. But

only in painful wiggles. The only sounds lepers can make are cries of pain. Slowly, but very, very painfully, they die. Leprosy is very contagious. The slightest touch can be enough to contaminate you. For that reason, and also because little was and is known about leprosy, lepers were sent off to rot and die on the island of Molokai. Blessed Father Damien volunteered to go to Molokai in an effort to bring the comfort and peace of the Lord Jesus Christ to these miserable wretches. He was warned repeatedly that he would contract the disease, but he went anyway. He knew what was in store for him. Miraculously, for many, many years Blessed Father Damien worked among these poor souls without contracting the disease. The comfort and hope that he gave those people was tremendous. Finally, he too became afflicted and, slowly, he too withered away, singing the praises of the Lord rather than the cursing of the devil, to his grave. No one knows much about this terrible disease. Many scientists and doctors have studied it for years and have discovered very little. It is said that Blessed Damien found that in almost every case he attended—and there were thousands—that each leper who had not contracted the disease from another leper had a serious addiction to the sin of self-abuse. Many were convinced that the sin of self-abuse had been the cause of their illness. From the time they were your age, they had abused their minds and bodies with that habit so much that their bodies literally started to decay. Many so-called wise men laughed at Blessed Damien's discovery, but none have been able to refute it. And if you think of it, it makes sense. So I must warn you, my friends, self-abuse is a dangerously serious matter. Don't take it lightly. Don't give in to the temptation, for the consequences are severe.

"One other thought I must leave you with, my friends, and it is simply this. When you confess your sins, you make a firm resolution to sin no more. It is upon that condition that the priest, Jesus Christ's representative in the confessional, forgives your sins. Most priests will say something like 'I forgive you your sins. Go in peace and sin no more.' If any one of you said that he did not or could not firmly resolve to sin no more, then no priest could forgive you because you are not truly sorry for them. To be truly sorry for them you must firmly promise to sin no more. It is not enough just to say those words. No, you must mean them. Now, I don't believe some of you understand that. When you come into the confessional week after week—and sometimes twice a week—and repeat week in and week out that you have sinned against the Sixth Commandment, then I seriously doubt that you have true contrition, that you are truly sorry for your sins when you confess them. And if you do not really intend to make every effort to sin no more when you confess your sins, then you have no contrition, and your sins are not forgiven, no matter what the priest says."

All through his talk I wanted to look at my hand to see if there were any signs of rotting, but I didn't want the others to see me. As he was leaving, I looked at it quickly, but I couldn't see anything. At noon, I studied it in the sun. The right hand. That was the one I used; that would be the one that would be infected. At first I saw nothing. Then on the inside of my hand, just below my little finger, I saw a tiny white flake or scab. I looked down at it all afternoon. I could hardly wait to get home. Once home, I locked myself in the bathroom and pulled down my pants. But there wasn't enough light to see. I turned on the light. She could see in with the light on. I pulled down the shade. That would make her suspicious. I rolled up the shade. I needed the light. I would have to take my chances and listen for the back door. Carefully I examined it, careful not to touch it with my right hand. What if I had already spread the scab and my dick rotted before the rest of my body? How would I piss? Slowly I turned it and stretched the skin. Then I saw it: a tiny white scab near the tip. I tried not to cry, afraid that she'd notice.

It didn't get hard that night. I prayed for a miracle. To go to a doctor, I'd have to tell her.

For three days I checked it every chance I got. It seemed to be spreading. But on the fourth day it was gone. I swore that I would never jack off again. It would be so much easier. I wouldn't have to worry about Communion and Confession—no broken fasts to tell her about. But three nights later, when I was sure it was gone, I touched it. It felt so good.

"*Cochino!*" she hissed, as I walked in. I had just come in from school. I didn't know what she was mad about. Then I saw the sheet. She was holding it. "Look at these spots. I know what they are, and I know how they got there. Liar! You say you broke your fast. Liar! Don't let me hear that again. You miss Communion again and you will pay."

But summer came and there were no more six o'clock masses because by six o'clock I had already gotten off the back of Don Miguel's truck at some ranch or shed. The days were long and hard. When I got home, she had already gone to work. Sometimes I fell asleep at the table while eating my dinner. But no matter how tired I was, it seemed like I always managed to do it once or twice a day. Because it felt so good. Besides, I had so many mortal sins on my soul that one or two more wouldn't matter. Hell was Hell. You'd probably burn as bad for a thousand mortal sins as you would for ten thousand. Besides, people didn't die at thirteen. Not many, anyway.

One day, we were working in the plums. I was eating my lunch behind some boxes when I heard a girl laughing. She was running towards the boxes, chased by a boy. Her tits were swaying under her T-shirt. They were big. Before she reached the boxes, she was out of breath and stumbling. He caught her from behind. She screamed, but she was happy. He buried his mouth in her neck and then grabbed her tits. She let him. "Oh! Oh!" She let him, rubbing the hands that were grabbing her tits. My dick felt as if it were going to burst. I couldn't believe what I was seeing. I had imagined it, dreamed about it many times, but this was different. This was real. She was letting him. She was liking it. She was hot. I wanted to get closer. I wanted to see more, to see it better. I crawled along the boxes. He had his hand under her T-shirt. If I could get a little closer, I might be

able to see her tits. I crawled closer. I strained against the
boxes. If I got flat on the ground at the edge of the boxes, I
could surely see her tits. I wriggled to the edge. I was just a
few feet from them. I pressed against the boxes so they
wouldn't see me. The boxes fell; some fell on me. She saw
me and screamed and ran. He saw me too, cursed, and then
started coming at me. But changed his mind and ran after
her.

I went back to my row, hoping they hadn't recognized
me. As worried as I was that he might come and find me,
still I kept thinking of what they had been doing. My dick
was as long and as hard as a pole. It hurt to go up and down
the ladder. It hurt to reach for a plum. It felt raw. It would-
n't go down. When I couldn't stand it anymore, I went back
to the boxes. I didn't care what Don Miguel said. There was
no one there, and I laid down where I had first seen them. I
had gotten so that I didn't like to do it until towards the end
of the day. When I did it in the morning, everything seemed
to go wrong the rest of the day. God was quick to punish.
But now I had to do it, and I did, there in the open, besides
the boxes, looking at the place where they had stood. Anyone could have seen me, but I didn't care, at least not until
it was over. Then I hurried to cover myself and to get back.

As I got back to the orchard, I remembered the picture
of Adam and Eve at school. They had just eaten the apple
and were being driven from the Garden by a huge angry
angel. I felt their darkness in the shadows of the orchard.
Stooped, each had an arm around the other, helping each
other away from the wrath of God. I was watching for Don
Miguel. I got back to my ladder unnoticed.

I had left an almost full bucket of plums on the ladder. I
jumped on the ladder and skipped up the steps before Don
Miguel could come. The bucket started falling on me. I
grabbed onto the ladder to catch my balance. Instead I
tipped the ladder over onto me. I fell on my back and the
ladder banged on my forehead. Every part of my body hurt.
I was lying in smashed fruit. Then Don Miguel was there.

"What the hell are you doing, boy? What a fucking

mess, if I've ever seen a mess. Get your ass up and get this
fruit out of the rows and get your ass back up in those trees.
You're not worth the space you take up in the back of my
truck. Now get your ass up and busy before I kick it up."
     I got up and did as he yelled. I expected that, and more.
And I got more. Another bucket of fruit fell. A wasp stung
me. The boy that had been with her found me. He grabbed
me by the collar. "Look, you little son of a bitch. Don't you
ever be spying on me and my girlfriend again! You hear!"
     They were yelling at me from the back of the truck to
hurry up. I was the last one out of the fields. Hurry. I
expected that. Don Miguel had the truck idling. I broke into
a run and started to boost myself on the truck when I saw
her. The truck was moving. It was the girl by the boxes, and
she rode with me every day. I lost my grip, but tried to hold
on. The truck dragged me over the asphalt until I let go. I
scraped and then stopped hard. It hurt. I expected that. I
started to cry. They stopped the truck and came back.
Some of them were laughing. I expected that too.
     When the plums were almost over, I went to another
stack of boxes to eat my lunch. She was there, lying on top
of two boxes with her arms across her face shading her
eyes. She saw me and then looked away. I kept looking. Her
tits were sagging into the edges of her T-shirt. I remembered them swaying under that T-shirt. I remembered her
gaspings, and how she liked it, and how she rubbed his
hands wanting more. She didn't move. She was hot. I looked
at those tits for a long time. She knew I was looking. She
didn't care. She didn't move. She was hot. I took a few steps
toward her. She still didn't move. She was one of those kind
of girls that the boys were always talking about; the kind
that always wanted it and needed it and had to have it. I
kept staring at her. It was getting hard to breathe. Still she
didn't move. Now I was sure she wanted it, that she wanted
me to grab those tits like the other guy had. I was shaking.
I moved a few steps closer. I knew she was hot. I knew she
wanted it, but I didn't know how to do it. I didn't even know
her name. What would I say to her? I tried to control my

breathing. It was too loud. She would hear. But she was just laying there waiting for me. I moved a few steps closer. I'd grab her the way the other guy had. Then she sat up. "Get the hell out of here! Go, you goddamn creep. Get the hell out of here! Shooo!" I ran.

𓇼𓇼𓇼

It was late that summer that Father Martínez had his novena. That was the third year he had come. Each year it had been at the end of the summer. They were waiting for him. I heard them talking. Padre Galván would be gone for a week, and he would be there for at least three of those days. They kept talking about his coming. Even some of the men were waiting for him.

She made me serve the novena.

"He won't have anybody to serve for him, and it doesn't start until 7:30, and Don Miguel said he'll be bringing his people home early this week."

"But I'm tired at night, and you didn't make me do it last year or the year before that."

"This year is different."

It was 7:15 when I left the house. The sun was down far enough so that most of the street was in shadows. But there was still heat. It seeped out of the houses and the sidewalk and the street and the earth. It was that time of day when it was hotter inside houses than outside. People who had sweated through their dinners were outside, waiting for their houses to cool. I knew them all. I nodded to some of them.

The little church stood high enough so that one side of it was still catching the sun. It was going to be hot in there. Then I noticed that there were a lot of people going to the novena. When I reached the front of the church, I saw that there were even more people than I had thought. There were more men than I had ever seen at church. I went up into the church and through it, rather than around it, to get to the sacristy so I could see how many people there were. The church was packed. I went around and behind the altar, down the stairs that led to the sacristy.

He was standing in the shadows of that orange heat.

"Who are you?"

"I'm Jesús Olivas, Father."

"What do you want?"

"I'm your altar boy, Father."

"Who said I needed an altar boy?"

"My grandmother did, Father."

"Who is she?"

"Soledad Olivas, Father."

He looked at me. He was a small, thin, dark man with a pock-marked face. He combed his hair straight back which made it stick up. He wore a black cassock. The sash at the waist showed how small he really was. There were big beads of sweat on his forehead.

"You serve here all the time?"

"Yes, Father."

"Maybe I do need an altar boy. Light the candles."

"Which ones, Father?"

"All of them."

"All of them, Father? Padre Galván only lights all of them at Christmas and Easter, Father."

"When Padre Galván is here, you do as he asks. When I'm here, you do as I ask."

"Yes, Father."

I put on my cassock and surplice, got the big candle lighter, and started upstairs. The little priest had put on a white surplice and was standing in front of the chest where the hosts and chalices were kept. It was hot up there. Someone had opened the windows, but the air wouldn't move. There were more people there than I had ever seen. Some were even standing in the vestibule. And they were talking. People didn't talk in church, but now they were.

"Do they usually talk like that?" he asked downstairs.

"No, Father."

"Do this many people usually come to your services?"

"No, Father."
He was an ugly little man. He wiped his brow. It didn't
do much good. I wasn't sweating like that. He thought for a
moment. Then he went to the closet where the vestments
were hung and took out the big gold cape that Padre Galván
used for benediction. He put it on. It was way too big. It fell
on the floor all around him. But he didn't take it off. Then
he took out the big gold fan where Padre Galván put the
Host—the Body and Blood of Jesus Christ—during benediction. In the center was a round glass case that held the
Host. Padre Galván called it the monstrance. The gold was
cast so that it seemed that golden rays came out in every
direction from the glass case. He blessed a host and put it in
the monstrance.
"Go get the censer and the charcoal and the incense."
"Now, Father?"
"Yes, now."
"But we always save it for the end."
"Please do as I say."
"Yes, Father."
I took the censer and charcoal from the closet under the
stairs, but it was too dark to find the incense. I turned on
the light.
"Turn it off."
"But I can't find the incense, Father."
"Turn it off."
I turned off the light and felt for the incense. It was
quiet in the dark. How had he known they were talking
upstairs? I could feel him in the other part of the sacristy. I
found the incense.
"I'm ready, Father."
He had his back to me.
"I'm ready, Father," I repeated.
Then the priest turned. He was holding the vessel and
in it the Body and Blood of Jesus Christ. He thrust it
towards me, and I fell to my knees and bowed my head.
"Rise, my child, there is nothing to fear. God is Good."
I was afraid. In the quiet darkness of the sacristy, in the

fading evening orange light, I was afraid.

"Get up, my child, because tonight God has chosen you. Tonight you will help carry out His Divine Will. So listen to me carefully. Light the charcoal . . . Go on, light it. Then go upstairs. Station yourself at the altar bell. When you are sure that everyone has seen you, put some incense on the charcoal and then ring the bell. Ring it hard. When I come out, wait until I reach the center of the altar. Then follow me closely, no matter where I go. Do you understand?"

When they saw me come out with the smoking censer, they quieted down. But when they saw that he hadn't followed me, they got louder. I thought they were angry. I hurried to put the incense on the charcoal. The puffs of the sweet smelling smoke almost choked me. I rang the bell hard. It seemed like he would never come out. I kept ringing it. What was he waiting for. Then he came out, with the Sacrament held high. Their words became whispers. He didn't go up to the altar; he walked right to them. When he reached the Communion railing he started singing, a hymn or a chant in Latin. His voice was loud and strong. It shook with feeling. It smothered everything. No one would have expected so powerful a sound from so small a man. Aside from his voice, there wasn't a sound in the church. And most of them had fallen to their knees.

But that wasn't enough. He pushed past the railing gate. I followed. He went to the first pew and thrust the golden Sacrament, the Body and Blood of Jesus Christ, at them. Those who were not already kneeling, knelt. Their backs were bent and their heads were bowed. His voice got stronger. He crossed over to the other side of the aisle and thrust the Body and Blood at them. Slowly he zigzagged down the aisle, leaving behind kneeling, bowed bodies. When he reached the vestibule, he didn't stop. With thrusts of the Sacrament, he pushed the frightened people back. Kneeling, they wiggled backwards onto the church steps. When he had cleared the vestibule, he stopped, looked up to heaven, and sang Glorias. Then he started back toward the altar, slowly zigzagging, singing still, and pausing at each pew to remind them.

But he didn't go to the altar. He went to the pulpit instead, taking the Sacrament with him and placing it directly before him. He looked out over them. They were still kneeling. It had taken a long time to weave through the church. He studied them. His forehead was a mass of sweat. Gradually some of them began looking up at him. They seemed confused. He watched them. Finally, when some of them began moving around in the pews, he bellowed, "You are in the House of God!" He was shouting. His eyes were bulging. "And when you are in the House of God, you must show respect!" They had put their heads back down. He watched them.

"I heard the loud talking and laughing that went on in this church earlier this evening. Either you do not know what respect is, or you forgot where you were. I guarantee you, if you knew the wrath of God as I do, there would have been none of that. I have seen Him strike down men for transgressions far smaller than what was going on here. Men have paid dearly for refusing to take their hats off in the house of God. Women have been crushed for not covering their heads. It is not the hat or the shawl that is important. They are but symbols. It is the respect. God's vengeance is swift and complete. I know of a man who blasphemed and was struck dumb. I know of a man who stole from the church and lost his hand. I know of a man who attacked a priest and in turn was beaten to death. This is the house of God! And I warn you, when you enter the house of God, you had best act as if you were in His house.

"And I am an instrument of God! And whether you know me or like me or detest me or agree with me, you must respect me. Whether you think I'm intelligent or stupid, vain or humble, handsome or ugly, weak or strong, you must respect me. Because I am His instrument. It is through me that He has chosen that He be brought to you. Here is His Divine Body and Blood. Look at it! I bring it to you. Only I can bring Him to you. Only I can touch Him. Only I can transport Him. If any of you dared touch His

Precious Body and Blood, not only would it be sinful, but the consequences to you would be grave. These are consecrated hands. He has chosen me as His instrument. And while many are called, few are chosen. It is not easy being chosen. And once you are chosen, you dare not refuse. Lucifer, the most intelligent and beautiful of the angels, refused Him. 'I will not serve,' he said. And immediately, he and his followers were cast down into the depths of hell. Alas, there are some poor souls who though chosen have said, 'I will not serve.' Because it takes courage to serve. It takes sacrifice and self-discipline to serve. They have been unwilling to give their lives to Him. And the consequences for them have been indeed grave. Every now and then I will encounter an individual who is truly miserable or destitute along the path he has chosen to take in life. Probing some, questioning him a little, it doesn't take long to learn that at some point in his life he turned his back on a vocation.

"It is not easy to serve Him. First He asks that you leave your home and your loved ones. Then, there are years of study and self-discipline . . ."

"Self-discipline! Don't talk to us about self-discipline when you have none yourself!" A man was standing and shouting from the rear of the church. "We know what you did last year! You're not fooling us!" Then the man looked around. He was trembling. The priest watched. The two waited. The others kept their heads bowed. When the priest was sure of that, he picked up the Sacrament and began shouting, "Begone, Satan! Begone, Satan!" He got down from the pulpit as quickly as he could, stumbling on the gold cape, and with the Body and Blood held high, he hurried toward the man. When he had almost reached him, the man pushed his way out of the pew and ran out of the church.

The little priest was in the aisle. He watched the man force his way through the people in the vestibule. When he was gone, he burst into a hymn again and slowly made his way back to the altar. Everyone was kneeling. Slowly he returned, watching them, making certain that they stayed in place. But this time when he reached the altar, he went around it and down into the sacristy. They waited for him. People started stirring. Then some started leaving. I went down to the sacristy. The priest was gone.

When I left the church through the basement door, there were people waiting.

"Where is he, Jesús?"

"I don't know."

The next morning she had questions, too.

"What happened last night, Jesús?"

"Nothing."

"Nothing?"

"Nothing."

"Was Doña Petra there?"

"Yes."

"And Doña Agripina and her husband?"

"Yes."

"And you say nothing happened?"

"Nothing happened."

"Didn't they do anything?"

"No."

"Did they say anything?"

"No."

"What did Father Martínez do?"

"He did the novena."

The next day we finished a ranch about mid-afternoon and, rather than start another ranch, Don Miguel brought us home early. I was anxious to get to the church. Something was going to happen. I got there before 6:30. The church was locked. No one was there. It was never locked at 6:30 when Padre Galván was there. There was no answer at the rectory. I went around the church to crawl through a closet window that was always unlocked. Slowly I let myself down. The basement was dark. I closed the window, turned, and then jumped back. He was standing there, dressed in the gold cape with the Sacrament held in front of him.

"You scared me, Father."

He just looked at me. He didn't move and he didn't

speak. I tried to smile because I didn't know what else to do. Then he said, "God works in strange ways, my child." He walked away and placed the Sacrament on top of the vestment drawers and stood before it with his head bowed in prayer. It was quiet in the basement sacristy. The sun hadn't sunk enough to come straight through the ground-level windows. But the dark light was starting to turn orange. The novena wouldn't start for at least an hour and I didn't know what to do. I took down my cassock. It was too hot to put it on then. I hung it back up. The sounds of my movements fell hard on his silence. I stood by my cassock not wanting to move again. Time wouldn't pass. My legs ached. We hadn't worked long that day, but I was tired. Finally I said, "Is there anything you want me to do, Father?"

"No."

"Can I open some windows?"

"No."

"It's getting hot down here."

He didn't answer. I didn't care about the windows, even though it was getting hot. I just wanted him to talk to me, to say something. But he wouldn't answer. He didn't make a sound. The silence made me nervous. I couldn't stand still.

"Did you know the church is locked, Father?"

No answer.

"Don't you think I ought to unlock it, Father?"

"No."

"All the windows upstairs are closed, too, and if it's this hot down here, it's going to be boiling upstairs. If I don't open some windows up there, the people won't be able to stand it. Do you want me to open some windows, Father?"

"No."

I sat down on the floor. There was nothing else to do. My shirt was soaked. I felt trapped. I wanted to get out of there, but I didn't dare move. I watched him. He kept his head bowed. His hands were folded under his chin. It was too dark to tell if his lips were moving. The light was turning orange. It darkened his cape. Who was he?

Then the door rattled and the priest whirled around

with the Sacrament in his hands. "Shhh! Don't move! Don't
let anyone know we're in here!" The door rattled again.
They were trying to get in. "Anybody in there?" Shhh! he
motioned. Someone put their face to the window screen and
flattened it against the glass. "Get behind the closet!" he
whispered. I got behind the closet. He was standing in the
middle of the sacristy floor with the Sacrament held in front
of him. There were big stains of sweat on the cape.

The face at the window said, "I can't see too good in
there, but it doesn't look like there's anybody in there."

Somebody else said, "He's got to come sometime. Let's
just wait."

I crept to a window. There were fifteen to twenty people
outside. "Father, there's a lot of people out there."

He didn't answer. He was watching the door. Sweat was
running down his face. I could hear them talking. "Are you
sure he's not in there?"

"Yes, I'm sure."

"Did anyone check the rectory?"

"He's not there."

The sacristy was getting darker. The orange light
brought more heat than light. I could hear him breathing.
Time dripped by. Outside they said, "Are you sure he's not
in there."

"Check for yourself."

"It's getting close to 7:30."

"Maybe he won't come. Maybe we scared him out of
town."

"No, he's still here."

"How do you know."

"I just know." The priest looked at his watch. "Jesús,
that window you came through. Where does it lead to?"

"Out the back of the church, Father."

"Do people go back there?"

"No, Father."

"Listen to me carefully. Get dressed. Get the censer
ready. Then go upstairs. Take the censer and the candle
lighter with you. Light the candles, but don't turn on the

lights. Leave the censer at the top of the stairs. When you're finished lighting the candles, take the altar bells and put them with the censer. Then go open the doors."

"What about the windows, Father?"

"Don't worry about the windows. As soon as you open the doors, get back to the altar. Don't let anybody stop you. If they ask you where I am, tell them you don't know. If they ask you if I'm here, tell them no. No one will follow you past the altar railing, so it's important that you get back as soon as you open the doors. Then turn on the lights and get the bell and censer. Ring the bell hard. Ring it even before you start to walk out to your place. Ring it as you walk there. Ring it the whole time, and ring it loud. Keep ringing it until you hear me singing."

I surprised them when I opened the doors. Two men followed me down the aisle. "Where is he, Jesús?"

"I don't know."

"How is it that you don't know?"

"I don't."

Their women said, "Stop it! You're in church. You're not in the street. You're not at home. Believe him, he is the grandson of Soledad Olivas. She's taught him not to lie."

They stopped at the railing. I could hear people coming into the church behind them, lots of people. I rang the bell, expecting the priest to come up the stairs. He didn't come. I rang it again. There was no sign of him. I rang it as I walked out there. It didn't quiet them. I kept ringing it, wondering how long I could keep ringing it before they got mad enough to come after me. Then I heard him singing. It was coming from the back of the church. That same booming voice. Slowly he came towards the altar, zigzagging. Everyone knelt. His footsteps were so heavy for such a little man. His eyes were bulging. When he reached the railing, he stopped and turned.

"Tonight we will begin our novena by asking each and every one of you to come up here and kneel before the Sacrament. To be within inches of It and feel the presence of His Body and Blood. And while you are feeling that pres-

ence, I want you to think about your life, about your sins
and the lack of love you have for Him and your fellow man.
Think of how you must change your life in order to be with
and in Him forever . . . Now starting with you. Yes, you in
the first row. Come up here. And when she's finished, the
rest of you in that row follow her, one at a time. And when
that row's finished, let the next row come and so on until
each and every one of you has had an opportunity to feel
His presence and meditate within it."

The first one was Doña Juventina. She was a Guadalupana. She was afraid. She stopped after each step. He
kept motioning her with his fingers. The closer she got, the
more hunched she became. When she was a few feet from
him, he burst into a hymn. That startled her, and for a
moment made her stand straight. He kept motioning her.
Her mouth was quivering. She covered more and more of
herself with her shawl. She glanced at the Sacrament. She
was afraid to get too close to it. But he kept motioning with
his fingers, and when she was inches away from him, he
pointed for her to kneel. She knelt and bowed her head.
When he stopped singing, he reached for her chin. "Look up,
my child." She was old enough to be his mother. "Look at
His presence, my child. Remember what you are, and
remember what He is. I say, look at Him!" I looked too. The
golden monstrance was giving off a brilliant light. He
brought it within inches of her eyes. "Look at Him!" I saw
Him too; in the center of the vessel, in that pure white Host,
an infant wrapped in swaddling clothes and curled as if
lying in a manger. "Forgive me!" she cried, "Forgive me!"

"Forgive her, Father," he said, "for she knows not what
she does." Then he sang again while she knelt bowed at his
feet. When he finished singing, he reached down and
touched her gently. "There, there, my child, God is all-
knowing, all-merciful, all-forgiving. Rise and go in peace."

She went back to the pew weeping. He sang again, sig-
nalling for the next person with his fingers. Some of the
men started leaving. "Stay, my sons. Come and deal with
your Maker." They didn't stay. Some of the women followed.

"Stay, my children. There is nothing to fear. God is all-good, all-powerful, all-knowing. He knows what you carry in your hearts." The closer to the doors they got, the louder his voice got. "He will forgive. He knows what you dare not tell others. He still loves you. Stay! Come and feel His presence as I must each day!" He was shouting. "Stay, my children! You came for a novena, did you not! Or did you come for some other reason! What is there to fear in a novena! Stay!"

Some did stay: mostly women. One by one, he brought them to Him. Each begged for forgiveness. Most of them wept. When he was satisfied that each had felt His presence, he would gently raise them from the floor. When the last of them had risen, he said, "Now kneel, all of you. Close your eyes for a minute or two and reflect upon what has happened to you tonight." When they opened their eyes he was gone.

She questioned me again the next morning. "What happened last night, Jesús?"

"Nothing."

"Don't tell me nothing. That's what you told me yesterday. But the women told me what happened. Why do you lie to me?"

"Nothing happened."

"Liar! If you didn't have to go to work, I'd fix you. The women said he was acting like a crazy man. Disgraceful!"

"He's not crazy."

🕯🕯🕯🕯🕯

A crowd had gathered near the basement door. They were kicking up dust. I thought they had him. A man ran from the crowd. I thought it was him. He ran down the basement steps and kicked on the door. "Open up, Father. We know you're in there!" Then he ran back to the crowd. "He's in there! He's in there! I know he's in there!" Another man ran to a window near the door and pressed his head against the glass. "Come on out, Father! Father! You're no

Father! Hey, you, Martínez! Come on out! We know you're
in there!"

Then I saw Chole. She was in the middle of the crowd.
She was wearing one of those dresses that showed everything. I couldn't tell if she was drunk or not. She was surrounded by women who wore shawls and skirts that fell to
their shoe tops. They were laughing and talking with her.
They were the same women who had chased her from the
church. I had seen them do it twice. There were probably
other times. Once she was drunk, but the other time she
didn't seem drunk. She kept saying that she just wanted to
talk to God, that she had to talk to God. One of them had
hit her with a stick. Now they were all friends. Their men
were behind them, sneaking glances at Chole. They
stretched to see a little more of her ass. She wore high
heels, but she seemed naked.

They were egging her on. "Go on, Chole, get him to come
out. Go on, Chole." She liked it.

"Frankie," she called.

They laughed.

"Frankie, baby, come to mama."

One of them was laughing so hard she started to choke.
"Again, Chole, again."

"Frankie, baby, come to mama. Look what she's got for
you." Someone gave her bottle and she took a big swallow. I
knew she was drunk then.

"Get him to come out, Chole. You know how to do it."

She left the crowd and walked toward the church,
swinging her big ass. She put her hips against the basement window and, leaning her upper body against the brick
wall of the church, rolled her hips. "Frankie, why don't you
listen to me and come on out here and do me a little favor?
Remember how much you liked it, Frankie. Remember how
hot and wet it was. It's that way now, Frankie. So hot and
wet. Come on, Frankie. Mama's got this hot thing all ready
for you."

They were laughing and screaming. "Give it to him,
Chole!"

"Frankie, you know you like it. Remember all those sweet things you said about it that last time you were in it? Only please, Frankie, this time promise me that after you're done, you won't kneel down and cry and pray like a little boy. Come on, Frankie, let me in so I can let you in."

Two men went to her side. They urged her on. One of them put his hand on her big round moving ass. "Stop it!" screamed a woman. "Stop it! Stop it! This is the house of God!"

Chole kept grinding her hips against that window. Women came out of the crowd. One of them grabbed her by the hair and another grabbed her by the neck. Then Chole was on the ground, surrounded by women who were kicking and beating her. "You whore! You filthy whore! This is the house of God!"

When they were finished, she staggered past me. There was blood on her face and her dress was torn. She was crying. "They wanted me to do it," she sobbed.

Women were arguing with each other. They said that the men had let it go too far; that they had let it get out of hand. The men said that they hadn't had anything to do with it, that it had been the women's idea to get Chole, that the women had gotten Chole. Doña Agripina said, "Why are we fighting among ourselves? He is the one to blame, and he sits in there undisturbed."

A man said, "I've had all I want from him. If he won't come out, I'm for dragging him out." They yelled.

I ran around to the other side of the church and let myself in through the closet window. They were banging on the door. He met me with the Sacrament.

"No, Father, not this time. They want to get you."

He was staring straight ahead. The gold cape was soaked with sweat. There was a big bang at the door. They were going to break it down.

I took hold of his arm, "Come on, Father."

He wouldn't move. He was mumbling, "God is good." There was another bang. This time he moved. I took him to the tiny room under the stairs. There was a false ceiling in

that room and a crawl space above it. I pushed aside part of
the ceiling. "Come on, Father. Step up on those shelves and
climb up there. They'll never find us there."

He wouldn't move. He kept repeating, "God is good."
Then there was a shattering of glass and they started
crawling through the broken window. He climbed up those
shelves with the Sacrament in one hand. It was completely
dark up there. I couldn't see him, but I could feel the Body
and Blood of Jesus Christ just inches from me. My sins of
self-abuse felt as if they were strangling me.

They looked for him everywhere. After a long time they
left. I waited until I was sure they had gone. Then I said, "I
think we can go now, Father. I think it's okay now, Father."

He didn't move. Instead he said, "Stay."

ÔÔÔÔÔ

"I don't know where or when I was born or who my parents were," he told me. "I do know that I was raised by Mexican missionary nuns in an orphanage in El Paso. When I
was twelve they told me that I was entering manhood, and
that soon I had to decide what I wanted to do with my life.
A few months later I was in a seminary at the foot of the
Sangre de Cristo Mountains in a remote part of northern
New Mexico. I had decided to follow the highest calling of
all: to become a priest and give and dedicate my life to
Jesus Christ, the Only Begotten Son of God, the Father.
The halls and rooms of the orphanage had always seemed
so cold and bleak to me, even in the summer. They were
always so bare and empty, but the darkness and dampness
of the seminary's adobe buildings were even worse.

"I guess I was weak from the beginning. They used to
wake us up every morning at 4:00. It was always hard for
me to get up at 4:00. The others didn't seem to have that
problem. There were cracks around my window. Cold was
always coming in, and on some winter mornings, it seemed
as if all the icy winds off the plains had filtered through. We

had to be at chapel by 4:30, dressed and with our morning prayers said. At first I was always late, and at first they excused it because I was the youngest one there. We said the Mass in the stillness and darkness of those mountain mornings on the sanctuary floor. We either knelt in prayer or lay flat on the floor with our heads covered, with every part of us covered in penance or adoration. I hated that floor. It was made of stone and too often it seemed frozen. It was hard to lay there and soak up that coldness. Twice during the first two weeks, I fell asleep on that floor. They excused that too because I was so young. But shortly after, there were no more excuses. I was told that I had to do penance. That wasn't hard because I could punish myself whichever way I chose, and usually I felt better afterwards anyway. What was hard was that they wouldn't talk to me. I guess they didn't think I was worth much. We were only allowed to talk twice a day: during the noon meal and at the common hour after dinner. If I asked a question during the meal, they would answer in one or two words. If I went up to them at the common hour, they would move away or stop talking or just ignore me. I knew I wasn't as good or as strong as the others, and I knew they thought I was weak. But I needed some human contact with them, with anyone. I guess contact with Jesus should have been enough. But it wasn't.

"During the Christmas season when I was still at the orphanage, families in El Paso used to invite us into their homes for Christmas dinner. I guess it made them feel good. And it was nice to go—too nice, so nice, in fact, that towards the end I didn't want to go because it made it all that more difficult to return to the orphanage after just a day in those homes. One Christmas, I asked the people if I could stay and live with them. Afterwards, the nuns were very angry with me. But all day long, the mother and father were giving me so much attention that I thought they really liked me. The mother was hugging me all day long. She even brushed my hair and said I had pretty eyes and what a fine looking man I'd be some day. The father showed me how to use a hammer, a measure and a saw, because when I grew up, he said, I'd always need to fix and build things. He showed me how to box, how to stand and how to hold my fists up because as a man I would always have to defend myself. There were two other children from the orphanage with me, but they paid almost no attention to them. So at dinner when the mother and father were saying how nice it had been to have me there and how they wished I could come back and often, I just asked them if I could stay, if I could live there. Everything became silent; you could have heard a pin drop. I guess I didn't want to accept what the silence meant, so I kept asking if they would please let me stay. The nun was giving me dirty looks, but I kept asking. They didn't answer. I knew what that meant, but I kept asking anyway. I said that I wouldn't take up much room, that I could sleep on the floor or even in a closet; that I was good at chores and would be a big help around the house; that I would even shine shoes downtown to pay for my food, and that I wouldn't keep any of the money; that I'd give it all to them. Try me out for just a week, I said. They didn't answer, and finally I stopped talking. The nuns were mad at me for weeks.

"So maybe I thought that by going to the seminary I'd escape the loneliness. Perhaps from hearing the nuns, I thought the seminary would be like one big happy family. Perhaps I've been running from loneliness all my life. But once in the seminary, I was lonelier than ever.

"It was built on a mesa ten miles from the nearest village, over a red dirt road that rose gradually through the trees. If you looked back when you reached the mesa, it seemed as if you had crossed an ocean of trees. Beyond the adobe building was a mighty tan-orange mountain that went straight up like a huge wall. The building itself was long and low. Half of it was divided by a long hall. On each side of the hall were twenty-three small narrow rooms. We slept in the rooms on the east side, facing the trees. Those on the west, facing the mountain, were where we studied. Each room had a window. The rooms on the east side had a cot and a candle and a corner for worship and two pegs on the door to hang your clothes. Those on the west had a desk and a chair, a kerosene lamp, bookshelves and a corner for worship. In the morning after breakfast, we had study and meditation. Afterwards, depending on the weather, we went outside and worked in silence until noon. We raised as much of our own food as we could during the short summers. The gathering and preparation of firewood was a year-round occupation. After lunch we would work another two hours and then meditate and study. About then, the afternoon winds would start up. They were cold winds, even in the summer, and they were loud. You could hear them everywhere.

"For many years, I watched the days come to an end against that mountain. Whether I was studying Latin, the Scriptures or the Lives of the Saints, I'd see the mountain fade, see it turn yellow and then disappear. Then I would light my lamp. There's something about the end of the day that frightens me still. But there, next to that mountain, surrounded by that wind, it seemed too often that all I was would also soon come to and end, that everything I was and did and would do was hopeless and pointless. And then finally it would be night and it didn't seem so hard.

"One day just after I lit my lamp, I slipped outside. I don't know why. There were only twelve of us then. I walked away from the building toward the base of the mountain until I could see all the twelve lighted windows. They were all at their desks: young boys and men in black cassocks, hunched over holy books in a remote wilderness. I was in my second year then, and it appeared likely that I'd be there another ten years. They seldom spoke to me, and ten years seemed like an eternity. From the orphanage I had come to this. I should have left then, but there was no place to go.

"She came one night last year when I was here. I had already gone to bed when there was this banging on the door. She was hysterical. I didn't know who she was, and at first, I thought that something had happened to her husband or children and that she had come to get me to give someone the Last Rites. It took me a long time to calm her down, just enough so that I could understand what she was trying to tell me. Finally I understood what she was saying: that she had seen the devil; that he had tried to have sex with her; that it had almost happened when she recognized him. It made sense. She was terrified and had little control of her body; every few minutes, she convulsed. In her hand she had a five dollar bill that she said he had paid her with. She kept telling me to touch it, to see how hot it was. I touched it. It was warm. Then after one of her seizures, she fell asleep on the floor. She was too heavy for me to move, so I covered her and went back to sleep, but not before I blessed her with holy water and encircled her with holy pictures and statues. She was still there when I left to say the six o'clock Mass the next morning. By the time I returned, she was gone.

"She came again the next night just after dark. She said she thought he was following her and could she come in for a little while. By then, I had a pretty good idea who she was. Your parish is small, and it wasn't too difficult to find out. She made her confession, and then there was no doubt who she was or at least what she was. I read to her from the *Lives of the Saints*, and also an account of Mary Magdalene. I wanted her to know that God's love is great, that no matter what she had done in the past there was still hope for her. When I finished, she said she was afraid to go home or even to go out into the night. She was sure he was following her. She asked if she could sleep on the floor again. When I hesitated, she pleaded. I didn't see what harm there could be, and so I said yes. I got her a blanket and told her she'd probably sleep better on the couch. She said no one had ever been that good to her and kissed my hand. As I went to bed, I remember thinking that I liked her, that she really wasn't as bad as they said, and that with guidance and understanding, she could leave her wayward life and find God. I couldn't sleep. I kept hearing her deep breathing across the hall in the front room. She's a big woman. By that I don't

mean that she's tall or fat, but, you know, you've seen her.
You know what she looks like. I mean she's full. What I
mean is that I'm sure she's bigger than I. And that night
she seemed to fill up the whole house, and I couldn't sleep
just listening to her breathe.

"Sometime during the night she called out, yelling for
help. I went to her. She was having a nightmare. She
thought she had seen him again. She was very frightened. I
calmed her as best as I could, and when I stood up to go, she
asked me not to leave her. So I brought a blanket and laid
down on the floor beside her. Every few minutes, she'd
touch me and say she was sorry; that she just wanted to
make sure I was still there. Then she got up and said she
couldn't sleep. But if she could just lay down next to me, she
knew she could sleep. She pressed against me. I could feel
her fullness. I could feel her breathing. I could smell her. I
had never been that close to another human being. There
was nothing sinful about it, at least not then. It was warm
and it felt good. It was close. I felt needed, but not as I was
usually needed—as an instrument of God, as someone who
was bringing Him closer to people. This was different. It
was I who was needed. What I didn't realize at that time
was that I was also in need.

"She was gone when I returned from Mass, but she
came again that night. I read to her and asked her if she
wanted to make her confession. She said that she had nothing to confess, and that made me happy. We talked about
her and then I told her some things about myself. I don't
usually talk about myself. People aren't really interested.
They come to tell me their problems. But she seemed to
care. She asked me about the orphanage and the seminary.
And then she asked if she could stay again. 'Yes,' I said.
And was it all right, and she didn't mean any disrespect by
it if she slept next to me again. 'Yes,' I said again.

"We lay there. We weren't touching, but I could feel her.
I could smell her. Every time I breathed, it was as if I were
breathing her. I didn't move. I was afraid to move. I knew if
I touched her, if any part of me touched her, it would be sin-

ful. So I lay there for hours, unable to sleep, unable to move. I wondered if she was really asleep, if her deep breathing was real. Did she want to touch me? I must have dozed off because when I awoke, she had curled herself up against me. It was still dark. I was lying on my side with my back to her. She had cupped my buttocks in her lap, she had her stomach and breasts against my back, and had pressed her face into my hair. She had wrapped one of her arms around me. I was aroused, yes. There is no doubt about it. But she was asleep and, more than being aroused, it was simply a matter of experiencing the warmest, safest feeling I had ever experienced. She seemed to be holding me, protecting me from anything that could ever threaten or harm me. I felt so good that I cried. Tell me, was there anything wrong with that? Tell me, I want to know. Was there anything wrong with that?

"I confessed it that night to my confessor as a sin, but I still don't know if it was a sin. There was never any doubt about the next night though. That was a Friday night.

I was leaving on Sunday after the twelve o'clock Mass. That night was different from the moment I answered the door. She was dressed the way she was dressed tonight: hanging, bulging out of her clothes. Every time she looked away, I stole a stare. I hated that dress; I hated what it did to me. She was everywhere I turned. I tried, but I couldn't read *The Lives of the Saints*. She took my hand and asked if we could lay down. We didn't use any blankets; we didn't use anything. We did it there on the floor. It was the first time I had ever had sexual intercourse. She had to help me. It wasn't like what I had thought it would be, and when it was over, the guilt was immense. Yes, she was right. I knelt and begged Him for forgiveness, right there next to her nakedness. Yes, I cried. She got up and dressed and kissed me on the forehead while I was still on my knees and then she left without saying a word.

"The next morning during the celebration of the Mass, I ate of His Body and drank of His Blood even though I was steeped in sin. It was probably the worst day of my life. All morning I prayed, but all my prayers and meditation didn't remove the pain. I had to see her. Just once more before I left. Then it was time for me to hear confessions, to forgive those who could never forgive me. It was hot, but I made myself wear three sets of clothes under my cassock as part of my penance. Still I wanted to see her, if only to wish her well. The church was burning, and the confessional was even hotter. I knelt instead of sitting in that tiny booth. I knelt the whole afternoon, wrapped in four sets of clothes. When I heard the first footsteps of a woman, I whirled and pushed the curtains aside. But it wasn't her. The next footsteps weren't hers either. Then I just peeked, so they wouldn't notice, whenever I heard a new set of footsteps. She didn't come that afternoon. I had to see her. I even thought of going to her house. I knew it was one of those three shacks across the street. But I told myself she wouldn't be there if I went, even though the truth was I was afraid someone would see me. I went back to the rectory instead and prayed some more. I prayed because I didn't know what else to do. I prayed until it was time to hear evening confessions.

"I kept telling myself she wouldn't come. Still, I looked out the curtain each time I heard footsteps. She didn't come, and at nine o'clock I locked the church and went back to the rectory. I tried to pray but I couldn't. I laid down, but I couldn't sleep. She was a Chinatown whore—I hated calling her that or thinking of her in that manner, but it seemed to make it easier—and Chinatown was just a block away. I wanted to see her just once more, if only to give her my final blessing. That was all I could give her. That was all I had planned to give her. I knew she lived across the street from the church, but by then—I was certain—she wouldn't be home. It was Saturday night and I knew she was down there, somewhere in Chinatown. I wanted to see her, even if it was in Chinatown, just to urge her to change her ways and to remind her of the promises she had made to God. It wouldn't be hard to find her, but someone was bound to recognize me. Finally I thought of wearing some of Padre

Galván's lay clothes. I even wore a cap and dark glasses.

"I went down the alley and around the block, down a side street into Chinatown. I looked into every bar and business that was open. I went up the main two streets and then down the side streets. I didn't see her, so I started again. This time I went into the bars and restaurants and hotels. But I didn't see her. In one bar I asked the bartender if he had seen Doña Chole. 'Doña who?' he said. 'Chole,' I said, 'Chole, you know, the whore.' As soon as I said it, it hurt. He laughed. 'Oh, you mean *puta* Chole, Chole the *puta*? What's this Doña Chole shit. You mean you want a little ass, don't you? Well, there ain't nothing wrong with that. And besides, she's pretty cheap. But I'll tell you, my friend, she's pretty dirty, too. You stand a good chance of getting the clap. She was here earlier, but she left with some guy. She might be hard to find. It's Saturday, you know, and everybody's got money. But she usually uses the San Joaquin Hotel or the Washington Rooms.'

"I went to the Washington Rooms, but the door was locked. I went across the street and looked up above the store fronts. Some of the windows had lights on. Two of those didn't have shades drawn. I backed myself up against the buildings to see if I could see anything. A man getting out of one of those big trucks said, 'Hey, man, you get your nuts off looking into windows?' I went to the San Joaquin Hotel. It had a tiny lobby. An old Filipino sat there. He spoke to me in English and Spanish, but I could barely understand him in either language. I asked him if he had seen Chole, the *puta*. He kept staring at me. Then I thought he said, 'I know you. I know who you are.' I ran out of there. But I didn't go back to the rectory. I must have walked those streets for at least another two hours. I walked them over and over again. I had to see her. I was leaving in a few hours, and if I tried to see her, then they would all see me.

"A policeman asked me where I was going and I said home. But as soon as I was out of his sight, I walked those streets again. I had given myself plenty of reasons for having to see her. But as it became later, as it appeared more and more that I wouldn't see her, all I wanted to do was see her. I even thought of waiting outside her house until sunrise, until the first Mass if I needed to. It would have been enough just to see her for a moment, just to look at her, just to say . . . I don't know, anything, something.

"Everything was closing. I went into a bar and had a beer. Where was she? It was almost two. In a few minutes the bars would close. Then what would I do? I signaled the bartender to come over. 'Have you seen the *puta*, Chole?' He shook his head no. A man started watching me from the other end of the bar. I left. I hurried back down the street. Then I saw her. She was sitting on a bar stool, dressed like she was tonight, talking to a big bellied man who was sitting on a stool next to her. He had his hand on her leg. Behind her, another man, in a dirty white T-shirt, was pawing her. When he put his arms around her stomach and started working his hands up, I went in. She had a silly grin on her face. When his hands reached her breasts, she said, 'If you can't pay, don't play.' I grabbed him and I think I hit him, but the pounding he gave me I thought would never end. He chased me into every corner of the bar, and I thought he would never stop pounding on me. Someone called the police, and he stopped when we heard the siren. I was bleeding badly, but I staggered and ran as best I could through alleys and yards to the rectory. I left Fresno that night."

He stopped talking, and we sat there for a long time. Finally I asked him to hear my confession. He forgave me my sins.

Chapter Eight

"**W**hy didn't you go to Communion this morning? And I don't want to hear that you broke your fast."

"But I did."

"When?"

"Last night."

"When last night?"

"Last night after I went to bed I got real hungry and so I got up and got something to eat."

"What did you eat?"

"Some tortillas."

"How many?"

"Just one."

"If you were so hungry, why did you just eat one?"

"I don't know, I just did."

She slapped me. "Liar. I counted those tortillas before I went to work. There were eight then and there are eight now. Look! Count them! I know what you've been doing. I've seen your underwear. I've seen your sheets. Get out of my sight! Get into the pantry. Lucky for you that you have school today, or you'd be in your crib all day. What a disgrace. Have you no shame? Don't you think Padre knows? What must he think? To think I have this in my own family. Get in there. And when you get home, get into your diaper."

The worst of it was that she knew.

The next morning she didn't let me go to Mass with her. "I know you're in sin, and he knows it, too. Have you no shame? If you don't go to confession Saturday, if you don't receive Communion Sunday, you'll pay dearly."

I went to confession on Saturday, but not before I did it again and again, so that I wouldn't be tempted before Mass on Sunday. "Bless me, Father, for I have sinned . . ." He knew it was me. It didn't matter. He knew I was in sin anyway. I hadn't gone to Communion for three mornings. Still, when he asked, "And how many times did you do it, my son?" it was hard.

"What are you doing in there?"

"I'm going to the toilet."

"Why is it taking you so long?"

"Because I have to go bad."

"Are you sure?"

"Yes."

And then, when I came out, "Why doesn't it smell in here?"

"It does smell."

"I don't smell anything. Come here. Touch this seat, it's not warm."

"It is warm. Feel over here."

I locked everything, even when she was at work. Someday she'd jump out of the toilet bowl and catch me on the floor just as I was coming.

"You stay here while I change these sheets. Understand?"

"Yes."

"What's that?"

"What? Where?"

"Don't act dumb. There, what is that?"

"I don't see anything."

"This. This. Don't tell me you don't see it. It's a spot and you know what it's from."

"I don't know what it is. It's always been there."

"Liar. But I warn you, you miss Communion one more time and you'll pay dearly."

After that I started my night runs. There were confessions at St. Sebastian's on Monday nights, at St. Francis' on Wednesday nights; and with Padre Galván on Friday nights and Saturday afternoons. If I was careful, I could go to Communion every morning and still jack-off. St. Sebastian's was the furthest away. I ran part of the way to get there in an hour. I had to be careful because there were no Mexicans on that side of town, and the people would wonder what I was doing there. They'd call the police, or the police would stop me if they saw me. So I would always wait until it was dark or getting dark, and then I'd begin my run. But it was worth it. The priest at St. Sebastian's was old. He never scolded me, and he forgave everything. His penance was always just ten Hail Marys.

I always wore myself out on Mondays, knowing it would be him that night. I'd do it as soon as we got back from Mass, as I was changing in the closet. She didn't suspect the closet. And on Mondays, I'd see Sally and Rosie at school again. Their tits were so big. I watched them out of the corner of my eye, or I'd take a good look at them whenever I turned in any direction. Sometimes they would be sitting, especially Rosie, so their tits were plopped on their desks. My dick would get so big that it hurt and I couldn't sit. Sometimes I'd raise my hand and ask to be excused, and I'd run down to the toilet and take care of it. I'd do it one or two times after she went to work. I couldn't do it on Tuesdays.

I was hard at it again on Wednesdays because I couldn't do it too many times on Friday and Saturday. It was Padre

Galván's confessional on those days. So I had worked it over
pretty good by the time I started my night run to St. Francis. St. Francis was closer than St. Sebastian's, but not by
much. If I ran a good part of the way, it would take fifty
minutes. I had to be more careful on that run because I had
to go through downtown and the police were always around.
At first they stopped me a lot.

"Where you going, boy?"

"I have to get something from my grandmother, and she
cleans at the Power Building." Or, "I have to take something to my grandmother, and she cleans at the Power
Building." On some rainy or foggy nights there was nobody
else on the streets.

The priest at St. Francis didn't care how many times I
did it. I think he was drunk most of the time. I could smell
him through the curtain. Once he started snoring right in
the middle of my confession. I did everything I could to
wake him. I couldn't miss Communion the next morning.
They'd know. Finally, I went into his part of the confessional and shook him.

Padre Galván got mad if I said I did it more than twice.
So I had to watch myself towards the end of the week. I was
never sure if he had told her or was going to tell her. And I
didn't like to look at him when he knew. But he always
thought I had just done it two times for the whole week. He
never asked how long it had been since my last confession
and I never told him. He thought he was the only one I was
confessing my sins to. If he only knew.

ᛞᛞᛞᛞᛞ

It was one of those mornings when—after Mass, after I
had put out the candles and put away the wine, after I had
hung up my cassock and surplice—'Amá was praying so
hard that she didn't see me. I could almost tell by the tilt of
her head. As I got closer, as I passed between her and the
altar, I knew. She didn't blink. She was seeing something

on or beyond the altar. Her lips were moving fast, but they never made a sound. I went home alone on those mornings because there was no telling how long she would be. That morning as I got to the corner, I heard, "Jesús, help me. Help me, Jesús." I knew it was Chole even before I looked. She was sitting on the sidewalk across the street, propped against the fence. She was drunk. "I can't get up, Jesús. Help me." I didn't go to her right away. I was afraid 'Amá and Padre Galván would see me with her. "Please, Jesús!" I wasn't going to go to her except that she gave me money almost every week. I couldn't tell how drunk she was, but I thought if I didn't help her, she'd probably remember and then not give me money Sunday.

I crossed the street. She was a mess. Her black and red makeup was spread all over her face. Her hair was sticking straight up. Her dress was stained and creased all the way up to her stomach. I looked, but her thighs were too thick. She could barely keep her eyes open. "Thank you, m'ijo." And she stank. But her giant tits were almost out of her dress and, drunk as she was, I wasn't afraid to stare at them. Oh, they were big. Next to them, Rosie's were like mosquito bites. I got hard, and my breathing got heavy. She bent her leg and tried to lift herself. I looked again, but her thighs were too thick. "Help me, Jesús." I wanted to help her. The more I helped her, the closer I'd get to those tits. I bent over and put my arm around her. They were so full. The crack between them seemed to go for miles. I pulled, but I couldn't lift her. "I'm too heavy for you, m'ijo. I'm sorry I'm so fat."

"No. No. You're not fat, Chole." They were gigantic tits.

I tried again. This time I stooped and put both hands under her arms. I struggled up. Slowly she rose.

"Thank you, m'ijo. You know I'll never forget this."

Then one of her tits fell out of her dress. I stopped. It was the biggest, roundest, brownest thing I had ever seen. I couldn't move. She kept pulling on me, and then we both fell. And then I was right under it, looking straight up at it. The giant nipple seemed to spread across my face. I was so

close to it that I could have touched it with my nose by just
tilting my head a little. I would have never dreamed that
there could be a tit that big. My dick ached. I was stiff all
over. But a car came. It slowed and passed and then
stopped. I got up and ran.

"Jesús! Help me! Come back, Jesús! Help me!"

ὄὄὄὄὄ

They talked about Chole.

I heard them in my house on Sunday afternoons when it
was too cold or wet to go out.

"We're going to move. I can't take it anymore. That
woman is driving me crazy. But it's so hard to find another
place. And the rent is so cheap, and the landlord never
bothers us."

"What did she do this time, Agripina?"

"For some reason, she won't take them in her house . . ."

"That's because they'd come running out if they saw
that filth. Bums or not, there's a limit. That woman has no
water in there. Can you imagine what it must be like?"

"Well, she does most of her filthy business in those
rooms in Chinatown. But at least once a month, or probably
more, one of them will follow her home. She'll be drunk,
they'll both be drunk, and they'll make such a racket in the
alley—because she always goes through the alley—and, you
know, our little house sits right there. And my poor *viejo*
works so hard. It's not so bad in the winter, because then all
the windows are closed. But once it gets hot and we have to
keep the windows open at night . . . I can't bear that
woman. But the other night was just too much. I already
told my *viejito* that I'm starting to look for another place."

"What did she do this time, Agripina?"

"I really don't know if I should repeat it in the Señora's
house. It's so crude."

"There isn't any of us here who doesn't know what she's
like, Agripina. You won't offend us, and certainly not me.

And it'll probably just tell us why she needs our prayers so badly."

"My poor *viejo*, he works so hard. Well, remember this week, those days when it got real hot? Our house was burning even late at night. One of those nights I couldn't sleep. Even the sheets were hot. My poor *viejo* was tossing and turning, sweating. His side of the bed was soaked. His body had passed out from all the heavy work in the sun all day. You could imagine what it must have been like working on the track those days. But his mind must have been telling his body how hot it was because he couldn't rest, he couldn't lay still. I tried fanning him, but it didn't do any good. Then I heard her. You know how loud she gets when she's drunk. Well, she was really drunk and really loud that night. Right away I wanted to get up and close the windows because I was afraid she'd wake up my *viejo*. And he hates her worse than I do. If she had woke him up that night, I think he would have killed her. But it was so hot that if I had closed the windows, my poor *viejo* would have probably suffocated.

"Then I heard her last victim of the night. He was pretty drunk, too. They were arguing because he only had two dollars. She wanted another dollar for a room. But I don't know how they would have ever made it anywhere in the shape they were in. He kept swearing on everything that was holy, and even on his mother's grave, that two dollars was all he had. She didn't believe him, and he kept telling her to search him. She must have, because after awhile she said, 'Okay, we'll do it here, on this clump of bermuda grass where it's soft.' Can you imagine that, on bermuda grass. She kept telling him to hold himself up because the bermuda grass was scratching her. I would have closed the windows, but I thought that would wake up my poor *viejo* for sure. So I had to lay there and listen to their filthy noises. But that's not the half of it.

"Pretty soon there was this loud commotion, and she started screaming. This time I did get out of bed. The Rojases had turned on their porch light across the alley, so I could see everything. Another man had come, and she was struggling with him as best she could while the first pig was on top of her. Only, the second man just wanted her money, which she must have had in her brassiere because she kept yelling for somebody to call the police and for the first man to get off her so she could call the police because this other man was trying to rob her. But the first man kept saying that he couldn't, that he was stuck. 'I'm stuck!' he kept saying, but he wasn't so stuck that he didn't keep up his dirty little movements. She was pushing on him to get off, and there for awhile they did look like they were really stuck. You know, just like two dogs in the street, one yelping and trying to get free, but both of them stuck. Finally she stopped pushing on him because the other man had run off into the night with her money. And then she just lay there and started crying while the first man finished with his filthy little movements. Imagine the nerve, crying over that filthy money."

They talked about her in the fields.

"You know, *compa*, I hate to say this, but I've been watching you lately, and what I really think you need is a good fuck. I don't mean no offense to my *compadre*, *compa*, but I've been watching you lately, *compa*; I've been watching the two of you. It's none of my business, *compa*, but it's plain that the two of you aren't getting along. And it's getting you down. I always say there's nothing like a good old fashioned piece of ass to pick you up."

"Maybe you're right, *compa*. I wouldn't say this to just anyone, *compa*, but you know I consider you my friend. But it's been a long time since I had a good fuck. The *vieja* is always sick or she don't feel like it tonight or her back's been hurting her all day or she's got an infection. Or if she does give it to me, once every six months, she just lies there like a slab of meat."

"Well, what the fuck's the matter with you, *compa*.

There's plenty of cunt out there."

"It's easy for you to say, *compa*, because you got a way with women."

"Oh, man, if you got to fuck, fuck. Fuck Chole if you have to. It'll only cost you three dollars."

"Chole."

They laughed.

"Well, I mean, if a man's got to fuck, he's got to fuck."

"I don't have to fuck that bad."

They laughed.

"What's the matter with Chole? She got some mighty big tits and a big juicy ass."

They laughed again.

"Yeah, and you'd better be ready to have your dick drop off the next day, because she must be carrying every kind of syph known to man. And does she stink! Whew! Remember what those old billy goats used to smell like? You couldn't get near them bastards they smelled so bad. Well, she smells worse. She smells like she's been fucking three or four of them billy goats every day."

"How do you know, *compa*?"

And they laughed again.

They talked about her at school too.

"We got Chole, the whore, last night. You know how she's always staggering home drunk and everything. Well, there was six of us, and we had Larry Ramírez's old man's panel truck. We saw her coming down Mariposa St., you know, where it's real dark, and we jumped her and put her nasty ass in the back of that panel truck. And before she knew it, we had her out in the country. And we fucked her. Man, did we fuck her. We fucked her every way you could think of. One guy even put it in her ear. I'm not lying. I swear to God. Those were some crazy motherfuckers. One guy squeezed a bunch of lemons he got off a tree all over her

so she wouldn't stink so bad. And another guy shoved a coke
bottle up her cunt."

ôôôôô

Chole waited for me on Sundays after the 12:15 Mass.
She knew 'Amá never went to the 12:15 Mass with me.
Chole would wait between the produce sheds on C St. where
no one could see her. She would hiss and whisper at me as I
went by. "Jesús! Jesús! Come here, m'ijo. Come here for just
a minute." I always went over to her. She gave me money.
"I know you're ashamed to be seen with me, m'ijo. I
know that. It's okay I understand. Maybe when you get
older you'll understand . . . Maybe you won't. Maybe
nobody ever understands. But look, m'ijo, I got cleaned up
for you. I got dressed up for you. You like my new dress,
m'ijo? It's a special dress. I knew you couldn't be ashamed of
me in this dress. I could even go to church in it. Someday I'll
go to church, and you won't be ashamed. You'll see. Come
here, m'ijo. Just let me touch you."
She would put her fingers through my hair and part it
over to one side.
"That's how your father wore his hair. You look more
and more like him every day. If only he could see you. I
should have been your mother. For a long time I thought I
would be. Maybe if I had been your mother . . ."
I'd let her stroke my hair. In a few minutes she'd give
me the money. I'd look down at it and shake my head no,
that I didn't want it, when I really did. And she'd say "Take
it, m'ijo, I want you to have it. I wouldn't offer it to you if I
didn't want you to have it." She'd hold the money out, and
when I'd reach for it, she'd clasp my hand in both of hers.
"Just let me hold your hand for a moment, m'ijo. Don't pull
away, please don't. Just let me touch you for a minute. Then
I'll let you go. You know that Chole never hurts you, m'ijo.
Let me just touch you."
Then she'd let go, and I'd take it and hide it in my sock

so 'Amá wouldn't find it, until I could go downtown. I couldn't spend it in Chinatown, because they knew we didn't have any money and someone might tell 'Amá or guess where I had gotten it. I tried not to think of where it came from: not from her, but from them, her men.

And I tried not to think of her whenever I took my hand to myself. But after I had seen that huge tit, it was hopeless. No matter how hard I tried, there was always some hint of her. No matter how smelly and filthy she was, no matter how much they made fun of her, there was always some sense of those giant tits and, later, of her big thighs and the black magic between them. "Mijo, you know that anything I have is yours." I couldn't shut that off. She whispered it as I got nearer and nearer. And after I had taken my pleasure, I stood or lay there shaking my head no, no, I could never have anything to do with her, I would hear her again, but then it was only: "Just let me touch you, *m'ijo*."

▵▵▵▵▵

The first sign of it was when I found the bloody rags in the bathroom. I must have been eleven or twelve. I took them into the kitchen.

"What are these, 'Amá? Where did the blood come from?"

When she saw them, she snatched them and slapped me.

"Give me those! They're none of your business, that's what they are! How many times have I told you not to be sticking your nose into what's none of your business! This is none of your business!"

I understood. Her look was enough. Those rags were none of my business. It didn't take me long to forget them. I only saw them twice over the next few years. And when I did, I didn't touch them. I didn't get any closer to them than when I noticed them. Once I saw them on the bathroom floor again, and once I saw them in her room. They were none of my business.

Saturdays were the only nights she didn't work. One Saturday night she screamed for me from her room. "Jesús! Jesús!" I ran. The door was closed. When I opened it, I saw her sitting on the floor. Both of her feet were wrapped in bloody rags. She was holding one of them.

"Go to the bathroom, hurry, and get me the blue bottle where the medicines are. The big blue bottle. You know which one. The big one. Hurry! The bleeding won't stop and every time I try to move, it seems to get worse."

There was a razor blade on the floor near her feet.

When I brought her the bottle, she said, "I've told you many times that what goes on in this house is only for our eyes and ears. Do you understand?" She looked at me. I understood. "Now get out of here. I have to take care of this."

After that, I watched for her feet. I didn't see much because her full black skirt touched the floor and her feet were always somewhere under it. One day while we were eating, I spilled some food. While I was under the table cleaning it up, I saw her feet, or at least her shoes. The tongue of each shoe had been cut away and so had the parts for the shoe laces. There was a big hole in the front of each shoe. Her feet puffed out through those holes. And though she wore black stockings, I thought I saw the redness of blood on one foot. The next morning at Mass I studied the crucifix. I wanted to make sure where the spikes were.

I started watching her hands. I knew exactly where the Roman soldiers had driven the spikes. I expected to see wounds on her hands any day. But I never did, instead I saw the other wound.

It was hot, a clear afternoon heavy with heat. The house was storing heat. She had taken off two blouses and was wearing her white cotton underwear over her skirt. She reached for a bowl and I saw the slash of a bloodstain on her side just above her stomach.

From then on, when she closed her door on a Saturday night, I wondered. But I never asked. It was none of my

business. Then one night she called me again. "Jesús! Come
here! Quick!" As I opened the door, she said, "Don't come in.
Just get me the blue bottle. Quick!" The room was dark. I
couldn't see anything. When I came back, she said, "Give it
to me! Quick! Now go!" She was on the floor again, except
that this time she was lying on her side. I couldn't see
much, but it did look like she was sweating blood.

ooooo

"Do you think of me, *m'ijo?*"
She was still holding on to the money. It was a dollar
bill. She had held my hand in hers longer than she usually
did, but she wouldn't let go of it. She had taken longer to
fool with my hair and stroke my shoulders than she usually
did. And now this babbling. I wanted to leave, but she
wouldn't let go of the money.
"Look at me, *m'ijo.* Tell me. Do you ever think of me
during the week, when we don't see each other? Tell me. I
want to know."
I wasn't going to get it unless I told her.
"Yes, Chole. I think of you."
"No, no. Not bad things. Not about the bad things they
say about me. No. Just about me, Chole, somebody who
loves you and treats you good."
"Yes, Chole."

ooooo

They told her about the holy nun on a Sunday. It was
the first thing they talked about. I was just leaving.
"Señora, did you hear that the nuns from Mexico came
back yesterday? Yes, they did. But the thing of it is that
they say they brought a very holy nun with them. She
might be a saint any day now. They say they're working on
the papers. They say the Virgin appeared to her and left her

image on her habit. They say it's a better image than the Virgin, Our Lady of Guadalupe, left with the Indian. Everybody's talking about her. Padre Galván's all excited. What's the matter, Señora?"

"Nothing."

The women kept talking about the holy nun and how holy she was. 'Amá didn't say much. And when 'Amá didn't say much, the meetings didn't last long. And when the meetings didn't last long, 'Amá was in a bad mood afterwards. I got out of there.

I stayed away as long as I could. It was easy. I heard the music from a block away. It sent chills through me. They had started early. I stood by the door so I could feel the sounds whenever it opened. They didn't care.

"What you want, boy?"

"Nothing."

"What you waiting for then?"

"Nothing."

"Aw, man, leave him be. Can't you see he's digging the music?"

The slow pieces made me sad. They were always about someone leaving someone and how hard it was to be without her. I hadn't had a girlfriend, but I knew how it had to feel. The fast ones made me glad. They made everything all right.

A green neon clock looked at me every time the door opened. I stayed until 4:20. It would take me five minutes to run home. That would give her at least fifteen minutes, and if I wasn't there before she went to work, I'd pay for it the next day.

"Where you been?"

"At the track."

"You know I have to be to work. Why did you stay so late?"

"There's no clock there, and I didn't know what time it was."

"Liar! You can tell what time it's getting to be."

"But the days are getting longer. They fool me. I think

it's early and it's not."

"Good for nothing! I don't know why I put up with it. All these years, and for what? I raised my child and now this again. I don't know of any other grandmother who's done what I've done for you. You'd better sit down and eat if you know what's good for you."

She went on. I had heard it a hundred times. I looked at the clock. Nine more minutes. I thought of them dancing. The later it got, the more they danced. But then she switched.

"We haven't been praying enough. You haven't been praying enough with me. There's too little time spent in this house with God. That's why He looks so unfavorably upon us. But that's going to change. You'll see. Starting tomorrow, as soon as you get home from school, and I want you home early, we'll start."

I felt my knees hurt and my back ache. All those rosaries and meditations, and now we were going to do more.

"And we're going to fast."

"'Amá, you know I faint when you make me fast."

"Well, I'm going to fast and you're going to eat less. Don't expect me to be cooking for you. If you want to eat, then you fix it."

ôôôôô

"I'm tired of it, Jesús."

It was the first time he had said my name.

"You come here week after week and tell me the same thing. That you've abused yourself twice since your last confession. Then you say you're sorry and promise to sin no more. But you're back the next week with the same thing. How can you be sorry? I'll forgive you your sins this one more time, but next week, if you bring me the same confession, I won't forgive you. Is that clear?"

I knew that he had known, but that changed everything. It was hard to look at him every morning after that. I came as late as I could and left as early as I could. I stayed out of his way. I took as much time as I could lighting the candles so that I wouldn't have to be with him too long in the sacristy. I changed in the corner. He looked at me differently. I knew what he was thinking. He didn't talk to me very much anymore, and when he did, it was rough. He blessed the wine I took him, over and over again. He had never blessed it so many times before. It must have been because the wine cruets were in my hands, and he knew what I did with my hands. When he gave me Communion, he was slow in blessing the Host. I thought maybe he didn't want to give it to me. Maybe he had found out about my night runs.

I took him his confession, the one he wanted. "Bless me, Father, but I haven't sinned since my last confession."

"Well, that's good. It's good to know that you can come in here without two sins of self-abuse on your soul."

He didn't say my name. He didn't need to.

"Still, none of us are perfect. Few of us can get through a day without committing a sin of anger or pride or jealousy or without telling a lie. Are you sure you're free of those?"

"Yes, Father. I haven't committed any sins since my last confession."

Except that my dick was still swollen and sore from Wednesday. To bring him his confession, I knew I'd have to go five days without doing it. So I did it so many times on Wednesday that by the time I left for St. Francis', it looked like a little brown beet.

🕯🕯🕯🕯🕯

"I need more, Chole."

"Why, *m'ijo*?"

"Because she's on a fast, and she's not cooking for me. It started out that she wasn't cooking for me. But now it's worse. Now she's gotten so bad that she's not buying food."

"But why, *m'ijo?*"

"Because she doesn't think she's holy enough."

"Here."

"Is that all?"

"It's all I have. Look."

"You got more. Those men give you plenty. Everybody knows that."

"*M'ijo*, I'm broke."

"You got more."

"*M'ijo*, try to understand. I don't work every day. I just work now when I need to. I don't like it, and I've done it for so long. But I don't know how else to feed myself and buy myself the few little things that I like. And I drink when I work. When I have to work, I start drinking at home in the afternoon. It's easier that way. I don't feel it as much, and after awhile, I don't even care. But that works against me too, because I lose track of the money. They steal it from me or don't give it to me, or I just lose it somewhere. Somedays I wake up without a penny when I know I should have at least twenty dollars. But here, take this for now. And I'll work tonight, and I won't drink. Or I'll watch myself anyway, and I'll have some more for you tomorrow."

"I have to go to school tomorrow."

"I know, but I'll meet you after school."

"Where?"

"Here."

"People work here tomorrow and they'll see."

"Then come to my house."

"I can't go to your house. Somebody will see."

"Then pick a place. Any place. I don't care where, and I'll meet you. And I'll be careful, and no one will see. We don't even have to talk. I'll just pass by you and drop it and keep going."

She was talking to somebody else, but we were the only

two in the house. She wasn't praying. She wasn't kneeling
or fingering her rosary. They were conversations. She was
waiting for answers and then answering them. But I could-
n't hear anyone else saying anything. There were more conversations each day. I knew it was the fast, but after
awhile, I didn't even see her taking water anymore. I tried
not to hear. No matter how much I hated her, I didn't like
seeing and hearing her like that. But I couldn't help hearing, because it wasn't long before I figured out that most of
the conversations were with my mother. She spent most of
her time scolding her. And as many times as she said how
much she loved her, as many candles as she lit for her, she
didn't seem to like her at all. She always came back to my
father. "Why, Gloria, did you do that to me? If you wanted a
man, if you wanted a husband so bad, there were plenty
here who had an eye for you. Good ones. Respectable ones.
You were such a pretty girl, you could have had your pick.
And look what you picked. Yes, we were poor. But we were
gente decente, decent people, and you could have had any of
the Vásquez boys. They all used to look at you. Think how
rich and happy you would be and how proud I would be."

⚐⚐⚐⚐⚐

She sent me on ahead of her. She got to Mass later and
later. I told Padre that it was because she was weak from
fasting. And she left right after Communion. There were
lots of people at the six o'clock Mass those days. They had
come to see the holy nun. 'Amá didn't seem to notice any of
them, not even the holy nun. She would come up slowly,
among the last, receive Communion and then leave.

"Tell her I want to see her. Tell her to wait for me after
Mass tomorrow morning so we can talk. She didn't look so
good this morning. But with Sister Dolores here and all this
excitement, things just haven't been the same around here
lately. Tell her I'm a little worried about this fast, and that
I want to talk to her about it. I've never questioned her

judgment. She's such a devout woman. But maybe this time she's gone too far."

She waited. A Mexican man in a suit and tie came down to the sacristy after Mass. He was a reporter for a Mexican newspaper in Los Angeles. He had come all the way from Los Angeles to our church to do a story on Sister Dolores. Padre was pleased. I knew she was waiting, so I went upstairs to tell her that Padre would be there in a little while. Outside, I could hear the people trying to get near the holy nun. The other nuns surrounded her, but the crowds were big then and they weren't much protection. Only two days before, they had torn her habit, and yesterday Padre had asked them at the Mass to show some respect, to talk to her, yes, if she wanted to talk to them, but to keep their distance, to respect her person. They were bringing their sick and their old, and were waiting with them outside until she came out of Mass. They tried to touch her. Some threw themselves at her feet. It was enough if they could just get her blessing, so they screamed and made funny noises and threw things, hoping that she would turn in their direction and bless them. Because that's all she did. She didn't stop or talk or smile or even nod. She blessed them, and everyone and everything that was in her path. She blessed them when she chose to stop praying and raised her hand without raising her head or eyes. She blessed them without seeing them, and then went back to praying.

'Amá didn't like it.

"Blasphemous!" she said. "It's a wonder He doesn't appear and drive them all from His Temple. Only God should be worshiped, not his saints or their statues or their pictures. And surely not a living person. And no living person except God and his priests has the power or right to bless others. It's blasphemous. But it's his fault. Not only has he let it happen, he's helped it. He wants it. He likes all of this."

Padre came up from the sacristy with the Mexican man in the suit. 'Amá fixed her shawl and straightened her knee.

She got ready to talk to him. But he went by without noticing her, talking lowly but quickly to the Mexican man in the suit, as they hurried out to where Sister Dolores might still be.

She started seeing things, different things. She saw a bright blinding light come out of the Sacred Heart, right from the spot He was pointing to. She saw the Holy Spirit, the Third Person of the Blessed Trinity, in the form of a dove, spitting fire down on a dark empty field. She saw a huge black bat, bigger than me, she said, that chased her through the house leaving her shivering in sweat. She saw three black spiders, as big as my head, running down every wall she looked at. When she saw green snakes in every room, I told her I was going to get Padre. "No," she said. "It'll all be gone tomorrow." And then she was calm.

The next morning Padre had a High Mass in honor of Sister Dolores' patron saint. It was the first time High Mass was said for the six o'clock Mass. He had been announcing it for weeks. He asked me to come early so I could get out the Easter candle and help him with his vestments. He got the choir to sing. People came from all over. There were cars and trucks with license plates from Texas and Arizona. That morning they had their sick and their old inside the church to get the special blessing that had to come from this special Mass.

'Amá was still dressing when I left. She had gotten me up, but that was all. She could barely move. There were pauses between the sounds of each step. She had to eat that day. She couldn't go much longer.

He had me turn on all the lights and light every candle. He brought out all the gold vessels and chose his red vestments, the ones he only wore at Christmas. We were still downstairs when Sister Dolores came in. We could hear the excitement and movement above. "She's here," he said, more to himself than to me. His face was gleaming. He went to the closet, opened the door with the mirror, and looked at himself. Then we went upstairs. As soon as we walked out to the altar, the organ started. Its first full sounds pushed the lights and the smoke and the excitement to the sides and corners of the church. Each time he turned to answer the choir, he seemed happier. His weak voice wasn't weak that day. It was as much his Mass as it was hers.

'Amá came in just before Communion, when there was no singing. It wasn't a moan that she used so much as a low steady groan. I knew it was her. I knew it even before the others who could see her knew. She fell next to Sister Dolores' pew. She was barefoot and had left a trail of blood behind her. The wounds on her feet were open and deep. But what scared people most was the bleeding slash across her ribs.

🕯🕯🕯🕯🕯

"Hurry up, Chole. Give me the money. I want to go."

"I just want to talk to you for a few more minutes, m'ijo."

"You're not talking. You're just messing up my hair. You've already talked to me. You started talking to me when I first got here."

"I know, m'ijo, but I just want to see you for awhile. I hardly ever get to see you."

"Do we have to do this every Sunday? Do I have to let you mess up my hair before I get the money?"

"No, m'ijo. It's just that I don't get to see you too much."

"If I didn't need the money, if I didn't need to buy my own food, if she wasn't still sick, I wouldn't still be standing here waiting for your two lousy dollars. Come on, Chole. I got to get going."

"But where are you going m'ijo?"

"I got friends to meet. That's where."

"You have friends. I'm glad, m'ijo. For a long time I've been worried that you didn't have any friends. It's no good not to have any friends."

"What do you mean, do I have friends? Sure I have friends. I've got a lot of friends. A lot more than you do. How many friends do you have, Chole? Name me one."

"I don't think I have any."

"You're back to your old ways, Jesús."

He didn't have to say my name.

"What do I have to do? Do I have to threaten you each week? How long has it been? Five, six, seven, eight weeks since you brought me a week free of self-abuse? How patient must I be? When will you bring me two weeks free of sin? Don't you understand by now that you just can't give in to yourself whenever you feel like it? Life is hard. Satan is everywhere. You must practice some form of self-control each day or you'll be swallowed up. Is it so difficult to keep your hand from yourself for a week? For a week at a time? Surely you can't be that weak?"

The next morning he wore his white vestments. He was all in white, white trimmed with gold. He looked pure. He didn't look at me, except once. That was just before we went up to start the Mass. I was on one knee, tying my shoe. I looked up and saw him looking down at me. I looked down.

During the Mass, when I washed his fingers with wine, with the Blood of Jesus Christ, his fingers seemed so clean. He wanted a lot of wine that morning. He kept tilting the chalice, clinking it against the cruet. More. My hand shook, and I couldn't pour much. I knew he was thinking that I shouldn't have been holding what would be the Blood of Jesus Christ. When I came down from putting out the candles, he was gone. He hadn't said anything to me that morning.

They came from everywhere to see 'Amá. They came from Reedley and Dinuba and Orosí and Tranquility and Five Points and Raisin City. There were times when there

were people waiting in their cars and on our porch and in
our front room to see her. Padre said there should not be
more than five people in her room at one time. Agripina
came every day to wash her sheets and nightgowns because
'Amá had to be clean. She never showed them her wounds;
she showed them only to Padre. But they all knew. The
word had spread, from camp to camp, from field to field.
Some said they had even heard about her on the Mexican
radio program at 5:00 o'clock in the morning. I was glad
'Amá was getting famous, and for a week I got up at five to
hear for myself. There was lots of talk and bouncy music on
that half-hour program, and the announcer sold everything
from flour to diamond rings. But I never heard him talk
about 'Amá.

The men came too. This was different than going to
church. There was something real here, something you
could see. They came in freshly-ironed shirts with their hats
already in their hands. The women were all covered up,
their shawls wrapped around their heads so that you could
only see their eyes and noses. They brought their problems
and their sick and their old. She listened. "I am nothing. I
am but a crude tool of God. For reasons known only to Him,
He has chosen me to help bring you closer to Him. He is
good and He loves every one of His children. Believe me, I
know. You Have but to listen to Him and love Him, and
there will be great peace and happiness in your lives. Of
this I know." They came out of her room nodding. Clearly
she was a holy woman.

One day a great big fat woman with glasses came. 'Amá
was resting then, not seeing anyone. But when she heard
that the woman was from Texas, that she had come because
they were talking about her in Texas, 'Amá asked them to
bring her in.

They talked.

"Yes, people ask me why I don't have any wounds on my
hands. All I can say is that God in His infinite wisdom often
acts in ways that must appear to us who understand so little to be of great significance. They in fact have no signifi-

cance at all. But what was this that you were saying about people in Texas?"

"I'm sure I've seen you before and your boy, too."

"That's my grandson."

"Oh. Didn't you used to live in Brownsville?"

"No."

"Corpus?"

"No."

"But you have lived in Texas, haven't you? Because I'm sure I've seen you there."

"No."

"You're sure? Well, you've been there, haven't you?"

"The only time I've been to Texas was when we crossed the Rio Grande. But where did you hear these things in Texas that you were talking about?"

"Señora, my life is so full of problems right now, I don't know what to do. They say that life gets easier as you get older, but mine seems to be getting harder. Right now it's these sores on my legs. Maybe you can help me, Señora. I hope you can help me."

"What were these things you said you heard?"

"I know it started with this man I met. He's a good man, Señora, he really is. No, to tell the truth, it really started with my husband. He never was any good."

"What part of Texas did you say you're from?"

"Del Rio."

"Is that where you heard these things?"

"Yes. But like I was telling you, Señora, my husband was bad, real bad. He always beat me and chased women, and me and the kids always had to fend for ourselves. Then seven years ago next week, he disappeared. One day he went to the store and he just never came back. Those were hard years. Thank God that some of the kids were old enough to help me. Then I met this wonderful man, Señora. I want to marry him. The Padre in my town is fixing up the papers to make my husband dead. Next week, the seven years will be up, and the Padre can say that my husband's dead and I can marry this man. Except I have these sores.

I'll be honest, Señora, I've let him touch me. But that's all, by all the saints, that's all I've let him do. Only God punished me, because where I let him touch me, I now have these sores. Help me, Señora. They say you can make people well. Take these sores away from me. I'm not a very pretty woman as it is, but if he sees these sores, Señora, I think I'll lose him."

"You must have faith, my child. I am nothing. At most I am His crude tool. Come, kneel beside me and let us pray. Good. But before we begin, tell me, what did you hear about me in Texas?"

𖤐𖤐𖤐𖤐𖤐

"Chole, it's hard. They don't like me. Nobody likes me."

"I like you, *m'ijo.*"

"But nobody likes me. They all hate me."

"No, *m'ijo.* They just don't know you. Give them time. It takes time, *m'ijo.* Everything takes time."

"But it's been this way ever since I can remember. They've always made fun of me. They've always chased me. I've always stayed out of their way."

We were standing in the hot spring sun between the produce sheds. I was crying, and she was holding me. I didn't know where the tears came from, or what caused them. All I knew was that on that Sunday when I saw her, I started crying. And she held me.

"Easy, *m'ijo*, easy. People don't know what they're doing when they do these things. When they hurt like this, it's usually because they're hurting or somebody's hurt them. And they start it all over again. I know that doesn't mean much to you right now, but try to understand it because it will help."

She had pressed my head to her breast. My tears and sweat were running down into her dress. I could feel the thickness of her body. I could feel her stomach against mine. I could feel her warmth.

"But I never hurt anyone, Chole."
"Some of us never do."

Just a few days before the holy nun was supposed to go
back to Mexico, 'Amá got very sick. Padre had been coming
every day, trying to get 'Amá to show her wounds to somebody from the bishop's office. Only God knew what could
come of it. Maybe they would decide 'Amá was a saint, like
the woman in Germany that bled every Good Friday. What
a blessing that would be for everyone. 'Amá wouldn't do it.
"Do you want God's work to become a circus?" On the day
she got sick, she was so feverish that Padre wanted to give
her the Last Rites. "No," she kept telling him. "Just let me
see the holy nun."

It was October when Sister Dolores came. It was fall
and the air was finally carrying its own coolness. Women
were crowded inside and outside of our house, and there
were some on the sidewalk, too. She came on foot with the
other nuns from the house behind the rectory. Padre was
leading them. They were all praying. 'Amá was in bed resting on clean white sheets and pillow cases that Agripina
and I had changed that afternoon. I couldn't tell if she was
asleep, but when they told us that she was coming, Agripina bent over and whispered to her and 'Amá smiled without opening her eyes. The closer Sister Dolores got, the
more excited and louder the women became. Still 'Amá kept
her eyes closed. I knew she was pleased.

When they reached our block, some of the women went
to meet her. The other nuns drew closer around her. When
they came into our yard, women left the porch and went out
of our house to see and touch the holy nun. They pushed
and pressed the other nuns. Sister Dolores kept her eyes
down, praying. They grabbed for her. There were screams
and Padre shouted, "Stop it! Get away from her! This is not
a circus! Have some respect! This is a very serious matter!"

The women backed away. Then he said, "Wait here, sisters, until I can clear the house."

He didn't like me then, and I knew he'd never let me stay in the room, so I hid in the closet behind the clothes. He told everyone to get out. Agripina didn't believe him. "Even me, Padre?"

"Even you."

Then he went back out to get Sister Dolores. 'Amá still had her eyes closed. He brought her in and closed the door and whispered something to her. I couldn't tell if Sister Dolores heard him. She kept her eyes down, praying. She was facing the bed. No one moved. I could hear 'Amá breathing. I knew she wasn't asleep. I knew she knew the Sister was there. But I didn't know who'd move first. The Sister did. She went straight to the bed and stood over 'Amá. 'Amá opened her eyes. I thought she was smiling. Sister Dolores gently pulled back the sheet. Slowly she raised 'Amá's nightgown. It didn't matter that Padre was there. I had never seen 'Amá's legs. They weren't brown like her hands or her face. They were yellow. The flesh sagged from her bones. Then the holy nun bent over the wound on 'Amá's side. She traced it with her fingers. She got right next to it, looking at it from one side and then from another. She nodded. Yes. Yes. She covered 'Amá. Then she moved to 'Amá's feet. Carefully she examined the wounds, touching them lightly with her fingers. She nodded again. Yes. Yes. Then I saw that she was crying and that tears were falling on and around the wounds. She kissed the wounds and gently wiped the tears away with her lips. She looked at the wounds again. Yes. Then she pulled back the headpiece of her habit, and with her short black hair wiped 'Amá's feet. Then she knelt and kissed them again and said, "You are truly a holy woman, Señora."

CHAPTER NINE

For years I had watched them walk up that small hill to Jefferson High School. They came in waves, up in the morning and down in the afternoon. They were Mexicans and blacks, and they stayed in their own groups. Everyone knew they fought near the beginning of the school year. What that settled no one knew, because afterwards they still walked in their same groups, in their same order, side by side or back to back, but not together, never together. Near the school, there were groups of whites; they lived there. There weren't very many of them and no one fought with them.

When the day came for me to walk up that hill, I wasn't ready. She had nothing to do with it. "Hurry, Jesús, you'll be late." She would have rather that I worked, but there was no more work. "Did you hear? Jesús, you'll be late." When I left, they were still walking by. I didn't walk with them. Instead, I waited in the alley, behind garbage cans, until they had all passed. Then I walked up alone, a block behind the last group. It was easier that way.

At the school it was worse. There were kids everywhere, most of whom I had never seen. I watched from bushes across the street. Some were walking, but most were standing in bunches laughing and talking. I had the feeling that

if I left those bushes and walked across the street, they'd all
see me and laugh. So I stayed there until a bell rang and
they disappeared. Then I went over on to the lawn in front
of the main building. I couldn't go home and I couldn't keep
hiding behind someone's bushes. I looked at the building,
hoping that somehow it would come and get me. All that
came was a big man with hairy arms who wanted to know
who I was and what I was doing there. He took me to the
office, asked me some more questions, and then took me
down that long dark hall to one of the classrooms.

They laughed when I walked in. Somebody knew me.
"Hey, Dopey Jess, school started half an hour ago and three
weeks ago yesterday." More laughing. The teacher asked
me my name and I said Jesus. More laughing. She didn't
want that name. Somebody said, "His name is Jesus, but
they call him Jess Olivas. Dopey Jess Olivas." There were
three empty seats, and I went to the one in the back of the
room in the corner. A big black guy with wild hair sat next
to me. He stared at me the rest of the period. 'Amá always
said: "Just leave them alone, and they'll leave you alone." I
didn't look at him.

I didn't know what the teacher was talking about, and I
didn't care. The last thing I remembered was that she had
someone read from page fifty-one. I didn't have a book and I
had never read fifty-one pages of anything. The desk was all
carved up. It had initials and names and nicknames and
crosses; it had fucks and shits and love signs. Ink had been
poured into most of the carvings. Somebody wanted to make
sure we saw them. I could feel my body relaxing. Nobody
was looking at me anymore. Except for the black guy.
"Leave them alone . . ." I didn't look at him. I thought of all
the people who had sat in that desk and carved. How could
they have used their knives without her seeing them? One
of the carvings said: Joe 1930. Who was Joe? Where was he
now? Who ever gave a shit about Joe? Why would Joe want
to carve out Joe 1930? What made Joe think anybody would
give a shit? Maybe he didn't think that. Maybe all he
thought was what a long, fucking, boring class this was.

One person probably poured all the ink because the desk was all sloppy. Still, it made Joe's scratchings stand out more.

The bell rang. The black guy was still looking at me. I could tell. But I didn't look at him. Everybody was trying to get out of there. Sammy Ortiz said, "Hey Dopey Jess. School starts at 8:30, and that ain't no field-hand time either." But that was all, and then he was gone and the black guy left too and the classroom was empty and quiet. When I opened the door, there was a burst of noise, of kids jammed together in that hall, moving in different directions, laughing and talking. I didn't want them to see me. I stepped back into the classroom. All of a sudden the man with the hairy arms was at the door. He took me by the arm and led me down the hall through a jumble of students, brushing and bumping them as we went. I saw them all, and I saw none. A few saw me. "Look at Dopey Jess, you guys. He found somebody to lead him around. Somebody to protect his tender little body. Hey, *puto*! Ain't you got no shame!?" This time the man opened the door and let me go in by myself. The teacher told me to wait at his desk until he got the class going. I stood at the front of the room, with my side to the others, looking out the window. I could feel their eyes. There was some giggling, and I thought somebody said Dopey Jess. Then the teacher told me to print and sign my name on a card and to find a seat. There was a seat in the front and one in the back. I went to the back. The shame passed more quickly this time. Before long, I didn't think anyone was looking at me anymore. I looked around me. It was an arithmetic class. There were Mexicans and blacks, pachucos and pachucas in the back part of the class. The teacher was at the board. No one was paying any attention. A few were talking but most of those in the back were just sitting there, slouched, looking at nothing, seeing nothing, hearing nothing. One of the chucos saw me looking at him and I turned back to my desk. I looked around again. I knew what I was looking for, something I had caught a glimpse of: long brown chuca legs, bare almost up to the ass. I went back to them. If I sat the right way at my desk, I could look at them without anyone knowing I was looking at them. I looked at them until the bell rang.

He was waiting for me at the back door.

"I'll go," I said.

"You'll go where?"

"To the next one."

"Where is it?"

"I don't know."

He took me by the arm again. This time there were whistles and cat calls. "Look at Dopey and his pimp." I tried walking faster to get away from him. I bumped into two blacks. The first one warned me; the second one shoved me. "I'll go to my next one," I said, before I went into my third class.

"And where's that?" he said.

I had brought my lunch, but I didn't know where I had left it. I went back to the first classroom, but a teacher said I wasn't allowed in there during the lunch period. I didn't want to go outside, but I didn't want to stand in the hall either. Too many people would see me. I thought of the stairs to the second floor. As I went to them, I almost walked into Johnny Soto and Lilly Patiño and Bobby Zúñiga and two other guys and two other girls that I didn't know. When I saw them, I turned and started walking the other way. But Johnny Soto saw me and said, "Hey, Dopey Jess, don't run away, man. We want to talk to you."

They were dressed like chucos and chucas. If I hadn't known them, I would have thought they were real chucos and chucas. They hadn't dressed that way at Our Lady of the Angels. The guys wore long-sleeved black shirts with white buttons that were buttoned at the collar and the sleeves. The shirts were tucked into black-pegged pants that ballooned from the thighs to the calves. They wore black shiny shoes with layers of leather soles that were at least two inches thick and heels that were an inch thicker. Each wore a thin strip of a black leather belt. Their hair was greased, rolled into a wave in the front, combed back on the sides and swished together in the back and parted. Johnny and one of the other guys wore silver chains with small silver crucifixes that hung at their chests. The girls wore loose black sweaters over the points of their tiny tits, sweaters that hung over and covered half of their short black shirts. The skirts were tight, like big black bandages, strapping their brown thighs together and ending just under the cheeks of their asses. They wore sandals that made their legs look even more naked. Their streaked hair was in giant rolls across their foreheads and then fell straight back. They used lots of lipstick, eye paint, rouge and powder. I had known them in cotton dresses and corduroy pants and T-shirts. Somehow Lilly still seemed the same. She was still fine and pretty, and that softness was still in her eyes.

"Hey Dopey, where you going? How come you're trying to run away from us, man? Don't you like us?"

Johnny had a new way of talking. He cocked his head back and held it to one side. Then he barely moved his lips and he almost closed his eyes.

"I wasn't running from you, Johnny. Honest."

"Don't be lying to us, Dopey. We saw you trying to run, man. Don't be calling us liars."

"I ain't calling you no liars, Johnny. Maybe I was running."

"No maybes about it."

"Yeah, I was running, Johnny. But it's not because I don't like you guys."

He had a new way of standing, too: leaning back to one side with his head cocked and his hands dug deep in his pockets, so that when he looked at me, it was out of the corners of his eyes.

"Now look, Dopey. I don't want to have to get bad with you because I know you don't mean nothing and because I've been knowing you for a long time. What I'm trying to do is do you a favor and introduce you to some of my friends so they'll know you're okay and not get bad with you when the shit comes down. Because there's going to be a whole lot of

shit come down around this place before too long. Them
fucking niggers are starting to think they're pretty bad.
Were going to have to show them who rules. But before we
do that, we're going to have to shape up some of our own
brothers. Those guys from Snake Road are going to have to
learn that chucos mean business. So is that gang from Elm
Street."

He nodded his head as he talked. Slowly, just enough to
be noticed. And he narrowed his eyes even more when he
wanted to show that he meant business.

"This here's Alex and that's Ralphie and you know
Bobby and Lilly. That's Dolly and that's Connie. I've
already told them that you don't bother nobody, that you do
as you're told and you don't want no trouble. But you know,
Dopey, I can't be letting you slide forever. You got to be
shaping up, too. This is high school, man. This ain't grammar school no more, Dopey. And you got to be realizing
that. Look at you, man. You're still dressing the same
raggedy way you did in grammar school. It was bad enough
there, but there ain't too many people gonna put up with it
up here, man. I ain't saying you got to look sharp, Dopey,
because not everybody can be a chuco. It takes more than
rags to be a chuco, man. I'm just saying that you could at
least take off them corduroy pants and them J. C. Penney
T-shirts. On top of that, they got holes in them. They're all
worn out. Can't you see that, man? You been working in
them fields all summer, man. You could be buying some
new clothes. And that hair. Man, you look like a fruiter.
You better start letting it grow and give your grandma back
her wave-set and start using some of that good pomade.
Because if you don't, Dopey, some people are going to start
thinking that you're trying to shame us Chicanos by the
way you look. And I know you don't want nobody to start
thinking that, do you, Dopey?"

"No, Johnny."

"That's right, and I know better than that and that's
why I ain't giving you a bad time. I know it's always your
grandma who's steady on your ass and makes you live in

church and all those things. And I've told my friends that. But you know, Dopey, she's a little old lady who ain't over five-feet tall. And it's about time you start showing her who's boss. If she fucked over me that way, I'd let her have it. Set her on her ass a few times, Dopey, and you'll see how fast she'll cut all that shit out. There comes a time when you got to show them old folks where it's at. There wasn't one of our people that wanted us to be chucos and chucas. So we had to set them straight. Because that's where it's at and that's where it's going to be."

'l'hen he got right up next to me. "Dopey, the plain fact is that you got to start looking and acting like something besides a little queer. You hear?"

They laughed.

"Yes, Johnny."

I didn't think Lilly laughed.

"You like looking like a queer?"

"No, Johnny."

"Then why do you look like one?"

"I don't know, Johnny."

That time she laughed.

"Now go on, get out of our way, man. Only I'm telling you, you better shape up. Now go on, get. And make sure you walk behind us because you're a disgrace to the Mexican race. That's pretty good, huh? A disgrace to the Mexican race."

When the bell rang that afternoon, the man was right there. He came out of nowhere. There were more whistles. "*Joto!*" "*Puto!*" "*Joto!*" I walked as fast as I could.

"Can I go to my next period by myself, please?"

"Tell me where your next period is."

"How should I know?"

"I gave you a card this morning and told you it had your classes on it. Remember? Where is it?"

I didn't know.

At the start of the last period, the black guy said, "What's the matter with you, boy? You blind or got polio or something that you can't be walking around by yourself?

Why you need that man to be grabbing on your shoulder? You sure are strange."

The last bell rang and everybody ran for the doors. When I got outside they were already going down the hill, wave after wave. Ernie Padilla was on the lawn with a bunch of guys. To get to the street I would have to pass them. I went back into the building. There were some of them still in the halls. I went to the top of the stairs, and from that window watched and waited until Ernie and his friends were gone. Then I went down the hill.

"Where you been!?"

She was mad.

"At school."

"Liar! I saw them going by half an hour ago. I make all these sacrifices so that you can go to school, and what do I get? The very first day you're an hour late, probably hanging around with all that *pachucada*. Those were the only ones that didn't go by, those animals in their black clothes. *Such men!* I'd better not hear that you've been hanging around Chinatown with those *pachucos*. I should have sent you to the oranges the way the Sanchezes did their kids. You don't know how lucky you are."

As soon as she left for work, I tried to escape with my hand. But the four years of school were everywhere. They came down on my mind like a thick fog, falling, covering everything. I couldn't even think of Chole. I kept telling myself about her big tits but my mind couldn't see it. After awhile I came, but from habit. And then the silence and the drop, way down. The four years followed me there. They settled softly on everything. If one day had brought that much pain, how much would four years of those days bring? If one day had taken so long . . . I tried to eat, but the food tasted of time, time that would never end. My stomach was raw. I was breathing the four years, and each breath was scraping the rawness. I tried to sleep. Sleep would stop it, at least for awhile. I closed my eyes. But those four years slipped in between my eyelids and my eyes, like two gray sheets that became one when they met at my eyebrows and slid up over my mind, covering it totally so that all I could feel and think and sense were the four years. And they'd never end. I'd never stagger through them. Because if one day took this much . . . Pacing just reminded me of how many times I'd have to walk up that hill in four years, how many times I'd have to walk through those halls, how many bodies I'd have to squeeze past, carefully, so that they wouldn't punch me in the mouth. I tried to run through or past or out of those four years on my way to St. Francis, but I couldn't. No matter how fast or how slow I ran, they stayed with me. I confessed from memory. I was awake when she came home. The four years were props in my eyelids. Through those four years I heard her sigh and grunt and move around and go to bed. They'd never pass.

The next day he came out to get me when I crossed over from behind the bushes. I ran to the other end of the building and into my class. Slowly it passed. Toward the end of the period I watched for him at the back door. Just as the bell rang, I saw him, and I went out the front door and down the hall to my next class. I watched the clock, minute by slow minute. I couldn't see the hands move, but they did move. The teachers called on me. "Jess Olivas." I wouldn't answer. "Is that your name? . . . You, in the back row. The one with his head down, in the green T-shirt, is that your name? . . . I'm talking to you." I wouldn't answer. Most of them just passed on. One of them came to my seat and poked me. "You. I'm talking to you. Can't you hear? Don't you speak English?" I wouldn't answer. He sent me to the principal's office, but I wouldn't answer the principal either. After awhile, the principal sent me to my next class.

Instead of Dopey, they started calling me Windy because I'd never answer. Two of the teachers called on me when they wanted a laugh. They knew I wouldn't answer. They'd say my name in a way that the laughs would start even before they had finished saying it. But one teacher kept after me long after the others had given up. She kept me after school. "Why won't you answer?" I wouldn't answer. But one day I said, "Because I don't like school." I was sorry I said it. It gave her a hundred more questions and kept me in front of her, looking down at my shoes for what seemed like another hour. Then one day I wanted to answer again. I felt the words in my throat when she asked once and then again, "What is it you don't like about school, Jess?" Everything was there, lumped in my throat, but I didn't know how to say it, how to get the words out of my throat.

So she left me alone, too, and I'd sit there, day after long day, without a book or paper or a pencil, watching the clock or a chuca's legs. I didn't look at the white girls because they all sat up in front. I wouldn't have looked at them anyway. Even the chucos didn't look at them. They weren't for us. I watched the black girls wiggle their asses up the hill in the mornings. And chucos used to whistle at them. But theirs was a different world. So I looked at chucas. Or rather, I snuck looks at chucas because they, like the other Chicanas, would have laughed at me if they had seen me looking. Anyway, they showed more and made it easy to get hard.

ôôôôô

One Sunday in November, Chole had a big paper bag with her at the produce sheds. "Oh, you saw it, " she said. "I wanted it to be a surprise. I didn't want you to see it until I was ready to show it to you." The bag was behind her, and she put her hands on my shoulders, stopping me. "Oh, m'ijo, I'm so glad you're excited. I can tell you're excited. Listen to me, m'ijo. I want you to know one thing. Chole loves you. She loves you more than anything else in this world. She would never let anything happen to you. Do you understand that, m'ijo?" She had brought her face to mine. She was looking for my eyes. I was looking at the bag.

She looked until she knew I wouldn't look at her. Then she let go. In the bag was a brown leather jacket with a fur collar. It was beautiful. "Do you like it, m'ijo? Here, try it on. Let me help you. Here, let me get the zipper. You know, I saw you going to school the other morning. I saw you, but you didn't see me. And you looked like you were in a hurry and I didn't want to slow you down, so I didn't call to you or anything. But it was that day when it was already real cold and you had on that green sweater that you've been wearing for years. Not only is it too small for you, but I could tell by just looking at you how cold you must have been. Do you like it, *m'ijo?*" It felt soft and warm. "The man at the store said it's what all the high school boys are wearing. He said if it doesn't fit, I could take it back. Here, now let's see. Turn around. It looks *so* good on you, *m'ijo.* Do you like it, *m'ijo?* And it fits just right. Oh, you look *so* good in it, my little man. You look more and more like your father every day." She walked around me, there between the produce sheds. "Do you like it, *m'ijo?*" I didn't want to say I liked it. But it was so warm and smooth and soft. "You do like it, *m'ijo.* I can tell. I'm so glad. "Here, let me help you with the zipper."

I yanked away from her. I didn't want her touching me then.

"I'm sorry, *m'ijo*, I didn't mean to grab at you. I didn't mean to upset you. It's just that I tried it on and I know how the zipper works. Don't be mad at me, *m'ijo.* If you only knew all the places I went to get it."

"I didn't tell you to go any place."

"I know, *m'ijo.* I went because I wanted to do it. I wanted to get it for you, *m'ijo.* Don't be mad. We should be happy now. Just look how good you look, and everybody will see how good you look."

I liked that. I liked the thought of walking up the hill, of walking through the halls and sitting in the classrooms and . . . then I remembered 'Amá.

"I can't take this, Chole. She'll know."

"How will she know? Tell her you found it."

"She won't believe that. She'll make me take it back to where I found it. She'll say I stole it."

"Tell her somebody at school gave it to you."

"She won't believe that either . . . Here, take it. I can't keep it."

"Tell her . . ."

"Oh, shit, Chole. Leave me alone. I know what she'll say. Take the fucking thing."

"*M'ijo*, I don't want you to be mad. I just want you to have it."

"I don't care what you want."

The next morning was cold. I thought of the jacket as I walked up the hill. At the top of the hill a bunch of guys were yelling and whistling. "Come on, bitch. I got ten inches for you. You'll like it so much you'll pay me!" "Why don't you come and suck on my big dick, whore?" It was Chole. She had the leather jacket. She was waiting for me. When she saw me, she hurried towards me. Their hoots and laughs followed her.

"*M'ijo*, I came because it was so cold and I thought of a way you could keep the jacket."

I saw them watching, and before she could reach me, I turned and ran, yelling at her, "Get away from me, whore!"

The first day I skipped school I already knew about Mr. Buckley, the truant officer. It was the stories they told about him that kept me going to school every day. Everybody knew the story about the two chucos in Chinatown who had pulled knives on the old man when he spotted them and stopped them and told them to get in his car because he was taking them back to school. Just about every version had them telling him to get his ass back in the car and get out of there. Then the old man pulled out his gun. After that, you could have your pick. The best one had the old man shooting the knives right out of each chuco's hand, right there in the street. Then he handcuffed the chucos, kicked them in the ass a few times, and took them downtown to jail. They said the judge sent them to Preston and they were still doing time there. He brought a lot of chucos back to school while I was there. I never saw any gun or even handcuffs. But they all said that the only reason they had come back with the old bastard was that the crazy motherfucker had pulled a gun on them.

I went to the railroad tracks. There were men working everywhere. It wasn't like Sundays. And they all knew I should have been in school. I thought I saw Mr. Buckley's green car everywhere. Twice I thought he was coming up behind me on foot. Everyone I saw was for sure going to call him. I hid in a big stack of turkey crates, and I stayed there until the 3:30 train to San Francisco came. It was full of feathers and big wads of turkey shit. It stunk bad.

It was awhile before I ditched school again. But one day, I just couldn't sit in those desks anymore. I just couldn't watch the clocks anymore. So I didn't go, and Mr. Buckley didn't catch me and nobody sent me to the office the next day. It got easier each time. Towards the end of the school year, I was only going to school one or two days a week.

🕯🕯🕯🕯🕯

I didn't go back to school the next year. I went to the King Theatre instead. It was a huge white building on the edge of downtown, less than a block from the railroad tracks. It had a black fire escape along its back side that went up from the alley to its roof. The roof was flat and tarred. There was a three-foot wall around it. On the roof was a door into the building itself. The door was covered by a shelter that made a tiny room. The door to the shelter was never locked. It was to that roof that I went on the first day of school.

I didn't plan it that way, it just happened. Because I did wait in the alley and I did start up the hill. But I didn't want any more of it. So I went to the turkey crates, except now they were empty chicken crates, and they stank worse. I didn't stay. I went through the downtown alleys. There were cars and people there too. Then I thought I saw Mr. Buckley's green car, and I ran out of that alley and over into the next alley and up the fire escape to the roof of the King Theatre.

I had been up there a few times before on Sundays. Once I got up there, I knew it was a good place to hide. For one thing, the show wasn't open on weekdays. There was no one in it. For another, I could sit along two sides of the wall of the roof and not be seen from the other buildings. And by stooping or crawling next to the wall, I could move around most of the roof without being seen. When the sun got too hot, there was shade in the shelter. When the tiny room got too stuffy, I could stand unseen against one side of the shelter and look out over the west side of Fresno. And the three-thirty train to San Francisco told me when it was time to go home. It was better than being in school.

I went there the next day and the day after that and the week after that and the month after that. I'd make my lunch and eat my breakfast and go out the back door just as if I were going to school. I'd wait in the alley and follow them up, but only half-way, because then I'd jump into the next alley and run to the roof.

But it wasn't as easy as I had first thought. For one thing, the sun was still blazing. Outside the tiny room, the only shade on the roof was for part of the morning on a side of the shelter facing other buildings. If I stood there, they'd see me. I couldn't sit for long against the wall of the roof because by ten o'clock the tar was burning. By noon, it burned through my shoes wherever I stood. Sooner or later, the sun would drive me into that tiny room. It was hotter in there than it was outside, but I needed the shade. The shelter had been built to keep the weather out of the show. It was four feet by four feet with walls and ceilings of thin pine planks that were covered by tar paper. I couldn't leave the door open because it faced a building and someone might see me. Walking in there was like walking into an oven. As soon as I closed the door, it got hotter. And I was always afraid of being bitten by black widow spiders. I couldn't leave the door open long enough to be sure that I killed them all. Besides, they came back on weekends, when they knew I wasn't there, and built new nests. But I had to get out of the sun, and I couldn't bring a hat with me because she'd get suspicious. I had seen people get sun strokes in the fields. One of them died. If I got a sun stroke up there, I'd die because there'd be no one to find me and help me. So I'd stand inside that tiny baking room, ready to jump if I felt a spider. And the sweat would pour out of me. My clothes would get soaked, and I'd have to go back into the sun to dry them. At other times, I'd have to go back out because I couldn't breathe in there. There didn't seem to be any air left. The heat was burning it up. But it was better than being in school.

Then one day it rained. It was a warm rain at first, but once I got soaked I got chilled. The warm wind made me shiver. I went into the tiny room to get out of the wind. The roof leaked. It was worse in some spots than in others, but it leaked on me wherever I stood. Soon, I was standing in water. The shelter didn't drain. My shoes were soaked, but I had to stay out of the wind. When I got home, I saw that the soles had separated. They were my new shoes, and for weeks I hid them from her. But it was better than being in school.

The day after it rained, the weather changed; it got cool. And the day after that it was cold. The roof was still wet and I couldn't be on it very long without getting wet. She had been mad for two days because my clothes had been soaked for two days. Today, I wouldn't have any excuses. The shelter smelled of wet wood. The pine planks oozed with water. The floor hadn't drained. If I stood in there, the soles would come off my shoes. I spent the day standing against the west side of the shelter. The wind was cold and the sun was blurred all day long behind a thin sheet of clouds. And it never got hot. It was a long cold day up there. But it was better than being in school.

Once it got cold, it stayed cold. I took a sweater. Then I took my jacket. Then I took my other sweater. The roof was too cold to sit on. The shelter was still wet, and the wetness made it colder. So I'd stand against the west side of the shelter. The cold came up through my feet. By nine o'clock, my feet were numb. It spread up my legs. There was usually a wind by noon. When it came, I was already hunched up with my arms folded and my chin buried in my neck. But the wind made it colder. It got so cold that I asked Chole for the leather jacket. I was going to leave it in the shelter and just use it when I was up there.

"I don't have it, *m'ijo*. Somebody broke into my house and stole it."

"Somebody's always breaking into your house."

"I know, *m'ijo*. But it's not my fault. There's nothing I can do to make them stop breaking into my house."

"Yes, there is."

"What, *m'ijo*, what?"

"Stop being a drunken, fucking whore!"

"Oh, *m'ijo*, don't be mad at me. It really makes me sad. I'll get you another jacket. I'll get you a better one. I'll work and get the money. I'll have it for you in a couple of days."

"Keep your fucking money! Shove it up your cunt! It's big enough anyway. I don't want your filthy money buying me a jacket that I'm going to wear on my body!"

"*M'ijo*, don't say those things. I know you don't mean them. I know you're just mad, and I can't blame you for being mad. Your father used to get mad at me like this and it hurt. Please don't you do it too. I love you, *m'ijo*."

"Don't tell me you love me! I hate you! I hate you!"

But when I took my hand to myself up there, when I went into the shelter and did it, it was Chole. My face would be sunk in that giant tit and my body would be buried in those giant thighs. When my seed splattered all over that tiny room, it was always Chole.

It rained again. And the next day the fog rose from the valley floor. It hung there like cold white smoke, day after day. It covered the other buildings. I could walk around. I had to. Because the fog brought its own special cold, one that went right through me no matter how many undershirts or T-shirts I wore. It made the shelter an ice-box. I hated to go in there. One day I carried up matches, paper, and two pieces of wood. I lit a fire. It was nice and warm until the tar caught fire. I tried to blow it out, but that made it worse. I tried to stamp it out, but my feet felt like they were burning. I used my jacket, but I thought it was catching fire. Finally I smothered it with my sweater, but after that I had to throw the sweater away. It was one of the two sweaters I had. I froze the rest of the day. That day I thought about going back to school. But the next morning I thought about the classrooms and the halls, and went back to the roof of the King Theatre.

The days were long. I tried not to think of time because, like the fields, it just made it pass more slowly. But the harder I tried to forget about it, the more I thought about it. There were two-hundred and forty minutes in the morning and two-hundred and ten in the afternoon. Every morning, I began by wondering if I had been through the first forty minutes yet. Later, I wondered if I was already in the hundreds. If I wasn't there the first time I thought about it, I was by the third or fourth or fifth or sixth time the thought came to me. A hundred and ninety-nine minutes was still a lot of minutes. It was more than three hours. If I didn't think about it, it went faster. Don't think about it, I'd tell my mind. But my mind would think about it anyway. Until I'd drop off into a blank. And then I'd remember that I hadn't thought about it, and I'd think about it some more. Was it in the hundred-seventies yet, or did I still have more than three hours? At noon, a whistle blew. I couldn't tell where it came from. Only two-hundred ten minutes left. That was today. The thought of tomorrow or the day after tomorrow twisted my gut.

I tried to think of other things, nice things, things like having a girlfriend, or having everybody like me. But I couldn't think of any of those kinds of things for more than a few seconds. My mind wouldn't hold them. Dirty thoughts were different. They came and stayed all the time. On the days of my night runs, I'd roll in them, taste them, feel them, until I jacked-off. And then I'd tumble in them again, and do it again and again. Thoughts of women and girls, any woman, any girl. And Chole. On days when I had another night to wait for confession, I'd fight them. Then they would swarm on me, tickling my dick and stirring my balls. I'd shake my head; I'd bend over; I'd do sit-ups; I'd do push-ups; anything. I had to go to Communion.

Toward the end of February, the fog left for good. The first winds were cold. Then for a few weeks, the sun was warm and the air was clean and it was easy being on top of the King Theatre. But it got hot in April. The shelter dried out fast. The black widow spiders moved back in. The heat was worse than the cold, just as the cold had been worse than the heat. Sweat poured out of me. I hadn't gotten that wet on the rainiest of days. The spiders wouldn't let me move. I couldn't lean or squat or lie on my side as I had in the winter whenever I took my hand to myself. And I needed the shade. I needed the shelter worse now than in winter. The sun got stronger each day. It was like steel. It didn't give. It was steadily beating on me.

ôôôôô

I went to work in the fields with Don Miguel the day after school let out. And I stayed in the fields when the others went back to school. Because I didn't have to hide, either in the hallways or on the roof. The people that stayed never bothered me. They didn't care what I looked like. One old man used to tell me that I had made a mistake; that I was wasting myself. Without an education, I would end up working in the fields like him for the rest of my life. He liked to talk.

'Amá was happy. She thought I was old enough and that I should have done it last year. I was the man in the family. It might have been different if I had a father, or a father that cared. It might have been different if my grandfather was still alive. But she was getting old and tired now, and it was time I helped her. It was time I became a man. She hadn't seen school do anything for any Mexican yet, and she couldn't see why it would do anything for me. It seemed like all I was doing was going there to eat my lunch. Besides, if I stayed in the fields, she would let me keep part of my check. Five dollars, she said, which was a lot.

ôôôôô

The cotton ended in December. Don Miguel told most of the men that he'd have work for them in the pruning about the third week in January. He told me that he wouldn't have any work for me until the thinning.

"But that's not until April or May," I said.

"I know," he said.

"But what am I supposed to do until then?"

"I don't know."

"Why won't you let me prune?"

"Because you need experience to prune."

"But I can learn."

"No, the bosses only want people with experience."

"But how can I get experience if you won't give me a chance to get it?"

"That's your problem."

"What am I supposed to do?"

"What everybody else who's ever pruned has done. Wait for the trucks every morning until somebody's short. Then you hope they're short enough to take a chance on you. If you're good and learn fast, then you might catch on. Chances are you'll have to come back to Chinatown and wait until somebody's short again."

'Amá said I could sleep late the first week. Except for a few days when the crops had changed, we hadn't been together since June. She had come to my door every morning. "Get up, Jesús, it's time." But that was all. I'd leave the money on the kitchen table the nights I got paid. The next morning it would be gone. In its place would be two dollars.

The first day she said, "Rest," almost every time she saw me. She said it softly, the way the other women said it to their working men. By the second morning, she was reminding me of him.

"He's all alone, Jesús. Since you've been working, he's been saying Mass all by himself. There's nobody to help him. It's strange to see him serve his own wine and hold his own tray. I know he misses you. All those years you helped him, and now he's alone."

The next day it was, "You know, Jesús, he did a lot for you. I'm sure he would like to see you. I'm sure he would like to have you serve Mass while you're waiting for the pruning to start." I couldn't tell if she was asking. There was still some softness in her voice.

The next morning it was the voice I knew, straight and hard. "How long has it been since you confessed yourself?" I didn't answer.

"I'm talking to you, Jesús!" The voice scraped.

"Not too long ago." I didn't look at her. It was the same voice, all those years of that voice.

"When?"

"About three Fridays ago, at night."

"How long has it been since you received Holy Communion?"

"A long time."

"Then you should go on Sunday. There's no reason for you not to go on Sunday. There's no reason for you not to serve for him on Sunday. I'll tell him you'll serve for him on Sunday."

I had been going to Chinatown every day since I stopped working. There was no place else to go. Each day I went a little earlier. Each day I could feel her tensing earlier. That day I went to Chinatown right after she said that.

Chinatown was where the men went when they weren't working. I couldn't go to the bars there because I was too young. Besides, I didn't like them. I didn't like the darkness and the men hunched over on bar stools. The chucos ran the pool halls. They were young, but they would have pushed

me around from the time I walked in. It was too cold to
stand on the street. Only the winos did that time of the
year. So I went to the Michoacán Market and sat on an
empty milk crate with the old men who didn't work anymore. I didn't sit with them so much as behind them,
because they all had their places and crates that they went
to every day. They didn't say much to each other. I didn't
know that until I sat with them. Mostly they stared quietly
at whatever it was that happened to be in front of their
place, resetting their mouths from time to time. That was
all they did until one or two of the men who were still working came in, as some did every day, and talk started–the
news and the gossip and the comparing and the kidding and
the laughter. Then they would leave and it would be quiet
again. Until somebody else came.

That morning, as I sat in the Michoacán Market, I
thought over and over about what she had said. All those
months and nothing had changed. It was the same. Week
after week she had taken my money and had given me two
dollars, not five, not the five she had promised (without ever
mentioning it). She liked money. We ate the same. We wore
the same clothes. She hadn't bought anything. She had that
money someplace. And now him again. Together they would
put me back in line, their line. Mass and Communion every
morning. If I didn't go to Communion, they'd know why,
and they'd look at me with those looks. He knew what I
was. But I'd have to tell him every week that I was. I hadn't
stopped confessing myself during those months in the fields.
Every few weeks, my sins would weigh heavy on me. It
always had to do with death and dying. Some nights I could
smell death in the house with me. On those nights, I'd make
a night run. So it wasn't the confessing. It was that they'd
have me again.

On Saturday I told her I thought I had a job on Sunday.

"Who is this man?"

"They call him Don Faustino."

"How do you know him?"

"In Chinatown they said he was looking for workers."

"What kind of work could he have now?"

"He's pulling up vines. He needed a lot of people this morning, but I didn't know about it. He's going to be in Chinatown tomorrow morning at five."

"Well, I told Padre that you would serve for him tomorrow morning. I've let you rest all week. The poor man has no one to serve for him. And besides, how long has it been since you went to Communion?"

"I won't go if you don't want me to, 'Amá. It's just that they say he's paying good money. And I know we could use the money, because it could be a long time before I get on in the pruning. But if you want me to serve instead, I'll serve. It's just that I thought we could use the money."

"Who is this man?"

"All I know is that they call him Don Faustino and that he's Filipino."

"That explains it. Those Filipinos will do anything. You've got to watch them. They can't be trusted. They're so hungry. They'll do anything for a dollar. He probably does have work."

"Do you still want me to go to church with you in the morning?"

"No. No. We need the money. Everything is so high these days. Go. Let's see if you have some luck."

There was no don Faustino and there was nobody in Chinatown at five o'clock that morning, except for the drunks who were passed out in the doorways. I walked through Chinatown just in case she followed me. I crossed the tracks and went to the roof of the King Theatre. It was even colder up there in the dark. But I couldn't hang around Chinatown. There was no place to hang around at that time of the morning, and someone might see me. It was colder on the roof than it was in the fields, even when the sun came out. At least I could move around in the fields. And there were other people in the fields, even if they didn't talk to me. They were there, and I was with them. I was part of them. I had gone there in the back of the truck with them. But no matter how cold it was up there, it was better than being in Mass with them.

Don Faustino was good until Christmas day. I was ready for them by then.

He looked older. I hadn't seen Padre in more than six months. That was the longest ever. It looked like he had lost more of his hair. I had never thought his baldness went back that far. The lines on his face, especially around his mouth, seemed deeper.

"It's good to see you, Jesús."

I didn't expect that, and I didn't believe that. Except that he said it again.

He was surprised when I received Holy Communion, because I hadn't confessed to him. When I served him wine the second time, I almost grinned. It was the last Mass I served for him.

I spent the mornings of the next three weeks on top of the King Theatre. It didn't take much each night to convince her that someone might be hiring the next morning. Those hours just before daybreak were the coldest of any day. And then the sun hid, sending fog instead. I dug my hands deep and hard into my pockets. I buried my chin in my neck. I tried to control my shivering. But it was better than being at Mass with them.

The pruning came. I was at the corner of F and Tulare Streets before five. So were the others, fifty men, maybe more. The cold kept us together in small groups. "¡Ay, qué friazo!" That was almost all anyone said. Most of us shifted from foot to foot; somehow that kept us warmer. "¡Pinche brisa!" The fog hadn't lifted, it seemed, for weeks. It blurred the street lights. But everyone forgot the cold at the first sounds of the trucks. Two of them came, old flatbed trucks with wooden guard railings and wooden benches. Some of the men left us as soon as the trucks stopped; they got into the backs of the trucks, nodding to the contractors. Those

were the steadies. The rest of us crowded into the street
around the contractors.

"Get back or we ain't going to pick anyone. We sure as
hell can't pick you if we can't see you, and we can't see you
if you're right on top of us."

We moved back, but not much. The contractors examined us under the street lights. Some of the men called their
names and waved to them and took off their hats when the
contractors looked in their direction. The contractors didn't
say much. They picked men by pointing and jerking their
fingers. They only questioned a few of the drunks.

"You hung over, Pete?"

"Hell no."

"You telling me you're off the stuff?"

"I didn't say that."

"Can you give me a good, full week's work?"

"Sure, you know that, Joe."

"I'm not paying tonight. I'm telling you right now. I'm
paying once a week and that'll be this Saturday. And I don't
want you to start on me tonight, that you need your wages
or a few bucks. If you don't last the week, then you don't get
paid. It's as simple as that. So if you can't last the week,
then don't come, because I'm telling you right here in front
of everybody that I ain't going to pay you."

"Okay, Joe."

Then they left. They took almost forty men. The next
morning they picked a few more and the following morning,
one more. On Friday and Saturday, they didn't need any
more. Each morning there were fewer of us left, mostly
drunks.

Saturday night she asked, "You're going to Mass in the
morning, aren't you?"

"I don't know."

"What do you mean you don't know!"

"They say that some of the crews are going to work and
I thought maybe I should go down in the morning."

"There won't be that many working."

"They say they are."

"There won't be much hiring."

"They say Sunday is the best day, once the crews are picked, because a lot of people get drunk on Saturday night and they're mostly short on Sundays. The only way I'm going to get on is if they're short. But if you don't want me to go, 'Amá, I won't go."

"Maybe you'd better go."

There were just the four of us that Sunday: two drunks and a man who kept telling me that his baby had to go to the hospital and that his family was almost without food. If he didn't get hired that day, he didn't know what he'd do. I tried not to listen to him. He was telling me those things so I'd leave and he'd be picked. He didn't talk to the drunks. He knew they'd never be picked. Each time he finished telling me about his family, I'd move away from him. He'd wait awhile and then come over to wherever I was and tell me again. He was telling me again, when I heard Chole. She was pushing a man away.

"I told you, I'm too tired. Can't you leave me alone!?"

"But I have the money."

"I don't care about the money, I'm tired. I can't do it again. Not tonight."

"But you told me to wait. You promised you'd do it with me after you finished with my *compadre*. And I sat outside the room and I listened to the two of you and I waited. I have the money. Look. Please, Chole."

"Your *compadre* was an animal. He didn't know when to stop. I couldn't get him off of me. Don't you guys have women out there in Raisin City?"

"It's been a long time, Chole. I need it. Look. Here, look at how much money I have. It's all yours. You can have it all. And I'll be quick. Just let me get in there for a little while, Chole. Please."

"I told you I'm tired."

"Come on, Chole, please."

"Get your hands off me, you son of a bitch!"

One of the drunks didn't like it. "Leave that woman alone, you dirty bastard!"

Then Chole saw me. "Jesús, oh Jesús, help me! Get him
away from me, Jesús!"

He didn't follow her into our group.

"Jesús, walk with me! Take me home, *m'ijo*! You know I
don't ask you for much. Do me this favor, *m'ijo*. Help me."

I went with her, without thinking, without hesitating.

"Thank you, *m'ijo*. You know I don't ask you for much."

She put her arm through mine and leaned against me.
"You don't mind, do you, *m'ijo*? It's just that I'm scared and
all shaky. Some of these men have no respect at all."

I could smell the wine or beer on her. "Are you drunk?"

"Just a little, *m'ijo*. Do you mind?"

"No."

She stumbled and grabbed onto me. I felt the softness of
her thigh. My breathing quickened. She pressed against me,
and her tit, under her coat, had to be against my arm. I felt
a buzzing, a tingling in every part of me. I was breathing
hard. I held my breath so she wouldn't hear it.

"You're not mad at me, are you, *m'ijo*?"

"No. No." I was hard, sticking straight out. She had to
have seen. Still, she pressed against me. Our legs touched
as we walked.

"Oh, *m'ijo*, I'm so glad you're not mad at me."

I got closer so that most of our legs were touching. I
could feel the bigness of her ass on my thigh. My breath was
getting stuck in my throat.

"Are you drunk, Chole?"

"Yes, some, *m'ijo*. But you have to understand that a lot
of times I have to drink with them. And other times it just
makes it easier."

"I know." I liked it that she was drunk.

"Oh, *m'ijo*, you don't really hate me, do you?" She
turned and looked at me, and I felt what had to be the fullness of her tit under her coat.

"No, I don't hate you. I don't hate you at all."

"I'm so glad to hear you say that, Jesús. I never could
believe that you hated me, even though you said you did.
Even though you said worse things than that. I still loved

you. I know the kind of life you have with her. I know what
she is. I know what she must have put you through. I know
how lonely you must be. We're so much alike, Jesús. If you
only knew."

I wasn't like her. But I felt the side of that huge ass
sinking into my leg and I didn't say anything. She stumbled
again and this time her coat opened and for a moment I had
her tits on my arm.

"I'm sorry, Jesus."

"That's okay" I was so hard it was hard to walk.

A man jumped out at us. "Okay, bitch, I've had it with
you! If you won't take my money, then I'm going to steal it,
cunt!" It was the man who had been with her at first. He
had a knife in his hand. "I'd love to hear you tell the cops
that you got raped. Get this punk out of here! What's the
matter, can't you get your rocks off unless you're taking on
babies?"

I jumped back, but she didn't. Instead she went up to
him. "Get the fuck out of here, Fernando! You touch him
and I'll kill you myself. You keep playing these games and
you'll be dealing with Tommy. I don't need no cops. I pay
Tommy plenty. Ask Cuate what happened to him. Put that
thing away and get the fuck out of here!"

"I don't want no trouble, Chole. I pay for what I want.
Look, I've got a lot of money. I'm real hard up and you told
me to wait and I had to listen to you and my *compa*. It won't
take long. It'll be easy money. We could just go over in the
alley there and do it. It'd only take a minute. You don't have
to get dirty. We could do it standing up. Come on, I'll do it
real fast. The kid doesn't mind waiting, do you, kid?"

"I told you to get the fuck out of here, Fernando! I told
you I'm tired and I mean it. I'm tired. Can't you hear? I've
been fucking since two o'clock this afternoon. I'm tired and
I'm sore. I don't want to spread my legs for nobody else. I
don't give a fuck if I ever spread them again. Sometimes I
wish my cunt would be sealed. I don't want to see another
dick. I mean it! In plain language, I do not want to see
another dick! And if you don't get the fuck out of here right

now, Tommy Macías will be looking for you tonight."

He cursed her. He called her every name I'd ever heard.
But in between, he begged her too. And then he left, rubbing himself.

I had never seen her like that. She turned; she was
waiting for me. I wasn't hard any more. I didn't know if I
should go with her or not go with her.

"Come on, *m'ijo*." She came back for me. "Come on,
m'ijo. Let's go. Don't let him bother you. He's just talk.
Besides, he knows I'm not kidding about Tommy. I know I
sounded awful, but sometimes I have to sound like that just
to protect myself." She put her arm through mine again.

"Do you really need me to go with you?"

"Of course, *m'ijo*. You think I like walking these streets
by myself? Even though it's morning, it's still dark. You
never know what could happen."

She pulled at me and her coat opened and I saw those
huge tits. We walked. We had only a block to go. Our legs
were rubbing after the first few steps.

"Do you like me, *m'ijo*?"

"Sure I like you."

"Your father used to say some of those things you say to
me. He used to treat me like you do. Sometimes it was
awful. Sometimes it was more than I thought I could take.
But down deep I knew he loved me. He never told me he
loved me. Except once. He was drunk then, real drunk, but
that's when people really say what they mean. And besides,
he wasn't the kind of man who said those kinds of things.
He had lots of women, it's true. But I know he didn't love
any of them."

I didn't like her talking about him, not anymore. I used
to, but not anymore. And not then. But she was pressing up
against me.

"I was young when I met your father, younger than you
are now. From the first time I saw him, I knew. They said
he was evil and to stay away from him. But they didn't
know him. No one ever knew him. It was the way his eyes
flashed, like black fire. When he smiled there was nothing

you could do. So much flash in those eyes, in that smile. I was so much younger than you then. He hadn't met your mother yet. He had already turned me out onto the streets when he met her."

I saw the corner and then the lines of the church, through the fog, behind the street light. I remembered 'Amá. She'd be going to church. She'd see us. I stopped and she stumbled again. This time my hand, the back of my hand, was resting on her ass. My breath stuck. My dick felt as big as a tree again.

"What's the matter, *m'ijo*?"

"Nothing. Let's cross the street."

"Don't be afraid of her, *m'ijo*."

"Who's afraid! I'm not afraid! Where the fuck do you get that? There you go again with your stupid shit!"

"Don't be mad, *m'ijo*."

"I'm not mad! You just don't know what the fuck you're talking about! You never know what the fuck you're talking about!"

"I didn't mean anything, *m'ijo*."

"You never mean anything, but you never shut up either!"

"I'm sorry, *m'ijo*."

"You're always sorry!"

"Let's cross, *m'ijo*."

"Who the fuck wants to cross! I don't want to cross! I ain't afraid of nobody. You understand?"

"I know, *m'ijo*."

She put her arm around me. My hand stayed inside her coat, on her ass, against the silkiness of her dress. She moved us toward the street. I could feel that big ass roll. We crossed the street.

"You know, Chole, the only reason I said let's cross was because there's a lot of ruts up a little further in the sidewalk, and I was worried that you might fall with those shoes of yours."

"I know, *m'ijo*."

It was worse on that side of the street. 'Amá could see

us sooner. We should have stayed on the other side of the street. But my hand was on her ass, lightly. I didn't know if she could feel it. Her ass was so big. I wanted her to feel my hand. I wanted her to let me, to like it, to get hot. But I didn't press hard because I was scared she'd tell me to stop.

"I look at you and I see him. Not that you look exactly like him. But you do look more like him every day. There are so many things about you that remind me of him. You stand like him and you walk like him; and I know you've never seen him. You talk like him, and I know you've never heard him talk. And you have his temper. Your eyes get the same way when you're mad. Oh, I wanted you so much to be my son. He didn't want children and I went along with him for a long time. Then I lied to him. I told him it was safe when it wasn't. I got him to get me when it was my time. But I never got pregnant. For a long time I thought it was him. I never thought it was me. And it was all right that he couldn't because I loved him. But then your mother got pregnant. That day I felt my heart tear."

We were almost there then. She was always whining. But I had all of my hand on her ass and it didn't matter. Then I wondered what we would do when we got there. I was afraid I wouldn't know how to do it and that she'd know and she'd laugh. We were at the corner. No 'Amá. I didn't know how to do it. I thought of leaving. But my hand was rubbing full on her ass. I'd get that much at least. Couldn't she feel it?

"*M'ijo,* I've watched you since you were a little boy. I used to watch you from the corner playing on your porch when you could barely walk. I used to sneak into the back of the church early in the mornings and hide until you and she passed. And then I'd look at you through those glass doors. You didn't know that, did you? I loved to watch you when you were small. When I watched you serving Mass as a little boy, I used to think that angels had to look like you. I watched you grow up from behind those doors. I saw you grow from Padre Galván's waist to be taller than him. Lots of times, when I had had a bad night or just felt bad, I wouldn't go to bed. I'd wait and then go over to the church. Just seeing you made me feel better. . . . We're here, *m'ijo*, and I want you to come in. I'm ashamed of it. It's not very nice. And it's dirty. But I always wanted you to be in it. I always hoped you'd visit me. Now when I'm alone here, at least I'll be able to say, 'He stood right there,' or 'He sat here.'"

I squeezed her ass.

"If that's what you want, *m'ijo*, you know Chole will give it to you. But be nice. Easy. Go slow. Let's get to know each other first."

"I already know you." I grabbed at it with both hands and squeezed hard. She jumped. I couldn't see her. It was dark in there and it stank. That didn't matter. What mattered was that I didn't know how to do it. She came back to me.

"*M'ijo*, I like you to touch me. But do it nice and do it easy. You know I'll do what you want. Just be nice."

"Turn on the light. I can't see."

She put her arms around me and brought my head to hers. She kissed me and put her tongue in my mouth. It was fat and wet and felt dirty. 'Amá and I didn't even drink out of the same glass. I wanted to pull away, but I could feel her tits pressing against me, big soft things. She had an awful smell. She stank. But my dick was rubbing against her leg. She pulled back her tongue and bit my lip and laughed. She still had her arms around me. I couldn't see her in the dark, but I knew where her tits were. I grabbed them. "Ooww! Please don't hurt me, *m'ijo*." I wasn't hurting her. I was just grabbing them, squeezing them, making sure I had them, holding what I had dreamed of holding for years.

"*M'ijo*, you're hurting me."

She pulled away from me. I went after her. I couldn't breathe. I had to go after her. I had to have them. I had to breathe. She caught me by my arms and held me away from her. She was stronger than I thought.

"*M'ijo*, I love you. Listen to me, *m'ijo*. I love you. I'm

yours. Every part of me is yours. Just don't hurt me, *m'ijo*.
Take what you want. I want you to have me, but don't hurt
me. Don't treat me like they treat me. This is for love. It's
not for money. You don't know how long I've wanted this.
Don't make it bad. You don't know how many nights I've
come back here and finished myself off thinking of you. I
needed the money real bad today, so I took them on, one
right after the other today, until I couldn't do it no more.
You saw. I'm sore. But when I saw you, when you helped
me, I felt so good. And now I want to finish off with you. So
here, take my tits. Make them naked. Hold them in those
wonderful hands of yours. Do what you want with them.
Just don't hurt me."

   She put my hands on her tits. I felt them, I rubbed
them. I cupped them. I breathed easier. "Make them
naked," she whispered. I put my hands down the front of
her dress. So much flesh. But I couldn't get them out. They
were wrapped in too tightly. "Unzipper the dress." I didn't
know where the zipper was. It was getting hard to breathe
again. I couldn't find it. I heard the dress rip. I felt it give.
But I couldn't get at them. The bra was too tight. My hands
were all over them but I couldn't feel them. "Let me undo
it." They wouldn't come out. I pulled on them. "Stop, get
your hands out if you want me to undo it." I kept grabbing
and pulling. "I can't unsnap it with your hands in there." I
didn't listen. "You're hurting me, *m'ijo*. Stop." I pulled
harder. She screamed. And then the bra snapped and I felt
the weight of those huge things in my hands. I sunk my fingers into them. I squeezed them. I kissed them. The bra
kept getting in the way. It kept falling between my face and
her tits. I yanked it. "You're choking me, *m'ijo*! Stop!" She
grabbed my arm. She was stronger than me.

   She turned on the light. Her tits were huge brown mel-
ons with nipples as big as my hands. The bra was wrapped
around her neck. With one hand, she tried to undo it. Her
dress hung on her stomach and her hips. The room was a
mess. There were dishes stacked all around the counter
behind her. There were more dirty dishes on the table with

dried up food and opened cans. The smells made sense. Her tits sagged from her chest, bigger than I had ever imagined. Clothes and whiskey and wine bottles lay everywhere. The bed was a bare mattress, brown from use. There was a torn, stained blanket on the floor. When she freed herself of the bra, she let go of me. I lunged for her and we both fell. I grabbed and bit and sucked on her tits. "You're hurting me, *m'ijo.*" Then I unbuttoned myself. I knew what do do.

"*M'ijo*, I'm sore down there. Go easy. Please."

I pushed hard but I couldn't find it.

"Easy, *m'ijo*. Let me get the dress out of your way."

I pushed harder.

"No, *m'ijo*. Easy, *m'ijo*. I have to take off my pants, *m'ijo.*"

I pushed harder. I was sinking into something.

"No, *m'ijo*, this is crazy. You're taking my pants with you. You're hurting me."

As soon as I knew I was in her, I came. It had happened so fast. And then I smelled her again. Then I saw that her hair was greasy and that her ear was yellow with wax.

"Oh, my little bull, I love you so much. I want to give every part of me to you. I just wish I was clean and innocent for you. I wish I was everything you ever wanted. Did you like it, *m'ijo*? Tell me you liked me, *m'ijo.*"

We were on the floor. Just under my nose was a splotch of dried food. A few feet away was a cardboard box stuffed with papers and garbage. Next to it, a blood soaked rag had fallen from the heap. The blood was more black than red. I felt sick to my stomach. She was still kissing me, still holding me.

"*M'ijo*, I want you to come to my house whenever you want. Whatever's here is yours, and for you, I'll always be here."

The church bell rang. "I have to go, Chole." I had to get out of there.

"No, *m'ijo*, stay."

"I have to go."

"No, *m'ijo*, please. Just stay five more minutes."

I got up to go, but before I could reach for my pants, she had gotten to her knees and wrapped her arms around me. Then she took her mouth to me and I did it again. Not as fast as before, but too fast for her because she kept saying, "No, *m'ijo*, that was too fast."

I slept. It was a sleep in which I knew I was sleeping, in which I knew I didn't want to be sleeping. Not there. Not then. I woke with a dread because I knew it was noon or later. I shouldn't have come. I shouldn't have done it. I shouldn't have stayed. I had to get out of there. As I moved, I felt her. I knew it was her. I could smell her. She stank. She was lying next to me. The filth in that room was everywhere. Daylight made it worse; it made the smell worse too. I felt sick. I had to get out of there. I tried to move without waking her. But she moved too.

I looked at her. The tears had washed her makeup loose. It streaked down along the side of her face into the rolls of her neck. Her pores were filled with dirt and grease. Each one seemed like a pit of black grime. The mattress had stain upon stain. I couldn't figure out its color. I couldn't tell which stank worse, her or the mattress. I had to get out of there. I jumped up. "I've got to go."

"No, *m'ijo*."

I didn't want it this time. I was out of her reach before she raised herself.

"Stay, *m'ijo*. I'll fix you some breakfast."

She must have seen my face. "Never mind the mess, *m'ijo*, I'll go out and get us something to eat and bring it right back. What would you like? Anything. Nothing's too good for my prince. Just tell me. I've got plenty of money."

I started for the door and she grabbed me. I pushed hard. "Let go of me!" She fell over a chair and onto the floor. "*M'ijo!*"

I expected to be punished.

I had a taste of it while I was in her house. It was everywhere when I came out.

From Chole's door you could see the steps of the church across the street. The first thing I saw were people on the church steps. One of them was Raquel Ramos and it looked like she was looking at me. I jumped behind some bushes. There were people everywhere. Either the 12:15 Mass had just ended, or it was later than that and there had been a big baptism. I thought of going back into Chole's house but I could hear her crying and I didn't want any of that. Besides, it was late. I wasn't sure if Raquel had seen me. She was talking to another woman and kept on talking. As I looked around, I saw that people could see me behind those bushes. I ran around the house to the back yard. The back gate was locked with a chain. There was barbed wire across the top of the fence. I climbed the fence, but I couldn't get over the barbed wire. Agripina's house was half-way down the alley. The longer I stayed on top of the fence, the surer I was that she had seen me. Every time I put one leg over the wire, my pant leg got stuck and I was cutting my hands. Finally I jumped. My pant leg stuck, throwing me off balance. It ripped and I landed hard on my shoulder. I was afraid Agripina might have seen or heard me fall. I got up fast and ran toward Tulare Street, away from her house.

As I reached Tulare Street I saw Refugio Sánchez and his family walking on the sidewalk toward me. I turned and ran back down the alley. I didn't know if they had seen me. I ran hard. I didn't want them to see me. Before I knew it, I was at Agripina's house. Her house sat next to the alley. She was a nosy old bitch that saw everything that happened in the alley. She had her curtains fixed so that she could watch without being seen. I knew that's what she did because I had been in her house and had watched her watching. I knew she was watching me. 'Amá would know.

I stopped running once I left the alley. There were too many people in the street. But I walked fast. It was late and I had to get home. One of the old men from the Michoacán stopped me. "What's the matter with you, boy? It's Sunday.

How come you got your work clothes on?"
"Because I worked today."
"Who'd you work with?"
"With José de la Torre."
"They got back a long time ago."
I didn't know what I'd tell her. She knew by now.

I went through Chinatown so that I could go around our house and go in through the alley without her seeing me. People were working again. They had money again. There were more people in Chinatown than I had seen in a long time. It seemed like every few steps I saw someone who knew me. Except for the winos, I was the only one wearing work clothes. Half a block from the Michoacán, Doña Filomena's cart was stuck. She was a toothless old woman who lived alone up the street from us. Once every few weeks she'd go to Chinatown, pulling her homemade cart to do her shopping. The cart was a deep wooden box nailed to two two-by-fours, with half a roller skate nailed at the end of each. You could hear her coming and going. The old iron skate wheels ground into the sidewalk. She carried everything in the wooden box. On her way home she would stop to rest every fifty feet. Then she would re-wrap the end of the cart's rope in her fist and start again. Now the cart was heavy with a sack of La Piña flour. The worn iron wheels were caught in a crack in the sidewalk. She looked up at me and her watery old eyes said, "Help me, Jesús." I raised the cart and tried to get it going. But two of the wheels wouldn't turn. It felt like there was sand in the wheels. It was getting late. Doña Filomena didn't say anything. She just watched. Someone came up behind me and put a hand on my shoulder. I jumped.

"Easy, boy. Nobody's going to hurt you." It was one of the drunks who waited with me in the mornings. "Well, tell me, boy. How'd you do? Did you get any ass? Did she give it to you or did she make you pay?" There were people all around. "How was . . ." I dropped the cart and ran.

I didn't know what I was going to tell her. Lots of stories, lots of excuses started in my mind, but none of them took hold. I went into the yard from the alley. I expected her to be waiting for me at the back door with the leather strap. I still didn't have a story. She wasn't at the back door. The Guadalupana was there. I went into the bathroom from the porch as quickly and quietly as I could and locked myself in. She heard me and in seconds was trying the bathroom door.

"I'm in here."

"I know you're in there. Where have you been?" It was barely a whisper. She didn't want them to know.

"What?"

She asked me again.

"What?"

She went back to them. I knew she'd get rid of them. She did and she was back. This time she pulled hard on the door.

"Where have you been!?" She was yelling.

"I have to go bad, 'Amá. I can't talk right now."

"All right, you go. But you're not going to get away with it. I'm going to wait right here. You'd better have a good explanation when you come out. And I don't want to hear about some strange Filipino."

I didn't tell her about a Filipino, but I did tell her about a strange man. "There was this man who I had never seen before, who came this morning in a truck. He wasn't no Filipino and he wasn't no Mexican. He was an Okie. I should have known there was something funny about him from the start. Just the way he looked, and the way he talked, real funny like. I was the youngest one there and I had the littlest experience, but he wanted me."

She was mad but now she was getting confused too. She had always warned me about "those kind of men," but she never wanted to talk about them or even hear of them.

"He said he only needed one man and he picked me. He said he was going to give me a dollar an hour."

She slapped me. "Liar!" She was trembling, but she was confused too. It was her eyes, always her eyes. Now for the first time I didn't look away. I looked down at them and through them to whatever it was that was her. Because it was she that looked away. But not for long. "I don't believe you!"

"I'm not lying, 'Amá. All I can tell you is what happened." And I told her. "I should have known right from the beginning because he was acting strange then. He didn't say nothing. He didn't say where we were going. He just kept driving out further and further into the country." She didn't like it. She got an onion and started chopping it up. Her back was to me now.

"I asked him a lot of times where we were going. I didn't know where we were. I said I was going to jump out if he didn't tell me. He said something about an Armenian. I should have known then because he was getting real nervous. He took his hat off for a minute and I saw how funny his hair was. I should have known then."

"I don't want to hear anymore." She took the onions and went to the sink, went further from me and started rinsing some beans.

"I know you've always told me not to get in cars with strangers, but this was different. This was work and I'm older now and I thought I could handle anything. But this man was . . ."

"How many times do I have to tell you! I don't want to hear it!" She was just mad now. "¡*Pendejo*! You should know nobody's going to pick you for a dollar an hour! Don't you have any sense?"

I should have left it. I should have gone to my room or gone outside or anything. Instead I stayed in the kitchen. I sat at the table with my arms folded while she rinsed the beans. I pressed it. "I'm hungry, 'Amá. I know you don't want to hear it, but I left my lunch in his truck when I jumped out."

She didn't say anything. Not right away. "There's some beans from yesterday on the stove. Finish them. There's some *nopales* in the ice box."

I didn't leave it alone even then. I went over to where she was standing to get a spoon when I could have used the one on the stove.

"What's that smell?" she said.

"What smell?"

"That smell."

"I don't smell anything." At least I hadn't until then. I went to the stove to stir the beans. There was sweat on my forehead. I knew the smell. I stirred the beans just long enough so she wouldn't get suspicious. Then I went to the bathroom. I had just gone, so I couldn't be in there too long. When I pulled down my pants, the smell came roaring up at me. Chole. My dick was red and slimy; my hair was pasted together and there was a white crust on my thing and on my stomach. Chole. I didn't know what to do and there wasn't enough time to do it.

"Jesús!"

"I'm coming, 'Amá."

"You left the fire on the beans and you just went to the toilet a little while ago!"

"I'm coming, 'Amá."

I went back. The smell was worse. I had turned it loose. I served myself the beans and cold *nopales*. I didn't like cold *nopales*, but to warm them I'd have to get a pan and they were next to her.

"Are you going to eat cold *nopales*?"

"I'm real hungry." I sat as far away from her as I could. The smell kept coming up, like rotten steam.

"What's that smell?"

"What smell?"

"Come over here and you'll see. I think maybe something died under the house here. Maybe that mangy old gray cat. Come here. You'll see."

"No, that's okay, I believe you."

She put the fresh pot of beans on the stove and then left the kitchen and went to the altar to say rosary.

I sat there staring at my cold *nopales*. "I love you," she had said. She had said it over and over again. It didn't matter then, but it did now. If anyone knew. If anyone guessed. If anyone found out. I'd die. Ugly, smelly whore.

"Have you heard about Jesús?"

"No."
"Can you imagine what he did with her?"
"He didn't?"
"Yes, he did."
"Is that right?"
"I love you," she said. How dare she. I should have punched her in the mouth. "Don't you ever say that again, bitch! The next time you do, I'll knock your teeth out!" I should have said, "Look, whore, there's no telling your cunt from your face! They're both just as ugly! You're ugly! You have some balls telling me you love me! Do you think I could ever let anything as smelly and ugly as you love me? Your whole body's caked with shit! It's matted in your hair! It's stuffed in your nose! It's dripping from your tits and oozing from your ass! Take a bath, bitch! You stink, whore! How dare you say you love me! I'd die of shame if anyone heard you say that!"
"I love you."
"Stop it, pig."
"I love you."
"Stop it, you filthy, ugly beast! Stop it before I kill you!"
"I love you, m'ijo."
"What's the matter, Jesús?" She was standing in the doorway. "Why are you shaking your head? You've hardly eaten anything and you said you were so hungry."
I didn't answer.
"How long has it been since your last confession, Jesus?"

ooooo

I got a job the next day. I hadn't expected to get one. That morning I was sure I'd wait on the corner for two months and never get one. I was surprised when a Filipino, who called himself Matías, drove up after all the other trucks had gone and said he needed all six of us. He was a small, nervous man who spoke a mixture of Spanish and English and Tagalog. Everyone laughed at the way he talked and the way he moved. I laughed too, but I was afraid of him. I hadn't told him that I had never pruned before. He gave me a pair of shears and pointed to a row of vines like he did with everyone else. I watched the men on either side of me, and then I did what I thought they were doing. When he came back, he started yelling and slapping his hat on his leg, pointing at me and at the vines. He was saying a lot of things, most of which I couldn't understand. The others were laughing. He took the shears and showed me, mad, talking through his teeth and looking back at me after each cut. I knew what he was doing, but I couldn't understand him. He gave me back the shears and I did what I thought he had done. He watched and then left. He came back in a few minutes and watched some more and left again. When he came back the next time, I was far into the row. I heard him screaming long before he got to me. Then I saw him running at me. "Sum um a bitchee! Sum um a bitchee!" I threw the shears and ran. The others laughed. He was too old to catch me. I hitch-hiked home. I knew why I had gotten the job.

I didn't tell her. I just said that one of the contractors had told us to wait, that he might come back later. I thought she was going to ask about Sunday. But she didn't. Maybe nobody had seen me. Or maybe they just hadn't talked to her yet.

I went to bed right after I ate. There was nothing else to do. But I couldn't sleep. Candlelight was flickering at her altar in the front room. It reached me at the back of the house, faint. I watched it throb for a long time. I got up and checked the doors and the windows. Locked. I got back into bed. I still couldn't sleep. I had to either close the door or forget about the light. I didn't want the darkness, but the flickering light had to be what hell was like. Was there really a hell. I didn't worry about there being a heaven. If there wasn't either, then once they put you in the ground that was it. Once the worms started on you, that was it. All that was left was bones, and bones didn't say or feel anything. I couldn't imagine not being alive. Ever since I could remember, that's all I could remember, being alive. I couldn't remember not being or being someplace else or something else. I always was. I was me. It was the only me I knew. Being asleep was the closest thing I could imagine to being dead. Because then, most of the time I didn't know who I was or where I was. If I dreamed, usually I just remembered pieces of dreams, and usually what I remembered was too wild to make any sense. But mostly when I woke, those hours were blank. Sometimes before I fell asleep, I'd tell myself that I was going to try to find out what I did when I was asleep. But when I woke, there was just a big blank. Nothing. Sleeping had to be like being dead. Nothing. Except that you never woke up. People died in their sleep. Sometime, some place, they had to find out. They had to know that they hadn't woken up, that they were dead. A forever of nothing was something I couldn't imagine. Somehow there always had to be a me. I couldn't end, not really. But if there was no heaven or hell, that was it. That couldn't be. But it was. The old men at the Michoacán always talked about it. "You know who died?" Just the other day one of them came back from a funeral. He was still in his good clothes. A man from his town in Mexico had died. He said, "Pepe was there. They brought him all the way from Lemoore so he could see them bury Tomás. We're the only two left now from Jacapo. After the funeral Pepe put his arm around me. He was crying. He said, 'We're all dying, *compa*, and there's nothing we can do except wait.'"

The candles flickered like the flames did in hell, in darkness. Please, don't take me tonight. I thought it over and over again. I know what I did with Chole, but not tonight. I'll never go near her again.

It was stiff the next morning, sticking straight up, just like it always was. She was awake. She was always awake. I could hear her in her room. I thought she'd ask me about Sunday. But she didn't. She didn't say much except that, with our luck, I'd probably go the whole season without being hired. Maybe no one had seen me.

That morning there was a cold wind in the streets. I

had heard it the night before. There wasn't much winter wind in Fresno. When it did blow, it usually brought rain. It would start in the afternoon, chase away the fog, and blow in clouds. Now it came only to make us colder because it was still foggy. It came from every direction. There was no escaping it. No matter what building we hunched against, it reached us. It pushed the winos into a circle. They passed around two bottles of wine instead of one. Other workers asked them for a drink to warm themselves. The yellow truck came and the "steadies" pushed to get on first, to get closest to the cab. After the "steadies" got on, the contractor picked a wino.

The green truck came, and then there were only five of us. We waited. It wasn't six o'clock yet. I never knew who I was waiting for or how long I should wait. I waited because that's how you got experience. I was usually the last one to leave the corner. If some of them stayed after me, it was because they had passed out. That morning one of the winos offered me a drink.

"Here, kid, have some. It's so fucking cold. Come on, have some. You're old enough, aren't you?" He held out the bottle. "How old are you, anyway?"

"Eighteen." Almost true. I'd be eighteen next week.

They left early that morning, just after daybreak. "It's too fucking cold to be out here. Go home, kid. Don't freeze your ass off here. Nobody's gonna come anyway." I didn't want to go home; I didn't want to go home to her. So I waited, propped against the side of the Zacatecas Bar, with my shoulders raised to warm my neck and to keep the wind out. Cars had started passing. Barkeepers had already come, and now storekeepers were coming. I rubbed myself. It felt good. It warmed me up. I thought of Chole, of those big tits and how I had torn them out of her brassiere. Of her big legs . . . I shook her out of my mind. (I'd done enough already I'd have to pay for.) Still, she kept coming back. Then about eight o'clock, I saw her. I saw a car go by first. It was a big fine brown car driven by a Mexican. I had never seen a Mexican in so fine a car. I watched him go down

Tulare Street. She was there, about a block away, waving at the car. Fucking whore. Except that she shook her head, saying no, when he stopped. She walked away from him. The car left and she waved again. She was waving to me. I waved before I thought about it. She motioned for me to come. I got hard, but there were too many people around. I had to stay away from her. There was so much to pay for already. I thought of how badly she stank. No one had ever smelled that bad. I thought of the stains on her mattress. She pissed in bed, probably when she was drunk, and then rolled in it and slept in it all night. I thought of the splotches of worn skin on the inside of her thighs, where every smelly wino who could scrape up fifty cents had rubbed. But I was still hard. I thought of how ugly she was and how greasy she was and how ashamed I'd be if anyone ever found out. I thought of all those things and more, but I was still hard. Finally I looked down the street at her again. She was gone.

I waited until I couldn't take the cold any longer. Then I started home, but down Tulare Street, toward the church instead of toward Chole. I was still hard. I told myself that it would be good to go home the way I used to every day when I served Mass. When I got to her alley, when I got to where I'd have to cross the street to go into her alley, I shook her out of my head again. It didn't do any good. I stopped. But as soon as I stepped into the street, as soon as I took that first step towards her, I heard a loud screeching sound. I looked up and saw a car skidding toward me. I froze. It kept coming, and I couldn't move. And then, just as it reached me, just as it touched me, it stopped. It was the brown car. But the Mexican wasn't driving. Instead there was a black face behind the wheel, laughing. I knew who he was as soon as I saw him. I ran as fast as I could run, away from Chole's alley, away from the brown car. It was two blocks before I looked back. I didn't see him, but I kept running. I wanted to be home. He'd never go near 'Amá, and for sure not near her altar.

I ran into the front yard and around the house. I didn't

see the front door open, not then. The back door was wide
open. The windows were open. Everything was open. The
wind was blowing through the house. Everything was scat-
tered. "'Amá!", I yelled. "'Amá! 'Amá!" Then I saw her on the
floor in front of the altar. She was still twitching. Her
mouth was open and her eyes were blank. That was the way
she was after she had seen Him. But which Him had it been
this time? Or were They one and the same? I looked out the
windows to see if the car was there. I didn't see it, but I
knew I'd be safe at the altar. I took the crucifix off the wall
and sat down with it at the altar, making sure that I had it
in front of me at all times. They said that was one thing
that always worked.

She had told me about the devil years ago. He was all
over Mexico. People saw him there all the time. They usually saw him late at night, and those that saw him either
went crazy or died or, in a few cases, survived but never
sinned again. It was men who usually saw him. They said
he had a small furry stub of a tail, and that his horns were
not really horns but little knobs, like those of baby goats.
And he was a black man, but with white hair and white,
white teeth. I had always been scared of him, and there was
a time when I thought he was everywhere. Now I thought
he came only at death. With Death.

They said that at the time of death, he always showed
up and fought with an angel for your soul. People who had
watched people die said that the dying person always got
caught in the struggle. You could see the dying one start to
struggle, start to sweat, try to wrench himself free from
whatever side of the bed the devil was on. They'd scream,
"Get out of here! Leave me alone!" People had crucifixes
ready then, but if the dying one was in sin, he would never
stop struggling, even when the crucifix was placed on him.
Usually he'd knock it off with his movements. They said
that was the one time God let the devil stand up to the crucifix. But that was to punish the sinner, to begin casting
him from Him. And the devil fought hard, he wanted all he
could get.

Now I held onto the crucifix and sat at the altar under
the Flaming Heart of Jesus and under the picture of the boy
Jesus talking to the wise men in the temple. He'd never
come near me now.

But I was cold. I had been cold all morning. I got a blanket and sat there again, beside the altar. I must have fallen
asleep because I didn't remember being afraid anymore. I
didn't remember much until she said, "What are you doing
with the blanket? I'm the one who's lying on the cold floor."

I jumped up. "I got it for you, 'Amá, but everytime I
tried to put it on you, you'd throw it off. Honest." She was
mad. She was always mad. It was easier not to talk to her,
but I wanted to know. "What happened, 'Amá. Why was
everything all thrown around?"

"You know what happened. Why do you ask such stupid
questions? I saw Him again. I don't know how much more I
can take. It takes more and more out of me each time.

"Here, help me get up. I'm going to go to bed. I have to
rest for work."

That was one of the few days I didn't want her to go to
work. She slept, and I stayed at the altar with the crucifix. I
saw the brown car and the black face again and again, but
each time I looked out the window it wasn't there. The weak
winter afternoon faded. The house darkened. I was still
cold. I couldn't remember if I had closed all the windows.
But I didn't want to leave the altar. I had finished about
five Acts of Contrition. "I confess to Almighty God, to . . ." I
had started hundreds. If I ever meant them, I meant them
now. If they worked, those had to work.

"What time is it, Jesús? Why didn't you wake me? You
know I have to go to work."

I was kneeling when she came into the room.

"You see. It's like I've been telling you. There's something happening in your life that's showing you that you
need Him. Just remember you're going to confess yourself."

I didn't wait until Saturday. I went that night, taking
the crucifix with me, stuffing it into my pants under my
jacket. I left while there were still people on the streets. I

went to St. Sebastian's because there were still people on the streets. I went to St. Sebastian's because there were more lights along the way. I ran as fast as I could, expecting him to jump out at every alley and from behind every parked car, but keeping one hand on the crucifix. Downtown, I was sure he was the man behind me wearing the hat and overcoat to hide his horns and his tail. There was still some wind. I felt like I had been up all day and all night. I hadn't eaten since breakfast. I couldn't eat. I had buried my dinner in the back yard so she wouldn't know. I felt weak, but I kept running. It seemed safer running, like I had more of a chance against him if I was already moving. I got to St. Sebastian's just after six. I had an hour to wait. That was all right. I felt safe. He'd never come into a church. I started more Acts of Contrition with the crucifix in my hands. I said some more. An hour passed and the old priest didn't come. That was all right, I still felt safe. Half-hour later, I began to wonder. I didn't want to go to the rectory and ask for a priest because then they would know when I confessed that it was I, Jesús Olivas, who had fucked Chole, the whore.

"I love you, Jesús."

I shook her out of my head. She came back. I tightened my hold on the crucifix. She wouldn't stay away. So I thought of the slimy red rawness of her cunt. I thought of all the dirty dicks that had gone into that ugliness. All colors, sizes, and shapes. Each leaving what it had to leave. That cunt had to reek. And I was no better than any of them. My dick was going to rot. I thought of the insides of her thighs, darker, a purplish brown, like two big birth marks. It was from all the thousands of men she had held between them. It couldn't come off now, even if she scrubbed. Those breasts. All those years of wanting them, and then to grab them until there was nothing more to grab. They sagged and hung, useless. They hung almost to her navel, ugly.

"I love you, Jesús."

"No! No! No! No! No!"

From the back of the church an old man said, "We're closing up now." I hadn't heard him come in.

"But I thought they had confessions here."

"Not this week. The priests are away. They won't be back 'til Sunday."

I was still in sin and the devil was out there somewhere waiting for me in the dark. "Let me stay a little longer, please."

"I'm sorry, but I have to close up."

"But you don't understand!"

"I'm sorry."

"You're not sorry."

"I'm sorry."

I ran, crucifix in hand. My feet were sore, but I had to run. There was nobody on the streets now. The darker the block, the faster I ran. I ran in the street. It was darker on the sidewalk and easier for him to trap me there. A car came up behind me. It seemed to be slowing down. I jumped up onto the sidewalk. It wouldn't pass me. I looked back, but all I saw was a glare. I ran harder. I ran into a front yard and tried to run around the house. But the sides were fenced. Then everything lit up.

"Halt! This is the police! Get your hands up or we'll shoot!"

It wasn't the police. I knew that. It was him, but maybe he would shoot. The quicker to take my soul back with him. Someone kicked me and pushed me up against the fence.

"I said get your hands up asshole! Get them up! Up! Away from your body! Now up against the fence! Spread eagle!"

He pushed me again. I hit hard on the fence. I saw the gun and the uniform. It wasn't the devil.

"I said spread it, asshole!"

He kicked me again and stood me up against the fence. Then he ran his hands over my body.

"Find anything?" There was one behind me.

"No." He hadn't felt the crucifix. "Where you running to, boy?"

"Home."

"Where's home? . . . I said where's home?"

"On D Street."

"Give me an address."

"1486 D Street."

"You're a long way from home, aren't you, boy? What are you doing over here on this side of town?"

"I was going to church."

He kicked me again. "Don't get funny with me, boy. I asked you what you were doing running through a neighborhood you don't belong in."

"I was going to church, sir."

He hit me in the ribs. "Want to get cute, huh. Okay Where were you running to?

"Home."

"Where were you running from?"

I didn't answer. He didn't want that answer. I didn't want to give him that answer again.

The other one said, "It's not worth the hassle, Mike. We're just gonna be bothering a lot of people out here. Let's take him in. Any I.D. on him?"

"No."

"What's your name, asshole?"

"Jesus."

He hit me again. "He's really a wise ass. You're right though. Let's haul his ass down . . ." Then he felt the crucifix, and pulled it out. "What the fuck is this? . . . Oh, my God, we got a weirdo. Maybe he did go to church . . ."

They let me go. But when I got home I couldn't sleep for fear of losing grip of the crucifix. I was awake when she came home, and then the next thing I knew she was saying, "Get up, Jesús. It's time."

I was so tired I thought I could fall asleep leaning against the Zacatecas Bar. Still, I had a hard-on. I had promised myself that I wouldn't look down Tulare Street toward her house anymore, dark or not dark. And I didn't. I faced the other way. Nothing could make me look over to where I had seen her the day before. I had learned my les-

RONALD L. RUIZ

son. The two trucks came and went, and then there were
just four winos and myself. They were already drunk and I
didn't think they'd stay long. I was going to leave when they
left. I didn't want any brown cars pulling up when I was
alone. Then, not long after it was light, one of the winos saw
her. "Goddamn. Things must be pretty bad all over. Look at
old Chole waving at us. She's got to know we don't have no
more than twenty-five cents between us." I looked. She was
closer than she had been yesterday and she was waving.

"Ever fuck her, Joe?"

"Name me one guy in Chinatown who hasn't. I used to
fuck her almost every Saturday and Sunday. But her hole is
so big and smelly now you're better off with your hand. And
that's free."

They laughed. They were all sitting on the cold cement
now, getting drunker.

"Fuck, look at the goddamned old whore. She won't go
away. She keeps waving."

"Why the fuck don't she come over here and ask us if we
got any money?"

I didn't look.

She must have left because they didn't mention her
anymore. They stayed a long time that morning. The longer
they stayed, the drunker they got. And the drunker they
got, the meaner they got. They argued over the bottle. They
grabbed it away from each other. They punched for it. And
then one hit another over the head with the bottle and there
was blood all over the sidewalk. When they heard the siren,
some of them tried to leave, but couldn't get up. When I
heard the sirens, I ran home.

"'Amá,' I don't feel so good."

"Is that what you told the contractor when he asked you
if you wanted to go to work?"

"No, he never asked me."

She looked at me. "Go to bed if you're sick."

I did and I dreamed of Chole. I was washing the dishes,
looking out the window over the sink into the back yard.
'Amá was moving around behind me in the kitchen, doing

something. Chole walked into the back yard. She wore high
heels and one of her short dresses with her big tits hanging
out of the top. It was freezing outside. She saw me at the
window and waved just like she had that morning and the
morning before. She had a big smile on her face. I was
afraid 'Amá would see her, but I couldn't say anything or
motion because then 'Amá would see her for sure. She kept
smiling and waving and walking toward the window. When
she was a few feet from the window, she stopped and turned
and bent over and flipped up her dress. She was naked
underneath, and the red meat of her cunt swelled up at me
from between her big brown legs. She inched her way backwards toward me, and her great big red pussy got bigger
and bigger. Then the cunt left her and came floating
towards me. As it got to the window, I could hear and feel
the sucking sound its big red hairy lips were making. That
whole side of the house seemed to buckle. The window flew
out of the wall and disappeared into that cunt in one fast
slurp. 'Amá hadn't noticed. But now that red, raw hole was
sucking at me. I planted my feet and held onto the sink.
The upper part of my body was being sucked through the
window. I used all of my strength to keep from being sucked
in. Then the sink started to give. I could feel it coming out
of the wall. When it gave, I dove backward, out of the suc-
tion and lay quivering and exhausted.

The bed was all wet. I was all wet. There was jizz all
over everything. I knew it was a dream, but I dreamed of
her again anyway, except that this time I dreamed only of
her cunt. It hung over me, a slab of meat, floating in the air,
red and raw, its fat lips rubbing and wetting each other. It
hung no more than six inches above my head and a foot in
front of me, so that it was always there unless I kept my
eyes down. Even then, it cast a shadow down the middle of
my forehead, covering half of each eye. The outer halves of
each eye were in the sunlight or moonlight or whatever
light there was. It went everywhere I went. It followed my
every move.

At first I tried to ditch the cunt. I turned, I ran, I

jumped. But even as I moved, the cunt was there, moist and waiting. I swung at it, I took swipes at it. But each time, it was too fast for me. It jumped just out of my reach, and then it would settle back down again to half-cover my eyes in its shadow. I screamed and covered my eyes with my hands. I was standing in the middle of a street, and with my eyes covered, turned round and round, hoping that it was just a nightmare and that when I stopped turning, when I woke up, it would be gone. But when I uncovered my eyes, I saw where I was. I was right in the spot where the brown car had almost hit me, and I could hear it coming. I ran, but her cunt stayed in front of me so that I could see it all the time. I ran through fields back into town and up the fire escape. It was on the fire escape too. I tried to trick it on the roof, running across the roof at a zigzag and then jumping into the shelter and slamming the door shut. It was dark in there, and I heard it before I saw it. I heard the slurping, sucking sound, and then I felt the soft wetness of its lips brush my nose. I screamed and ran through the alleys and along the tracks, through the school halls and down the hill. But it stayed with me. Finally, I knew where I'd be safe, free from that hairy monster. I ran as fast as I could. It was less than a block away. I ran up the stairs into the church. I was right: it didn't follow me there. I sighed. Padre Galván was waiting for me. He was saying Mass and standing at the altar railing with the Communion chalice in his hands. He was waiting to give me Holy Communion. 'Amá was there. I wiped the sweat from my face and tucked in my shirt. Then I blessed myself with holy water and walked slowly, with my hands folded together and my head bowed, down the aisle. I was saying Acts of Contrition just to be sure. I knelt at the railing and he said the holy words and blessed me. I stuck out my tongue and raised my head to take the Host. For some reason, I opened my eyes and saw what he had in his hand, what he was about to give me. That big, red, raw piece of meat. I screamed.

There was another dream. This time I was living in her cunt. Everything in there was soft and warm and safe. And whenever I got hungry, whenever I so much as thought of food, one of her tits would plop through those lips into my mouth and fill me with chocolate milk shakes.

"Wake up, Jesús, it's time."

CHAPTER TEN

That was the longest I had ever slept, but it wasn't until I was leaning against the Zacatecas Bar that I remembered my bed. It was too late then. It was full of jizz. She had probably seen it. I didn't care. The yellow truck came first and then the green truck. That morning the winos left right after the green truck. One of them had stolen a case of wine and had hidden it in an abandoned house. I didn't know how long I'd wait. I didn't want to go home to her and the sheets, but I didn't want to be around for any brown cars either.

"Happy birthday, Jesús."

She was standing beside me. She had snuck up on me. My breath got heavy and I got hard. "Come see what I got for you at my house." I went with her. I didn't wait or think about it. There were cars on the street and some people on the sidewalk, but I went anyway. Someone would see me and tell 'Amá. Our thighs rubbed. It didn't matter if they told. Not then. When we were a block from the church, I wondered if it was one of those days when 'Amá stayed late in church. I must have slowed or stiffened because she said, "Don't worry, *m'ijo,* I saw her go home at least fifteen minutes before I went to get you."

"There you go with that big mouth of yours!"

"Don't be mad, *m'ijo*. I didn't mean anything by it."

"I don't care what you meant! You don't know what I'm thinking. How do you know what I'm thinking?"

"You're right, *m'ijo*. I'm sorry. Don't be mad. Wait 'til you see what I got you for your birthday."

I was mad. She shouldn't have said that. I wouldn't talk to her. We walked in silence for the rest of the block and through the alley. When we got to her yard, she said, "Please, *m'ijo*, don't spoil today. It's your birthday. Let's enjoy it. There are so few things to enjoy."

We stepped from the cold into packed dry heat. A small gas heater was hissing in the corner, giving off the only light in the shack. The stink was the same, but I didn't remember the heat. "Do you like it, *m'ijo*?" she said, pointing to the table. On the table was the biggest chocolate cake I had ever seen. It had eighteen yellow candles and yellow writing that said, "Happy Birthday, Jesús." Next to it was a big box wrapped in gold paper with red ribbon. "You like it, *m'ijo*. I can tell by your face." She reached for a mirror behind a stack of clothes. As she bent over, the short dress tightened and slipped up almost up to her ass. Her upper thighs told me how big her ass was. I saw the bottom of one of her cheeks, where it broke and sagged from her leg. She had to be naked under that tiny piece of a dress.

"Look at your face in the mirror, *m'ijo*, and tell me you don't like it."

I shoved the mirror aside and grabbed her. The mirror fell and broke.

"Oh, *m'ijo*, not now. You can have it after. You can have all you want after. Let's light the candles and you blow them out and then open your present and we'll eat some cake. Please."

I yanked at the front of her dress. "No, *m'ijo*, you're tearing it. Don't do that, please. It's my best dress. I wore it just for you." I ripped the dress away from her and pushed her back onto the bed. Then I was in her, digging and pounding as deep and as hard as I could. "You're hurting me, *m'ijo*. Wait a minute, please, *m'ijo*. You're hurting me."

I dug deeper. I wanted it all. Every corner and crease. But I kept slipping past it all. Then I stiffened. And then I had none of it.

I lay on her and in her. Gently she ran her fingers through my hair. "Do you feel better, *m'ijo?*" I felt worse. I wanted to cry. I put my face on her shoulder so that she couldn't see it. I was afraid. I felt empty, hollow. If I had gotten up, I think I would have crumpled over. I couldn't get enough air. I took bigger breaths; longer, deeper breaths.

"What's the matter, *m'ijo?*"

I couldn't coat the rawness inside of me. "Nothing." I seemed to be breathing fear instead of air, and that made it rawer. I didn't dare get out of her arms. I didn't dare leave her softness.

"You feel better now, *m'ijo?*"

I nodded yes.

"Good."

Spit was drooling out of my mouth. It was smeared all over my face and her shoulder. I couldn't stop it. Not even that.

"Get up for a second, *m'ijo.* No, don't get off me, just hold yourself up for a second. Don't get off me." I couldn't have gotten off of her, not then. "Good. That's it. I think it was your belt buckle in my leg . . . There, that's better. I got it . . . Oh, I'm bleeding. No. No. It's nothing. It's okay Stay on me. It'll stop. It's only a small cut. Let me have the closeness."

She put her arms around me again. "Oh, I like this." I looked at her. She had her eyes closed. I didn't know if she was falling asleep. I didn't want her to go to sleep. I didn't want to be alone. Not then. "Chole, don't go to sleep."

"I'm not, *m'ijo.* I'm just liking this."

She fingered my ear. The emptiness wouldn't go away. It got worse. It ached. I felt as if I were turned inside out and that all of me was down there in the deepest part of me, where the ache was. I held onto her. I expected to slip out of her legs, run down her legs and onto the floor like water. She rubbed my back. I thought of 'Amá. She was wondering where I was. I shook her out of my mind.

"What's the matter, *m'ijo*?"

"Nothing."

"Is my hand bothering you?"

"No."

I thought of Padre Galván and confession. I got rid of him, too, but without shaking my head. Her hand was moving slowly, smoothly down my back. As it got near my ass, I shivered and got hard inside of her. I did it again. Hard, searching, looking everywhere inside her cunt for someplace to hide or something to hang onto. It took longer that time. But after, the fall was further, deeper, tumbling over and over through the empty space of myself. I landed hard, in darkness, in a place that was mine alone.

I must have slept, because when she said "*M'ijo*, let's have some cake," I felt the pain gush back into my mouth. It had been gone. "Yeah, let's have some cake."

She got up first. I watched her walk across the room naked. "I'll get some dishes and forks." I had never looked at her as I did then. I saw the flesh of her thighs shake with every movement. Her ass sagged down into folds of fat that flopped as she walked. "I don't have any clean dishes, *m'ijo*. I'll have to wash some. It'll just take a minute." Her stomach stuck out further than her ass. There was a roll of fat at her hips. The crack of her ass was stained dark with years of shit that she had never wiped or washed. But the thighs, the thighs that had always looked so good under a dress were full of big pock-like marks that shook and changed shape with each step, each movement. For that, I kept telling myself, I'm going through all of this.

She couldn't find another plate. She broke one trying to get it out from under all the other dishes and pans and cans and garbage that were piled in a dried-up sink. She broke another dish, dropping it when a rat jumped out of the sink. I sat next to the chocolate cake, running my finger along the edges. It was good. I was trying not to look at her anymore, especially not at her thighs. I was trying not to hate her. The cake was big, and the box was huge. No one had ever done anything like that for me. She kept telling me how sorry she was for everything. She loved me. I knew that. I heard it every time she said she was sorry. But that just made it worse.

"Aren't you going to put on any clothes?" I said when she sat down across from me. Her tits had to be touching her thighs.

"The way you keep tearing off my clothes, I didn't think you liked me in clothes. Besides, it's hot in here." It didn't matter . . . It did matter. But I didn't know how to say it.

"Does it bother you?"

"No."

"If it bothers you, I'll put on some clothes."

"No, that's okay. It doesn't bother me."

"Good. I guess I don't like to wear clothes. In my work I don't know if that's good or bad. But let's celebrate. It's your birthday. Happy birthday, Jesús. It's so good to have you here. Oh, I forgot a match to light the candle. And I want a drink, too. Do you mind if I have some whiskey, *m'ijo*? I don't know why, but I've always thought you don't drink. Do you?"

"Sure I drink." She heard the edge in my voice.

"I didn't mean anything by it, *m'ijo*. It's just that I know your grandma doesn't drink, and you're just eighteen and . . ."

"There you go with your big mouth again."

"Don't get mad, *m'ijo*, don't get mad. I'll just get two glasses and that'll be it."

I had tasted the winos' wine and didn't like it, but that was all.

"This is all I have. It's not the best whiskey, but it'll warm you up. I take mine straight. That way you can taste it. How about you, *m'ijo*?"

"Sure."

"It's going to have to be straight, *m'ijo*, because I don't have anything to mix it with."

"Okay."

She poured them.

"Here's to you. Happy birthday, Jesús."

She gulped hers down in one swallow. I still had mine in my hand when she looked at me. I gulped mine down too. It burned. It was awful. I coughed. She laughed and laughed.

"Shut up, bitch! Stop laughing at me! Stop it!"

"I'm sorry, *m'ijo*. I didn't mean anything. It's just that it was so funny when . . ." She laughed again.

Every part of me tightened. I threw the glass as hard and as straight as I could. I heard the cry first, a wild cry. She grabbed her forehead and fell to the ground. I saw the blood on the edges of her hands. I was scared.

"Chole! Chole! What's the matter, Chole!"

She wouldn't stop making that sound. Someone would hear. "Chole! Stop it! They'll call the cops!" She stopped. She lay still with her hands over her forehead. I knew she wasn't dead, but . . .

"Chole, are you okay?"

"I'm all right. But get me a rag, please."

I got her a rag.

"Wet it."

I did.

"Are you all right, Chole?"

"Yes. It'll stop bleeding in awhile . . . Oh, *m'ijo*, you gave me my dress for a rag. It was my best one, the one you tore. I thought I could fix it, but not now."

"I'm sorry, Chole." I was sorry. I had no place else to go. "I'm sorry for everything."

"But why did you do it, *m'ijo*?"

"You were laughing at me. I can't stand for people to laugh at me. All my life people have been laughing at me."

"But I wasn't laughing at you, *m'ijo*. I love you. The whole thing was funny, but I wasn't laughing at you. It was just that you were choking on the whiskey. I don't mind that. That's probably good. I don't care if you can't drink. It doesn't make you any less to me." She held the piece of dress to her forehead.

"But I can drink." There was something stuck in my

throat then. "Come on, let's have another one. I'll show you."

"No, *m'ijo*, that's okay. We don't have to drink."

We drank.

I woke to the hiss of the little gas heater. I was naked, but it was hot in there. It was awhile before I knew where I was. My head hurt and my throat and mouth were dry. I had forgotten about Chole until I moved and felt her next to me. She was lying on her back, naked, staring straight up and crying.

"What's the matter, Chole." She had something sticky in her hair, and her face was dirty. "What's the matter, Chole?" She didn't answer. I asked again.

"You really don't know?"

"No. What's the matter?" She cried harder. "What's the matter?"

"You're not lying? You really don't know?"

"No, honest. I swear by Jesus."

"*M'ijo*, you got crazy. You threw the cake at me and tore up the suit I bought you. You kept calling me a filthy whore and kept telling me how ugly I was and how you hated yourself for being here. But you wouldn't go. You took the box and hit me with it. You kept saying that I was trying to buy you the way everybody buys me. I told you that wasn't true, that I loved you. That got you madder, and you hit me. You weren't for sale you said. You hit me and said you knew where the money was coming from. Blood money you called it. And then you hit me again, and the box came open and you took the suit and laughed at it and said what was I trying to do, make you my pimp, dress you up the way I dressed your pimp father. I didn't answer, and that got you madder, and this time you hit me with your fist and tore up the suit. You ripped it into pieces, and when you couldn't get it any smaller, you took a razor blade and cut it into still smaller pieces. I cried and told you not to, and when I wouldn't stop crying, you jumped over the table and pushed my face into the cake. You kept pushing and twisting on the back of my head until I think all of my head was in the cake. I was choking, but somehow I got my head out of the cake. I tried to get away from you, but I fell instead and you came at me with the cake and said, 'Here's your fucking Happy Birthday!' Then you smashed the cake on my head. You kept telling me to shut up, and when I wouldn't, you got the knife and I shut up. I just sat there. I was afraid to move or cry. Your father had done crazy things like that to me, but I don't think I was ever really afraid that he would kill me. I was with you. But then you started to cry. You got down on your hands and knees and cried and cried and cried and begged me to forgive you because you said I was all you had in the world."

"I didn't say that."

She didn't answer, and I didn't press it. She would have said anything I wanted her to say. We lay there for a long time. Then I said, "What time is it?"

"It must be close to four," she said.

"How can it be? It was way past four even before the cake."

"No, *m'ijo*, this is Friday."

"Friday?"

There was no going back now, ever. I could smell the chocolate on the bed. Her hair was matted with frosting. There were yellow streaks in it. She was ugly.

"Can I have another drink?" I wanted to forget again, everything.

"Oh, no, *m'ijo*. We can't start that again. I've got to go to work tonight. I'm flat broke."

I felt a stab, pain. "Chole, don't go! Please don't go, Chole!" I said it before I could stop it. But I couldn't have stopped it. "Please don't go, Chole."

"But, *m'ijo*, I'm broke. This is the slowest time of the year. I'm down to my last dollar."

"Wait 'til tomorrow, Chole. We don't need anything to-

day. Stay with me, Chole." I was holding onto her arm. "I'm
sorry for last night. I'll never do anything like that again to
you. I swear." She was watching me carefully. She wasn't
sure. She wanted to believe me.

"You really want me to stay tonight, *m'ijo*?"

"Yes, Chole."

"Then I'll stay."

She kissed me and put her leg over me so that her cunt
was pressed against my thigh. I went into her again. This
time she moved. She took hold of me with her thighs and
thrust and danced hard around me. I couldn't move. She
gasped and clutched.

"You need me, *m'ijo*, don't you? Tell me you need me."
Each time she said it, she moved harder. I came.

"Oh, no, *m'ijo*, no, no. I was so close. If you could have
just waited another minute. I want so bad to come by you. I
love you."

I fell further, way down. There was no going back, but I
didn't know where to go from there. I reached for Chole. I
touched her matted hair and felt the chocolate frosting
become powder in my fingers. There were tears on her
cheeks.

"What are you crying about, Chole?"

"I'm crying because I'm so happy, *m'ijo*. All my life I've
wanted to be needed. I've wanted some *one* to need me, to
make me feel worth something."

I thought she was crazy. She didn't have me and I didn't
need her. It was just that there was no place else to go. Not
then.

"Let's have a drink."

"No, *m'ijo*. You got crazy the last time we did, remember? I don't want that to happen again."

"I won't get crazy this time. It won't happen again. I've
already promised you that, haven't I?"

"But you haven't eaten anything."

"Neither have you."

"Yeah, but I drink all the time. Lots of times I drink
rather than eat."

"I want a drink."

"No, *m'ijo*."

"Look, we'll just have one. Nothing will happen."

"You'll get crazy, *m'ijo*."

"Not on one. You hold the bottle."

We drank, sitting across from each other at the table, naked. I didn't cough this time and it made me feel good. It took away the fear. Then we were laughing. Everything was funny. Until after one long hard laugh, I said, "How could anybody in their right mind pay good money to fuck somebody as ugly as you." She didn't laugh.

"I guess you don't think that's very funny, do you, bitch? I guess you know I wasn't joking, don't you, bitch? You'd better laugh. I'll give you three to laugh. One . . ." I hit her on two, as hard as I could. She screamed and doubled over. I kept hitting her, on her neck, on her head, on her back, wherever I could. "You were going to leave me, bitch, weren't you? You filthy, ugly whore you! You were going to leave me, weren't you!" I beat her and kicked her even after she was on the floor. I stopped only after she stopped moving and crying. Then I got some rags and tied her hands and feet as she lay on the floor. I remembered all that.

It was freezing outside, and it was dark, and I was naked. I stumbled around out there for a long time until I found them by feeling along the side of the house on my hands and knees. Then I took them inside. I threw cold water on her.

"Get up, bitch! I know you're faking it. You're not fooling me."

"No more, *m'ijo*, please. I can't get up, you got my hands and feet tied."

I remembered that, too.

I pulled her up to her knees. But before I cut her wrists loose, I told her what the rocks were for and made her kneel on two of them with her feet tied. As long as her feet were tied, she couldn't go any place. I put a rock in each of her raised hands. Then I got my belt from my pants and came back and sat at the table right next to where she was kneeling. I remembered that, too.

"Now as long as you keep those rocks raised just over your ears, there won't be no problems. I'm real tired. You've worn me out with all your shit. Now I'm going to close my eyes and try to take a nap. But I might not be able to sleep. The trouble is that you won't know when I'm sleeping or not. I'll be checking on you from time to time. If I open my eyes and you don't have those rocks above your ears, then you're going to have this belt on your ass. The trouble with you, Chole, is that nobody's ever made you pay for your sins. All you sinners just turn your back on God, while the rest of us are steady praying for our sins and yours, too. I can tell you, Chole, my friend. It's time you start doing a little praying, and I'm here to make sure that you do." I remembered that, too.

"And cut all that crying shit out, too. I'm going to give you 'til three, but it might only be two or maybe even one, to cut it out. Then you're going to get this belt across your mouth." I remembered that, too, and I remembered hitting her once with the belt. But that's all I remembered.

Then there was blood all around her legs. Her feet were still tied and she was lying on the floor. She screamed when she saw me move.

"Leave me alone, *m'ijo*, please. Please go!"

"I ain't going and you're not going either. And you better shut up before someone hears you and I have to beat your mouth shut."

"No more, *m'ijo*, please no more. I love you, don't you understand? Don't hurt me no more. And if you don't want to go, let me go. You can stay here. I won't tell anybody. Honest."

"Oh, you want to leave me again, huh, bitch! You want to run out on me just when I need you! I'll show you!"

"No more, *m'ijo*, please! Look what you did to my legs. You were crazy again. You said they were ugly and you cut them. You took that razor blade and said you were going to make them even and pretty, so you wouldn't be ashamed of me. You'll always be ashamed of me, *m'ijo*. You'll always be ashamed of yourself, *m'ijo*."

"Shut up, whore!"

I hit her across the mouth, and then I dragged her to the bed and tied her to the bed. I spread her arms and her legs out, and I tied each one to a post. I don't know how long I kept her tied there. All I know is that I made her shit and piss there, and I fucked her there too while she was spread out. I kept her there until they came. Until I heard them pounding on the door. I cut her loose before they kicked the door in. It was only 'Amá and Padre Galván. When they saw the two of us naked, they began yelling at her and beating on her. I ran. Through the alleys and around the back of 'Amá's house to get some clothes. And then I began the wait.

CHAPTER ELEVEN

It was in the middle of nowhere and it didn't look like a prison. The first thing I saw was lawn, lots of it. Then there were white houses and then the long, long, yellow building that seemed to stretch for a mile, three stories high. But there was no wall. Instead, there was a high chain-link fence with barbed wire on top, but no wall. Prisons were supposed to have walls. When we got to the gate, one of the deputies got out of the car and waved up to a tower. The shadow of a man with a cap and a rifle appeared and nodded. Then I heard the loud click of the gate. Slowly the gate slid open. It was a prison.

We drove along the building. I saw the bars on the windows. Soon I'd be behind one of those windows. We rounded the building. On the other side, we drove down a ramp and stopped beside a steel door. The upper part of the door had a thick square of glass. The deputy got out again and spoke into a box. "Fresno County Sheriff's Department. We brought you another one." There was another loud click, and that door slid open, showing the bars of a large cell. The deputy opened the car door. "Okay, Olivas. Out." It was hard getting out of the car. They had put two sets of chains on me.

As soon as we were past the steel door, it shut behind

us. In front of us was another cell, the same size as the one in which we were standing. Beyond that cell was a guard station. Once the steel door clanged shut, there was another click, and someone said, "Slide that one open by hand . . . Okay, now close it. This door won't open until that one's closed."

Then the voice recognized one of the deputies. "Hey, Fred. Fred Rodgers. Christ, I haven't seen you in a hell of a long time. Where in the hell have you been? Como ou lii here. Shoot, I didn't even recognize you. You put on some weight, didn't you? What the hell brings you here?"

"Hi, Bill. Just thought I'd bring you another one, seeing how they tell me you're running short."

"Short my ass. Jesus, it's good to see you. But why the hell couldn't you put this little twerp on the bus? The way you got him chained up, you'd think you were bringing us Pancho Villa himself."

He was a red-faced fat man standing behind a counter. His voice sounded more like that of a black man than it did of an Okie or a Texan, which I thought he was. He had sergeant's stripes on the sleeve of his khaki uniform.

"I suppose we could have put him on the bus except that this little fellow is kind of peculiar. He acts up in some strange ways, and the captain didn't think it was worth the savings to put him on the bus because sometimes he gets plain crazy."

"Shoot, we'll take care of that. We get a lot of them that think they're crazy or are just acting crazy. Once we get a hold of them they get real normal real fast. But don't worry about him anymore; he's our problem now. Stay and visit awhile. Stay and have dinner with us before you go. You got a long drive back."

It was a big concrete room that funneled into a hall at the far end. Along one wall was a varnished yellow counter. Along the other wall were doors to rooms or cells that had glass from about waist up. We were the only ones in the big room. I could see two black prisoners bending over something inside the glass-covered room that was further away.

"Good idea. Bill, I'd like you to meet Jim Spencer. He's a
new man in the Department. Jim, this is an old friend of
mine and a hell of a guy, Bill Tucker."

"Pleased to meet you, I'm sure. Where'd you say you
were from, Jim?"

"Indiana."

"How long you been in California?"

"Since the war, like everybody else. I was stationed out
here when it ended, and I liked it so well that I stayed.
Knocked around for awhile. Then I was lucky enough to
land this job. Don't think I'll ever go back to Indiana. Too
damned cold in the winter and too damned hot and muggy
in the summer."

The sergeant was bald. His forehead went back to the
top of his head. I didn't like him.

"Hear him, Bill? Like I been telling you for years now.
It's a damned good job. Make the move. Join us. What they
pay you here ain't worth it. The shit you have to put up
with from these characters just ain't worth it. This isn't
police work. You're just a paid baby-sitter. Trouble is, the
pay's bad and the babies are as mean and as vicious and
dangerous as you're going to find."

"I know. Besides that, we can't get anybody worth anything to work here. Not that I blame them. Not for what
they pay here."

"It ain't too late, Bill. I know you could make the transfer."

"Well, I'll tell you. Sometimes it wouldn't take much.
But I best get them niggers out here so we can start pro-
cessing this boy, and I can get you fellows something to eat
and we can relax and talk."

He looked at my papers. "Let's see here. Oh, we got a
violent little man here, don't we? Mayhem. Assault with
intent to commit murder. Assault with a deadly weapon. A
barn-burner, too. Arson. We don't get too many of those.
Well, just looking at you, I would have never thought that."
He looked at me. "Small and skinny as you are, I would
have said you were another typical-type burglar. But no, I
guess you want to be bad. Well, I'm sure we can accommo-

date you. We got a lot of people here who think they're bad, or at least thought they were bad. Where are those god-damned niggers . . . I realize you fellows don't have that much going on in Fresno, but why all these chains? He's such a little twerp. Hell, either one of you could sit on him and damn near kill him."

Two blacks in prison blue came into the room. I looked over at the glassed room. They were the same two. The big-ger one had shaved his head completely. He said, "You buzzing us, sergeant?"

"You goddamned right I'm buzzing your asses!" He sounded more black than the blacks. "We got a new one to process here. But be careful. This little fellow thinks he's a bad ass. Shoot, I bet either one of you could handle him with both arms tied behind your backs. Don't take any shit from him. Kick his ass if he so much as looks at you cross-eyed. Now, if these good deputies would be so kind as to unlock all those padlocks on those chains."

"Oh, I'll take care of him all right, sergeant. Don't you be worrying about that. Fact is that we just need but one of us. Roy, why don't you go back and finish that floor while I take care of this here youngster?"

The deputies took off my chains, and the black put his hand on my shoulder. "Over this way, boy." He took me to the end of the counter. "Strip," he said. My stomach dropped. I tightened. "I said strip." I stripped. "Now bend over. Come on, bend. I got to look at your asshole." I bent over. "I said *bend*, motherfucker!" He grabbed my back and in one motion had the top of my head on the floor. The sergeant and the deputies laughed.

"What'd I tell you, fellows? That little runt isn't kind going to be any problem here."

"Now spread your legs, boy. I mean spread them. I got to see up that hole." I felt his hand on my leg. I spread them as far as I could. I didn't want his hand anywhere else on my body. My finger tips were on the floor. I was tight and scared.

"What's the matter with you, boy!? Open that ass! I ain't

gonna hurt you. Least ways not here. I said open."

My body was tight. I couldn't have moved a muscle. He slapped me on the ass and I shit all over the place. He yelled and kicked me, slamming me into the wall. "You rotten son of a bitch! You dirty son of a bitch! You went and shit on me!" The deputies roared. He kicked me again. "You dirty son of a bitch! Get up and clean that fucking mess!" He didn't wait. He yanked me up. He picked me up and threw me into my shit. "There! How you like that! Clean it, asshole, clean it!" The deputies were still roaring. He threw me some rags. "Clean it all!"

When I cleaned it, he picked me up again and dragged me over to the wall again and had me bend over again. "Look, sucker, I got to look up that asshole of yours. That's part of my job. But I ain't gonna fuck around with you no more. You pull something like that on me again and I'm gonna give you a whipping you ain't ever gonna forget." He grabbed each of my cheeks and pushed down on my legs. I was shaking all over. I tried to stop shaking, but I couldn't.

"What is the matter with you, boy? You sure are afraid Otis is gonna fuck you, aren't you? Well I would, but the sergeant's here. Now let me see that stinking ass of yours . . . Oh, my God, what a mess. Don't you people believe in baths where you come from? You probably never heard the word 'bath.' Now I know why they call you people greasers. That is the *dirtiest* asshole I have ever seen! Whew! What a man does around here to be a trustee . . . But I'll tell you, that is one small, tight hole. Somebody's gonna have a ball tonight."

I was still shaking. "Hold still, goddamn it." I shook all the more. They laughed. He pushed down on me harder.

"Tell you what, sergeant. Put him in with me tonight and I guarantee he'll be behaving in the morning."

"I can't do that, Otis. You know that. Shoot, if I did that, I'd have a race riot on my hands in five minutes. No, he goes in F wing with all the other greasers."

"But don't nobody need to know, sergeant."

"Shoot, tell me one thing that happens around here that

the whole goddamn prison doesn't know about in five minutes. Imagine me putting this little greaser in with all you niggers and nobody knowing. Shoot. If I did that I'd have all you niggers and greasers killing each other off before morning."

"So what's wrong with that, Bill?" one of the deputies said. "The taxpayers would love it." They laughed.

"Trouble is, if the niggers and greasers killed each other off there'd be nobody left here and I'd be out of a job. Then I really would have to go to Fresno." They laughed some more.

I was still bent over, afraid to to take any other position.

"Hey, Otis, I think he likes it. Look at him still bent over like that. No, I think he likes you. Why don't you look up his ass again? Why don't you give him a little goosing? Look at him, he's just waiting."

He spread my cheeks again, hard. But this time I felt something and I screamed and broke loose. He chased me and caught me and beat on me.

"Didn't I tell you he was a crazy bastard, Bill?"

"Yeah, but we'll take it right out of him. Otis, shower him and give him his blues and blankets, and then have Williamson take him to F wing. Tell Williamson to tell Brown that I want him housed with AH-NEE-MAHL, as the greasers call him. Animal will take damned good care of him. No, get Williamson down here so I can tell him myself. That way there won't be any fuck-ups, or at least no excuses."

"Why don't you let me have him for the night, sergeant?"

"Cut the shit out. I told you what to do. Now do it."

🕯🕯🕯🕯🕯

Animal. The word went back and forth in my mind. Animal. Not a person or even a thing. A word. Animal. And then it went a little further. Housed with Animal. He wasn't doing me any favors. His voice said that much. Animal. The

RONALD L. RUIZ

black man was pushing me through the door of one of the glassed rooms. "Get in there and shower. You are one filthy mess." Animal. I turned on the water. My mind was trying to tie that name to something: man, beast, dog, what? And then I saw the black man looking at my ass. He grinned and I looked away and got into the middle of the shower, as if the water would stop him. "What's the matter, boy? Don't you like Otis? Otis likes you." He was watching the sergeant and the deputies, too; he was waiting for his chance. Then he lunged and grabbed my ass and I jumped away. He grabbed again, and I jumped out of the shower, and he fell into the shower. "You dirty cocksucker! You dirty little son of a bitch!" He got up and stalked me, keeping the door behind him. "Come here, you son of a bitch!" The room was just big enough that he'd have to leave the door to get me, that he couldn't move more than a few steps from it without leaving it. "If it takes me all day, I'm gonna get you, you little cocksucker!" I watched him. My breath was stuck in my throat, but every part of me was ready to spring for the door.

Then the door banged open and the sergeant was standing there. "God-damn it, Otis! Can't you leave that boy alone!? Are you that fucking hard-up? I'm out there waiting to take my friends to dinner, and you're in here trying to corn-hole this sorry little bastard. Get the fuck out of here and go get Williamson! . . . Where's the lice solution? God-damn it, you're so fucking hard-up you didn't bring the lice solution!"

The black man turned and threw a small bottle at me. It hit me and fell to the floor.

"Wash your hair out with that. Use all of it," the sergeant said.

I watched him, watched the sergeant chew Otis out in the big room as I showered. I watched him even when the white stuff burned my eyes. I saw him start back towards me, and I tightened. I was ready to jump out of the shower. But when he opened the door this time, he just threw down clothes and a towel. "I'll get you yet, cocksucker." I watched him leave the big room, leave the sergeant and the deputies, and I turned off the shower, relieved. But as I dried myself, the thought of Animal came back. A man, a gorilla, a freak. I didn't know. A man would just punk me, but what about the others? I put on the denim pants and shirt and the new brown shoes. Animal was with my every movement. Housed with Animal. Animal. I wanted to cry, die. "Move it, asshole! The sergeant's getting pissed!" The black man was there again, with the door open, waiting. But the sergeant was watching.

There was another guard, a giant, in the big room. "This is him. Be sure that Brown puts him in with Animal tonight. I don't care who's in there with Animal, tell Brown I said to move him and put this guy in there instead. This little man thinks he's a bad ass. We'll see how bad he feels tomorrow morning. In fact, I want you to check later tonight to make sure that he's actually in there with Animal."

"Sure, sarge."

🕯️🕯️🕯️🕯️🕯️

He took me down the hall—Animal—and up some stairs. He was taking me to Animal. He walked at my side, just a shade behind me. He was making sure I got to Animal. Those were his orders. If I ran, I'd have to run forward, and I didn't know where that would take me. Maybe to Animal. The pictures of the Ape Man who came with the carnival for two years in a row kept coming back to me. I never saw the Ape Man; I never had the money. But I did stare at the two big painted pictures on either side of the trailer. "More man than ape! More ape than man!" the ticket seller kept saying. And I did hear the roar from within the trailer every few seconds. At the top of the stairs, was another steel door. This was it. I pictured a hairy Animal, stooped so that his hands were almost touching the floor, grunting, waiting for me. If I ran, there was nothing to lose.

But he unlocked the door before I could run, and instead

of Animal, there was a huge tunnel. It was the corridor that
ran the length of the building, at least a quarter of a mile
long. It must have been fifty feet wide and twenty feet high,
with barred windows near the roof. Wings ran off it on
either side. From the sky, it must have looked like a big
caterpillar. There were just a few cons in the tunnel then. I
expected one of them to be Animal. But they kept moving,
coming from one wing and going to another. There was a
guard stationed outside every fifth or sixth wing. The late
afternoon sun was jamming its way through the windows
above. Animal was seeing that sun. We stopped at a door
under a big red F. I was trembling again. A guard came
from two doors over.

"Want in?"

"Yeah."

I must have moved because the big guard put his big
hand on my shoulder and said, "No, not that way. We're
going in here."

It was dark in there, but I could feel Animal everywhere. A peacock-like cry came from the second tier. Animal. It had to be him. The guard took me to the guard
station. There was no one there. Another cry. That came
from another place.

He was everywhere. And then there was a scream, "*Ay,
nalguitas!*" and an answer, "*Nalguitas tiernitas!*" One of them
was Animal. He was already looking at my ass. I couldn't see
into the cells, but he could see me. A trustee came.

"You want to just leave him. Officer Brown's on count
and it could take a long time."

"No, you go tell officer Brown that I have to talk to him
right now. Tell him that the sergeant wants this guy housed
with Animal starting right now, and that he sent me over
here with him to make sure that happens."

"Where you from, youngster?"

I didn't answer. He didn't look much older than me.

"I'm talking to you, motherfucker."

"Hey, goddamn it. Cut out that spic shit and go get
Brown."

"All right, all right, I'm going." And then he yelled up to the second tier, "Es tuyo, Ahh-nee-mal, es tuyo." He's yours, he's yours.

And then the cries burst out everywhere, like big birds, peacocks, telling everybody that I had come. The cries became words: "AHH-NEE-MAL! AHH-NEE-MAL! (Es tuyo), AHH-NEE-MAL!"

He punked me after dinner. It was too close to dinner when they put me in with him, so he waited until after dinner. I wouldn't go to dinner. "All right, sweetheart," he said in his thick, raspy voice, "I'm gonna let you slide this time. But I don't like skinny asses." He squeezed my ass. "Starting tomorrow you're gonna start putting some weight on." When he came back he waited until lock-down. As soon as the cell door clanged shut, he grabbed me. I screamed and he punched me, not hard enough to knock me out, just hard enough to shut me up. My scream set off screams everywhere. "AHH-NEE-MAL!" "AHH-NEE-MAL!" It hurt. I could feel the ripping and tearing. It hurt more than anything had ever hurt. Every part of me hurt. I must have screamed some more because they hooted some more. "AHH-NEE-MAL!" "AHH-NEE-MAL!"

I woke up lying in blood. My thighs and hips were stuck in it. Animal was snoring on the lower bunk; his feet were hanging over the side. Every few minutes he'd clear his nose with one hard, dry snort. There were no other sounds. What little light there was came from the tier deck. Slowly the punking came back. My ass hurt. The blood was from my ass. My new denim pants were wrapped around my ankles. Cries of "AHH-NEE-MAL!" "AHH-NEE-MAL!" hung in the shaft of the wing's tiers. They all knew. I tried to get up, but the slightest movement drove pain up my ass. I fell back into my blood. And I cried without a sound until I saw the first sign of light, and the floor was as wet with my tears as it was with my blood.

Day came through the cell's small barred window. I got up. I didn't want them to see me. Animal was sprawled on his back. His dead dick was caked with my shit. Each time I moved, my ass hurt. I knelt down and wiped up the blood and tears with toilet paper because I didn't want them to see. Slowly, quietly, I moved toward the bunk. I didn't want to wake him. I didn't want it to happen again. I didn't know how I'd boost myself without stepping on his bunk, without making noise. I stood there not knowing. It was getting lighter. After awhile I was able to look at him; but not at first, because at first I was afraid he'd wake up and see my fear or my hate. His face was as thick as the rest of him, thicker because of his fights.

"They call me Animal because that's what they called me in the ring." He unplugged his plugged nose with a burst of air. "I just kept coming. No matter who it was, no matter how tough a hitter, I just kept coming. 'Like an animal,' they used to say. I used to be the light heavyweight champ of West Texas and all of New Mexico."

Hair seemed ready to jump out of every pore in his face. There was less than an inch of skin separating his eyebrows from his hair line. Hair grew across his cheeks right up to his nose.

"Look, I don't take shit from nobody." He snorted. "But I don't give shit to nobody either. You're my new woman. Treat me right and I'll treat you right. Won't be anybody in this whole joint that will fuck with you so long as they know you're my woman."

He was a block of a man: almost six feet tall and way over two hundred pounds. His arms were as big as my legs, and his legs as big as my waist.

"Let me tell you, I get my share of anything in this place. And my bitch gets shit that no other bitch sees. So treat me right."

He cleared his nose: a hot dry stream of empty air. Now as he slept, the snorts didn't come as often; but they still came, short puffs of air.

"I don't like head that much, so you won't have to blow
me too much, except maybe sometimes, when I get too used
to you and I can't get it up. But usually, I only like it once a
day and that's usually right before I hit the sack for the
night. I sleep better that way."

I moved toward the end of the bunk, raising one foot
and placing it, and then the other, as much for the hurt as
for the fear of waking him. I decided to use the pole that
supported the upper bunk from the lower bunk I boosted
myself, slowly. My ass sagged with pain as it hung over the
edge of the upper bunk. I inched my way up, trying not to
shake the bunk. I had heard that the Japs stuck sharpened
bamboo poles up prisoners' asses. Now I knew what it felt
like. I was sure I was bleeding again. I could feel the warm
blood running down one of my hanging legs. My ass felt as
if someone was trying to cut it away from me, from the hole
out. But I didn't stop. He'd be getting up soon. I wanted to
be in the bunk before he woke. Slowly, I pulled my legs over
the edge. It seemed that as soon as I was on the bunk, a
buzzer sounded and somebody hollered, "First call! First
call!"

He didn't move. Others were getting up. The buzzer
sounded again. "All right! Let's go! Second call! Second call!"
This time the bunk shook. I felt my ass tighten. The bunk
shook again, harder; it shifted and then stopped. He cleared
his nose. Hard snorts. I couldn't see any part of him, so he
had to be sitting on the edge of the bunk. He cleared his
throat to clear his nose. He spat twice. Then he cleared his
nose again. When he stopped he said, "Get your ass out of
that rack; it's time to go to chow. I don't plan to miss my
food because of you." I didn't answer or move. If I went with
him, they'd see me, and now that they knew, now that they
had heard, I didn't want any of them to see me. There was a
stillness. He snorted. I was stiff. Then, in one motion, he
grabbed me, yanked me out of the bunk, onto the floor, on
my feet, and pressed me to him, his face next to mine.
"Look, you little whore. You gave me some shit last night,
and I should have kicked your ass but good. The only reason

I didn't was because I don't like a limp fuck. But don't press your luck, because I'll beat the holy fuck out of you. I'll make you goddamn sorry that you ever thought of fucking with me. Now get your shirt on, cunt, because I want my breakfast."

He shoved me toward my shirt, which was on the floor near the wash basin. But I didn't move anymore than the shove carried me. I was still a few feet from my shirt and I didn't move toward it. If I were to put it on, then he could force me out, and everyone would see me.

"I said put your fucking shirt on, pussy!" He came up to me. "Put it on, bitch!"

I didn't move. He hit me. When I came to, I was on the cell floor alone.

I was on my bunk when he came back.

"Get out of that fucking rack before I kick your rotten ass! You're coming with me today."

I was going to get up, but I knew the others were watching, and that made me hesitate. He yanked me off the bunk again and slapped me across the face. Blood spurted out of my nose, and I cupped it with my hand, looking down at the blood instead of him. That made him madder.

"I'm talking to you, asshole! The bull says you should come with me! Now get your fucking shirt on, and this time I mean it!" He pushed me toward the shirt again. This time I was almost stepping on it.

"Put it on!" I didn't want them to see me. I felt the first blow, and then the guard was there.

"Jesus Christ, Animal!"

He punked me again before dinner. I must have at least whimpered because I heard the hoots and the cries: "AHH-NEE-MAL! AHH-NEE-MAL!" He left me there on the cell floor when he went to eat. He punked me again when he came back. All night long I tried to get off the floor and into my bunk. I didn't want the others to see me in the morning lying there like that: with my pants at my ankles and my naked ass and blood oozing from it. But I seemed stuck in my blood, and I couldn't lift myself. That morning two bulls from the goon squad dragged me out of the cell, out of the wing and down to the hole.

I must have known that I was naked. I remembered being cold the whole time and trying to cover myself, but there was nothing to cover myself with. I remembered curling and bunching myself up to keep warm, but it must have been so that they wouldn't see me either. I tossed and turned. There was nothing restful about it. I was moving and worried the whole time. But I didn't want to wake up. At least twice I heard the sound of the slit; it was more than twice. And then I came awake in stages, putting it off, telling myself that I was tired, that I needed more sleep, until I was lying in the darkness with my eyes wide open. And the stillness kept telling me what I had known all along: I was in the hole.

It was completely dark. My eyes were useless. There was never any getting used to that dark. But that was part of it. They knew that. That was part of the isolation, part of the punishment: total and complete darkness. I felt my way around it, eight-by-eight maybe. The walls were cushioned, not soft, but they gave. The floor and ceiling were the same. It would be hard to hurt yourself in there. That was part of it too. Once you hurt yourself, they'd have to take you out. There was nothing in the cell except the hole. It was in the middle of the floor, perfectly round and about five inches across. Its smell told you what it was for. Everything sloped down towards it. They wanted you to use it. That was part of it too. Once you started eating your own shit and drinking your own piss, it was only a matter of time until they would have to take you out. As long as you kept your shit and piss away from where you ate and slept and sat, like any caged animal did, the longer you could suffer what they wanted you to suffer. Nature was on their side.

As I felt my way around the cell, I tilted a tray, spilling soup on my hand. I drank what was left of it and ate the two slices of bread that were there, too. But that was all there was. I was hungrier after I ate than before I ate, but I couldn't find anything else to eat. I was still cold. There were goose pimples all over me. The floor and the walls were cold. They were warmer when I sat on and against them. So I picked a spot to sit in. It was the right hand corner of the cell opposite the door. Everybody needed a spot. 'Amá had her spot in the kitchen, the chair by the window; she had her spot in her room and at our altar and in church. Padre had his spot in the confessional, against the back part of it from where he would hunch. Chole had her spot in Chinatown, at the corner of Tulare and F Streets. I had my spot on the roof, both in and out of the shelter. Now I had a new one.

Now, as I sat in my spot I noticed there was no sound. Nothing. Late at night, it was quiet. But you could always hear the hiss of the pilot light or the tick of the clock or an insect or the whir of a far-away car. But now there was just the thickness of silence. I listened, I strained to listen. Nothing. I put my ears to the walls. Nothing. To the floor, to at least feel vibrations and know that something was moving and making sounds. Nothing. I talked to myself; I whistled; I sang. I wanted sound. I was afraid I'd forget. I screamed. "Hey, you lousy motherfuckers! You rotten cocksuckers!" Nothing. No one came. No sound unless I made it. The silence got thicker. I could feel it, as fine as the fluff that floated off the cotton balls when you picked them.

And so I sat, not knowing how long I'd been there or how long I'd be there. Because the judge had said, ". . . for the term prescribed . . ." which everybody said probably meant life. Always there had been a limit. I only had to stoop in a field so long. I only had to kneel in the pantry so long or stand in the rain-soaked shelter so long. Even at the Fresno County jail they were only going to keep me for so long. But now I could be there forever, for the rest of my life, for the only forever I'd know in my life. I could be there until the day I died, without knowing whether it was day or night. I wouldn't even know that much. I jumped up. I beat and pounded on the door. "Open up, you dirty lousy motherfuckers! Open this fucking thing! Open it! Open!" I beat on it until my hands hurt. I yelled until I was hoarse. Then I sank in front of it and cried. I laid there and my mind slipped off—for how long I didn't know—to that place where I didn't have to think or feel or remember. Numbness set into the rest of my body. I wasn't asleep but I wasn't awake either, and I wasn't ready when a slit near the bottom of the door slid open and a hand reached in. It felt for a tray, but found my hip instead. A voice came through the slit. "All right, asshole. I'm only gonna tell you once, so listen. No tray, no food. Understand? From now on if you don't have that tray lined up next to this slit so that I can just pull it out, then you're not gonna get any food. You're gonna starve, and I don't give a fuck if you do." Before I could answer, before I could say anything, the slit closed.

In the darkness I found the tray that I had tipped over earlier and the cup I had drank from. I was hungry again. No tray, no food. Fuck him. I didn't need no food. But my stomach hurt. He'd be coming again. But I didn't know when or how many times he would come. I put the tray and cup under the slit and moved away from the door. I was hungry, and I didn't want anything to go wrong. I didn't want the tray to bump against me or get stuck against me when he came. I wanted the food. He could come any minute. A minute went by, but he didn't come. And then another and another and he still didn't come by. I went back to my spot. Maybe he knew I wasn't in my spot, and that's why he hadn't come. Maybe he was waiting for me to get back to my spot. I waited quietly and patiently in my spot. I needed food. But he didn't come. Maybe he only came once a day. Was that yesterday or today that he had come? I lost everything in the dark. Would he come back? Had I gotten him too mad? I should have had the tray there. But I hadn't known. I should have known.

My head hurt. I felt weak. It was getting colder in there. I was shivering. I went back to the door. I kicked it and then buckled in pain. When my foot stopped hurting, I got up and pounded on the door. "I want some food! I need food, you fuckers!" But I was careful not to touch or budge the tray from its spot under the slit. No one came. Now my

hands were hurting too. I went back to my spot to keep
warm and to let the pain go away. I wasn't asleep, but I
wasn't awake either when the slit slid open and startled
me. The light from that small hole in the door blinded me,
but I heard the trays, and then, then it was dark again. I
crawled toward the slit so that I wouldn't spill any of it.
Carefully, I felt for the tray. What I felt first was the heat
from the cup. I drank the soup and ate the bread and then
licked the cup. It was still cold in there. I went back to my
spot, to huddle against the two walls, to make them warm
so that they could make me warm.

I slept. This time it was a deep sleep, so deep that when
I woke there was another tray there. I hadn't heard the slit
or the trays. It wasn't like most of the sleeps I had there,
sleeps that came with a worn mind rather than a worn
body, sleeps in which my worn mind kept wearing itself.
There were sleeps of fear. I would fall asleep and then see
myself naked and asleep in my spot, in my corner, with my
ass sticking out and a lot of Animals peeking through the
slit, waiting for me to be sound asleep. I'd try to cover my
ass, but always there was some part of it showing. And
always I was on the edge of falling asleep. There were
sleeps of struggle, sleeps in which I'd struggle to stay awake
or struggle to wake up but couldn't. There were sleeps of
watch, when I took to watching and waiting for the slit to
open. Then I slept only because I couldn't watch anymore.
But my body kept on watching, my skin tingled, my feet listened, the hair on my arms stood up, my eyes blinked wide
open, thinking that the slit had opened. But each time I
woke, the slit was closed. And each time, I was a little more
lost in the darkness.

After one of those many sleeps, after I had been there
for what seemed like months, I woke to a hard-on. I hadn't
had one in the hole. It stretched above my navel and rubbed
against my stomach. I tried not to think about it. I didn't
want to think about it. But it was so long and hard and big
that its touching on my stomach made me shiver. They said
you wore yourself out jacking-off in the hole. That's all you

did. That's all there was to do. You did it 'til you couldn't do
it anymore. Some guys even learned how to eat themselves.
But I hadn't jacked-off once. I hadn't been hard once. Now I
was, and it was one of those that wasn't going to go away. I
tried to picture Chole. I concentrated and brought her into
my mind, brought her huge thighs up to my nose. But somebody else was there, too, and he got bigger and bigger until
it was his thighs I was looking at. Animal. My ass hurt and
my stomach tightened. I shook him out of my head. I
brought back Chole. But just barely, fuzzily, but clearly
enough I thought, and so I stroked it. It felt good. The
motion was easy. I stayed with the motion for awhile. Then
I wanted more and reached for Chole. But I got Animal
instead. I felt his weight and the tearing. I heard the hoots
and saw my blood and shit on his dick. The hard-on disappeared. It shrunk to a stub in my moving hand. I cried.

Some time later, as I was eating a slice of bread, I
thought it smelled of shit. I stopped chewing, held the slice
away from me and then brought it back to my nose. It did
smell like shit. Were they baking shit for me to eat? I
smelled it again. Yes. But my hands smelled of shit, too. I
put the bread down and smelled my hands. Yes. Was it the
bread or my hands? I got down on my knees and smelled the
bread on the floor. Shit. I smelled myself—my knee, my
arm, my other arm. Shit. I went to the tray, and without
touching the other slice of bread, smelled it too. Shit. The
soup was still warm. I smelled it too. Yes. I sipped it. It
tasted of shit. I smelled the tray. Shit. The walls smelled of
shit; the corner I never used smelled of shit. I went to the
hole itself and found it. They never thought I would, but I
did. They were pumping vapors of shit up through the hole.
But they were smart. The vapors were so faint that you
could barely feel them. I had to stick my nose as far down
the hole as I could to feel them, to make sure that's what
they were. I made a plan of my own. I decided to sit on the
hole, to sleep on it, to cover it for as long as it took to force
the vapors back down the hole. To have them pile up on the
end they were coming from until they exploded in their

faces. I covered it through two slit openings. Then I must have passed out because the next thing I knew I was eating another slice of bread and there was no smell of shit on it.

ÔÔÔÔÔ

I took to waiting for him right from the beginning. The slit was in the center and bottom of the door. It was no more than eighteen inches wide and six inches high, just big enough to slide a tray through with a cup on it. Whoever was bringing the trays could slide open the slit, pull out the old tray, shove in the new tray, and shut the slit before I could count to five. For awhile, I thought he was one of the guards. But this same guy kept coming every day—I knew it was the same guy—and guards had days off. So it wasn't a guard. This ruthless bastard who played with my mind every day, who gave me all the pain I could take in less than five seconds, had to be a trustee. At first I was sure he had to be a nigger. They were always sucking on the white man's ass, laughing and joking, playing the clown, bending and bowing so smoothly with everything the white man said. But they were the most vicious, violent snakes when they got a Mexican alone. It had to be a nigger, until one time I was sure I saw part of his hand. It was a white hand. I should have known. Those fucking butchers who really believed they were better than anyone with darker skin. They made fun of the way we walked and talked and dressed and ate and stood and combed our hair. It had to be one of those white motherfuckers. Except that one day he called me *"puto"* only the way a Mexican could. That made sense. Having been in the hole so much himself, he best knew how to torture.

He was all that happened; he was the only thing that happened every day, or night, or whatever it was. Everything began and ended with his last coming or his next coming. I had so much to tell him, always so much to bitch about or beg for. Usually I missed him. I was either dazed or asleep or just not ready when he came. If I was ready, there was never enough time. I started by screaming at him. "Hey, you rotten motherfucker, get me out of here!" It didn't do any good. I was never able to say more than a few words and he was gone. I tried talking to him, too. I'd lie on my side, as close as I dared to the tray, facing the slit, lining my mouth up with the center of the slit. "Sir, can I talk to you for a minute, please?" That was worse. It was hard to start talking with one side of my face on the floor. He was gone before I could get to the "talk." Once I touched his hand. I was at the slit at the right moment. I touched his fingers as he reached for the old tray. He rammed the slit shut and didn't leave a new tray.

After he had come twenty or forty or sixty or a hundred times, I don't know, my ass started bleeding. It happened when I was crouching over the hole. When I stood up, I felt a warmth running down the back of my leg. I rubbed it between my fingers. It felt like blood; it tasted like blood. I banged on the door. "Hey, get me out of here! I'm gonna bleed to death!" The movements made it worse. I lay down, but near the door, and then, pushing the tray aside, next to the door. The bleeding wouldn't stop. I put my lips on the slit. I'd start talking as soon as the slit moved. I had to tell him that I was bleeding to death. I waited, but he didn't come. I kept the tray away from the door. I was going to stay next to the slit for as long as it took. Then the bleeding stopped. I stayed there anyway. But I must have fallen asleep because the next thing I knew was feeling his fingers brush my cheek. I grabbed for those fingers but the slit closed, without a tray.

I bled some more later, though not as much. I still had to tell him. He had to know what was happening to me. I made another plan. I decided to take the next tray and save some of it, and then get ready for the tray after that because, when he came that time, I planned to jam my arms through the slit and press my body against the door. He'd have to chop off my arms to close that slit. And before he did, I'd tell him about my bleeding. I got myself ready. I slept as much as I could before the first tray came so that I wouldn't be sleepy for the second tray. When the first tray came, I saved my soup and ate only half a slice of bread. Then I sat and lay by the door with my arms next to the slit. I pinched myself when I felt myself getting drowsy. When that wasn't enough, I got up and took two quick steps across the cell and back again, across and back again. Then I added a bump against the wall to those steps, a little harder each time just to make sure that I'd be ready and awake. Until I bumped myself so hard that I thought I had made myself bleed again. I hadn't, but that made me realize that I hadn't bled since before he brought me the last tray. Still, I had to tell him. He had to know what was wrong with me. When he came, I had just bumped myself against the opposite wall. By the time I got over to the slit, he was gone. I beat on the door. He had to know, and I had to tell him. He had to know that I could die from bleeding. It didn't matter that I hadn't bled for two trays now. He had to know. So I decided to try again, to take the next tray and ration my food and get ready for the tray after that.

I did that. I took the next tray. I rationed it and got ready. It didn't matter that I hadn't bled. I sat this time, bent over, facing the door with my fingers spread against the slit. I didn't let myself lie down this time because that's when I got drowsy. My back and arms ached, but the way I was sitting, the way I had my fingers pressed against the slit, my hands had to fall through the slit as soon as he opened it. And before he could get my hands out of there, I could tell him. It didn't matter that I hadn't bled again. He had to know. So I waited, with my back aching and my fingers numb with soreness, but making sure that even when I got drowsy they stayed pressed against the slit. Except that when he finally did open the slit, the sound, the movement startled me and I fell backwards rather than forward. He felt for the tray, for a second or two, and then the slit closed, without a word, without an extra sound.

"Oh, please talk to me. I have to talk to you. I have to talk to someone, anyone. Please talk to me. You don't know how hard it is to be here like this, alone. Let me just touch your fingers for a moment. Please."

From then on, I was always watching and waiting. "Hey, you, mister. Hey, you, wait a minute. Please just wait one . . ." "Carnal, ayúdame. ¡Carnal!"

"Hey, I don't want no trouble. All I want to do is talk for a little while. Just for a minute. That ain't asking too much. I just want to hear you and see you, too. I just want to know you're there. This place does funny things to you. After awhile, there's nothing but this darkness. I can't even feel myself in this darkness. I touch myself, but I can't find myself. I can't feel myself. I'm part of it, too. It's all one big dark silence. I've been by myself a lot before, but never like this. Always there were other things, other things I could see or hear or touch or smell. And somehow, that made it easier. But here . . ."

Still, when they came to get me, when they opened the door, I tried to hide. "You ready to program, Olivas?"

I was lying on my side, in my spot, when the door opened. At the sound of the door, before the light, I curled, bringing my knees to my chest. With one hand I tried to cover my ass, with the other I cupped my dick and my balls. The light was blinding. I couldn't open my eyes.

"You ready to program, Olivas?" I didn't know what that meant. "Look, asshole, we ain't got all day. If you want some more, we can give you some more."

"No more. Please no more."

Animal was at the plates shop when they took me back to the cell. I waited, dreading his coming. I stood by the small barred window even though my eyes were still bothering me. I opened them more and more. I saw more and more of the sky's blue and the rich green of the late winter grass. It didn't matter that he'd punk me again and again. I'd get used to it. The flag was blowing hard in the wind. Three cons were working in different parts of the prison grounds, feeling that wind. A lone car, small in the distance, was slowly making its way up the hills across the highway. Some free man was driving it. It didn't matter that the others knew. It didn't matter that they would hear and know and see. I looked at the flash of the sun until my eyes and head hurt. It did matter.

He came back late in the afternoon, when the sun was like fire in the window. He didn't waste any time. He pinned me against the bunk. "Look, you skinny piece of shit. I'm not gonna fuck with you this time." He cleared his nose and I felt the hot snort on my face. "You give me any shit this time, and I'm gonna give you a beating you'll never forget. You hear me!? Wash your face, pig, and comb your hair. We're gonna be eating pretty soon, and I don't like any of my cunts embarrassing me in public. You know what I mean?"

When I followed him out of the cell, there were a few hoots. "AHH-NEE-MAL! AHH-NEE-MAL!" I knew what they meant. I kept my head down. As we stood in line waiting to go out into the tunnel, some of them made cracks. I kept my head and my eyes down. I stayed right behind Animal. When he moved, I moved. The chow hall was at a door on the left, about a block down the tunnel. It was full, Mexicans on one side of the room, blacks on the other. There was a long line. Animal didn't get in it. "Come on," he said, and went to the head of the line. As we pushed our trays through the line, he told the servers, "This is my new old lady. When I send her back for more, fill that fucking plate up good."

I didn't look up at any of them. One of them said, "Hi, sweetheart."

We ate at a table right in the middle of the whole chow hall. Nobody ate with us. As soon as we sat down, Animal took my plate and from it took half of my potatoes and almost all of my meat. "I never was too much of a meat and potatoes eater until I came to the joint." Then he drank my glass of Kool-Aid and his too. "Here, go get us some more

Kool-Aid. Take your plate, too and tell them I need more meat." When I came back, he reached over and pinched my ear lobe. "You know, sweetheart, you . . ." I yanked my head away. Even as my head was still turned, he hit me, knocking me and my tray to the floor, splattering food all over me. The hoots started. "AHH-NEE-MAL! AHH-NEE-MAL!"

"Goddamn, you're bad, Ahh-nee-mal!"

"Motherfucker's still champ."

Then he said to me, "Don't you ever pull away from me when I touch you! Hear!? Now get up, and eat something, cunt, 'cause I don't like skinny asses!"

He punked me right after lock-down. I must have screamed, or maybe some of them saw, because the hoots came, "AH-NEE-MAL! AHH-NEE-MAL!" It was at least a week before the hoots died down. At first he punked me twice a day: once right after lock-down and again two hours later when the lights went out—to put himself to sleep he said. At first my ass bled and it got infected. I thought for sure that the bleeding and the infection would kill me. I didn't care. But then the bleeding stopped and the infection went away. But the soreness never went away. It was always there, everywhere I went and every move I made. And the pain never went away either. Each time he did it, the pain gushed out my ears. It felt like it was splitting my head open.

They kept me locked up my first week, waiting to see my counselor. When he hadn't come by the second week, the bull told me to work in the plates shop with Animal until he did. They made license plates for cars, trucks, and buses. And Animal and a short, fat, red-headed bull named Warren Sanders ran a dope ring out of there too. Every morning, Monday through Friday, Animal met Sanders at 7:25 as he came into the tunnel at the central gate. Together, they walked to the plates shop. Sanders looked like any other bull on his way to work: in his khaki uniform, with his gut pushing past his open jacket and his black lunch pail swinging in his hand. There were some things different in those morning walks. First, few cons walked with any bulls. And if some did, no con walked with the same guard every morning. And everybody knew Sanders wasn't carrying his lunch in that lunch pail.

Animal was the foreman at the plates shop. That allowed him to move around the shop as he pleased, to deal with his five pushers as he pleased. Animal alone picked his pushers. They were all junkies. Some were that way when they got to Animal. Others weren't. He kept them that way; he kept them in heroin both for themselves and their customers. And he kept replacing them, one at a time, about every four or five weeks, when it was clear that another one was too strung out to do him any good. He gave them free heroin every day, a little more each day, until they were hooked. Then he made them beg, a little at first, but more each week, until they'd do anything for a fix. The trouble was, that when they got that bad, they couldn't do anything.

At 7:30 every morning, Sanders and Animal met behind the windows of the shop's office. That's where they packaged and split up the heroin, everyone said. But no one knew how or when Animal got it out of the office, because there was never anything in his hands, never anything bulging in his clothes when he came out of the office. When he did come out, he went straight to his first pusher, the one that had been with him the longest. It was easy to spot him. His eyes were sunken the deepest—grim, frightened eyes in dark pits. He was hunched over, and he looked like he hadn't slept in a week. He was sweating, always sweating, and his was the grayest of the yellow-gray skins. "Let's have it," Animal would say with his hand flat open. And I could see or hear the answer depending on where I was standing or whether the big machines were on.

"I need a fix, Animal. I ain't gonna make it if I don't have a fix."

"I said let's have it!" The open hand nudged him.

Now when the hype answered, he was fumbling in his pocket. "I need one bad, Animal, real bad."

"I want it all," Animal said as he got the rumpled bills.

He did want it all, because as the morning passed, the junkie was going to get more and more desperate until it didn't matter where he got it from or how much he paid for it.

"I've been good by you, Animal. I've made you lots of money. I'm not asking for much, just a quarter. That's all I need right now, Animal. I don't wanna be sick, Animal. Please, you gotta give me a quarter. I won't let you down. These guys from Los are looking to buy a piece. I almost put the deal together for you today. I'll have the money sincho for you in a couple of days. Cash and carry. I already told them."

"This all you got?"

"Yeah, but I need a fix, Animal."

"Give me your card."

"I didn't cheat you, Animal. I just need a little taste."

"Fuck off."

Then he'd walk away from him and the junkie would follow. "Just give me half-a-quarter, Animal. I'll get by on that." All the life he had left was in his eyes, quick, frightened, terrified eyes. "Get the fuck out of here."

"I'm gonna be sick, Animal. Please, Animal, you don't know what that's like!" The eyes were bright, burning what was left.

"If you don't get the fuck out of here, I'm gonna knock you on your ass, punk."

That didn't scare him. There was only one thing he was afraid of now and that wasn't Animal's fists. But towards the end, just before Animal had him sent to the hole, he'd hit him, down him right there, just to get rid of him.

Animal would go to the second pusher who probably had been watching Animal and the first pusher. The second pusher who, by now, knew that in a few weeks that would be him, and that there was nothing he could do about it. He turned over his money quickly, and he didn't beg, not then. But just as Animal was leaving, the second pusher would say, "It'd be nice to have a little taste, Animal," his eyes already sinking.

When Animal got to his fourth and fifth pushers, it was

different. He was different. He still had months in each one
of them. He dealt with them separately, but the treatment
was pretty much the same. He laughed with them, joked
with them; put his arm around them and slapped them on
their backs. He told them not to worry, that they'd never be
like the other asshole pushers because they had class. He
could tell. And then he'd give them a taste; he'd do their
jobs while they went behind the stacks and fixed.

The cons argued over who ran the dope ring, whether
Animal worked for Sanders or Sanders worked for Animal,
even though they all knew that Animal was boss. Sometimes they came up with different answers in one day. If
they hated Animal or were jealous of him at the time, then
Animal was nothing but Sanders' flunky. If they were hating Sanders or the prison, then Sanders was nothing but
Animal's tool and the cons ruled. Everyone said that Animal was the richest con in that joint and probably in all the
joints. But no one knew where he kept his money, and no
one ever saw him spend any of it. He took what he wanted.
The word was that a lot of it went to buying off bulls inside
the joint and cops outside the joint as protection for his
business. The word was that a lot of it went to buying
judges on the outside; that he needed to buy four of them to
win his case. And that he had three judges bought and was
working on the fourth, but that the fourth judge had found
out what the other three had gotten and was holding out for
a hell of a lot more.

Animal never used dope, and he never said why, except
that had it not been for dope, he probably would have been
the light-heavyweight champion of the world. He still had a
shot at it, he said, if he could just get out of the joint soon
enough. The only thing I ever saw him take was home brew,
and only a little on Sunday afternoons, our day off.

Nobody messed with me. They knew I was Animal's old
lady. But there were always cracks: "He gets tired of his
cunts real fast," or "I'm gonna try you out, baby, when Animal dumps you."

I followed Animal one step behind everywhere he went.

He wanted it that way, to cover his back, he said. That was part of the routine which began every morning with the first buzzer. By the second buzzer, I was washed and dressed and had pissed, because that's when he got up and the toilet and wash basin had to be free for him to use. While he sat on the toilet, I spread and smoothed his clothes and took his shoes, which I had polished the night before, and put one on each side of his pants, just free off the bunk, so he wouldn't have to stretch and stoop. I stood behind him with a towel as he washed, and then dried the back of his neck and behind his ears. I laced and tied his shoes while he yawned and snorted on the edge of the bunk, and then stood behind him, holding his jacket ready, as he combed and recombed his hair. At breakfast, he sat at our table while I brought him his food. It took several trips because he liked hot things hot and cold things cold, and because he got special things from the guard's side, like juice and fruit and sweet rolls, and because his eggs had to be done for two-and-a-half minutes, no more, no less. At the shop I'd hang his jacket and then sharpen the pencils he'd use on his pusher's cards. Animal liked sharp pencils. Then, I'd hide two sandwiches that the coffee man smuggled out of the kitchen for him every day.

My job at the shop was to watch for snags on the lines. If I saw one, I was supposed to throw a switch. To do this, I was on a raised platform from which I could see the whole shop. Animal said my real job was to watch his back, to watch his every move. If I saw anything suspicious, like someone following him or waiting to ambush him, I was supposed to press a hidden buzzer. If anyone ever jumped him, I was to press another hidden buzzer that would bring the goon squad running. No one ever jumped him while I was there, but I often wondered how long it would take me to press that buzzer if they did.

Lunch and dinner were times when orders and complaints and deals were made. As soon as we walked into the chow hall, Animal went to our table. Cons walked past him, dropping notes and saying what few things they could as they walked past. I spent most of those meals standing in line. What they couldn't give or say to Animal, they said or gave to me in the line. On the way back to the wing after dinner, there was always a crowd around Animal. They always talked about dope, and I always thought about the punking a half-hour away. He would belch and burp and snort and start rubbing his dick and balls as soon as we got into the cell, waiting for the lock-down. By then, he had me kneeling against the edge of the bunk, bracing myself against it so that he could thrust harder. Though I didn't bleed anymore, it always hurt. It hurt just thinking about it. As we walked, I could feel the pain shooting through me and stuffing itself into my head. I could feel him belch and snort. I could feel his huge stomach folding over my back, as if it were swallowing up all of me. But it never swallowed my hate.

After nine weeks, Animal told me he was tired of me. I wasn't expecting it. He had told me that I was the best old lady he'd ever had. I had paid so much attention to him, that by the last weeks there were times when I was able to tell what he wanted or what he was going to do faster than he could. Maybe that's why he got rid of me. He told me on a Sunday, right after we got back from lunch. Sunday was our "recreation day" and there was no lockdown until after dinner. He said he wanted to talk to me up in the cell. I followed him up the stairs to the second tier, confused. I thought I knew by then when he was going to punk me, and there hadn't been any signs of it.

"You know," he said as we walked into the cell, "I'm gonna cut you loose."

I didn't know what to say.

He laid down on his bunk and said, "Stick around."

That confused me more. He pulled out a bottle of home brew from under his mattress. It was too early for Animal to be drinking, because on Sundays he helped the bulls put away the loaded cons. It was good for his business that the cons got loaded, but it was also good for his business that they didn't get out of hand. So he helped put them away.

Even loaded cons were afraid of Animal.

"Yeah, I'm gonna cut you loose. They brought in this tender young thing just yesterday, and they're saving him for me. I need something new. A man needs a change. He's a pretty thing with a pretty good build on him. At least he'll have some meat on him. At least I won't have to keep beating my balls on bone when I'm humping. Nobody should have to do that. And I'm gonna tell you again for your own good—like I've been telling you every day since you got here—you're gonna have to keep your asshole cleaner. There's way too much shit in there. Not everybody's gonna put up with all that shit on their dicks like I do. The guys in this wing like clean assholes, and somebody with a dirty asshole like yours is gonna have a hard time hooking up with somebody. And you better hook up with somebody as soon as I cut you loose, because you're young and skinny and weak, and unless you have somebody covering your ass, you're gonna be in some big trouble. That's why I asked a lot of guys to stop by this afternoon, kind of look you over and see if they'd like to make you their old lady. Shit, it's gonna cost them. 'Cause you know Animal doesn't do anything for free."

Guys did stop by that afternoon, a lot of them. And Animal wasn't doing me any favors either. He tried to pimp me to every one of them. When the first ones came, he said, "Pull your pants down! Take the fucking things off! Let them get a good look at your ass." As I took them off, I moved to a corner of the cell, not yet knowing, so nobody else would see. But when one of them, a fat little Mexican, gave him three dollars, I knew. And when he moved towards me, I hit him. Then Animal came over. "You no good dirty little bitch!" He back-handed me, knocking me to the floor. Then he picked me up and put me in the position. I heard the little one's heavy breathing, and I felt his fat little hands on my back, and I heard myself moaning.

He kept me in that position all afternoon: on my knees and elbows, with my ass sticking up, pointed to the door of the cell. It sounded like everybody in the wing came to take a look. They loved it when somebody was punking me. They hooted and hollered. They liked it so much that Animal started charging them to watch. After awhile, it didn't matter how many of them watched. It didn't matter how many of them grunted their way into my ass.

They left just before lock-down. Little by little I let myself slump. He was on the bunk. I could hear him breathing, but I couldn't tell if he was asleep or drunk or what. They had brought him a lot of home brew. The more he drank, the easier it had become for them to buy my ass. Now I expected him to yell to get my ass up there or to get over to him and give him some. But he didn't yell, and finally I let myself lie flat on the floor. I didn't think I could ever get up again, ever move again. I didn't want to. But sometime during the night he nudged me. "Look, cunt, I'm gonna show you that Animal ain't all that bad. You made me a lot of money this afternoon, and I'm gonna give you a taste free. And if you mind your shit, there'll be more free tastes. Who knows, I might even think about letting you be one of my pushers." He had a needle in his hand. I didn't want a taste. But it didn't matter as I lay there. I felt him poke my ass with the needle, and in awhile I started to jerk and then heave. I kept on heaving. My whole body was one big heave. I couldn't stop heaving.

They kept me in the infirmary three days. When they took me back to the cell, Animal was at the shop. I crawled up into my bunk. I still felt weak and sick. My ass hurt. I tried to sleep, but I kept thinking of Animal. I didn't think I could take another punking. I would rather have died. I thought of ways of killing myself. He had a shank stashed in the cell somewhere. But I didn't know where, and I didn't dare search for it because he knew how everything, down to his toothbrush, was arranged in the cell. By the time I heard the first ones coming back, I had decided that he'd have to kill me to punk me again.

I thought he'd try before dinner, but he didn't. Instead, he stood beside the bunk and said, "Look, cunt. I'm gonna give it to you straight. Once I turn out one of my old ladies,

I never touch her again. I don't share my cunt with nobody. Never did. Not only that, but you can pick up all kinds of diseases, and I like my dick too much. It's good to me. You've had it pretty easy around here because everybody knows you've been my old lady. Once I turn you loose, it ain't gonna be that way. I've been taking good care of you, but there ain't nothing in this world free. You ought to know that by now. I tried to give you a way out the other day with a little taste of smack. I was thinking of making you one of my pushers because you ain't dumb. You catch on fast, and you know my business already. You see, if you were pushing for me, I'd still be keeping an eye out for you. But, shit, you go get sick, dying almost, on a tiny bit of smack. But I'm still thinking about letting you do it, because I think you'd be good and I take good care of my pushers. I watch out for them, and you're gonna need that. Ain't nobody fucks with my pushers."

I had seen him take good care of his pushers. I had seen him slap and kick and beat them. I had seen them get on their knees and beg for a taste, and had seen him laugh and walk past them. I knew their oily, yellow-gray faces. I knew the wild desperation in their sunken eyes, and the constant running of their noses, and the sweat that was always pouring out of their foreheads. He took real good care of them.

After lock-down that night Animal said, "You know, I think the problem last time was that I gave you too much. I forgot that you were probably a virgin. I never did ask you if you chipped on the streets. This time I'm gonna give you a lot less, and this stuff's been cut quite a bit." He had a needle and I backed away from him. "Come here, you little motherfucker." He grabbed me by the throat. "You're gonna earn me some bread!"

That time they only kept me in the infirmary two days, though the heaving had been worse. When I came back to the cell on Saturday, Animal didn't say a word. He left me alone on my bunk. I didn't eat that night, and I was still in my bunk when he came back from lunch the next day. I didn't know he was mad until he pulled me out of the bunk.

"Get your fucking ass out of that bed, asshole! We're gonna have some more visitors. You're gonna earn the protection I give you."

When I struggled with the first one, Animal hit me and left me sprawled on the floor. That didn't stop them—one of them held me up while another punked me. Animal was laughing and drinking home brew. My ass was bleeding. There were so many. After each one, I'd fall flat on the floor. They were all drinking, and as the afternoon passed, they let me lie on the floor longer and longer. Then, late in the afternoon, one of them said that he didn't need anyone else to hold me up, that he'd take me on by himself. He raised me easily and high. He was a big man, but I couldn't feel him inside me. I felt his thrusts against my ass, but nothing more. Except that he kept scratching me, long scratches across my back with his fingernail. He kept grunting and making funny squealing noises as if he were coming. But he didn't come; he didn't finish. He kept on pumping. I couldn't feel him inside me. He scratched me more. They were longer and deeper, all over my back. I felt something warm and wet on my back, and I thought he was drooling on me. It seemed like he'd never finish. I felt the drool running down the sides of my back, and I looked down and saw blood. I screamed and bolted free. I saw the razor in his hand and screamed all the more. I tried to run out of the cell, but there were a lot of them standing in the doorway. They jumped me and gagged me. They jumped him too. Animal was lying on his bunk drunk and smiling.

He was still lying there, naked and snoring, when I came to on the floor. My back hurt. Each time I moved it felt as if I were breaking the crust of my skin. The wing was quiet. The tier light showed up my blood on the floor. I wanted to die, but I didn't know how. I had heard of guys hanging themselves in their cells. There was nothing to hang from in that cell. I studied the walls and even the floor. Then I saw the razor. He must have dropped it when they jumped him. I crawled to it. It was a long flat piece of metal that had been filed so much it would have cut anything. I felt the edge, and it sent shivers through me. I knew what I was going to cut. I'd have them cut off before he could feel it, and then I'd cut off his dick, too. He'd have to kill me to make me stop and he probably would. That didn't matter.

Inch by inch I crawled toward him, shivering and trembling, afraid that I'd wake him. He was lying with one of his legs hanging over the edge of the bunk. It couldn't have been better. When I reached him, I just lay there for awhile, feeling the razor's edge, trying to imagine the pain, trying to imagine what he'd be like without balls and a dick. The thoughts excited me, and my breathing got heavy. So heavy I thought I'd wake him. I couldn't wait any longer. Slowly, carefully I rose. Trembling I bent over him. Carefully I reached for his balls. And then I had them, and I pressed and cut as hard as I could. They gave way with his first scream. When he grabbed me, I was already hacking on his dick, feeling the flesh give and blood squirting, pressing as hard as I could as he choked me.

CHAPTER TWELVE

It was about the time that the other guard was talking to me about exercising that I looked at the face in the glass. Before that, it seemed like it was always there. But I never looked at it. I would see it without looking at it, pressed against the small thick square glass in my cell door. I had taught myself to sleep curled up in the right hand corner of my cell, so that I could hide myself from those eyes. Because they never turned off the lights in my cell then, and the face was always pressed against the glass. I had taught myself to sit in my spot with my knees drawn up to my chin and my legs crossed to cover my ass, and my dick and balls tucked in between my legs and stomach. That way, he couldn't see anything either. I would always keep my eyes down, or at least looking off in another direction. Still, I knew the face was there, and I knew it was watching me. I used to think I knew who it was even before the other guard mentioned him. But then, I didn't really know for sure who it was until the last day. Until I saw him behind the wire fence, and then at a distance and only for a second.

I had a dog for a few weeks when I was ten or eleven. 'Amá was always mad at it because no matter where we tied it, no matter how much we beat it, it kept on digging big holes. I could remember being mad at it because 'Amá

was mad at it and mad at me and threatening to make me
get rid of it. I'd scold the dog and then stand over it. The dog
knew I was mad at it, and it would never look at me. It
would keep its eyes down or to the side. Every now and
then, it would lift its eyes and run them uneasily past me,
not looking at me and stopping them just to one side of me.
For a long time, I felt like that dog on the cell floor. It was
as if I woke to that face, because all those years after I got
Animal were like a sleep and a dream, a nightmare of which
I remembered just disconnected pieces. I remembered that
they moved me, three times by bus and three times by car,
from hole to hole. I remembered being on top of a mountain
and looking down at miles and miles of soft white fog. "Hey,
gooney, that's the San Joaquin Valley down there. That's
where your people are."

"Your people." It kept turning in my mind. "Your people." The holes got worse and then better and then worse. If
I went in a bus, they got better; if I went in a car, they got
worse. The bad ones felt like they were buried in the middle
of the earth. I went from darkness to light and then back
again; from double doors to single doors to double doors. I
never knew why they bothered, why they kept me alive. I
wanted to die. I told myself that again and again and again.
But I kept eating. The other guard said, "Hey, Olivas, you
ain't fooling me. I know you want out. You know how I
know? . . . You keep eating. If you didn't want out, if you
really wanted to end it, you'd stop eating, like I seen others
do." I kept eating.

On the day I looked at that face, what I saw was the
eyes, blue eyes, because the rest of the face was pressed
against the glass, smeared against the glass. They were
strange eyes. The whites of the eyes said more than the
blue. The huge, bulging, round whites of the eyes, with
their twenty or fifty tiny, broken streams scared me. The
blue and black of the eyes said nothing. Still, I looked into
those eyes until the face left the glass. It was right after
that that the other guard said, "The captain's gonna let you
exercise, Olivas."

I knew the other guard's eyes well by then, sad brown
eyes. Though he spoke to me through the slit, he always
looked in on me before and after he spoke. The sadness was
in the brown, around the outer edges of those eyes. "You're
just a step away from the main line, Olivas, and from there
it's just another step to the streets. You can do it, Olivas, I
know you can." Or, "I was here when they brought you in
fifteen years ago, Olivas. I'm an old man now, but you,
you're in the prime of your life, Olivas. You can still get out
and enjoy life, Olivas. It's up to you. Nobody can do it for
you."

I'd watch him put his head down, watch the brown baldness of that egg-shaped head, as he got ready to try again.

"Look, Olivas, you ain't bullshitting me. I know you can
talk. I know you can hear and understand everything I'm
telling you. I know there ain't nothing wrong with you. I've
seen the doctors' reports in your jacket to prove it. They all
say you can talk if you want to. They all say there ain't
nothing wrong with your hearing and seeing. But you're
gonna have to talk, you're gonna have to open up and program, if you ever want to get out of here, if you ever want to
leave this place." Leave, I didn't think about leaving. "Look,
you little asshole. I don't know why I keep sticking my neck
out for you. If the captain ever caught me down here like
this with you, he'd have my ass. If he ever heard me trying
to shape you up, he'd shit-can me. Look, I'm tired of trying
to shape you up. One of these days, I'm just gonna stop trying." I knew he'd be back.

And it was right after I looked into the whites of those
blue eyes that he stuffed a pair of white coveralls through
the slit. "I know you ripped up the last two pair of these
things that we gave you, but you'd better not rip these up.
You better start putting them on and wearing them every
day, because I'm convinced the captain's serious. He's gonna
let you exercise. And he's even gonna let you do it alone
first, 'til you get used to it. Then he's gonna put you in with
your countrymen on Tuesdays when they exercise. And once
you start exercising, Olivas, then it's only a matter of time

'til you'll be back on the main line. In all the years I've been working this hole, it's only been six months at most from the time a fellow starts exercising to the time that he's back on the main line. The only one I know of that hasn't is Taylor down there on the end. But he's a special case. I don't know what got into the captain, but he means it. In fact, it wouldn't surprise me if he let you this week. He didn't tell me to bring you these coveralls for nothing."

I didn't put on the coveralls that day nor the next day. And I hadn't put them on when he came again. "Goddamn it, Olivas, would you put on those goddamn coveralls! The captain's gonna let you exercise tomorrow. And if there's one thing the captain does, he watches every exercise period. You come out of your cell naked tomorrow, and he'll send you back to the Adjustment Center so fast it'll make your head spin. I've seen him do that to guys for a lot less than that." I didn't put on the coveralls.

And I didn't have them on when my cell door opened the next morning. There was a big clang, and then the door tugged slowly open. For the first time that I could remember, there was no bull there waiting. It stopped with another clang. Then everything was quiet and I was staring at a steel-wire fence five feet beyond the door and another five feet beyond that, a solid concrete wall. I thought the door would close as soon as I started toward it, but it didn't. Then I was standing in a five-foot wide walkway that ran about fifty feet in one direction and forty feet in another. On one side were doors to cells like mine; on the other was the steel wire fence that went from the floor to the ceiling. On the other side of the fence was another five foot walkway, but with no cells along it, just a wall. There was no one there but me. I looked for the captain. I looked down the end of the walkway where the guard's area was. There was no one there. I was in the biggest area they had let me into since I got Animal.

My first steps were shaky. There was too much space. I wanted too much of it. I took bigger steps than I could ever take in my cell. I made sure of that. Near the end of the

walkway I jumped up and forward and landed against the
steel fence. Then I broke into a run. Not since that night at
Chole's had I run. That almost stopped me, but I shook it
away. I ran up and down the walkway. The morning the
devil chased me, my night runs, bits of them came back. I
ran as fast as I could in as big strides as I could, until I was
breathless against the caged end of the walkway again. I
was smiling to myself—it felt good. As I bent over gasping
for air, I saw the black face looking at me. It was pressed
against the glass of the cell door nearest me. It had the look
that Animal's face had, that the faces of the cons that had
come with their three dollars and their home brew had. I
knew I was naked again, and I covered myself with my
hands. But the look was still there. He was looking at my
ass and I had covered my dick and balls. I turned my ass
from him; I faced him. I covered the outer cheeks of my ass
with my hands and moved away from him with little side-
way steps. I moved into view of another black face in the
next cell who had the same look on his face, except that this
one seemed to be looking at my dick and balls, and so I took
my hand from the cheek farthest from him and covered
them. There was no one at the glass in the next cell as I
inched sideways towards my cell. The next cell was dark.
But then there was a Mexican, and he had that look too. I
couldn't move fast enough. It didn't seem like I'd ever pass
him, so I ran instead until I was sitting with my legs
against my chest in my spot in my cell, wanting the door to
close, wanting to shut them out.

　　Later that day the other guard came. "The captain said
he let you out this morning for awhile. I wasn't around, but
he said you did real good. I'm glad you had enough sense to
put on your coveralls."

　　The next day was their exercise day. First the blacks
and then the Mexicans. They all looked in on me, not for
long, because the captain must have been watching, but
long enough for me to see that look on their faces, long
enough to make me cover myself as best I could. When I
was sure their exercise periods were over, I got up and put

on the coveralls.

But I didn't go out the next week when my door clanged open, even though I still had on the coveralls. The other guard came after the door was closed.

"Goddamn you, Olivas, what the hell is the matter with you, man!? The captain was madder than hell when I came in this morning. He said he let you out, but you wouldn't come out. He was ready to send you back to the Adjustment Center, but I begged him to give you one more chance. I told him you just weren't used to all that freedom. You know he's one tough bastard. He'll send you back right now. And you're so close. You've never been closer to getting out of this fucking place since you got here. Don't mess yourself up like this, Olivas. You're doing it to yourself, Olivas. You're doing it to yourself."

He came every day during that week. "You're going on sixteen years, Olivas, and it's all been hard time. You've done hard time, boy, no two ways about it. But I ain't feeling sorry for you because you don't want to help your own self out. The captain's been letting you out the day before the others get their exercise, so you better be ready to come out on Monday. I know you can hear me. I know you're hearing everything I'm saying." He'd straighten up and look down at me through the glass. He was a dark-skinned man, yet I knew from the first that he wasn't a Mexican. It was his nose: a big, sharp, hooked nose. "If you don't come out on Monday, and I don't give a good goddamn if you do or don't, then you're never gonna get out of this place. You're never gonna go home. Because you're so close now, if you don't do it this time, I hate to think what's gonna happen."

I never thought of going home. Not anymore. Still, I went out on Monday, with my coveralls on. I didn't run. It was hard enough walking. But I did, up and down the walkway, keeping my head and eyes down and not once looking at the cell doors. I did it, I guess, because that's what the captain wanted me to do, even though he wasn't there. I did it the next week and the two weeks that followed, knowing that each time brought me closer to exercising with "my countrymen," as the other guard called them. But I never saw the captain.

On the fourth Monday, he didn't let me out. I knew what it meant. All day long I told myself that I wouldn't go out the next day. They could do what they wanted to me—the cons, the captain—I wasn't going out. The other guard didn't come that day. I had hoped all day that he'd come and talk to me. I didn't sleep much that night. I kept waking up from dreams of them dragging me out. But the next morning, when the cell door clanged open, I went out.

I went out, I told myself, because I was afraid of what all nine or ten of them would do to me in my cell. But when I got out, when I was standing in the middle of the walkway, there were only three of them: one on each side of me, just a few feet from me, and another one at the far end of the walkway. I froze when I saw them, and so did they. At least the two closest to me did, because I didn't look past them. We were like three dogs that had suddenly noticed each other. I moved first. I took another two slow steps to the steel fence in front of me, and then slowly sat down on the concrete floor. Slowly I propped my back against the fence and brought my legs up to my chest even though I had my coveralls on. The two kept looking around, as if they were looking for someone else, as if they were looking for the captain. Then they started toward me, one from each side. I kept my eyes and head down, hoping they would pass me. They didn't pass me. They stopped in front of me. One of them said to me in Spanish, "Hey, where you from, *loco*?"

I didn't answer, I didn't look up.

"Hey, I'm talking to you, asshole."

"He's talking to you," the other one said in Spanish too.

"What's the matter, man, ain't you got a tongue or don't you like Mexicans?"

"He's in pretty bad shape if he don't like Mexicans because, looking at his black ass, there ain't much he could be except maybe a nigger." They laughed. But they were still looking around.

"Hey, I'm talking to you." He kicked me in the ribs with

his bare foot. It hurt. But I didn't move; that would have made it worse. I kept my head down.

"What's the matter, man, you think you ain't a Mexican? You think you're too good to be a Mexican?"

The other one kicked me on the other side of my ribs. "Hey, *puto*. The man's talking to you."

"Yeah, I'm talking to you. And you best not be talking to anybody but Mexicans in this joint, understand, *joto*!" He kicked me again.

"Leave him alone, assholes!"

I looked, and they looked too, towards the guard's area. But it didn't come from there. It came from the other end, from the third guy that was in the walkway with us. Because he said it again. "Leave him alone, assholes!" And they did back off, slowly, threatening me, cursing and bitching.

"So that's who's been punking you, huh, *puto*? You get off on them white dicks, huh, punk? Well, I'm gonna show you what a brown dick can do before you leave here. I'm gonna cure you of them white dicks, punk."

But they did leave, in opposite directions, and then they sat down on the concrete floor like I was sitting, across from their cells. The one that told them to leave me alone stayed down at the far end across from his cell doing exercise. They were weird exercises. He kept stretching and putting himself in funny positions. He didn't leave his end. I didn't even see him look in our direction. And he didn't say another word. He was a white man with a beard and the longest hair I had ever seen in the joint.

A new bull walked into the guard's area and said, "Okay, time's up. Everybody in."

I didn't see the captain that day and I didn't see him on the next two Tuesdays. On those Tuesdays, I just walked out of my cell and sat down against the fence across from it. The other two Mexicans sat across from their cells cursing me and the white man. The white man stayed down in his corner the whole time, not talking, not looking at us. On the third Tuesday, one of the Mexicans was gone. The other sat across from his cell between myself and the white man. I didn't hear him curse us that day. The new bull told us when it was time. I took the same three steps back into my cell. I still hadn't seen the captain.

That last Mexican went back to the main line a few days later. He made sure I saw him leave. He rapped on my glass until I looked up. Then he flipped me the finger, plastered against the glass. Then he said, "I'm gonna fuck you yet, punk," and left.

They brought in two more blacks the next day, but they were the only cons they brought in that week. So on Tuesday only the white man and myself were in the walkway. I watched him out of the corner of my eye. I didn't trust him. Even though he had helped me, he was just like everybody else. They were all the same. He got hard-ons too, and sooner or later he'd try to punk me too. He'd probably act like my friend, remind me what he had done for me and then try to punk me. Except that there was something different about him. The other guard had said so. He had mentioned him a lot of times: the one down at the end, he'd say. He had a name for him too, but I couldn't remember it and I couldn't exactly remember what he'd said about him except that he was different. I hadn't seen the other guard for weeks. And I still hadn't seen the captain.

The white man exercised the whole time. For awhile, I thought that was what the other guard meant. I had never noticed how many push-ups he did. It must have been in the hundreds at least. I had only noticed his strange exercises. As soon as the new bull hollered that it was time, I took my three steps back into my cell. I went back to my spot to think about that crazy white man and all his exercises when suddenly I saw him standing in my open door. I sat up, hitting my head against the wall, and brought my legs up to my chest. I lowered my head, waiting. But he didn't move toward me.

"Easy! Easy!" he said. "Hey, I don't want to hurt you. I want to help you, man. I know all about you and where you've been, and I want to help you get out of this fucking place, or at least, make it easier to be here. But right now, I got to get back to my cell before they lock it. And it's not cool to be seen talking together because the captain's watching. I know that son of a bitch is watching somewhere. And if he catches us talking, it'll be bad for both of us, but really bad for you, because he can only fuck with me so much. I've got people on the main line protecting me. But you ain't got nobody."

I watched him the whole time the next Tuesday without letting him know that I was watching. Near the end of the exercise period, when I was beginning to feel safe for that week, when there wasn't enough time left for him to punk me that week, he started moving toward me, exercising as he moved. I was sitting against the fence with my legs against my chest and my arms wrapped around my legs. He stopped when he reached me, and I tightened my grip around my legs.

He must have seen it because he said, "Hey, easy. Easy. I'm not gonna hurt you, man. Believe me, I don't want to fuck over you in any way. Still, we got to be careful, because if the captain comes, if he sees us talking, it'll probably mean the Adjustment Center for you. And I know that motherfucker's watching from somewhere, at least part of the time, because it ain't like him not to watch, because watching's the way he gets his kicks."

I had never seen him before. He was older than I had thought. His body movements were those of a much younger man. Close up, the lines in his face were too deep and too many, even though hair covered most of his face. Much of his hair was gray and the long hair on his head was greasy, but his eyes were steady and dark.

"I know you can hear me, Jess, and I know you can understand me. If I didn't think so, I wouldn't be wasting my time. Andy, the bald-headed bull, the good bull, has told me all about the doctors' reports. He's told me all about you, all that I didn't know. Because I followed you for a long time. I kept tabs on you until I lost track and thought you were dead. I knew all about that guy you castrated. Everybody in the joints did. He was one bad motherfucker and

292 RONALD L. RUIZ

nobody would have guessed that a little fart like yourself could have done that to him. Now he's just a big fat fuck that everybody fucks.

"Easy. Cool it. Relax. I don't want to mess with you, man. I want to help you, really. I know that's hard to believe in this place, but I do, and the reason I do is because you're worth helping. You did something that every asshole in this place would have liked to have done but didn't have the balls to try. That cocksucker terrorized everybody for years, but no one had the balls to take him on. But you did, and what makes it better is that you got him and survived. You survived all their fucking holes, all their fucking Adjustment Centers. You survived all his friends and all those loonies in those holes, and you're here, man, alive. I know you're a little fucked up, but you're here, and you're alive, and now you're even exercising. There's got to be something extra in that little body of yours. Believe me, Jess, I've seen a lot of dudes come and go. Most of them would have never gone after that cocksucker. Of the few that might have, most of those would have gotten killed trying, and those that didn't get killed trying would have gotten eaten up by the holes. But you're here, man, on the comeback trail, a step away from the main line and two steps away from freedom. You deserve to be helped, man. I want to help you. I want to help you get out of this fucking place . . . But I ain't gonna be helping either of us if the captain catches us talking. I better get back to my end. I'll see you next week, man. Be cool."

Throughout the week I thought of him. A Friend. I liked the hushed sound as I whispered it to myself again and again. A Friend. Would he talk to me next Tuesday? Would he still be my friend? By Tuesday I was sure that he wouldn't.

He didn't, at first. At first he wouldn't even look at me, even though I kept looking at him. It didn't surprise me. I'd been expecting it. He stayed down at his end, and I knew he didn't want me going down there. It wouldn't have taken much to find out what I was really like. And though he had only been my friend for a week, it seemed like I couldn't go on without a friend, without him. But then, about half-way through the exercise period, he came over to me again, and with his first few words, I knew he was still my friend.

"What do you say, man? I would have come sooner, but that fucking captain. I know he's watching. He's got to be watching. In the two years I've been here, he's watched every single exercise period I've ever had, until now. And he's watched every single son of a bitch that's ever been locked up in one of his cells, until now. He's watched them for days on end, hoping they'd crack. So I keep telling myself that he's got to be watching; he's got to be watching from somewhere. But I've looked and looked. I've looked at every crack, at every window, at every cell even, but I haven't seen the son of a bitch since you started exercising. And I talked to you last week and nothing happened to us this week. So maybe the fucker died. I don't know. Because for him, one of the main sins was that you weren't supposed to talk to each other. But them two Spanish dudes, the ones who were giving you a bad time, they talked to each other and nothing happened to them. Shit, they got a reward. They went back to the main line right after that. So maybe the fucker did die and go away. But what's strange is that Andy, the good bull, you know the one with the hooked nose and the bald head, he's disappeared too. Both him and the captain are gone and you know sure as shit that they both didn't die in the same week. And I can't get anything out of the new bull. He's just a kid, still full of ideas and ideals. It won't last long once he's been here a little while, but right now he's so stopped up with what's right is right that I can't get anything out of him. All the asshole will tell me is that he doesn't rightly think it's any of my business where they're at. And I don't dare try to bribe him because the stupid asshole's liable to turn me in.

"So I don't know. I don't know what to think. Because watching was the way he used to get his kicks. No, watching was the way he kept his control. It was the way he used and kept his power. Watching him watch us exercise every week always reminded me of what I used to do with ants when I was a little kid. You ever play with ants much? I did. Back home in Oklahoma it seemed like there were a hell of a lot of ants. I was always running into piles of ants and anthills in our yard and in this big field next door. I had these games where I'd play with those ants. They were really only one game because they always came down to the same thing. Anyway, my favorite one was that once I had spotted an anthill, I'd dig a circle around it with a stick. The circle was big enough to put most of the ants in it, but small enough so that I could reach any part of it without having to move too much. Then I'd fill the circle's line with water, like a moat, cutting off the ants from everything outside that circle unless they were willing to swim across the water. And I can tell you, ants don't like water. Then I'd fill in the anthill and watch them go crazy. I loved to see them scatter in every different direction until they reached the moat. Then they'd run along the moat looking for an end to the water. Some would go round and round, but they would never find an end to the water. I always wished that my ears had been good enough to hear their panic. Lots of times I'd put my ear to the ground, never close enough so that they could jump on me, get back at me. I'd put it down as close as I could get, but I could never hear their screaming and hollering which I knew they had to be doing from the way they were running around. I just had to be content imagining it. Once I had them running, I'd block off their path with a stick. They'd scramble in other directions, and I'd block off those directions too. They'd go crazy. I completely controlled them. I could do anything I wanted with them. Some I forced into the moat, and others I squashed when I got tired of playing with them.

"What the captain used to do . . . because he's stopped doing it now, and what's strange about that is that he stopped doing it just when you started exercising. And Andy's always told me that the captain really didn't like you, that he would have always liked to have gotten to you, and so he stops doing it when he could get to you. And he doesn't like me either and so he could get both of us. But, no, he stops doing it now when he could have us both and that just doesn't make sense. Because I've watched that fucker for over two years I've watched him watch every god-damn exercise period I've ever had here 'til now. And Andy's told me he's watched every exercise period for the last five years . . . but what he used to do was soften us up first. You know, the staring through your door's glass. He did it to me. He did it to you. He does it to everybody. He always did it before he'd let you out to exercise. Sometimes it was months before he'd let you exercise, and so he'd stare for months. Some guys never made it past that. That staring did a lot to you. It made you scared of him, and that's what he wanted. Sitting there, usually naked, stripped of everything, there's suddenly those two eyes looking down at you with as much contempt, with as much hate as you've ever seen. And he could stare down at you whenever he wanted for as long as he wanted. And he did, every day. More guys than you think cracked then, and he was only too glad to dump them, to send them to the Adjustment Center. 'Unamenable to treatment' he'd put in their jackets, and off they'd go. He taught you real fast who was boss here. That stare told you that in two minutes. And he controlled everything about your life, except maybe when you shit and pissed, and maybe that too, depending on if he let you eat or drink or what he let you eat or drink. And that stare convinced you of what no con needs any convincing, and that's that he's not worth very much.

"Anyway, he'd always be sitting next to the gate down in the guard's area over there when he let us out. He never said much except for his standard piece. And nobody wanted to hear him talk after that anyway because, when he did say anything—what little he said—it usually meant that someone was on his way to the Adjustment Center. Everyone knew enough to stand still and listen to his stan-dard piece. He always started by saying that he was Cap-tain Scott no matter how long we had been exercising and no matter how many times we had heard it. Then he'd say that he was in charge here, as if no one knew, and that there was to be no talking. Everyone of us had been sent to the hole, he'd say, and the idea of the hole was that we do our time in solitary confinement. A judge was making him give us thirty minutes a week of exercise, and just 'cause the prison wouldn't fight that order didn't mean that he was caving in. So we were not to indulge in something, talking that is, that wasn't ours to indulge in. The trouble with us, he'd say, was that we had no self-discipline, and because we had none, we couldn't, even if we wanted to, follow authority. That was why our lives were so fucked up. He didn't say fucked up because he'd never use a cuss word. That was why we hadn't been able to function in the society outside the prison, and that was why we couldn't function in the society inside the prison. But now we were in his society, the society of the hole, and he was going to teach us about self-discipline, and how to respect and follow authority. He said that he didn't think he should have to be wasting his breath on us since, but for that judge, we wouldn't have even been out of our cells. And so he warned us that he only spoke to any one person but once, and that the second time he was gone.

"They say that at the very start of all this exercising some guy laughed at the captain when he was talking about his society. They said that before anybody knew what was happening, there was the biggest, baddest goon squad inside the walkway just kicking the holy shit out of that guy. They say that when they had beaten him to a pulp, the captain came, and in front of the other cons, jammed his hands into the con's mouth and actually tore it. Ever since then, and that's been quite a few years now, there's been only one guy who gave the captain shit. But I knew that guy, and he was blowing it anyway.

The only other thing the captain would say was that when he tapped the bar with his stick, you had to start walking toward him until he tapped his stick again. But that when he tapped it then, we were to turn and go back the other way until he tapped again. When he tapped three or four times in a row, one right after the other, that meant we were to speed it up, not turn. So we had to be listening carefully, because he didn't want us turning when he meant for us to speed it up. If it was exercise that we wanted, then it was exercise that we were going to get. But we'd better move the way he wanted us to move. And if any of us fell out of step, we'd better get back into step quickly, because he didn't want to have to speak to us.

"Then he'd tap his stick and we'd start toward him and he'd tap it again and we'd go the other way. And he'd tap it three or four times in a row and we'd go faster. Every fucking week we did this, until you started exercising. You can imagine what we looked like. Guys who hadn't walked all week, now stopping and going, faster and slower; some stumbling, others falling at times, but always jumping up and getting into step because if he said, 'García, I don't like the way you're acting,' that was it. That was the first time he spoke to you. The next time it was, 'García, get in your cell!' and you were on your way to the Adjustment Center. The trouble was that you never knew what it was you were doing that made him speak to you. And it wasn't always stumbling or even falling, because he let a lot of guys slide when they did. So you just didn't know, and every time he spoke after his standard piece, it'd just scare the shit out of you. Because he had the habit of clearing his throat before he spoke, you always knew when he was going to speak. And he knew it scared the shit out of us and he loved it. And so a lot of times he'd just clear his throat and not say anything just to watch us jump. He even had me scared, and I got two guys on the main line that have been paying him plenty to keep him off my ass, to keep me here safe because I've been writing them writs for two years. And once he spoke to a guy the first time, he'd keep him on the string, sometimes for weeks. He loved it. He loved watching the guy jump all over the place, scared that he'd talk to him a second time, not knowing what it would take to make him talk to him.

"I'll never forget the guy that blew it, the guy that went

after the captain. He was a white guy, and he had a cell next to mine and the captain kept him in there for one hell of a long time before he let him exercise. We all knew why, because we could all hear the guy always screaming, and we all knew that the guy was screaming when the captain was staring in on him. And the more he screamed, the more the captain stared in on him. But somehow the guy never cracked. He never snapped. He'd scream like hell, so that we were all sure he was gonna crack, but he never did. And after awhile, he started sending me these notes, and then they became long letters. Andy would smuggle them to me. He sent them to me because I was the only other white guy here with him then, and though he couldn't exercise, he'd see me exercising with the Mexicans. The captain didn't want to waste his time watching me exercise by myself, especially because he wasn't going to do anything to me anyway because those two guys on the main line were paying him too much. And so he always had me exercising with Mexicans, except for the few times—and I can count them— we had another white guy in here. He put me in with the Mexicans because he figured that there were more Mexicans with more white blood in them than there were niggers with white blood in them. And no matter what, he still had some regard for white blood. So this white guy saw me exercising with all these Mexicans and he got Andy to smuggle me all these long notes. In each one he begged me to nod twice when I walked past his cell during my exercises once a week, so that he'd know that I was with him, so that he'd know that he wasn't alone and maybe that would give him the strength not to crack. He said over and over again that the captain's staring at him was driving him crazy, but that he was fighting it. He had to fight it because he knew that once he cracked, it was gonna be all over for him. But the thing that was really driving him crazy was that when he was on the streets he had been living with this young broad who had a little baby girl. Well, this broad used to work nights to support them, and when this baby was about fourteen months old, he started staring at her.

As soon as it got dark every night, he'd put the baby to bed and then start in on her. He'd leave the door open just enough so that there was enough light for her to be able to see him. Then he'd stare at her. He'd stare until she started crying. Then he'd leave the room, but come back in just as soon as she stopped crying and stare at her some more. This time he'd stare at her longer, even after she was crying. He'd hold her and make her look at him, even when she was crying, until she got dry and hoarse. And then he'd leave and wait until he thought the baby had fallen asleep, and then he'd go back in and shake her and wake her and stare at her some more no matter how much she'd scream. He did this every night, for hours. He said that he started staring at her because she was spoiled and he wanted to teach her some discipline; how to obey, how to get ready for the real world. After awhile, she learned to lay perfectly still and not cry, but look down, but not with her eyes closed, just down because that's how he liked it. He said that within a few months she was the best behaved baby you ever saw. She slept most of the day. She never cried. She stayed out of his and the broad's way. She never did anything she shouldn't have done or got into anything she never should have gotten into. And he never had to lay a hand on her. He just had to look at her and she'd back off of anything. But the longer the captain kept staring in on him, the more he kept writing about that baby. She was two when he got busted on a parole violation, and she was broken by then. She wouldn't look at anybody, and she wouldn't try to talk to anybody or at least go up to them. But it got so that she wasn't afraid anymore. It was more like she didn't care about anything anymore, like nothing mattered any more. Imagine, at two years old, nothing mattering anymore. The broad started taking her to doctors, but every doctor said it was a different thing, a different virus, and the baby got worse. She wasn't eating, she wasn't growing, she wasn't developing, she wouldn't have anything to do with anybody. She'd just sit or lie there. She was in the hospital when they busted him for crossing the county line, but it was really for living so long with a woman without working. And he kept writing towards the end that he knew that if he cracked, if the captain broke him, he'd never make it back. And towards the end, he kept writing that that baby hadn't really been his fault. That she needed discipline. That she was probably okay by now. But all the time he kept saying that he couldn't let himself crack.

"Finally, the captain must have figured that he wasn't going to crack, not there, not in the cell. So he let him out to exercise. Just me and him, the two whites. And on the very first day, he went after the captain. In fact, on the first approach, the first time we got close to the captain, he jumped at him and somehow managed to get his thumb and finger through that screen and grab the captain's ear. It looked like he was trying to pull it off, and for a minute, I thought he might. But the captain and the other bulls beat on his thumb so badly that I think he lost it. Not that it mattered to him then, because by then he was raving mad.

"But we have to be careful. I probably shouldn't be talking to you except that, if that fucker was around, he would have nabbed us by now. And he'd go after your ass more than he would mine. And so maybe I ought to just let you alone. Andy told me that the captain really didn't like you, that he told everybody that he thought that you ought to be snuffed. Just came out and said it like that. He was always saying that there was nothing that justified your living, your being kept alive at state expense. You know he's got all our jackets down there. He makes sure the office sends them to him. Andy said that the captain went through those jackets all the time, that he knew more about us than our mothers did. Andy said he went through your jacket all the time. The more he stared in on you, the more he went through your jacket. He hated you. He thought you were a vicious, worthless zombie who couldn't be trusted in here or on the streets, and yet had to be supported. He was always saying how every day of your life you were taking up space and guarding and food, and that the taxpayers, the state, were getting nothing for it and would never get nothing for it. It became like his own personal mission to do something with you. But he couldn't get you to react to anything, and that used to drive him up the wall. He couldn't understand why, after all this time, you hadn't snuffed yourself or somebody hadn't snuffed you. And you know, I can't either. Because over the years you've had to have had too many reasons and too many chances to kill yourself and you haven't done it. For some fucking reason, you still want to live. I can't understand it. I don't think there's too many of us that want to live that badly. I don't. And I guess that's part of what fascinates me about you. What is it that makes you so desperate to live?

"The captain hates me too. He hates my writs. They're one of the few things he can't control, and they bring intrusions from the outside. I've sprung quite a few guys, everybody except myself, it seems. And the writs have brought some changes in our conditions here too. So he hates them, and he hates me. But he's a whore too because he takes the money and lets me do to him and his society what he hates. The fucker's got to hate himself.

"But there's so much of this I don't get. He'd like to snuff you; yet he lets you exercise, he puts you right up next to the main line. We're talking here, or at least I'm talking, and he hasn't done anything to us. Maybe he's not here any more, maybe he really is gone. I haven't seen him, and my people on the main line haven't seen him, and I think he's quit staring. So I don't know where the fucker is. Or maybe some new court decision came down. I don't know and I can't get anything out of this new young bull. But you've got to talk, Jess. That's what they call you, isn't it? That's what I've been calling you. You've got to talk. You'll never get out of this fucking place if you don't talk. And you can talk. I know you can. Andy said that all the doctors said there was no reason why you couldn't talk except that you didn't want to. Well, I don't blame you for not wanting to, not where you've been. But it's different now, Jess. There's hope. You're next to the main line. But you've got to talk. Come on, man, don't let me down. I know you can talk. Say something . . .

"Okay. Maybe next week. But exercise at least, man. Do
a few push-ups. You've got to exercise. But I'm gonna get
going because the bull's gonna be coming. But do some
push-ups in your cell, man. I don't know how you've survived without exercising. It's important. It'll keep you from
cracking, because it toughens you. It strengthens your body,
but it strengthens your mind, too. The body's weak. It's lazy.
It wants to lay back. It wants to take it easy, walk a little
slower, bend a little less, sleep a little more, sit instead of
stand, and lie instead of sit. It wants to eat a little more and
yawn a little more. And each time it takes the easier way,
the mind gets a little softer, a little duller. And then the
mind's not ready. It's not fit for the daily shit and the daily
battle. It won't resist, let alone fight. And then they've got
you. If you don't exercise every day, then they've got you.
Because that's all that exercising is, getting ready. Each day
you exercise until it hurts. And each day it hurts a little
less; each day it takes a little more to make it hurt. You get
so the daily shit doesn't bother you anymore. You wait for
the bigger stuff. You're ready for the bigger stuff . . . the
bull's coming. I got to get out of here. For starters do the
push-ups, the plain old basic push-ups. You know, like this.
I do two thousand of these every day. I do a lot of other exercises, but the push-up is a good place to start. I'll show you
some more next week. And all of them you can do in the
smallest of cells, because sure as shit, they'll take this little
chicken-shit exercise period away some day."

I tried the push-ups that day. I did five the first time
and after awhile I did six. Awhile later I did five again and
then four, three times. My shoulders were sore the next
morning, but I was able to do seven on the third try. Seven
was the most I could do the next, but all together I did
forty-eight. I did ten at one try the next day and sixty for
the day. The white man was right. Each day it hurt a little
less, and each day it took a little longer to hurt. Each day I
felt a little stronger. I was getting ready.

And I tried talking, too, talking out loud. But something
kept getting stuck in my throat. It seemed to hold my

tongue. The only sound I could make was a dry gasping
sound. I tried saying, My name is not Jesus, it's Jess. Dry
gasping. I liked that white man. More gasping. Jess. I
couldn't say Jess. As Tuesday came, I tried harder. My
throat got sore. I spat blood twice. I stopped trying for a
day. I bore down on the push-ups instead. I knew he was
going to be disappointed in me for the talking, so I wanted
to take him a lot of push-ups. On Monday I did a hundred.

And I thought of him. There was little else I wanted to
think of. He would be doing a writ for one of the big shots on
the main line, so he got a special cell and he told them I had
to be his cellmate. I made it easier for him to write his
writs. I kept the cell clean and made sure that he got his
extra coffee and extra sandwiches. I got clean sheets for him
every day. And I collected the money for his writs. It got so
that people who wanted writs had to deal with me, because
he was too busy. He kept winning everybody's case. He was
famous all through the joint. Cons wrote to him every day
begging him to take their cases. He got letters from cons in
other states, from cons in the federal joints. He got so
famous that they made him a lawyer. And I became his
investigator and we got rich. And we'd drive down to Chinatown in our big brand new Cadillac convertible. Except that
I would be driving because it was my job to be doing those
kinds of things now. And we'd drive up and down the
streets of Chinatown with our big, fine white women, with
their platinum blonde hair all fluffy and blowing in the
wind. He with two of them, one on either side of him, in the
back seat, and me with mine hanging all over me in the
front seat. And all the guys would be waving and yelling at
us, all jealous, filling up both sides of the street. And we
would just nod, real slow like, and keep on driving by.

Tuesday finally came. I knew by the sun in the windows
above what time they'd open my door. I was standing next to
it, waiting, when they did. I squeezed out while the door was
still sliding open. I saw him come out of his cell. I saw him
begin to exercise. I waited for him to look down towards me.
But he didn't. That scared me. I looked away from him, but

then looked back, again and again. He still wouldn't look at me. I was panicked. I didn't know what to do when, finally, about half-way through the period, he came over to me.

"What do you say, Jess? Did you do any exercises? You ready to tell me about them? You ready to talk? I know you're ready to talk. Just say something easy, like, 'Hi, guy.' Then you can tell me about your exercises and I'll show you some more. Come on, easy now, just a word or two."

I tried. My throat was still sore. The only sounds I made were the dry gaspings.

"Come on, Jess, relax. If you just . . ."

Then there was a loud rattling above us. The ceiling seemed to be caving in. Bits of concrete fell on us. I heard the voice up there before I saw part of the light well move.

"All right, Olivas, you little goon." Somebody was up there, but I couldn't see him through the tiny opening. But then, I didn't need to see him. "You've been feeding us this crap for all these years that you can't talk, that you can't understand. And everybody but me's fallen for it, and you've been getting special treatment instead of what you deserve. But you're going to start getting what you deserve. I saw you with my own eyes and heard you with my own ears talking to that writ writer, trying to plan your way out of here. Well, you're going to get what you deserve, believe me. You better get out of the way, Taylor. I don't care how much money your pimps have. There's a limit to your privileges."

I heard the goon squad coming. I saw them at the second gate with their rubber hoses. I ran to my cell. I got down in my corner and curled myself, covering my head with my arms and giving them my back. They beat me until they thought I was unconscious.

I thought of him all week. I knew he'd get us out. I saw us running free in the streets. I tried to talk. I practiced until I spat blood again. I thought I could say "I," but I wasn't sure. I couldn't exercise. My arms and back were swollen, blackened and sore. When Tuesday came, my door slid open at the right time. I was surprised. I didn't think they'd let me out. For awhile I thought it was a trap and I didn't go near the open door. Then I thought I might miss a chance to see the white man, so I went out anyway. But he wasn't there. I was the only one in the run. I stepped on something cold. There were two knives on the floor. My foot was on one of them. I looked to see if anyone could see me pick them up. Then I saw the captain. He was sitting on a chair on the other side of the second gate. I knew it was him. I knew the eyes.

"You'd better pick them up, Olivas. You're going to need them." I knew the voice. "You'd better hold onto them, smart boy, because in a minute I'm going to let out four of your black friends who haven't had a piece of ass in months. I've got to do something for those poor fellows, wouldn't you say, Olivas? I suspect you're going to have to defend your virtue against those niggers, although I know you've always been a punk. So hold onto those knives. But I'll tell you what I'm going to do, just to show you how fair I can be. The niggers won't have any knives, and I'm going to open the doors of two of your friends to let them help you, to kind of even it up. One of the doors belongs to one of your countrymen. We brought him in this morning and I thought he would naturally come to your rescue. Except that he already told me this morning that he doesn't want any part of it. But I'm going to open his door anyway because I think countrymen should help countrymen. And I'm going to open your big buddy's door, too, down at the end there. He's always bragging about how much he helps cons. Let's see how much he'll help you, Olivas."

I heard the door locks pop, and then the four blacks came out, two on either side of me. I backed against the wall and waved the knives in both directions. Nobody was going to punk me again. The captain was laughing. "Okay, niggers, she's all yours. All you got to do is take those two knives away from her and, I guarantee you, you'll have the tightest, sweetest piece of ass you've ever had."

The blacks came towards me, tiptoeing, keeping their eyes on the knives. "Look here, man. You better give us them knives. We don't want to hurt you, but we will if you keep fucking with those knives."

Another door slid open. "Come on out, Messicun." The captain was laughing as he yelled. "Come on out and help your brother. Don't you want to help your countryman?"

The blacks kept coming. Then they surrounded me. They were within arms reach of me, big bastards.

"Come on, man. Don't be giving us no trouble. We just want a little ass. Captain said some dude used to pimp you. What's a few more dicks gonna do to that ass of yours? Be sensible. You know what it's like when a man ain't had no ass for a long time."

"Maybe he don't like niggers."

"Yeah, maybe."

"Now look here. Give us them knives. Don't make things bad for everybody."

The captain was yelling, "What's the matter, Taylor! I thought this spic was your big buddy! Why don't you come on out and help him! The door's wide open!"

One of the blacks said, "Now, man, I'm gonna count to ten. If by that time you haven't turned over them knives, I guarantee you, you're gonna be sorry. One, two . . ." I couldn't wait for them to come after me. " . . . three, four . . ." I jumped at the two on my right and slashed both of them. I turned as one was about to jump me. I sank one of the knives into his gut. The further it sank, the harder I jiggled it. His screams were everywhere. Another jumped me. I went down. But as I did, I cut another one. They were beating on me, trying to get the knives. They took one, and just as they did, something landed on us. There were screams, and I saw the white man choking one. There was another one on his back. One of them still had a hold on me and was still trying to get the knife. We struggled and then he slipped or something, because the next thing I knew was that he was screaming and the knife was in his throat. And then I heard the white man cry, "Help me, Jess. Help me." The one on his back kept plunging the knife into him. The white man fell and the black fell with him, pulling and plunging the knife until I buried my knife in his back as deep and as hard as I could.

The white man was dead. I pulled his body from the black's and dragged it to the far end of the run, where he had exercised. I was bleeding and my blood fell on him, fell on his blood and the blacks' blood. When I got to the end of the run, I sat against the steel fence and put his head on my lap and cried, "White man, I love you. White man, I love you."

CHAPTER THIRTEEN

I took out the chalice. And then the Host. This was His Body. A weak, frail Body that I could have ripped up and torn up and spit on and pissed on then. But I didn't. Instead, I took It in my fingers as I had seen Padre Galván do thousands of times, and I bent over It like he had. But I didn't pray to It, I talked to It, whispered to It, real close. I said, "All right, Cocksucker. On the third day You rose again from the dead. But on this third day You and everything here is gonna die. And it's gonna be a slow, ugly death. I want you to think about that, a slow, ugly death. Because three hours wasn't enough. You only hung on that cross for three measly hours, and I've seen three million hours of pain and hurt and suffering. I've seen three million hours of hanging. So You're gonna get more than three hours this time. Let's see if You can stop me, Big Guy." Then I left the church, careful to cover my tracks and to unlock a basement window.

I went to the Reno Rooms. That was where the old chink had been staring down at me. If that motherfucker stared one more time he was a dead man. An old cream-colored, white-haired nigger came to the tiny desk. "I need a room," I said. And I did. I needed to sleep, to rest. I only had tomorrow to find her.

"Only thing I got will run you four dollars fifty cents."

"Did I ask you how much it was?" The old nigger just stared at me.

"Give me it," I said.

As he turned to get the key and a card, I asked, "Have you seen Chole?"

"Cho-lay?" he repeated. "Don't know nobody by that name."

"She's an old whore who used to work these streets."

"Mister," he said, "this is a respectable place, mostly elderly gentlemens and . . ."

"Don't hand me that shit," I said, pulling out my wad of cash.

His eyes jumped on the money, and I pulled out a ten and said, "Keep the change."

"Yes, sir," he said.

I lay on the bed and closed my eyes. But as soon as I did, I knew I wouldn't be able to sleep, not there. I knew I had to be back at my station, back at the church. So I left the room and walked through the night's thick white fog to the church, hidden from everything and everyone twenty feet away. There I went back to my spot in the small loft next to the organ. But not before I looked down at the tabernacle and said, "I'm back, Asshole, and three hours wasn't shit." Then I lay down. I needed my rest. I was going to have to find her tomorrow. I thought of the executioner on Death Row. Where did he sleep the night before? It didn't matter. This Guy needed to know He was going to die. Through the night, I got up and yelled. "Three hours wasn't shit. It'll never be enough. I've seen three million hours of hanging."

At five minutes to five in the morning, I heard the front door and then the basement door. Padre Galván. This time he would have to go. But when the priest came out it wasn't Padre Galván. It was a young white priest who didn't look much older than twenty. He was alone; no altar boy. He rang the bells himself, answered himself, poured the wine himself. He said that Mass to no one but himself. I watched

him through the slits in the railing wondering what had
happened to Padre Galván. I thought he was alive. The only
death notice I ever got in prison was a telegram from the
Warden's Office telling me that 'Amá was dead. I was in the
hole then, and I wiped my ass with it.

I waited until it was light before I left the church. I had
a lot to do, but there was nothing I could do until the stores
opened. As I went down the steps I saw a small thin Mexican woman step out of the fog. I waited for her. Even
though it was biting cold, she wore only a thin cotton dress.
Her legs were bare down to her worn shoes. It had been
years since I had seen the copper-brown Indian color of
those thin legs. Wrapped around her upper body was a
black cotton shawl that covered her head and much of her
face.

I said, "Dispénseme, señora, pero que le pasó al Padre
Galván?"

She looked at me for a moment and then said, "Oh, he's
been gone for many years now."

"Where did he go?"

"He went to Rome."

"Rome?"

"Yes, the poor man could barely see out of one eye. He
could barely walk and he couldn't use his right arm, but he
still went to Rome."

"Why?"

"Well, that was before I came here, but we had a very
famous holy woman who lived and died here. Padre Galván
always said she was a saint. It was always on his mind. So
one day they gave him permission to go to Rome to see if
she could be canonized."

"And was she?"

"I don't know because I've never heard. But I hope so,
because I pray to her all the time."

"But where is Padre Galván now?"

"I don't know. He never came back."

I went to the only hardware store in Chinatown. The
Jap owner said to me as I paid him for the pick and shovel,

"You going to dig in those clothes?"

I looked at my sharp new clothes and then looked at him and said, "Yeah."

I drove slowly out Whites Bridge Road—fucking fog wouldn't let me see more than five feet in front of me—hoping it was still there. I didn't know what I'd do if it wasn't. But it was. Holy Cross Cemetery. I had served a lot of funerals there, and Padre Galván had showed me where she was buried. Otherwise I would never have known because 'Amá didn't go to visit her grave, just like she didn't visit me in prison. Her grave was in the poor part of the cemetery. The poorest part, next to the brickyard. There was no lawn, no trees, no road, no tombstones or statues. It was just dirt, hard Fresno dirt. The markers were small pieces of wood with names and dates scratched into them. Gloria Olivas 1919-1939. For years there had been a rusty empty can on top of her grave so that I could always tell at a glance where she was, even though I was too ashamed of the grave to go there. But one day, after a real fancy funeral, some of the women went crazy and others were passing out and Padre Galván had to help with them. And while everybody was busy with the women, I stole some of their flowers and ran to my mother's grave, put them in the can, and told her, "I love you, Mamá, even though I never knew you."

But today I would know her, meet her for the first time, even if it were only her bones. And then I would find Chole.

The cemetery had changed, but the poor part was still there. Except that the fog made it hard to see the brickyard, and most of the wooden markers were gone, and there was no can around. I walked to the brickyard fence, and from there got an idea where her grave had to be. I started digging. The ground was like rock. After more than an hour, I decided that that couldn't be my mother's grave. I moved a few yards over, dug there for awhile, and then moved to another grave. It was early afternoon when I started looking for a worker who might help me find her grave. I put the pick and shovel in the car. I walked around the cemetery. The fog made it impossible to see anything more than fifty feet away. Finally I heard some coughing and found a worker. When I told him what I was looking for, and gave him ten dollars, he said, "Sure I know where that grave's at. Come on. Follow me."

I went with him across the huge lawns towards the brickyard. But he stopped long before we got there and said, "This is it. People come here all the time." Before us was a giant tombstone, as big as any in the cemetery. Beside it were smaller tombstones with writing on them. There were statues of angels and saints and one of Jesus Himself around the grave. There were vases of flowers everywhere. "This is the Olivas woman. The one everyone calls the saint."

I looked at the tombstone again and saw 'Amá. There she was, in the center of the stone, in a round, glass-covered picture. She was praying, looking up to the sky, her hands folded with a gold halo over her head. She looked like a saint, and what I saw of the writing said she had gone to God.

"People come from all over every day to pray to her. They come from all over the valley, from Pixley and Wasco and Lost Hills. I've seen them come from as far as Texas. But this fog has been real bad, and people have been afraid to drive. But, believe me, in a day or two . . ."

"This ain't the grave. I wanted Gloria Olivas'. She's over in the dirt part."

"Chances are you won't find her. We're changing things around here and some of those graves have been dug up . . ."

The Jap said, "You weren't kidding about digging in them clothes. I got some overalls that are a lot cheaper than your dress clothes."

"I don't need no fucking overalls. Give me my change."

I went back to the cemetery. The dark day was getting darker. I didn't have much time. I found her holy place again. The first swing of my sledge hammer was at her praying face. I swung and I swung and I swung until it was too dark to see. But most of the tombstones and statues were gravel when I left.

𝟸𝟸𝟸𝟸𝟸

It took me four trips in and out of the church to get my cans of kerosene and gasoline and shit and piss in. Through the night I yelled, "Three hours wasn't shit! Three hours is bullshit! There's too much out here for three hours!"

Just after midnight I took my cans of shit and piss and walked calmly to the altar, opened the tabernacle, opened the House of God, and poured all my shit and piss onto His Body. There were five hours to wait. He was such a young priest, such a boy, probably just out of a seminary high up in the mountains of New Mexico. I waited for him near the light switch, and when he turned on the lights, I jumped him and stabbed him again and again. When he stopped moving, when he stopped quivering, I ripped out his heart and put that in the tabernacle too. Then I spread the kerosene and the gasoline and lit it and ran to Chinatown and began looking for Chole.

As the fire engines screamed, I went from bar to bar. No one knew her or had ever heard of her. But two bartenders told me that if anyone knew anything about her it would be an old Filipino named Silvestre. I found him, and he took me to her. She was living in what had been an old chicken coop in one of the Chinatown alleys.

At first I couldn't tell if it was really her because it was so dark and she was so old and all covered up and she wouldn't talk to me and she had shrunk so much. But when I got right up next to her, when I held her and smelled her, I knew it was her. The sky was bright with the church fire and I pointed to it and said, " I got them for us, Chole. I got them." But she didn't answer or nod or nothing, and I started to cry, and I held her, and I kissed her, and I said, "Chole, I love you."